Readers love
the Flophouse Stories
by AMY LANE

Shades of Henry

"Ms. Lane can always pile on the angst well, and leaves no stone unturned for Henry and why his life is a mess."

—Paranormal Romance Guild

"I really adored this book. Part of that came from seeing characters I've grown to love over the years, but also because it's rare to see two men who are so perfect for each other and deserve one another wholeheartedly."

—Rainbow Book Reviews

Constantly Cotton

"If you're looking for something sweet that also give you some thriller vibes, I heartily recommend Constantly Cotton. It swept me along and I couldn't stop reading until it was done…"

—Love Bytes

By Amy Lane

An Amy Lane Christmas
Behind the Curtain
Bewitched by Bella's Brother
Bolt-hole
Christmas Kitsch
Christmas with Danny Fit
Clear Water
Do-over
Food for Thought
Freckles
Gambling Men
Going Up
Hammer & Air
Homebird
If I Must
Immortal
It's Not Shakespeare
Late for Christmas
Left on St. Truth-be-Well
The Locker Room
Mourning Heaven
Phonebook
Puppy, Car, and Snow
Racing for the Sun • Hiding the Moon
Raising the Stakes
Regret Me Not
Shiny!
Shirt

Sidecar
Slow Pitch
String Boys
A Solid Core of Alpha
Three Fates
Truth in the Dark
Turkey in the SnowUnder the Rushes
Weirdos
Wishing on a Blue Star

BENEATH THE STAIN
Beneath the Stain • Paint It Black

BONFIRES
Bonfires • Crocus

CANDY MAN
Candy Man • Bitter Taffy
Lollipop • Tart and Sweet

DREAMSPUN BEYOND
HEDGE WITCHES LONELY
HEARTS CLUB
Shortbread and Shadows
Portals and Puppy Dogs
Pentacles and Pelting Plants
Heartbeats in a Haunted House

Published by DREAMSPINNER PRESS
www.dreamspinnerpress.com

By Amy Lane (cont)

DREAMSPUN DESIRES
THE MANNIES
The Virgin Manny
Manny Get Your Guy
Stand by Your Manny
A Fool and His Manny
SEARCH AND RESCUE
Warm Heart
Silent Heart
Safe Heart
Hidden Heart

FAMILIAR LOVE
Familiar Angel • Familiar Demon

FISH OUT OF WATER
Fish Out of Water
Red Fish, Dead Fish
A Few Good Fish • Hiding the Moon
Fish on a Bicycle • School of Fish
Fish in a Barrel

FLOPHOUSE
Shades of Henry • Constantly Cotton
Sean's Sunshine

GRANBY KNITTING
The Winter Courtship Rituals of
Fur-Bearing Critters
How to Raise an Honest Rabbit
Knitter in His Natural Habitat
Blackbird Knitting in a Bunny's Lair
The Granby Knitting Menagerie
Anthology

JOHNNIES
Chase in Shadow • Dex in Blue
Ethan in Gold • Black John
Bobby Green • Super Sock Man

KEEPING PROMISE ROCK
Keeping Promise Rock
Making Promises
Living Promises • Forever Promised

LONG CON ADVENTURES
The Mastermind • The Muscle
The Driver • The Suit
The Tech

LUCK MECHANICS
The Rising Tide

TALKER
Talker • Talker's Redemption
Talker's Graduation
The Talker Collection Anthology

WINTER BALL
Winter Ball • Summer Lessons
Fall Through Spring

Published by DREAMSPINNER PRESS
www.dreamspinnerpress.com

By Amy Lane (cont)

Published by DSP Publications

ALL THAT HEAVEN WILL
ALLOW
All the Rules of Heaven

GREEN'S HILL
The Green's Hill Novellas

LITTLE GODDESS
Vulnerable
Wounded, Vol. 1 • Wounded, Vol. 2
Bound, Vol. 1 • Bound, Vol. 2
Rampant, Vol. 1 • Rampant, Vol. 2
Quickening, Vol. 1 • Quickening, Vol. 2
Green's Hill Werewolves, Vol. 1
Green's Hill Werewolves, Vol. 2

Published by Harmony Ink Press

BITTER MOON SAGA
Triane's Son Rising • Triane's Son
Learning
Triane's Son Fighting • Triane's
Son Reigning

Published by DREAMSPINNER PRESS
www.dreamspinnerpress.com

SEAN'S SUNSHINE

AMY LANE

DREAMSPINNER
PRESS

Published by

DREAMSPINNER PRESS

5032 Capital Circle SW, Suite 2, PMB# 279, Tallahassee, FL 32305-7886 USA
www.dreamspinnerpress.com

Sean's Sunshine
© 2023 Amy Lane

Cover Art
© 2023 L.C. Chase
http://www.lcchase.com
Cover content is for illustrative purposes only and any person depicted on the cover is a model.

Trade Paperback ISBN: 978-1-64108-540-3
Digital ISBN: 978-1-64108-539-7
Trade eBook published March 2023
v. 1.0

Printed in the United States of America
∞
This paper meets the requirements of
ANSI/NISO Z39.48-1992 (Permanence of Paper).

One hundred and twelve books? Seriously? This is my 112th? Dude. Thanks to EVERYFRICKIN'BODY 'cause you don't do this shit alone.

Author's Note

IF YOU like the ficlets following the novel—and would like to read them as they come out—don't forget to follow me on Patreon: https://www.patreon.com/AmyHEALane

The Nurse

SEAN MICHAEL Kryzynski was going to kill Jackson Leroy Rivers. It was a fact. He'd come to accept it, plotted the man's demise, and had embraced the consequences. Everything was settled. How bad could prison be for a gay police detective anyway?

Dammit.

There had to be another option.

"Dammit," he said, this time out loud.

"You can't kill him."

Sean glared at the source of his problem, the baffling irritant that was all Jackson Rivers's doing.

"I don't know what you're talking about," he lied.

Billy—probably *not* his real name—gazed levelly back, and Sean swallowed. Audibly. God. It just wasn't fair. The kid had fathomless, *cynical* brown eyes, an almost perpetually arched eyebrow, a square jaw, a nose that had probably been broken once, and the body of a gym-addicted Adonis. He was in his early twenties, which put him and Sean in the same decade, but as far as personal experience was concerned, Sean wasn't even sure they were on the same planet.

And Billy, whose usual profession was making movies naked with other men—and given his looks, he was probably damned good at his job—was going to help give Sean a bath.

"You're thinking that you're gonna kill Rivers for putting you in this position. You can't. He was right. You can barely walk, you can barely breathe, and you're going to need help in the shower. Don't stress, man. I've handled naked shit before. It's no big deal."

Jackson, who against all of Sean's original prejudices had turned out to be a really decent friend, had hired Billy to be Sean's nurse as he recovered from a stab wound that had punctured his lung and broken some ribs and generally made Sean's entire body hurt in unexpected ways. It was a nice idea—Billy could probably bench press three grown men with those muscles—but… but… well… there were those eyes.

And that full, sardonic mouth.

And the fact that Sean's last boyfriend had ditched Sean *in the hospital* and left all his DVDs strewn across the floor as a parting gift when he'd gone through the stack and taken his own out. And liberated some that *weren't* his own, because apparently Sean sure could pick 'em.

As a rule, Sean wouldn't have minded being in the company of a man who looked like Billy No Last Name.

But there was that whole "Mom, this is my boyfriend, the porn star," thing.

And the "I just got stabbed through the lung and can't breathe," thing.

And generally the "My life is a mess, and how can I even be thinking about his eyes?" thing.

But still… there were those eyes.

"Mr. Kryzynski," Billy said with the same patience he would have shown a ninety-year-old man insisting he could still drive, "you were hurt. You were hurt *really bad*. And I know you want to shower. Like I said, I handle this shit all the time. I'm not going to lose my mind and molest you because you're naked, okay? I think we can both deal with this like adults."

Sean tried to take a deep breath and failed, hating himself because his knees wobbled where he stood. "But will you laugh at me?" he asked, feeling helpless. He was no Adonis, but he did work damned hard to keep himself fit. God, he must have lost twenty pounds over the last week in the hospital, and he could barely stand for longer than it took to walk across a room. It felt like an affront to humanity that he could work so hard on his body and have it all ripped away as he was walking under an overhang and was temporarily blinded by the shade on a sunny day.

Those infinite, cynical eyes did something unexpected then.

They softened. "No, sir. I wouldn't laugh at you. From what I understand, you're one of the good guys."

Sean sighed. "How would you know that? I'm a plain white cop, Billy. I'm practically the devil."

Billy gave a smile that held surprising faith. "Nossir. You come recommended by Rivers and Henry. They wouldn't lie to me. You're good."

And just like that, Sean no longer wanted to kill Jackson Rivers. "Okay," he said with a sigh. "Let's get this over with."

Reluctantly, he allowed Billy to help him undress in the clean sterility of his white-tiled bathroom and then allowed the young man to assist him into the bathtub and onto the shower seat, where he was able to wash his parts with a minimum of fuss. He stayed there for a moment, eyes closed against the spray, savoring the opportunity to be clean before he sighed and gave it up.

"I guess I'm done," he said, knowing Billy was waiting patiently on the other side of the curtain.

"Hang out for a minute," Billy urged. "I know you've been dying to shower for real."

He'd gotten sponge baths in the hospital but had been told he was free to bathe when he'd been sent home. However, he had strict instructions to keep his stitches dry. Billy had spent a good ten minutes with medical tape and a plastic bag, securing the stitches under his ribs where the knife had slid through his flesh like butter, facing upward, the better to puncture his lung.

"There's a drought," Sean said weakly, going almost boneless in the hot water.

"Come on, Saint Kryzynski. Indulge a little."

"I'm not a saint," he mumbled, suddenly exhausted. *If I was a saint, I wouldn't be drowning in your eyes, would I?*

He heard movement on the other side of the curtain, and a hand intruded to fiddle with the spigot. The blissful water shut off, and Billy was there with a giant fluffy towel—one of his favorites—ready to wrap Sean up and dry him off like a child.

Sean was embarrassingly weak as Billy helped him up.

"Crap," he muttered. "We forgot to bring clothes."

Billy snorted. "This is your place!" he said. "What's to dress? You walk commando to your room, let the boys get some air, get dressed there. Jeez, you really *are* a saint."

Sean grunted. "I have three siblings," he murmured. "I'm not used to having room for the boys to fly."

"Yeah, well I had five, so the minute I was in a place where nobody cared about my boys, they got all the air I could handle."

"Had?" Sean asked, suddenly very curious about this beautiful boy helping him through the weakest period of his life.

Billy's face, which had softened for a moment, closed down. "No Catholic family for gay boys, Kryzynski. I learned that lesson good."

Sean made a hurt sound. "You need to tell my mother that," he said, and then right when he was about to make his first step unattended, his knees went out.

Billy caught him, swept Sean's scrawny ass into his arms like Sean was a damsel in distress.

"If it's all the same to you," Billy told him, hauling Sean down the hall to his bedroom, "I don't really need to meet your mother."

Sean had enough oxygen to snort. "What makes you think you'll have a choice?" he said, trying not to wheeze. "She's been waiting for me to get out of the hospital before coming to visit. She lives in Turlock, so it'll probably be this afternoon, with a reprise in the morning."

Rivers, his boyfriend Ellery Cramer, and their assistant, Henry, had left shortly after they'd cleaned up Sean's living room from Jesse Carver's DVD tantrum—which was almost immediately after Billy had arrived. Sean's partner on the force, Andre Christie, had stayed a little longer, until Sean had dozed off in his recliner like a grandfather. Sean had awakened soon after, sweating and disoriented, *begging* for a shower.

He had obviously not thought that plan through.

"Aw, man," Billy muttered as he shouldered his way through the doorway of Sean's bedroom. Sean gave a weak look around to make sure Jesse hadn't had a tantrum *here* and was somewhat reassured when he realized that his cuff-link box was right where he'd left it and his toiletry kit was perfectly arranged on the vanity.

"You have a problem with mothers?" Sean asked Billy, finding himself deposited gently on the bed with minimal fuss.

Billy gave him a dark look. "Could you not tell her what my day job is?" he asked, looking really uncomfortable.

Oh.

"You're a friend of a friend, working his way through school. Your apartment got crowded, and I needed help. How's that?"

The gratitude on Billy's face was humbling. "Thanks for that," he said. Then he straightened up and adopted a crisp, military attitude that Sean sort of appreciated. "And now I get to dry off your skinny body and see you naked. Don't worry, I won't take advantage."

Sean glared—but it took his last drop of energy. "You're really, really awful. I can see why Jackson picked you."

Billy gave an indelicate snort. "Backatcha. Now drop the towel and get used to me seeing your junk."

Sean had no choice but to let the towel hit the floor while Billy helped him into his boxers, some sleep shorts, and a T-shirt, but he vowed then and there to break all sorts of healing records so he would under no circumstances be obligated to let this kid with the cynical eyes be in any way responsible for his junk.

THEY BARELY made it. Sean had just gotten completely dressed, and Billy had helped him back to his couch, when there was a knock at the door. Billy gave him a meaningful look, one that screamed "stay put," and then moved to open the door.

The woman on the other side had frosted blond hair, warm blue eyes with crinkles in the corners, and seemed decidedly bemused.

"Sean?" she asked, peering inside.

"I'm…," Sean wheezed, and Billy scowled at him.

"Come on in," Billy said smoothly. "I'm Mr. Kryzynski's helper until he's back on his feet."

"Oh!" Cathy Kryzynski wasn't a big woman, but she had a sort of vitality that pushed its way into any room. In this case, she powered past Billy with only a little difficulty—hampered partly by Billy's suspicious presence and partly by the bags of groceries she had in her hands. "Sean, I didn't know you'd have a helper, so I brought some food. Uhm…." She smiled at Billy expectantly.

"Guillermo Morales," Billy replied, surprising Sean greatly. "But, uhm, you can call me Billy."

Sean's mother gave a brilliant smile. "So nice to meet you, Billy. Here. If you take this into what passes for a kitchen back there, I'll talk to Sean for a second, and then I can give you instructions, deal?"

"That's fine," Billy said, taking the bags of groceries. "But…." He gave Sean a narrow look. "You need to do most of the talking. He really isn't healed, and it's going to be a while before he's up to long conversations."

Sean straightened, having a thought about protest, and then Billy added the kicker. "And seriously, he needs his nap. His friends just left, and I checked over the doctor's directions. He's about maxed out on company today."

Sean gaped, and so did his mother, but Billy glanced from one to the other with an absolute lack of fucks given.

"Let me put this away," he said, completely composed, and Sean's mom gave Sean one of those glances that came with pursed lips and a haughty tilt of the head. While the words "Well I *never*," were a bit passé in California in this day and age, Sean always thought that's what his mother *would* say if she didn't know someone would have a comeback to that, like, "You should, it's fun!"

"He's… determined" is what she *did* say as she drew near Sean on the couch. And Sean had to give it to Billy—*Guillermo*—because his mother's usually effusive personality seemed to have been instantly tempered by Billy's warning.

"He's doing this as a favor to a couple of friends," Sean said, knowing it hadn't only been Jackson Rivers, but also his assistant, Henry Worrall, who had helped arrange the situation. Henry worked as a PI, but his, well, *hobby*, was mentoring the guys in Billy's apartment. Helping them "adult," in his words. So if this kid's two best adult role models asked him for a favor, apparently that meant Billy had to take shit seriously.

"He has to be rude?" Cathy asked.

"He wasn't rude, Ma," Sean told her. "He was just very firm. I…." He took a deep breath that was only a little exaggerated. "He's right," he said on the exhale. "I'm not up for much."

Cathy's expression immediately shifted from offended to concerned. "You're right, honey. I didn't mean to stress you out." She went suddenly still, all of that vitality somewhat shrouded. "Is this why you didn't want me in the hospital?" she asked, obviously hurt. "I mean, I know I can only visit for a couple of days, but…."

He gave her a quiet smile. "You're a lot, Ma. And there were balls to the walls cops." Or there had been after Rivers and Christie had gotten done giving his entire precinct hell about how nobody had shown up. Yeah, lots of reasons Cathy Kryzynski should not have been in the hospital. "Christie told you I'd be okay, right?"

"Andre is a good boy," she said, and her wistful tone told him she was still hoping devoted family man Andre would start playing for Sean's team.

"He is," Sean said. "And his wife is lovely." He took another deep breath. "Now tell me if I missed anything in the last week, and then go help Billy." Jackson had left all sorts of microwave meals in the fridge. Billy was going to need some help playing refrigerator Tetris with everything his mom had brought.

"Well, school's starting this week, so Suzanne and Leah are both up to their eyeballs in fixing up their classrooms," his mom started, talking about his sister and his sister-in-law, who were both teachers. "Charlie's still in Germany, but he heard talk that his deployment might end and he might be stationed back in the States pretty soon."

"Marcie will be pleased," Sean said, because she seemed to expect some sort of response.

"Well, she needs to be more self-sufficient." Cathy sniffed before launching into a detailed description of everything Marcie's kids from her previous relationship had been doing and why most of it was bad. Poor Marcie. Charlie Kryzynski must have seemed like a catch until Marcie met his mother.

Sean didn't catch all of it, though. He was asleep before she finished the next sentence.

When he awoke, it was night, and Billy was urging him off the couch and to his bed.

"This couch is going to break your neck," the kid was saying. "I've set up the pillows on the mattress so there's less stress on your chest. Come on. Let's go. That's right."

"Where's my mom?" Sean managed to slur.

"Where tornadoes go to charge up for their destruction path the next day," Billy muttered. "My God, that woman's a lot."

Sean managed to chuckle weakly as Billy offered his shoulder. Sean took it and allowed himself to be helped to his feet.

"You were great with her," he said, not even self-conscious about it. "Man, haven't seen anyone put her in her place like that since Dad."

"What happened to your dad?" Billy asked, walking him slowly and steadily down the hall.

"Died on the job," Sean said. "Right when I was graduating from the academy. Believe me, you haven't *seen* drama."

"Sounds dire," Billy muttered.

"It was, *Guillermo*." Sean was a little miffed about that, and he couldn't figure out why.

"Sorry, man, it slipped out. Which is weird because nobody at the flophouse besides Henry even knows my real name."

Oh.

"Why Henry?"

"He helps us fill out our paperwork," Billy said. "I was going for my student loans."

Sean let go of the grudge against Henry he hadn't known he'd been carrying. "What're you studying?" he managed, not sure why it was necessary he and Billy indulge in dating conversation at this moment, but too interested to do otherwise.

"Engineering," Billy said shortly. They'd gotten to Sean's room, and once again Sean found himself deftly handled, lifted, positioned, and cared for until he was on his back, propped up just so, and able to both breathe *and* sleep.

"Too bad," Sean said, yawning as he fell into the pillows. "You're one hell of a nurse."

The faint sound of Billy's bitter laughter followed him into his dreams.

Nurse Billy

OH LORD. Billy had texted Henry for, of all things, a two-way intercom to help him with his new job. Henry had dropped it off the night before, after Billy had gotten Mr. Scary Cop with the Super Scary Mom to bed, and now, as Billy enjoyed the clean sheets on the double bed in the guest room, he could recognize the sounds coming through the electronic device.

His patient was waking up. Which mean Billy was about to be on.

Being "Nurse Billy" was possibly the easiest thing Billy had ever done for room and board—or it would be if his patient was a little more excited about being a patient and less excited about being super independent immediately.

"I hear you in there," Billy called, pulling himself upright on the super-comfy bed. "You don't even get to go to the john without me in there to—"

Thud. "Oolf!"

"—help you, you fucking asshole."

Goddammit. If this guy killed himself on Billy's watch, Billy was going to be pissed.

Billy hadn't been looking for an alternate gig from the flophouse—but he hadn't *not* been either. The flophouse—and hell, the porn gig at Johnnies—wasn't awful. He'd spent twenty years under the old man's roof; he *knew* awful. Rooming in an apartment with a bunch of guys was no big deal. He even liked the guys. They looked out for each other, and he may not have been the most demonstrative asshole on the planet, but he could appreciate that.

But porn was… exhausting. He'd been doing it for two years now, and he was so *tired*. The constant physical upkeep. The constant emotional seesaw. It felt like he'd spent a *lifetime* jumping up and down on his emotions to keep them in the right box. When he'd been living at home, the box had been heterosexually shaped, and it not only hadn't fit, it had been *excruciating*. When he'd been outed—and kicked out—the best part was not having to fit into that box.

Initially, porn had been sort of freeing that way. No strings—strings got messy, complicated, and embarrassing. No family. Just doing the things to make the other guy come. It had almost been a competitive sport, really. He remembered being a kid and challenging the other kids on the block to different tricks skateboarding. Porn was like that.

"Make that guy come with your hand. With your tongue. With your asshole. With one finger up *his* asshole. What other tricks can you do?"

So easy but so… detached.

He'd actually tried a girlfriend, thinking that maybe he was one kind of sexual and another kind of romantic—but that had been an on-and-off disaster, so maybe it was just the porn.

And he was one semester away from moving on to Sac State from Sac City. Not a big deal in *miles*, but *such* a big deal in terms of his long-term plans. So there he'd been, his situation not ideal but not awful either, and some hero had to get himself shot. And the only place to hide him?

Well, apparently Billy and Cotton's room in the flophouse.

Cotton, Billy's roommate, had taken one look at that soldier, half-dead and out of his mind with fever, and had practically transformed. One minute he was a big sloe-eyed *mess* who couldn't film one more damned porn scene without self-destructing and had no idea what to do with his life, and the next he was almost-dead guy's angel with a flaming sword. Selfless healer, advocate warrior, nurse extraordinaire. Cotton was going to save that hero if it was the last thing he did! Billy was all for helping with that—the guy had been running a mission to protect children, and Billy had been the oldest of six, so he got it. You did everything you could to protect the short people. But Cotton? Cotton apparently had dibs. Saving that guy had been the moment Cotton had been waiting for his whole lost life, and Billy had gotten moved to an inflatable mattress, which wasn't a problem, except the mattress was a little rough on the back.

And then Rivers, who apparently knew all the people, called Henry, the resident den mother, and said, "Hey, send someone over here. We need another nurse."

And Billy was so… so *impressed* by watching Cotton transform himself into that angel with the flaming sword that he stepped up.

He hadn't realized how easy Cotton'd had it. *His* hurt guy was mostly unconscious and apparently hadn't seen another gay man in a thousand years. *Billy's* hurt guy was a cop recovering from a punctured lung and a pneumothorax, and his ex-boyfriend had apparently stolen half his precious fucking movie collection on his way out the door.

Cotton's guy was all moony-eyed and shit.

Billy's guy was *pissed off.*

And Billy sort of got it. He understood pissed off—hell, *he* was pissed off, and had been since getting kicked out of the house. He'd been pissed off before that, even. Pissed off when he realized not every dad was so fucking heavy-handed with his fists. But a pissed-off cop was a whole lot different than an exhausted soldier; that became crystal clear with every moment.

Including this one, in which Billy was hauling ass through pissed-off cop's neat and charming little house to make sure the guy hadn't just made himself dead in his attempt to take a leak without some goddamned help.

"You couldn't fucking wait?" he asked, hands on his hips as he assessed the situation.

"I took a leak by myself in the hospital," Kryzynski defended from his crumpled-up position on the bedroom floor.

"Rails, right? You had rails from the bed to the little bathroom and inside the bathroom. Everything but a rail up your tight ass to make sure this didn't happen."

"Yes," the cop wheezed. The young detective was, thank God, still wearing the sleep pants and T-shirt Billy had helped him into the night before. He'd apparently gotten up, taken a few steps, and gotten almost as far as the door frame before, what?

"Did you get dizzy?" Billy asked, arms crossed over his bare chest. Unlike half the kids in the flophouse, he didn't sleep naked, and his boxers were in pristine condition—but he wasn't putting a T-shirt on in August. Ick.

"Yes," Kryzynski said again. "I… if you could give me a hand up…."

He sounded miserable and defeated, and Billy scowled. That hadn't been his intention. "I can't just leverage you up like a buddy at a party," he said. "And I don't want to jostle you too much, or I'm afraid of opening up your lung again or inflaming all that tissue. Don't look so surprised. I read up on your wound, asked Lance a few questions. I'm not hopeless." Lance had been a guy who worked for Johnnies, the same porn studio Billy did. But Lance had gotten his medical degree and gotten out. Or maybe he'd met Henry and gotten out. Billy didn't know how it all happened, but Lance and Henry were an item now. Lance was a doctor and no longer worked in porn, and they lived in the apartment downstairs where Lance could answer Billy's dumbass questions about how not to kill the guy he was supposed to be nursing back to health. And the first item on the list was not letting him crumple up around his chest like that because he needed a fully inflated lung.

"I just... wait," Billy said. "Okay. Here's what we're going to do. Sit up, your back against the dresser." He got to his knees and gave the guy his arms to use as leverage and then more or less took over, hefting him up by his shoulders and shoving him backward, then positioning his feet. It took more effort than Kryzynski probably anticipated, and he was breathing heavily before he was in position, but that was fine. This way, he would *wait* next time so Billy could do his freakin' job!

Finally they were both in the position Billy had planned, but Billy let him catch his breath.

"Does this suck?" he asked as Kryzynski struggled to even his breathing.

Kryzynski nodded his head.

"Does this suck enough to wait for me next time?" he prodded.

Kryzynski glowered at him with enough anger to take Billy's head off at the neck, but Billy just stared back. Yeah, he was a big bad cop and all, but Billy's old man had been pissed off *and* violent. Billy could deal with all bark and no bite. And after two years working out for top muscle tone, he could also knock someone's teeth in if they tried to bite him.

"Well?" Billy prompted.

"Fine," Kryzynski wheezed. "I... just... didn't...."

"Want to bother me so you could go piss by yourself," Billy finished, because he had no patience at all. "I get it. We all want our dignity. But you know what? I work in a job where three different people tell me how to achieve maximum poop, and then I have to have a buddy check my asshole to make sure maximum poop has been achieved and all traces eliminated. Dignity is a fucking illusion. You call my name, I come help you to the bathroom, and with any luck, I don't even remember seeing your wiener. With *bad* luck, you need help wiping your own ass, but let me tell you something. You would not be the first, and I literally have no shits left to give. Are we clear?"

Kryzynski's eyes were huge. "Understood," he rasped.

"Excellent. Now I'm going to get on my knees in front of you, and you're going to wrap your arms around my neck like we're dancing. As I stand up, you're going to push with your legs, I'm going to hoist under your arms, and maybe we can get you to the bathroom for your morning piss. What do you say?"

There was a sudden wash of heat between them, and Billy caught his breath.

Oh God. All that talk—all that Billy-gives-no-shits talk—about how it's all a body function and who cares? And suddenly Billy was bare-chested and in close proximity with this rather nice-looking police officer who had lied to his mother the day before to make Billy more comfortable.

Billy blinked slowly and met Detective Sean Kryzynski's big country-boy-blue eyes.

And tried not to think about how the man's heat blush had warmed Billy's chest, right down to his now-tingly nipples.

"What, uhm, do you say, Kryz... uhm, Sean?" he asked, hating himself for fumbling with his words.

"Ready, captain," Sean whispered.

Billy nodded and tried for a reassuring smile. "If we can do the bathroom thing, I promise I'll do the coffee thing. I'm much less of an asshole after coffee."

Sean gave a sudden surprised smile, and Billy began the slow, steady rise to his feet.

HALF AN hour later, Billy was dressed in cargo shorts and a tank, and Kryzynski was in exactly what he'd been wearing when he'd fallen down on his bedroom floor—minus five pounds of "dignity."

"I don't want to talk about it," he mumbled as Billy helped him walk down the hall.

"I told you, you're not the first guy I've ever had to do that for," Billy told him. He wasn't exactly *enjoying* the young detective's discomfort so much as *appreciating* it. The thing with living in the flophouse for two years was that boundaries had completely disappeared since day one. It was absolutely not unheard of to hear someone belting from their *one* bathroom, "Hey! Anybody out there? I did arms yesterday for my workout and I need someone to wipe my ass!" The fact that this filled Sean Kryzynski with mortification was like a sort of affirmation of the best of mankind.

"Please?" Kryzynski begged. "I can pretend it didn't happen in the hospital, but here…."

Billy let out a sigh as the hallway opened up and they neared the dining room table, and what looked like really uncomfortable padded metal chairs.

"Look, I get it," he admitted, helping his patient sit and then scooting him to the breakfast table. "I promise, this can be our last discussion about the matter. I don't want you to feel bad because you're still hurt."

He straightened and turned toward the kitchen in time for Kryzynski's weird little "*hunh*."

"What? What is that sound?"

His startlement was met with a pair of puzzled blue eyes. "It was a '*hunh*'—I don't think you'll find it in the dictionary."

"*That*," Billy said accusingly, "was a *Jackson Rivers* sound."

"What, the guy has his own lexi—" Labored breath. "—con now?"

"I don't know what that word you just used was, but yes. Believe me, in our world, that man is sacred. We study his ways. Did you steal a Jackson Rivers sound, and why?"

"I didn't steal it!" Kryzynski argued before taking a deep breath. "And I was just… you were nice. I was confused. You're only nice sometimes."

Great. He was *supposed* to be nursing the guy back to health, but apparently he was being a big fat dick.

"I'm not trying to be a bastard," he admitted, opening the refrigerator door and studying the contents. "I was the oldest of six and in charge of mustering the troops. If a shoelace was untied or a backpack missing, guess who caught hell?"

"Guillermo?" Kryzynski asked, and Billy glared over his shoulder, damning himself for letting the name slip when Mommy Kryzynski had shown up.

"Could you forget you ever heard that name?" he asked soberly.

Kryzynski cocked his head as though thinking about it, and then gave a negative little shake of his chin. "You are far too interesting as a

Guillermo and not just a Billy," he said, and then gulped a breath of air and coughed.

"Stop trying to talk," Billy muttered gruffly. "Anyway, I loved my siblings. Like, you would not *believe* how much I miss the little assholes. But I sucked at hiding bruises, so I got real good at not fucking around." He sighed. "The old man ran his house like he ran his unit, and I was his first lieutenant. You learn to be an asshole if you need to be, you know?"

"Yeah," Kryzynski said, nodding. "I get it."

Billy didn't want to talk about it anymore—hadn't wanted to talk about it in the first place—so he went back to the refrigerator, trying to remember Henry's rudimentary cooking lessons. Oh! Eggs, cheese, onions, mushrooms…. Henry's snarky commentary inserted itself into his head. "I know what's for breakfast," he said proudly, gathering ingredients.

"What?" Kryzynski asked.

"A make-you-a frittata!"

"What?" And now the guy sounded riled and irritated again, and there were no personal revelations or sudden intimacies between them.

Perfect.

"You'll see. This is Henry's first cooking lesson. Easy enough for a little kid to do it."

Chuckling to himself, Billy set about preparing a basic egg scramble, remembering the words to the song he and the other flophouse guys had made up to sing to the old Disney standard and belting it out.

Make you a frittata,
With just a couple of eggs.
Make me a frittata,
There's plenty of ways.
You won't have to worry about food the rest of your day.
It's a gluten free
Ensemble feed….
Make you a frittata!

He finished the song as he turned on the burner and started cracking eggs. Behind him he heard Kryzynski's rusty chuckle and figured he'd dodged the intimacy bullet using quick thinking and bad singing.

A few minutes later he dished up a plate full of eggs and cheese for Kryzynski and a much smaller plate of egg whites, tomatoes, and chives for himself.

His patient looked happily at his own breakfast and then eyed Billy's plate with surprise.

"That's it?" he rasped. "That's all you're going to eat?"

Oh no. They had to get this all out of the way right quick. "Look, before you ask or it's a thing?" Billy said. "Yes, we all have eating disorders. Yes, it's because we're naked on camera and we read the comments where people start discussing our BMI and giving us tips on living on iced tea and good wishes. No, I'm not going to change it just for you. And yes, I am getting treatment. You eat your frittata, and I'll eat mine, and we won't talk about it, okay?"

"Fine," Kryzynski muttered. "Great. Ketchup?"

Billy felt his professional pride as a frittata maker assaulted. "You taste that first," he ordered, stung. "And while it's hot!"

Kryzynski gave him a vaguely uncomfortable look. "I… I'm having flashbacks to living with my mother," he said, sounding baffled. "And it's delicious. But I still want ketchup because I'm a barbarian. I'm sorry. The heart wants what it wants. I don't know what to tell you."

Billy took a bite of his own and sighed. "You're right. Garlic salt, Detective Kryzynski. And chili powder. Your whole world would be so much tastier with a few more spices. I'm saying."

"Please?" Kryzynski begged.

"Fine." Billy stood up and grabbed the ketchup bottle from the fridge. And then a jar of salsa, which he preferred.

He handed Sean his bottle and grabbed his jar, doctoring his own food before he ate. He took his second bite and made a much more satisfied sound.

"And for the record," he said, after swallowing and savoring another mouthful, "if you have salsa *and* hot sauce, like you do, you're not a barbarian. Misguided, yes, but still kind of civilized. We won't have to throw you on your own island yet."

Kryzynski swallowed his own bite and grinned. "Good to know," he said.

Billy winked at him, feeling pleased with himself, and once the coffee was done, he really did feel like a brand-new person.

He settled his patient on the couch while he finished the breakfast dishes and ran to take a quick shower. When he returned, Kryzynski was falling asleep in front of an action flick and struggling to sit up.

"What are you doing?" Billy snapped. He'd timed himself. Between breakfast dishes and the world's fastest shower, the man had been on the couch for twenty minutes. "Why are you—are you trying to stand?"

"I can stand." Sean Kryzynski had, on the surface, a little boy's face, with a square jaw but a smaller nose and a vulnerable mouth. And, of course, the big baby blues. The almost perpetual scowl Billy had seen on that face made him look like a grumpy little man, and it was hard for Billy to take him seriously when he said things like that.

"Yes, you can. I've seen it. But why? Why do you have to stand now? You had a bowel movement, you had breakfast, you walked down the hall. You've been a productive little soldier, and now it's time to kick back and let your body heal. Why is this a problem?"

Kryzynski squinted at him. "Aren't I supposed to get better every day? I have a list of exercises I'm supposed to do. Shouldn't I, you know, do those next?"

Billy was going to smack him. "I have the list. But first kick back and rest for an hour. Trust me. It's like working out. You work out, you rest. When you work out hard, you literally give your muscles little tears and shit, and when you rest, they heal back together stronger. That's how you bulk up. This is the same thing, but the muscles you're building are all the things that let you pull air into your lungs."

That squint turned into a glare.

"What did I say?"

"I know how to work out."

In response, Billy ran a critical eye over Kryzynski's body, sweeping him from head to toe with enough blatant assessment to make the man's cheeks turn pink.

Good.

What he saw wasn't bad, really. The cop kept himself in good shape—lots of toned runner's muscle, some gym bulk, but mostly the sort of body that was kept tight and fed well in order to make it a more efficient machine. The runner's muscle was probably to catch bad guys. The gym bulk was probably to make sure Kryzynski had some power in a fight. Yeah, the guy had been in the hospital for nearly two weeks, and he had lost some mass, but once he got his wind back, he'd recover.

But it wouldn't do to let him feel all cocky and shit because then he wouldn't rest.

"*Mmm….*" He made the sound skeptical. "Do you? Do you really?"

For a moment Kryzynski tried to puff himself up, which made sense—he was maybe five eight, five nine on a good day. Billy knew what that was like, being five seven himself. Always trying to make yourself bigger because the whole world tried to make you feel small. Billy figured that on most days, Kryzynski did okay, made himself really big, the biggest cock of the walk. But it was hard to puff up your chest when you had no puff, and today, he let out a pitiful breath and sagged back against the arm of the couch.

"Can I at least move to the recliner so when I have to pee it's not a major production?" he begged pitifully.

"Yeah, sure," Billy said, feeling generous. "Let me help you—are you stupid? Did you hear what I said?"

The glare was back, but dammit, the guy had twisted to put one hand on the back of the couch to boost himself up, and Billy could see the grimace of pain from the back of the guy's head.

"I'm not stupid!" Kryzynski snapped. "I'm injured. You don't need to—" He fought for breath. "—treat me," he wheezed, "like a…."

"You don't want to be treated like a shitty little third grader? Then don't *act* like a shitty little third grader. Now you will sit there and wait for me to come help you because I've got manners and shit. Are we clear?"

"Fuck you," Kryzynski muttered, but all the fight had gone out of him, and Billy figured he'd heard.

"The list is long and well paid," Billy snapped back, and then he let out some of his own mad as he bent his knees and held his arm stiff, crooked at the elbow at his side. "Now grab my arm and let me do some of the work, okay? I'm not trying to piss you off, you stubborn asshole, I'm *trying* to help you. Fucking let me."

He felt the determination in Kryzynski's fingers as they dug into his arm and he let himself be escorted to the recliner instead of the couch. It was a solid piece of furniture—he was right. The next time he needed to get up, this would make it easier.

"We didn't get you on the recliner in the first place, why?" he asked.

Kryzynski grunted. "Because I usually save it for company. Andre loves it."

Billy settled him in and grabbed the throw from the couch to keep him snug against the admittedly stellar air conditioning.

"Well, this time you get the good seat," he said. "But I'm going to shore you up with pillows on your injured side because we want you to breathe there."

Kryzynski made a noise of assent. "You're weirdly good at this," he said grudgingly. "I mean, I wasn't expecting a drill sergeant, but I can admit, you're taking this really—" Breath. "—seriously."

"Like I said," Billy told him, "in my world, when Rivers asks you for a favor, you do it twice. In this case, the favor was taking care of you."

This time, the noise was of frustration.

"What? What do you want to ask?" he prompted.

"A thousand things," Kryzynski rasped. "No wind."

Billy nodded. "Well then, don't say anything. Here's the remote control. Point and click. You seem to have every streaming service known to man. I don't know why you're so upset about your DVDs."

"They're my favorites," he said briefly. "What do you—" Breath. "—want to—"

"Don't worry about me. I'm going to get my laptop to start my homework. My classes begin this week. Don't worry, we've got a schedule at the flophouse so you don't get left alone when I've got school or work. I was cutting down on my wait shifts anyway for school, so I only do that twice a week too."

Kryzynski frowned, and Billy knew what he was going to ask before he asked it. "What about…?"

"Shooting scenes at Johnnies?" he asked. "Yeah, I've got one in a couple of days. After that, I've got another one in about six weeks. I've got someone lined up to sub for me in a couple of days, and in six weeks I'll probably be long gone."

Kryzynski frowned again, but Billy didn't want to talk about porn anymore. He was going to take advantage of the fact that the guy was still out of wind and go fetch his laptop. He had some humanities classes that semester, and he was going to have to do a lot of reading before school even started if he didn't want to be behind.

Uncomfortable Options

THE KID sitting on the couch and captaining the remote control had bright red hair, freckles on his bare arms, neck, and cheeks, and the big sloppy smile of a Labrador mixed with a happy Great Dane. He wore the same uniform Billy seemed to, with a T-shirt stretched over his chest, cargo shorts hanging off his absurdly narrow hips, and, in this kid's case, a pair of bright lime-green Crocs, but Kryzynski could recognize the difference between the two kids even in the dark, and that was without seeing Randy's Crocs glow.

"You got everything you need?" Randy asked, big green eyes wide and friendly. "Billy said you probably didn't need to move a lot, but you might need help to the john. I'm good for that. I help the sick guy in our apartment all the time."

Sean tried to keep his smile friendly and not shocked. He was twenty-nine goddamned years old, but damned if between Billy and this kid he didn't feel a thousand.

"I don't have to pee right now," he said gently. "I'll let you know." Billy had more than drilled into him that he still needed help getting up and down, emphasizing that Randy had zero filters and really did not care one way or another about seeing another person naked. Sean had nodded his head at the time, not understanding, but now that he'd met the kid, he got it. Wieners were, apparently, no big deal for Randy. Sean suppressed a smile at the thought. "What do you want to watch?" he asked.

"You've got *all* the streaming services?" Randy asked excitedly. He looked around as though somebody might be listening in at the window of Sean's small neat duplex. "Even Disney+?"

Sean fought against a smile. "Yeah. Disney+."

"So we can watch *Aladdin*? Because that's my favorite!"

Sean's grumpy old heart twisted in his chest. He'd been expecting Marvel or Star Wars or something—he was on board—but... but *Aladdin*? That was for, well, little kids!

But then, the look on this giant kid's face was not exactly adult.

"Knock yourself out," he said. For the first two days after he'd arrived home, he'd been king of the remote control, and he was over it. He'd tried his damnedest, but he couldn't get Billy to confess to any preferences of his own. It was almost as though that whole "second in command parent" thing had precluded the guy from having any *likes* of his own, and, like much of Billy, it drove Sean to distraction.

The guy was crisp, military, and for someone who claimed he was going to be an engineer, damned good at the whole nursing thing when Sean was, admittedly, not the best of patients. But he was not exactly forthcoming about himself in any way.

Or he hadn't been until the emergency work call had come up—the reason Randy was there in the first place. After that call arrived, they'd begun forging a tentative relationship. It didn't mean Sean wasn't over being king of the remote—and it didn't mean he was comfortable with what Billy was doing that day either—but it did mean Sean felt a little more connected to his temporary roommate.

Sean just wished there'd been another way to break the ice than knowing that body—that glorious Adonis body—and those cynical, hurt eyes were out somewhere getting hard use by a stranger.

Billy had a scene.

SEAN HAD been watching an action flick in the recliner when Billy had picked up his cell phone the day after the make-you-a-frittata breakfast.

"Yo, Dex! What's up, man?"

Sean cocked his head—since he'd just done his exercises and couldn't move much else in his body—to listen. Dex was, he knew, Billy's boss and Henry's brother. How that all happened he had no idea... and didn't really care at this point. He'd thrown it all in a box in his mind, neatly labeled it Jackson's Porn Mess, and left it the hell alone.

What mattered here was that Billy had *thought* he wasn't going to be doing any scenes until Sean was better and Billy had moved out, the better for the two of them to never intersect again, and that had been fine with Sean.

Billy listened for a moment and then grimaced. "Oh no!" he'd muttered. "Hell. That's no good. Yeah, I can film it, but, you know, two days late. I've been eating like a horse."

He listened to the voice on the line and chuckled. "Civilian life for me means an extra egg white. Pathetic and sad, yes, but still looking forward to it."

Some more listening, and then Sean felt himself the object of some side-eye. "No, this gig's okay. No, no—he's a shitty patient, but you know me. Not exactly Florence Fucking Nightingale, right?"

There was a beat, and then Billy's mouth twisted with an honest-to-God smile.

"No, Dex, I don't know if that was her real middle name, because like you I'm not getting my degree in humanities." Dex said something else, and Billy chuckled, then sobered. "Actually, man—yeah. I need somebody to come watch my patient while I'm working. Please tell me not everybody from the flophouse is busy that day?" He grimaced. "Randy? Okay. Yeah. Well, no, you're right. Randy's a good kid. He's calmed down a *lot*. Okay, good. Yeah, I'll see you in three days. No problem, man. We're good."

He hit End Call, and Sean turned his attention back to the television before Billy could notice he was listening.

Apparently, he fooled nobody.

"You heard?" Billy asked.

Sean swallowed, unsure why this should bother him. He didn't even *know* this guy, except for the last two days he'd been a crisp, no-bullshit, pain-in-his-ass drill sergeant who had kept him fed, bathed, and yes, even kept his ass wiped, and Sean was indebted to him. What did this kid owe him? Obviously not anything personal—all Sean's attempts at conversation had been rebuffed. Sean's mother had called every day, and Billy had given her a professional-quality update and then kept her visits down to fifteen minutes, thank heavens. Billy knew Sean's brother's name, his brother's wife's name, and his sisters' names, but every time Sean tried to call Billy "Guillermo," Billy looked at him like he was violating his privacy.

The truth was, Billy didn't owe him *squat* in terms of loyalty or conversation or personal information, but still…. Sean was curious. And he felt the tiniest bit possessive. This was his boy, after all, right?

What does that even mean?

Sean shook off the obnoxious little voice. Dammit, he wanted to know, that was all.

"You have to shoot a scene anyway?" he asked.

"Yeah. Turns out their new guy needed a scene, and the guy he was supposed to film with broke his wrist BMXing, and he's going to be high as a kite for a week or so while they wait for the swelling from the surgery to go down so they can set it. Poor kid—I think the whole reason he's working this job is to buy more equipment for his bike. He's pretty well-ranked in the sport, or at least he was, you know, before he broke his wrist."

Sean sucked air in through his teeth, able to feel sympathy for this unknown kid who'd had a personal setback and a painful injury, but unable to figure out his feelings for Billy, the guy who was oh-so casually going to go have sex with a random stranger in BMX guy's place.

"That sucks," he rasped, and Billy rolled his eyes.

"Yeah, so now I have to. Sorry, man. I know how you probably feel about this job. I was trying to spare you the dirty details, but…." He shrugged. "Dex and John are pretty good to us—health, mental health, dental. They got a program started for after porn, 'cause not all the guys are thinking that far into the future, right? So Dex needs my help and…." He shrugged again, and Sean nodded, part of him touched because Billy was being sort of a stand-up guy.

But part of him was irritated, and he wasn't sure what to do with that.

He took a shallow breath—no deep breaths for him yet—and said, "I appreciate that you tried. I mean, you're right. I'm not comfortable with what you do for a living, but you tried to make me comfortable. That was nice. Thank you."

It was Billy's turn to cock his head. "That's it? That's all you got to say?"

Sean turned blindly toward the television set. "I don't own you," he said gruffly. "I don't own your time. You made a good-faith effort, and you're trying to do your boss a solid. I… even if I *did* have something to say about it, I wouldn't have any right to say it, would I?"

Billy let out his own breath. "No," he agreed. "But that hasn't seemed to stop you yet."

Sean glared at him. "What?" he tried to snap, but his voice didn't do that yet. Not enough force behind his vocal cords. It came out like a rasp. "Hhwwwhhhath?" That was fine, though. Billy apparently got his back up with Sean's intentions and not his actual tone.

"You got an opinion on everything is all. I should be a nurse and not an engineer. Rivers should be resting and not helping Cotton. I should stick to waiting tables and ignore the nice big cash influx that porn gives me—"

"I never said that," Sean protested.

"Yeah, but I could read your fucking mind every time I brought it up."

Sean glared at him, even though so far the glare had no effect on this kid whatsoever. "That is not my fault. I can have opinions on all sorts of things, but if I don't try to make them *your* opinions, you don't get to argue."

"Ha! That suits you fine, doesn't it? You just glare at me and wish I was fuckin' dead and call me a whore in your mind, but it's all my fault I'm taking it bad?"

Sean gasped and then coughed, and then scowled because he *needed* to answer that one and goddammit, he had no wind yet. "I never said that," he managed. "I never *thought* it. And if you heard it, you imagined it's what I thought. I may be a good Catholic boy with a lot of baggage, but I've worked at being better than that sort of judgy asshole, so you need to take that back."

It was true. Sean could admit it. A year ago he'd met Ellery Cramer while Jackson had been in the hospital. Sean had been hit hard with the crush, but Ellery had already been so far gone over Jackson that Sean hadn't had a chance. And Sean—who had only heard what the department had to say about Jackson, and none of it was good—had wondered why. For the last year, he'd made Jackson Leroy Rivers and Ellery Cramer his study, and the thing that had most impressed him—the thing that Ellery seemed to have fallen truly and deeply in love with— had been Jackson's ability to accept people without judgment. It was hard as a cop; it was his *job* to judge people. He arrested them, brought them to punishment, helped the DA make a case against them. Right and wrong were very concrete, right? So how could Jackson make his way through the prostitutes and drug addicts, through the petty thieves and drunks, and not see the dregs of society? The thing that cops were protecting nice people *from* as opposed to the nice people Jackson felt needed protecting from the police?

And the more Sean had worked with the two of them, the more he'd realized that every person had a story. Every person started as a human being. Even the bad guys—and there were some real pieces of shit out there—started out as people.

After a year of working to change his perspective, of working with Henry, who mentored these kids, with Jackson, who protected them, and with Ellery, who defended them without question, Sean had all but eliminated the word "whore" from his vocabulary, unless he was talking about a crooked politician. He was *damned* if this kid would call him out when he hadn't even been thinking the word—or any judgment really.

He'd mostly been wondering why he felt uncomfortable that *Billy* would be the one filming the scene.

"All right, all right," Billy said, holding his hands out. "I'm sorry, Mr. Soft and Sensitive. Forgive me if I didn't know you had a tender underbelly. You've been nothing but attitude since I got here."

Sean shook his head, hurt. "How would you know?" he asked. "I can't even get you to commit to a television show or answer my questions about music or books. How am I supposed to talk to you as a human when you're all 'Don't mind me, I'm a fucking island' while I'm stuck on the goddamned couch!"

The sound Billy made then was sort of like the one Sean had made when he'd been stabbed. Sort of a squeak and an *oolf* and a gasp all at the same time.

"It's not like you meant any of that shit," Billy retorted. "You were fucking humoring me because I make your damned meals and help you in the shower, right?"

Sean sent him a wounded look but didn't answer. Just shook his head and turned back to the television. He had no idea what he was watching, but it was supposed to be good, right?

Following a long silence, Sean actually *did* start to watch the show. Had *NCIS* really been on since 2003? Wow. He'd had no idea. Well, time to watch from the beginning because he was getting interested.

"I'm sorry," Billy said, and for once he didn't sound snarky or sarcastic. He sounded, well, sorry. "I… I figured you being a cop and all, you were probably just putting up with me."

Sean let out a breath, but he couldn't look at Billy now. He'd gotten used to the cynicism, the hardness in his eyes. "I used to be that kind of cop," he admitted. "I like to think I've grown."

"Well, I'm sorry. I didn't mean to be rude and shit. I didn't want to hear it if you thought I was a whore."

Sean was startled into looking over to the couch by the nakedness of the statement. The kid he saw there was… smaller somehow. Still the wide-shouldered Adonis with the impressive gym muscles—he used Sean's weights and treadmill every day—but also not the impressive drill sergeant with the attitude.

"I… I don't," he said, hoping it was true. "I wish you did something else—I'm just not comfortable about sex in public, I'm sorry—but I get it. Waiting tables doesn't pay the rent or the tuition. Like I said, you don't owe me shit. I just… you know. Wish you'd talk to me." He nodded at the television. "I mean, this show's not bad, but sometimes you want another human in the house for a reason."

Billy's mouth twisted into that familiar smile, but this time it had a softer edge. "Here," he said. "Hit Pause for a minute, let me finish this paragraph I was reading before Dex called, and I'll watch it with you. I used to like cop shows when I was a kid. Something about believing in good guys. Never gets old, even when you know it's all crap, right?"

"Right," Sean said sadly. *He* was a cop and it had once made him proud. What could he do to convince this kid it wasn't all crap?

He didn't know. But at that moment, it was enough for Billy to finish his homework, and then they snarked their way through three episodes of the show before Sean felt absolutely compelled to take a nap.

The three days since had been easier. Billy still had homework—and he still worked out when Sean was resting—but the time they spent watching television and movies together was more companionable and less Billy humoring Sean because that's what he thought his job was.

It had been… nice. Sean had mentioned liking jigsaw puzzles at one point, and Billy had ordered him one. He told Sean it had been on Jackson's dime when Sean protested, and Sean reminded himself that he should pay Rivers back, but he'd enjoyed listening to music and putting the puzzle together while Billy struggled with his first week's homework. The young man's pithy and often acid comments regarding the literature he was reading were interesting and often eye-opening.

"So Oscar Wilde was gay?"

"Very gay," Sean confirmed. *"Served four years in prison for being gay, if I remember."*

Billy snorted. "Well, I hope he's comforted by the fact that all the theater kids think he's a god."

It was a tentative friendship, and Sean was glad since that "need a nurse for a week or so" was bullshit, and he'd apparently need Billy's help for at least another month. But that didn't change the fact that in the meantime, Billy was still filling in on his job, having sex for a living.

SEAN TOOK a breath and tried to adjust himself on the couch, noticing as he did that Randy was sitting on his floor, arms wrapped around his shins, with a rapt expression on his face, completely intent on the opening credits of *Aladdin*.

As Sean watched, Randy's lips started to move as he lip-synced the opening songs.

Sean's eyes burned.

Oh my God—this kid. This kid was a *coworker* of Billy's, which meant he *shot porn* for a living, but… but… *look at him*. What mother had let this kid out of her sight to be naked with strangers when he still sang the words to cartoons with that rapturous attention?

In an effort not to start prying into Randy's life, Sean turned his attention to the screen, getting caught up in the story of the street rat with a heart of gold who really was a diamond in the rough.

Billy was gone until late afternoon, which meant Randy had watched *Aladdin, The Lion King, Zootopia*, and they were in the middle of *Madagascar 3* before the front doorknob jiggled and Billy called, "It's me. Everybody put away the cigarettes and booze."

Randy let out a dorky guffaw, and Sean—who had gone to nap through *Zootopia* but had been there for the ride through most of the other cartoons—felt a stab of relief for another adult in the room. He felt a level of exhaustion that usually accompanied babysitting his nieces and nephews and suddenly wondered if the rest of the flophouse guys felt like that around Randy.

"All put away," Randy called, scrambling to his feet. "Come on in." Suddenly he looked almost comically put out, as though he really *had* been put out. "Oh my God! I was going to put on mac and cheese and hot dogs for you! My bad. It's your favorite! It was the last thing Cotton said to me as I walked out the door!" He ran toward the kitchen as Billy let himself in. "Shit, Billy—my bad! I was gonna do the thing, but I got sort of distracted!"

"No worries. Here, put away the pots and pans, man. I brought pizza!"

Randy's eyes got really big. "Not with—"

"Your side's got feta and spinach—no lactose. No worries."

The look on Randy's face was pathetically grateful, and he went to get the box from Billy to set it on the table. "You're so good to me," he said happily. "I'm sorry about the mac and cheese. I even brought a bag of groceries!"

Sean remembered that—Randy had been in a rush to put the hot dogs in the fridge after Billy had left.

"I'll eat it tomorrow," Billy promised. "'Cause man, I gotta tell you, it's hitting me *hard* today."

Sean had watched him stare longingly at Sean's pathetically small meals over the last three days as he'd nibbled vegetables and drank chicken broth and apple juice to clean out his system. Sean had never really thought of it before—too much good-boy guilt to let him watch porn and really enjoy it, maybe—but cleaning out the system was apparently a real prerequisite for any sort of sex on film, particularly between men who waxed all their pubic hair, even what was in their ass cracks.

"Yeah," Randy said on a sigh. "I just *can't* sometimes. That's why—" He cast Sean a surreptitious look. "Anyway, thanks for the pizza."

Sean remembered Billy's comment that "all of us have eating disorders," and he remembered this kid watching animated features all day and practically wanted to cry.

"Definitely thanks for the pizza," he said. "If someone wants to help me to the table—oh."

Randy reached over the couch and put a paper plate in his lap, full of two slices of sausage, pepperoni, mushroom, and olive.

"Damn," he said, inhaling lightly. "Seriously, thanks."

Billy chuckled and came to flop down in the corner of the couch, his own paper plate full of spinach, goat cheese, and garlic, from the looks of it. Sean started feeling guilty all over again.

"You're not even going to have sausage?" he asked.

Billy looked back over at Randy and mouthed, "Later. He misses cheese."

"Oh!"

Randy came back and folded his legs to sit on the floor, and together they finished the movie. When they were done, the kid stood and dutifully took everybody's plates, lifting Billy's carefully from his lap. It wasn't until then that Sean realized he'd fallen asleep, head tilted back, snoring lightly.

"All fucked out," Randy murmured, and Sean grimaced.

"Uhm...."

"I mean, everybody thinks 'What a way to go,'" Randy said soberly, consolidating the plates and grabbing Sean's empty bottle of water, probably to refill it. "But it's exhausting. And all your parts hurt—your abs, your thighs, your asshole. If you run out of lube, you've got rug burn in unfortunate places, and you're starving, but your stomach hurts because you haven't eaten for three days. And the guys who have to take chemical aids and stuff to get it up are usually queasy and buzzing. It's a really shitty time after a scene." He grimaced. "It's why I was going to cook for him. We started doing that for each other in the flophouse, and I forgot. I mean...." He sighed. "The pizza was nice, but I think a homecooked meal would have been better."

"You can cook it now," Sean told him. "I've got plastic containers and stuff. That way, he can heat some up for dinner tomorrow, and you can take some to the flophouse to share."

Randy's face lit up. "That's awesome!" He hushed himself. "And that way, when I'm done, the Uber can come get me."

"Illgetchu," Billy mumbled, crossing his arms and burrowing into the couch a little tighter.

Sean laughed softly to himself. "Go ahead and start the water boiling," he said. "And when you're done"—he grimaced sheepishly—"if I could get a hand up to the bathroom?"

Randy grinned. "I knew you'd have to go *sometime*," he said. "Sure."

AFTER THE bathroom, Sean had Randy help him into bed. He wasn't quite ready to sleep yet, but he had his earbuds and his phone, and that way Billy could have the couch. He told Randy to find a throw in the closet and put it over Billy's chest because the air conditioning was finally starting to work and it would help him sleep better.

He must have dozed off at some point, though, because his audiobook had turned off automatically and the darkness through his bedroom window was complete, with only the outside light shining through, when the hall light went on and startled him awake.

Billy's silhouette appeared in the doorway. "Sean?"

"*Mmm*." He yawned and turned carefully to his side so he could reach to tap the base of the lamp for light. "Come in."

"Just checking on you," Billy said, but he came in anyway and sat in the chair by the bedstand. "Wasn't sure if Randy helped you get ready or—"

"He did fine," Sean told him. "Even offered to help me brush my teeth. I guess someone told him his gums were really important. We had a whole discussion about flossing. Scintillating stuff."

Billy chuckled weakly, and in the lamplight, Sean could see that Randy had been right. He looked sleepy and out of it and like he was trying to remember how to be the adult in the room.

"I don't even know how he got home," he said, confirming Sean's assessment. "I was supposed to drive him, since he doesn't have a car."

"He said something about an Uber," Sean told him. "He was going to make you mac and cheese with hot dogs before he left."

Billy smiled slightly and nodded. "Yeah. He did. It looks like he made a double batch and took some for the guys too. That was sweet. He's a mess sometimes, but he really is a good kid."

"So fucking young," Sean said, and then could have bitten his tongue. He didn't want Billy to think he was being condescending or pitying or anything, but there was such a difference. Billy was obviously a few years older, but more than that, he was wiser and more seasoned in almost every aspect of the adult world. With Billy the porn felt like a practical choice, but with Randy it felt like an accident that he just kept falling into.

To his surprise, though, Billy agreed with him.

"He drives us all crazy," he said. "Because on screen, it looks great. He looks at a guy and goes, 'I'm going to fuck your asshole until you scream,' and the porn is *fantastic* because he does exactly what he says, and the guy comes until his eyes roll back in his head and he can't use real words. But then you see Randy in real life and realize that he says that because he says *everything* as he thinks it, and you realize that he has *no* filter, and that it's only sexy in porn because you think it's attached to a grown-up who doesn't have six-thousand allergies and can't eat cheese."

"In a kid who still cries during *The Lion King*...." Sean tried to finish the thought, but Billy beat him to it.

"It's fucking tragic," Billy said, nodding. "And he's not stupid. I helped him with his GED, and I got to see his grades from high school before he got kicked out of the house. He was an honors student, man. But some kids are old at sixteen, and some kids can be married and have kids and still need someone to slap them upside the head and say 'Think, *pendejo*, think!' You know what I'm talking about?"

Sean let out a sad chuckle. "Yeah. Yeah, I do. Henry says it a lot— that just because the guys in the apartment have working penises, that doesn't mean they're adults. I don't think I really got it until today."

Billy shot him an evil grin. "You mean my big Bambi eyes didn't make you all melty inside?"

Sean snorted—or tried to, but still no air. "You've been kicking my ass six dozen ways to Sunday. I think we're pretty even on the adulting scale."

Billy let out a chuff of air that might have been a chuckle, but then he sobered. "Sorry about falling asleep. I always forget, you know? How wiped out you get."

Sean's mouth twisted. "Well, it's been a while since I had regular sex, so I wouldn't know either."

Billy cocked his head. "Mr. I-Stole-Your-DVDs didn't put out?"

Sean raised his free shoulder. "He was a fireman and still in the closet. He saw me when he could, and then I'd get the hose."

Billy's eyebrows went up. "Booty call? You were booty call?"

Sean sucked air in through his teeth. "I wouldn't put it like *that*—"

"That don't make it not true!" Billy protested. "Man, that's dirty. You shouldn't have to be a booty call."

Sean simply stared at him and raised his eyebrows, and Billy rolled his eyes in return.

"Yeah, so I just had sex on camera for money, but that was my choice. If I hadn't liked the guy, I could have told Dex no—we have that right. It's in our contracts. But this guy, he just calls you up when he's off and says, 'Hey, buttercup, let's have a relationship'? That's not right. I did that to a girl for a little while." He grimaced. "Not my finest hour."

Sean blinked. *That* was a curveball. "Bi?" he queried, feeling lost at sea.

"Questioning, I guess." Billy shrugged. "At least right after I started porn. I'd had exactly one relationship before porn, and I was like, 'This don't feel like what sex is supposed to feel like. Maybe I'm not gay.'"

"And…?" Sean couldn't help it. He was *dying* of curiosity about something that was absolutely none of his business.

"And I had an on/off thing with a girl I met in school. And when we were on, we went to movies and shit, and we had a good time. And the sex was meh, but she was great—which was why it was off and on, I guess. But…." He shrugged and, for the first time in Sean's recollection, seemed embarrassed. "I lived in the flophouse. There was sex and guys who wanted no strings on *tap.* And if you weren't having it, you were watching someone else have it. Eventually I had to concede, you know? That when I wanted it, and it was for fun, I'd rather it be one of the guys at the flophouse than this really awesome girl. I finally had to turn her loose, but it was hard." Another shrug. "I still miss her. If I hadn't fucked the whole thing up with sex, she would have been a really good friend."

Which was more than Sean could say about Jesse. "He was a fireman," he admitted. "You don't expect a fireman to be a douchebag."

Billy laughed softly. "I hear you. But hey, you should know by now. Any guy can be a douchebag. My old man was a lieutenant colonel in the U.S. Army, but he was an asshole with a heavy fist at home. Yeah, he looks like a hero on his service record. Me and the little kids, we got to see the wrong side of that coin, you know? Anybody can be a douchebag. The trick, I think, is to walk away from the people who are."

Sean had seen his share of domestic abuse survivors when he'd been a beat cop—had, in fact, been on first-name terms with the social workers assigned to his beat. "Not so easy to do when you're a kid."

Billy looked away. It was his turn to shrug. "No," he said quietly. "But it does give you something to shoot for when you grow up, right?"

"Yeah."

"Your old man was a good guy?" Billy asked, almost wistfully.

Sean suppressed the urge to deflect. "He… well, yes. Mostly." It served him right. Wanting to know about Billy. Prompting him to talk. There was always stuff about your own life that was hard to share.

"That was committed," Billy said, raising his eyebrows above those cynical eyes.

And it was the cynicism that did Sean in. He couldn't change his relationship with his father—his father had been dead for going on ten years. But he *could* keep his relationship with this young man honest.

"He was not comfortable with me being gay," Sean said bluntly. "He tried. I mean, I think if he'd lived longer, he would have gotten it. But he was still at the point where if my sister was razzing me about a crush, he'd shut down the discussion, when everybody else's love life was fair game. When I said I wanted to major in criminal justice, follow in the old man's footsteps, he…." Sean shrugged.

"He told you it was maybe not for you people?" Billy hazarded.

"Close. I mean…." He grimaced at Billy, knowing he'd still had it good. "Wasn't a beatdown. Could have been worse."

Billy nodded thoughtfully. "Still hurt." He rubbed his chest. "Am I right?"

"Yeah." The silence hung heavily between them in the dim room, and Sean realized how… how *happy* it made him that Billy came in to talk.

He would have to continue to be candid and real to make sure he did it again. "So to answer your question, my dad was a good guy. I wish he could have lived longer so he could have learned to understand me, but what I had wasn't bad."

Billy gave him a shuttered smile. "That's… I gotta say, that's good to hear. I mean, after the stories from the flophouse. There's not many stories in a gay-porn studio that start with, 'My dad's a great guy and he loves this job so much!'"

Sean's laugh surprised even him. "Yeah, that would be a tough sell. Even supportive parents might be a little bit, 'Oh, honey, I can pay your tuition, you know….'"

Billy nodded. "Yeah, although there *is* the occasional Mrs. Bobby's Mom."

Sean grimaced. "Mrs. Bobby's Mom?"

"Yeah, like, no shit. Bobby—he's one of John's biggest stars, and he only does a couple of scenes a year now. He does contracting work mostly—woodwork and construction. He's real good at that, and he makes a lot of money, but sometimes he just likes the attention. He fucks like a god. His boyfriend likes to watch. It's very weird, but it works for them. Anyway, when he started porn, it was so he could move his mom out of a bad situation. I don't know the particulars, but there was an asshole landlord and a small town involved. All the drama. So Bobby gets his mom out of the small town, and she needs a job. And she doesn't really *approve* of the porn, but John's old receptionist had quit and shit was *crazy*. Bobby tells his mom that the porn guys need a receptionist, and he apparently told her that they needed a mom too. And you know what?"

"What?"

"He was right. I mean…." Billy blew out a breath. "I mean, Dex is the mom and John's the dad at the studio—we all know that. But when you're done with a scene, having this nice woman offer you some crackers and ask you if you need some diaper rash ointment or witch hazel without judging you or telling you you're bad or need another job? It's like… it's like magic."

Sean remembered Randy telling him how hard it was to film a scene—to go without solid food for a couple of days and then knock yourself out doing something physical and demanding, and even emotionally difficult, depending on who was doing it.

"Was she there today?" Sean asked softly.

"Yeah. She remembered I liked horchata—had a can of it in her mini fridge so I could have some sugar water before I left. It…." The look he gave Sean then was particularly naked. "I was really not looking forward to coming back here. You haven't said anything, and I'm grateful, but you've got the nice mother and the solid family and… I just didn't want to drag my whoring ass back here to make you all squeamish and shit. It's funny how the smallest kindness gives you courage, you know?"

Sean caught his breath. "You… you don't need to be afraid of what I think," he said after a moment. "I'm a stupid cop. Who cares?"

Billy shrugged and swallowed. "I don't know. I didn't think I did. And then I stopped to get pizza, thinking you wouldn't know what a big deal it was, but you did. And you were super patient with Randy—not everyone is. I was worried. You gave *me* hell, but when I got here, Randy was looking like a kid who'd just had his best day with a big brother. I would have brought you pizza for that alone. And he…." Billy shook his head like he was trying to master himself. "Ignore me. I'm always sort of a mess after a scene. I don't usually get all squishy, but I get tired. Raw. Anyway, he left me mac and cheese and hot dogs, and it was such a nice thing. And I know that kid. He's got a good heart, but he needs prompting. So I wake up under a blanket, with my favorite comfort food in the fridge, and I know you might have given him a little nudge. And I wanted to say thanks, you know? For not being mean to Randy, not being shitty to me. I... it was stand-up. I just wanted you to know that."

Sean was still fumbling for an answer when Billy stood abruptly and yawned.

"And after all that, I've got to get to bed for real. I'll make sure the monitor's turned on, so you be sure to wake me up if you need anything, okay?"

Sean nodded, trying to pull in enough air to say something, anything, before Billy cleared the room.

"Billy," he rasped, as Billy reached the doorway.

Billy paused, his head dropping, his hand clutching the molding. "Yeah?"

"Thanks for coming in and talking. It... it was nice. Feel free to do it again if you want."

The young man straightened, his head came up, and his hand dropped from the door frame, as though the words had made him stronger. "Thanks, Kryzynski. I might take you up on that."

"And Billy?"

This time he looked over his shoulder. "Yeah?"

"You can call me Sean, you know. I don't have to be Kryzynski forever."

"You know first names are dangerous," Billy said, turning around just a little more.

"I know."

"You still don't get to call me Guillermo, you understand?"

Sean swallowed back the hurt but decided he could live with it. "Yeah. I get that." Maybe after some more conversations, some more bedtime stories, that would be something he could do.

"All right, then. Night, Sean."

"Night, Billy."

And then he was gone down the hall, and Sean switched off the lamp.

The Trouble with Heroes

"BILLY?" SEAN'S voice came through the baby monitor clearly at around 7:00 a.m., which was when he usually woke up needing to pee. "Can I try going by myself this time?"

"No." It was a week after Billy's scene, and while he had to admit Sean was healing nicely and could actually walk across the room unaided—and not get dizzy—Billy still didn't want a repeat of their first morning.

They were already uncomfortably close as it was.

If Billy ever ended up face-to-face with Sean Kryzynski's pretty blue eyes again, bad things might happen. There might be… closeness. There might even be *talking*. More talking. When they were close. Which could lead to highly inappropriate things between a nurse and his patient, right?

Billy sort of wanted to talk to Cotton about that. From what Billy had seen before he'd bailed on the flophouse, Cotton's sick guy had been scrawny and wounded and half out of his mind. Cotton wasn't, like, *attracted* to that, was he? Because no. Just no.

But *Billy's* sick guy was alert. He was awake. He kept fighting to get out of bed by himself and be independent and challenge Billy's authority in this whole nursing gig, and Billy was finding himself… well, interested.

Definitely interested.

Because it was hard not to be interested in a guy who pretty much got all your hackles up fourteen hours of every day, and Billy suspected it might be more once Kryzynski—*Sean*—got better and was not made of sleep.

But it was stupid to be interested in a guy who lived a whole different life than you, right?

But that didn't mean Billy wanted him to drop dead on the way to take a piss in the morning either.

"Come *on*," Sean begged over the intercom. "You've got to let me pee by myself *sometime*."

Shit. Billy could hear rustling of blankets and the scooting of that not-bad-actually-pretty-fine body in the sheets. If he didn't get his ass out of bed and go help, Sean really might give it another go by himself, and they'd end up face-to-face again, and Billy just *knew* that was a *bad* thing.

"Not today!" Billy yelled as he ripped off the covers and went thundering out the door and down the hall.

When he got to Sean's room, Sean was at the dresser near his door, leaning on it heavily and looking triumphant.

"I could have made it," he said mildly, but he was breathing hard, so Billy was going to assume he was fronting to make up for the fact that he'd done a dumb thing.

"Sure. You also could have crumpled down, repunctured your lung, and started all over again," Billy snapped. "Now here—you know the drill."

He offered his arm and Sean took it, allowing Billy to guide him to the bathroom for his morning ablutions.

This time Billy threw the guy a bone and waited outside the bathroom, which he'd been doing on and off for the last couple of days. The rule had been that Sean would ask for his help getting into the shower, and Billy was leaning against the wall, valiantly trying *not* to think about Sean Kryzynski naked and healthy and wet, when he heard the toilet flush, and then, before he could respond, he heard the water running in the shower.

With a grunt—and probably more panic than necessary—he threw the door open just in time to watch Sean safely grab the rails and help himself into the shower, completely naked.

The protest he was about to make dried up in his throat.

Lean and pale, with still-defined runner's muscle in his legs, at his hips, and in his abdomen, his surprisingly wide shoulders were the exact ratio to those lean hips that turned Billy's key.

Sean didn't see his assessment; he was too busy lowering himself into the shower chair under the spray and getting his sponge and soap.

Billy managed to make himself move in time to close the curtain, and he heard Sean's gasp of surprise.

"Thanks," he squeaked. "I'd forgotten."

"Yeah, well, save myself some cleanup," Billy told him, and because Sean couldn't see him, he held his hand to his bare chest and tried to catch his breath. Nice. Just... *very* frickin' *nice*. He'd been wondering when he'd get to look at that body as a man and not a person in charge, but he hadn't been expecting that sensibility to sweep over him like wildfire and destroy all his equilibrium in one heartbeat.

Sean—dammit, he couldn't call him Kryzynski anymore, not after that strange, intimate, *necessary* conversation in the lamplight when Sean's hair, growing long, had flopped over his brow and he'd stared at Billy like everything he said *mattered*—took short, efficient showers, so Billy had to ask.

"Hey, I'm running to my bedroom to grab a shirt, okay? Don't, you know, levitate out of your shower chair while I'm gone. It's slippery out here."

Sean's raspy chuckle did something to Billy's insides that he really hated, mostly because he didn't hate it at all. "Surprised ya, didn't I?"

He was so damned proud of himself Billy couldn't yell at him. "Yeah, you're something. Let me go put a shirt on and I'll try to deal with being obsolete."

He heard that raspy chuckle again and wondered what Sean Kryzynski sounded like when his lungs were fully functioning and he could run around the block.

And if it would do the same thing to Billy's stomach then that it did now.

"I DIDN'T mean to hurt your feelings," Sean said later over breakfast. Simple milk and cereal today, by Sean's request. Apparently the eggs were starting to make him feel bloated.

"What? No!" Billy shook his head and stuck to his fruit and cottage cheese. Which he hated, by the way. One of the great ironies of life was how much he'd hated cottage cheese as a kid and had been forced to eat it because it was good for him, and how much he hated it now as an adult and couldn't escape it for basically the same reason. "You didn't hurt my feelings. Just surprised me is all. I should have been paying better attention."

"It's a good thing. I do all the exercises. I can walk around the house now. Get out of the chair, get to the bathroom without help. But

I still need you in the house. Just, you know." He gave an embarrassed smile. "Not quite the same way as that first day."

Billy caught the smile and let it do what Sean had intended: help him relax. "Yeah, yeah. I get you. You're right. I've got a pretty cushy setup here. My own room. Free food and rent. Gotta admit it's been nice not having twenty-four-seven live porn going on around me."

Sean rolled his eyes. "Now you're bragging."

Billy was going to cackle and make light of it, but suddenly he couldn't. "Naw, it's not like that. I mean, I'm not really exaggerating much. Somebody gets busy in that apartment every night, and often more than one couple. Or throuple. Or whatever." He grinned and shrugged and was surprised when he felt his cheeks heat. He'd thought he was beyond that. "It's just, in the flophouse, you've got people who know the score. They have sex for money, so everyone knows they tested clean, so doing it all in-house is sort of a blessing. And it doesn't come with any strings—you don't have to worry about a date or if you find your soulmate the next day because these guys, they're friends, and they're not going to jam you up if you make a real emotional connection, you understand?"

Sean's eyebrows went up. "Sounds perfect."

Billy shook his head and became very absorbed in his cottage cheese. "I guess not," he said thoughtfully. "It didn't hit me so much until Henry came to live with us. And at first it was easy to write him off as a judgy bitch, right? But then it turned out Henry was in love with Lance—like, *really* in love with him. And you start to realize that somebody who can be that kind and who had his own problems too wasn't really judging us. He was *worried* about us. And... well, shit started changing."

"Like what?" Sean asked. He'd pushed aside his empty cereal bowl, and here they were, two dudes talking again, and Billy had a moment to wonder why this felt like the thing he'd been missing all his life.

"Well, first of all he made Fisher and Zeppelin realize they were in love and maybe should find a better job to support that."

Sean chuckled weakly. "That's fair."

"Yeah, but none of the rest of us caught it. And he just... did that. Caught shit. Like the fact that the super was charging some of the kids blowjobs in lieu of rent and not telling them, so he was getting blowjobs *and* extra money."

Sean made a pained sound, and Billy remembered that guy had been part of a case, and it hadn't ended well for him. "Rivers actually caught that," Sean told him.

Billy cocked his head. "You know this because…?"

"I was there," Sean said with a shrug. "Rivers didn't tell me in so many words. I think he didn't want you guys to have to talk to the cops."

Billy grunted. "God. That guy. You see? You see why Rivers is sacred with my people? But anyway, Henry was still part of that whole change. That idea that we could be young adults and not simply kids fucking our way through life. Henry's the one who sat Cotton down and told him to stop falling for every 'daddy' who asked him for a BJ, and it was a good thing too, because Cotton was dying by degrees. But even those changes didn't stop the fact that the guys who stayed in the flophouse—and the new guys just starting porn, like Vinnie, who got there last week—have no problem with sex on tap. And…." He shrugged, trying to remember where he'd been going with this.

"And it's nice to be staying in a place where that's not the focus of your day," Sean said dryly.

Billy remembered the wave of breathlessness, of arousal, that had swept over him when he'd seen Sean's bare and pale body in the shower not an hour earlier.

"Sure," he said, wanting to bang his head against the table.

"As flattering as that is, I do get it," Sean told him. "It's one of the reasons it's so hard to have a relationship. Sometimes"—he shrugged—"it's easier to keep your head out of that whole scene when you're focusing on your job." He gestured to Billy's schoolbooks piled in the corner. "You'll see," he said. "You already see. School's taking part of your focus now. You won't need that whole…." He made a little circle with his finger.

"Sex on tap?" Billy supplied.

"Yeah. You won't need that." It was funny that Sean seemed so sure, given how much sex he did *not* appear to be having.

"I don't need it now!" Billy said defensively, not sure why he felt so stung.

"Well, obviously not. I'm just saying, it does sound like a young man's game. You know, like counting how many socks you can wank off into—"

"Did you *do* that?" Because that sounded like a flophouse game to Billy. In fact, he couldn't believe nobody had done that before.

"God no. That was my younger brother. My mother made me talk to him. She was mortified."

Billy stared at him. "Wow."

"I'm saying. But eventually Charlie stopped doing that because he graduated from high school and was working his way through college, and he met a girl. Suddenly how many socks he could go through was not nearly as important as how much he could spend on flowers and decent restaurants."

Billy snorted. "I tried that once—"

"With a girl you didn't love," Sean pointed out, and Billy shook his head.

"This—*this* is what you get when you talk to a guy," he muttered.

"Someone who won't take your *shit*!" Sean retorted, but he was grinning when he said it, and Billy was forced to smile.

"Yeah, you talk a big game, but do I have to remind you...." He trailed off and looked behind him at the half-empty DVD shelf in the living room.

Sean gave him a narrow-eyed glance and let out a half-decent laugh, proof of his healing lungs. "Touché," he conceded. "Now can we go to the dog park or something?"

By the end of the first week, Billy'd had to admit even the nice, spacious duplex was stifling. Since exercise was recommended, Billy had been driving Sean to the local park. While it was not officially a "dog park," a lot of owners took their animals walking, some on leads and some not, and Sean seemed to get a kick out of getting his exercise by walking around one of the soccer fields at the park and then sitting on a bench and saying hello to all the "good boys and good girls" who came to sniff his socks.

Billy, whose old man had never let them have any pets at all, was starting to really enjoy that hour in the park. They had to leave early— September was still barbarically hot during a drought year, even two weeks in—but besides getting to pet the dogs, Billy got to watch *Sean* pet the dogs, and that was just as fun. He'd apparently never met a big dog he didn't like. Sure, Sean thought the little ones were okay—and Billy didn't tell him this, but he *adored* the little chi-whozits and terrier-poos and whatever—but the big golden retrievers and pit bulls with the sweet smiles and the giant wiggly bodies made the guy light up inside.

Watching his square-jawed face grow soft and sweet while baby-talking an animal nearly half his body weight was a thing Billy was starting to treasure. There was something very *pure* about dogs. All those people on the walk—they didn't seem to care if Billy was Mexican or both the guys were gay, and none of them knew Sean was a cop. What did they care about? Did these two guys on the bench love their *dogs*. That was all. Billy could believe in the world again, with people who loved their dogs.

And it got Sean out and about and exercising without overdoing it. He had to stop in the middle, right? On the good bench with the shade, because that's where all the dogs came to visit. Win-win!

And then on the way home, Sean usually had him stop at a drive-thru for a soda or something, and although Billy got a diet soda, he had to admit having a treat after they went to the park was like part of his childhood that he hadn't remembered. His mom had done the going to the park and the treating. As the family had grown, Billy had been more and more in charge of making sure the little kids didn't kill themselves falling off the playground equipment, and it had become less and less fun for *him*. But still that break from the apartment, that moment of knowing the people around him would be happy, and then the stop at the 7-Eleven for something sweet—it was a good moment in a day. And watching Sean practically glow with happiness as he wiped the retriever fur off his T-shirt made it better.

But today Sean was tired. He'd gone an extra lap around the soccer field, and he had to work really hard to keep his breathing even, particularly in air made smoky by recent wildfires. Billy was thinking grimly that getting him out of his low-slung Dodge Charger was going to be a *treat*. Billy loved the car, personally. Getting a chance to drive the thing in the last weeks had been an unanticipated perk that Billy could definitely live with, but it took a lot of leg strength to stand up from the folded position way down near the ground. He was thinking about saying something to that effect, because he hadn't yet told Sean that and it would probably be polite, when Sean's phone rang.

The ringtone was "Born Under a Bad Sign," and Billy snorted softly when Sean said, "Rivers! Sup?"

He listened for a moment and managed a low whistle. "Seriously? They're okay, though? Good." There was another pause, and Billy could hear Sean's breathing quicken. He was about to grab the phone and tell Rivers to stop yanking his boy's chain when Sean replied, "No. Not a problem. We can do that. No, I won't tell the police. Just, you know, keep that kid safe." Billy caught his sidelong glance. "No, you're right. They need protection. We're up. No worries." He let out a brief bark of laughter. "I'm all right? It took a shiv in the lung for you to decide I'm all right? I'll have to decide if it was worth it." Another pause. "Yeah, whatever. We're fifteen minutes away. We can take care of it. Yeah, fuck off yourself. See you later. Thanks."

He hit End Call and said, "Billy, you need to turn toward Davis Med Center. You know where it—"

"Yeah, I know," Billy muttered, not wanting to talk about his own trips to the doc. He'd managed to neatly avoid telling anybody at the flophouse but Lance, and that was because he was a doctor and Billy had needed to ask him some questions.

"Good. We're going to the ER, so I need you to park in the big open lot right there."

"I hear you. Who are we going to visit?"

Sean sucked air in through his teeth. "I need you to not panic when you hear this, okay?"

Billy knew his eyes got really big. "The actual hell?"

"Remember how you had to move out of the flophouse because there was a sick guy in Cotton's bed and you needed to make room?"

"Yeah?" His voice was rising. He *knew* his voice was rising. He couldn't help it. Cotton was their most vulnerable little soldier; he had eyes like some cartoon forest animal and the big upper lip and… and Billy had just sailed out the door, going, "Gotta go! Got my own sick guy to watch over! You try not to kill yours, I'll try not to kill mine!"

Cotton had given a tired laugh and waved, and that had been that. Billy had grabbed his backpack with his clothes, laptop, and shaving kit and vamoosed.

"Something happened to Cotton?" he asked. His voice squeaked, but he didn't care.

"Cotton's fine," Sean soothed. "There were people watching the flophouse to make sure the people after Colonel Constant—" He paused. "Cotton's sick guy," he explained, and Billy nodded.

"Yeah." Maybe at any other time, he would have gotten mad because Sean was being condescending or some such bullshit, but he was freaked out enough to appreciate the reminder. "I remember him. The hero." There had been no question about that. Billy was unclear on the details, but he knew that both Sean and Cotton's sick guy had been injured pursuing a case that involved getting children out of danger.

"Exactly. Anyway, there were eyes on the apartment, and those guys kept Cotton and Constance from getting hurt, but one of *them* was hurt. He's fine, but he's in the hospital, and I have to go smooth things over and get him out of there before they ask too many questions."

"Why you?" Billy demanded suspiciously. "Why can't Rivers or Henry—"

"Because they're running down a witness for something else," Sean told him. "You can't expect the same two guys to save the world *all* the time. If we don't start helping, they're not gonna make it."

"But what about the other guys from the flophouse?" Billy asked. "Are they okay?"

"Yeah. Nobody else was home. But…." Sean sucked air through his teeth, and Billy knew he wasn't going to like what came next. "There was some damage to the apartment, I gather, and there's a cleanup crew and shit. The goal here is to fix the apartment and get Cotton and the colonel out of town before anyone knows they're gone."

"Wait, Cotton's going with them?" Yeah, Billy and Cotton had hooked up, but that wasn't what Billy was thinking about. He was thinking about Cotton's absolute vulnerability, the way he had empathy for every living creature, including Randy before they'd gotten Randy on six dozen medications to calm him the fuck down.

"Yeah," Sean said, glancing at him. "I gather it was the boy's idea."

Billy bit his lip but kept driving toward Med center. "Man, they'd better not get Cotton hurt. He's so sweet. He cries at Disney movies. He cries at *cat food commercials*. I mean, if this is some hairy shit, I… I don't know if they can protect him enough."

Sean let out a breath that might have been a sigh. "Look, they've got Jackson's badass friends from the desert protecting them, I gather. At least one of them. I think Cotton would be their priority."

"Next to big bad military guy," Billy said bitterly. He'd *been* there when his mother had first tried to call the cops about the old man. He'd seen that shit in action. Cops and soldiers first, and everybody else took the back seat and the backhand.

"No, I don't think that's it," Sean told him. "I think Cotton volunteered. He didn't want Constance to be without care, and I guess he's gotten good at it."

"Rivers told you all that over the phone?" Billy asked irritably.

"We text. What's Cotton told you?"

Billy let out his own breath. Cotton had, in fact, been too busy to text anybody. But Curtis and Randy had both told him that the kid seemed to have a bond with the soldier guy. Not exactly sexual since nobody could be sexy when they were recovering from gunshot wounds and infection, no matter what the TV said, but Cotton had a sixth sense about when the guy was getting better or worse. Vinnie, the new guy— nobody knew him very well yet—seemed to assume Cotton and the guy had been a thing.

"Guys said he was getting attached," he admitted reluctantly. "God. Cotton and his daddies. I was really hoping…."

"What?"

"That he'd get his shit together before he found his next Mr. Right." Billy grimaced. "Stupid. I'm nobody's *mami*." He grimaced, hearing the lilt to the word that made it Spanish instead of English. He'd hoped to leave that behind, all of it, when he left home. Nobody had ever used that whole heritage shit to make *him* feel good, had they?

"No, not a mommy," Sean said. "You're watching out for a friend. It's nice."

"I'm not nice," Billy muttered, driving down Stockton. "And this place gives me the creeps."

"You didn't just spend a week here," Sean muttered.

"Spent enough time as a kid," Billy told him, the bitterness palpable on his tongue, and then he wished he could take it back.

Sean shot him a look of horror—and compassion—and Billy held up a hand.

"Not another word about it," he muttered. "It was a dumb thing to bring up."

"You keep doing that," Sean told him. "You know I need a nurse for another couple of weeks. Eventually you're going to have to tell me *something* about yourself."

"Man, not even my *shrink* knows about Guillermo!" Billy snapped. "Now shut up and let me figure out this parking lot, okay?"

Bigger Things

THE PARKING lot wasn't hard, but Sean figured Billy was feeling raw, so he kept his trap shut. But then as Billy circled, looking for a spot near the door, he broke the silence.

"You're going to have to walk."

Sean steeled his core; that extra trip around the soccer field had sucked. "Yeah, so?"

"Just saying. Do you want me to let you off by the door and park?"

"No." Sean sighed, hating how his chest hurt with the action. "I, uhm, may need help out of the car." He loved this car, but it was so low slung.

"Christ. Someone else couldn't do this?"

"No! And these guys did good shit. If me walking in there and putting them on the department dime and getting them out of the hospital before anyone starts asking questions is my only contribution, I'm glad to do it."

"Fucking hero."

"Whatever, man. Just park the car."

He was done with the argument. For one thing, he didn't have any more wind.

The situation wasn't improved any when Billy had to get in front of him and do the "put your arms around my neck" thing in order to get him out of his own car. It couldn't be helped—standing up from that seat required a lot of core strength he hadn't been aware he'd been using, and that meant tightening around his wound. It hurt too much to stand, and the effort had sweat popping out on his brow and a track of fire blazing along his wound path before Billy lost his temper.

"Come on," he muttered, sinking to a crouch. The position put them face-to-face again, irritation writ large on both their faces, he was sure. But as he held on to Billy's neck and allowed Billy's thigh and core strength to propel them both up, he felt something else, something that had nothing to do with pain and everything to do with their bodies, flush and hot, close together and against each other.

When they were standing, Sean found himself reluctant to let go.

"How're your knees?" Billy asked, sounding a little anxious.

"Knees are fine," Sean replied, wondering how fair it was that this kid's sharp cheekbones and full lips should be so damned appealing. My God, they were standing close, and he thought that he might be maybe an inch taller than the guy, but Billy's broad chest seemed to push him up in height.

A smile played on Billy's mouth, and it made him even more breathtaking. "Knees are fine?"

"Peachy." Oh. Hell. Sean knew what he was getting at, but now if he took his arms down like a startled teenager, Billy would have won.

"Then why won't you let go?" Billy prodded.

"Why won't you step back?" Sean goaded in return. Their chests were touching. Oh my God, *their chests were touching*.

And then a miracle occurred.

Sean felt the heat of it, sweeping up from Billy's stomach, along his chest, coloring the pale skin of his neck, turning his ears a dark red.

"Oh," Billy said, swallowing and—to Sean's chagrin—stepping back. "Sorry about that."

"No worries." Sean lowered his arms to his sides, keeping his back and shoulders as still as he could. "We should hurry in."

Billy nodded, and it was still a long molasses-slow minute before they turned and walked to the front doors of the hospital.

ONCE INSIDE, Sean had asked for a big Russian guy with a knife wound—that was all Rivers had told him to look for. Apparently he wasn't a common patient, but Sean's badge paved the way.

"Oh dear God," Billy murmured in his ear as they inched their way into the cubicle. "You sure that's the good guy?"

"So Jackson Rivers says," Sean murmured back, and they moved in to take care of business.

It turned out the big Russian had given his name as Dimitri Sartov, but Sean knew his name was Jai, and his last name was sort of up for grabs. It didn't matter. He used the department's agreement with the hospital to take care of confidential informants on the down-low to get the giant knife wound in the man's shoulder treated. A kid named Ernie—and he couldn't have been more than Billy's age—stood next to Jai and watched the entire procedure with a combination of sharp-eyed interest and dreamy regard that Sean, quite frankly, found unsettling. Billy, for the most part, was okay with letting Sean take the lead. For once.

"There," he said quietly to Ernie and Jai. "I just expensed your medical bills. The doc will be back with some pain meds and antibiotics, and then we can play musical cars and you can go."

Jai regarded Kryzynski narrowly. "Last I heard, you were in a hospital bed. What are you doing here?"

"Killing himself," Billy snarled. "Did you really have to—"

"This man is a hero, Billy," Sean told him, not sure how much Billy knew. "You weren't there when Rivers told the story. This man, Jai, and this young man's boyfriend just saved a busload of kids, and I'm pretty sure they saved Cotton's life."

Billy's eyes got large.

"I'll tell you later." Sean took a careful breath; it wasn't as easy as it had been that morning. "Right now let's get me to their car and them to ours. I promised Ellery we'd clean the blood out of their car and give them something that would let them get to LA today."

"Except our car is your doctor friend's," Jai said.

"You got blood in Lance's Mazda?" Billy asked, aghast. Then understanding dawned. "Which is why we need to take it—to clean the upholstery. Okay. I get it. It's all coming together." He shook his head. "You live a very interesting life, Sean. Sometimes. But you still need to get home for your nap."

Sean gave the kid an exasperated look. "We're getting there," he wheezed.

Jai eyed him with quiet disgust. "Everybody. Must everybody be a hero?"

"You are telling me," Billy muttered. "Anyway, here." He dug into the pocket of his faded jeans, then dropped the keys in Ernie's hand. "Now you give me Lance's."

"I can't believe I'm giving up my car for a week," Sean said weakly as Ernie returned Billy's gesture by dropping a key fob into his hand. "Love that car."

Jai grinned at him, his smile as big as the man. "What kind of car is it?"

"Dodge Charger." He sighed wheezily. "I only wish it was circa 1970, but no. Modern model."

"You should try a Ford SHO," Jai told him. "But we will treat your car well."

"Trust us," Ernie said. "This is the guy who helped Ace and Sonny make Jackson's car." He paused. "Before, you know. The thing."

Sean knew his eyes lit up. From what he understood, "The Tank," as Jackson and Ellery had called their modified SUV, had been totaled—or nearly totaled—in the whole clusterfuck that had started with his own stab wound and ended with the sick guy in Cotton's bed getting wounded. This right here—the bailing out of the giant Russian guy—was one final piece to that whole gigantic puzzle, which Sean thought was probably above his pay grade. But that didn't belie the fact that The Tank had been a prime example of vehicular beauty, and anybody who could treat a car *that* nicely had to be good people.

"They'd take a look at my baby?" he said, feeling a little bit giddy. "Because that would be—"

"Later," Billy muttered. "Come on. You're starting to sound loopy."

They shuffled out toward the front door, leaving Jai and Ernie to find their way home. Sean gathered it was somewhere down south, but again, above his pay grade.

"You stay here," Billy said, indicating the shaded overhang in front of the ER. "I'm going to go get Lance's Mazda and come back for you."

Sean didn't bother to argue—he couldn't even talk. He'd maxed out his stamina for the day, he thought ruefully. Fortunately Billy knew what the car looked like—had probably spotted it pulling in—and was back in a moment with a battered but sound two-door Mazda that would be a lot easier to get in and out of than the Charger.

A thing Sean barely noticed, because what he really saw was that Billy was no longer wearing his shirt.

Sean made a questioning sound as he limped forward and opened the door, and Billy nodded at the seat, which was sporting a new blue cotton tee cover.

"It was covered in that guy's blood," Billy said. "And it was tacky but not dry, and seriously gross. No, no—don't say a word. You look up upholstery cleaners close to the house, then I'm getting you home for your little nappy poo and then taking this thing out to get clean. Seriously, it's a good thing your giant Russian buddy didn't get caught with all this blood in the car. Dumbass cops would have arrested him before they realized he was bleeding."

Sean made a gasp of protest, but it was no use. He couldn't defend the people in his profession without the air to make a case.

An hour later he was lying in bed, barely edging sleep when he got the text from Jackson.

Thanks for helping out. What do I owe you for the upholstery cleanup?

He smiled a bit. *Nothing. We're good. Billy's getting it done now.*

Must be nice.

You're the one who sent him. Jackson hadn't even consulted him about it—just told him he'd arranged a nurse. Thinking about that now, Sean was thanking his lucky stars he hadn't ended up with Randy or Cotton or even Curtis, who seemed like a nice enough kid but who might have gotten mean when Sean pushed back. Billy was an ornery asshole, but he was never mean.

You got stabbed working on our case. Figured we owed you.

Sean laughed softly to himself. *I walked under an overhang and ran into a sociopath with a knife. As I recall, you're the one who administered first aid and called Officer Down.* It was funny, that moment—not funny "ha-ha" but funny "augh!" Sean had heard the scuffle on the balcony of Jackson and Ellery's second floor office and had been hurrying to help. There had been that dramatic difference between the shade and the sunshine, and as his vision was adjusting to the shade, Henry had shouted and a small heavily muscled man had run into him.

And Sean's chest had exploded in pain.

He frowned. *You never did tell me what happed to the guy who knifed me. I know he died, but I don't know how.*

There was a moment of thought bubbles across his phone, and then Jackson texted, *You know those two guys you just helped?*

Yeah.

The big scary Russian one showed up with Ace, their friend. Ace saw Ziggy—the asshole with the knife—about to get away and threw his knife at Ziggy's chest. Missed his heart by half an inch. And then Ziggy ran away, and Ellery opened the door to the Tank, and the guy ran into it, fixing that half inch.

Sean knew it was bloodthirsty... and didn't care. He knew it probably made him an awful, vengeful person, and still he didn't care.

That's the most beautiful thing I've ever heard.

Ain't it the truth. Get your nap, cop. You still have work in this world to do.

At that moment the door to the duplex opened, and he heard the sounds of someone moving about, putting keys in the key bowl, and grabbing a water from the fridge. A moment later Billy peeked into the bedroom.

"You should be asleep," he said.

"Any minute now," Sean answered on a yawn. "That was quick."

"That's going to take a day. I've got a rental. Texted Henry and told him I'd have Lance's Mazda back tomorrow. Don't know what *we're* gonna drive, but I figure we'll play musical cars until your Charger's back."

"I can't figure it out right now," Sean mumbled. "You're right. After my nap."

Billy chuckled and then said, "What're you smiling about? Someone send you a meme?"

Sean glanced at his phone and his and Jackson's last text. "Jackson told me what happened to the guy who stabbed me."

Billy's eyes widened. "Did he get arrested? Will you have to testify? Kneed in the balls? What?"

Sean let his evil grin sneak through. "Nope. You know the big Russian guy?"

"Yeah?"

"His buddy hit the guy in the chest with a hunting knife. Missed his heart by this much"—he held out his thumb and forefinger—"so the guy had enough energy to take off running."

Billy's face had lost its cynicism in this moment. He was animated and interested, almost like a little kid. "And then?"

"And then the guy ran by Jackson's big immovable car. Ellery was in the driver's seat, and he opened the door."

"Oh!"

"Apparently drove the knife that last little bit." Sean really wished he had the air to chuckle, but Billy did it for him.

"That's awesome," Billy said fervently. "Sometimes bad things really *do* happen to bad people."

Sean smiled at him, at peace as he hadn't been a moment before. "I appreciate a man who can see that whole sitch my way."

Billy gave a soft laugh. "I'm gonna let you sleep and go get some homework done. Uhm, Sean?"

"Yeah?"

"I meant what I said in the hospital. You and your friends are heroes."

Oh, if only that were true. Sean's mouth twisted. "That's sweet," he said. "But right now I'm just a guy who walked into a knife." He yawned. "Who needs his nap."

Billy bit his lip, and Sean could tell he wanted to say more, but Sean really was done. He closed his eyes and barely remembered the sound of Billy wandering into the living room to do his homework.

School Daze

BILLY SUPPRESSED a yawn and tried to keep his mind on his physics professor. He'd always been good at math and science and had *really* loved his classes, even the humanities ones that he complained about, but today he was so *not* feeling it.

"Mr. Carey," said the professor, "are we nodding off?"

Billy straightened in his seat and grabbed his pencil, doing his best to take notes and not wander off again.

He was starting to hate leaving Sean during his class days.

The night before, he'd been pulled from sleep by Sean's voice on the monitor rasping, "The fuck? Oh my God, Rivers, he's armed!"

Billy had been out of the bed and down the hall before the last word, but by the time he got to Sean's bedroom, the moment was over. Sean was on his uninjured side, clutching the sheet to his chest, shivering but already falling back asleep.

Billy adjusted the covers up under his chin and murmured, "It's all good now, *papi*. No scary monsters no more, okay?"

"*Mmm*… yeah. Sorry, Billy. Bad dream."

"Well, don't have them no more. I'll keep you safe, okay?"

"Yeah. Thanks."

Billy fought the urge hard—he really did—but as Sean's eyes fluttered closed, he lost the battle. He bent his head and kissed Sean's fair temple, smelling shampoo from the morning, a little bit of sweat from the walks around the park, and the scent marker that was unique to Sean only. Billy had slept with enough guys—both on screen and off by now—to know that every guy had one. Every guy smelled just a little bit *themselves*, as apart from other human animals. But there was something fresh and appealing about Sean's smell, like his animal was particularly designed for Billy's.

An ornery smell, but not boring, right?

So Billy didn't trust anybody to watch over Sean at night, and wouldn't even if he *had* been seeing anybody on the regular, which he hadn't.

And it was getting so that he didn't trust anybody to watch over him during the daytime either.

It wasn't that Randy or Curtis—or even Vinnie, the new guy— were incompetent or anything. But they weren't *him*. The week before, he'd gotten home—erm, to the duplex—to find that Curtis and Sean had watched two episodes of the mindless cop show Sean had been binging, and Billy had actually been jealous—*jealous*—of Curtis for watching the show with Sean instead of Billy.

It was stupid, absolutely stupid, to feel jealous in any way of watching the dumb cop show. If asked on any given day, Billy would have told people the damn show was idiotic and predictable and goddammit, why didn't the people on the show realize that just having lunch with the main protagonists could get them kidnapped or killed or tortured or some such shit, because guaran-fucking-teed, if Billy knew those assholes, the only way *he'd* communicate with them would be snail mail. Not even email; email could get hacked on those shows, and then where would he be? Snail mail, and he'd never fucking visit, because he chose *life* goddammit, that's why. The show drove him *batshit*.

But one day of seeing somebody else watching the stupid copaganda show with Sean and suddenly he wanted to be the *only* person watching it with Sean, and he didn't understand what his problem was. It wasn't like they were hitting on Billy's patient. And he hadn't gone to help Sean because was hoping for a hookup. He'd gone because everybody seemed to be getting into the cause of the kids who'd been saved and he'd wanted to be part of that. He'd had no idea he'd *like* looking after the fractious cop. In fact that possibility hadn't even entered into it. He'd wanted to help. Well, that and get off the air mattress or out of Henry and Lance's spare room, also incentives for moving into the sitch with Sean.

But he was starting to really like it there. Sean was up and about more. He spent an hour walking in the park now and even threw the ball for a couple of the bigger dogs. He was slow still, yeah, and he still tired easily, but he worked at building his stamina every day. He'd also started taking an online class in de-escalation and working with the mentally ill. The tactics weren't required by his department, which was a crying fucking shame as far as Billy was concerned, but the fact that Sean was working hard *not* to be the white cop who was the devil impressed Billy more and more every day.

And he was so much fun to talk to.

Billy had started to moderate the number of times a week he stopped by Sean's room after he'd retired. There was no more helping him to the bathroom, no more helping him to the shower or to bed. Billy still made himself responsible for meals and housekeeping and generally keeping an eye on the guy to make sure he didn't overdo it, but the fact was, if Sean gently insisted it was time for Billy to move out now so he could have his duplex back to himself, odds were good he would be okay. His mother still stopped by once a week—Billy seemed to be a good buffer for *that*—but Rivers, Henry, and Sean's partner, Christie, also managed to visit once a week to check on him. He'd be fine.

And Billy would miss their time together. He wanted to wander into his room for those quiet, intimate talks *every* night, but he couldn't.

How embarrassing. How needy.

He tried to limit himself to once every two or three days, but boy, did he savor them when he did give in. He hadn't given in the night before, and Sean had a nightmare. He'd gone in for a talk two nights ago, and Billy…. Billy had taken that talk with him to bed and hugged it to his chest, heard their quiet voices in the lamplit room, saw the sleepy sweetness of Sean's expression as Billy spoke.

Tasted the salty irritation Sean showed when someone hit his tender spots, even when Billy was doing his best not to be that guy.

Billy could remember the breathless moment when he'd asked the most obvious question in the world.

"So," Billy said into a sudden silence. "Did you… I mean, you *knew* what I did for a living when I got here. How'd you know?"

He was not prepared for Sean's fair skin to turn pink in the lamplight. "I've seen you before, remember? That first investigation with Henry. The party at Jackson and Ellery's house over the summer. Someone says 'the flophouse,' and it's almost a given what they do to end up there."

Billy had nodded, but he was still not convinced that was it. That flush—it was pretty strong. There had to be more to it.

"Be honest," Billy said, making his voice sly. "You've watched the porn, right?"

That pink grew deeper. "I don't have a subscription," he said with dignity, which told Billy he was skirting the truth.

"You don't need a subscription to cruise the website, my dude. And there's plenty of free samples."

And that did it. Sean squeezed his eyes shut and grimaced. "I, uhm, may have looked around this summer. When Henry first started working for Jackson. Curiosity and all that."

Billy chortled. "And...?" He held both his hands out with a "gimme-gimme" gesture. "Come on, let's have the critique."

Sean's blue eyes flew to his. "You've very beautiful," he said almost angrily. "You need to know that. I watch you measure your food and get on the scale and throw yourself into your workouts, but... but even if you weighed one forty and had a little pot belly, you'd still be, I dunno. Magnetic. So, you know, maybe don't worry so much."

Oolf. Billy dropped his hands—and his sly little grin—because he wasn't sure what to do with that. "But?" he asked, sensing there was more.

Sean's one-shouldered shrug was still half formed, especially when he was lying on the bed, probably because he wasn't comfortable yet, as much as he tried to do without painkillers. But that meant he felt strongly enough about what they were talking about to move his body to do it.

"But there was none of... this," he said, using his free arm to gesture. "This guy here. Who comes in and talks to me and makes me laugh and...." He smiled a little. "You started bringing dog treats to the park so we could feed them. I mean, the gorgeous guy without his shirt—"

"Or his pants." That part was important.

"Or his pants," Sean conceded. "He was there. But you? I didn't see any of the guy I know in that video. If I didn't know that was your job, I probably wouldn't recognize you."

Billy sucked in a breath, more bothered than he could even put words to. "Some detective you are," he rasped.

Sean's lips curled up slightly. "Well, I am young for the force."

Billy had smiled, then left the room shortly after that, but the conversation had stuck with him the whole next day. And then, the night before, he hadn't gone in to talk again, and Sean had cried out in his sleep.

And Billy's sense of protectiveness, his sense of gentleness that he'd thought he'd put away for good when he'd been forced out of the house, had risen up, and he'd placed that sweet, almost unconscious kiss on Sean's temple.

Had Sean felt that?

The thought had haunted him all day.

"Boy, were you a space cadet today," Curtis told him as they left the classroom. Billy hated to admit it, but he really liked having other Johnnies guys in his classes with him at Sac City. Something about having his porn friends there in what he was hoping would take him to his real life made him feel like he could actually make engineering that real life. He could be a Johnnies success story—like Henry's brother and his husband, or Reg and Bobby, or that guy Ethan who had mostly done porn to be hugged and held a lot. There could be life after porn, and he could be part of it. He knew it because his brothers were there with him working for the same thing.

"Yeah," Billy murmured. "Sorry. Thinking deep thoughts, you know?"

Curtis grimaced. "I was just worried about Cotton."

Oh Lord. Billy was a bad, bad friend. "Any news about him and his soldier guy?" Since that day he and Sean had taken Lance's car in to be detailed, Cotton had been off the radar. Apparently Cotton and his soldier had gone off into never-never land to keep soldier boy safe until he could get the people chasing him. There was probably a lot more to it than that, but nobody told the flophouse boys anything. It was weird. It was like their entire focus was porn and getting their shit together. Until he'd moved to Sean's place, it hadn't hit him how the whole thing was a trap for postadolescent narcissism. (Take *that* Psychology 101—Billy was starting to think he should have gotten a better grade in that class!)

"Naw." Curtis shook his head. "But I gotta tell you—you're gone, and it's only me, Randy, and Vinnie. I'm not sure if we should get someone else or—"

Billy shrugged. "I probably don't got too much longer," he said. "My sick guy—"

Curtis was African American, with pale gold-bronze skin, freckles, and a brown buzz cut. He stood about Billy's height, and aside from the race and the freckles, Billy had always felt like they were kindred spirits. Curtis too was an irritable bastard, and neither of them were big on charity or soft emotions. Henry had once described them as prickly, and Billy thought that was about perfect.

So when Curtis let out a guffaw and a disgusted snort, Billy took notice.

"What?"

"We all know his name, Billy. And he's sort of, you know, in the circle now. You can call him Sean."

Billy swallowed. "Man, whatever. He's getting better."

"Yeah, but he's got a spare room, and you're live-in help for when he goes back to work. He seems like a decent guy. You won't need to come back, you know?"

"You trying to get rid of me?" Billy asked, not sure if he should be hurt.

"God no. You're one of the few people at Johnnies I feel like I understand. But…." Curtis bit his lip, uncharacteristically diffident. "But I was thinking when Cotton left. Even if he comes back, he's going to be a different guy. Not the same lost boy, right? I mean, he'll still be all Bambi eyes and shit, but now we've all seen how strong he can be. We don't have to let him go back to being lost and afraid, but he probably won't anyway. And it's good to see someone move on. It was good to watch Lance and Henry move out and watch Lance quit the biz. It's not that I'm ever gonna be ashamed of what I did to get through school, but…." He shrugged. "I don't want to do it for the rest of my life."

They'd been walking together through the campus, but they'd come to a split in the path where Billy had to go to his Humanities 101 class and Curtis had to head for world history.

"Meet here after your class," Billy told him, probably unnecessarily, but it was always good to double-check plans. "I'll give you a ride home." Because the bus was never fun.

"You got the Charger back?" Curtis asked eagerly, and Billy couldn't help the grin that split his face.

"Oh my God. Whoever those guys were that took it down to the desert? They're fucking *geniuses*, man. That thing came back, like, with UFO speed, and the suspension? Don't even get me started." He kissed his fingertips at the perfection of it. "It's fucking amazing. It's one ride home you're not gonna wanna miss."

Curtis laughed gleefully. "Then hell yeah, meet here after class." He sighed. "I suppose we have to pick Randy up at Sean's and give him a ride home too, don't we?"

Billy grunted. "Yeah, and sorry brother, but…."

"But tall guy gets the front." He let out a sigh. "That's okay. It'll be worth it. Meet you here!"

A GOOD plan, but not to be. When Billy arrived back at Sean's place, he found Jackson Rivers and Henry in Sean's living room, with Randy and Vinnie and two pizzas—one Johnnies guys friendly—on the coffee table, and news.

Jackson, as always, looked like magnificent hell. He'd put on some sorely needed weight and muscle tone over the summer, and his boyfriend apparently nagged him into a haircut every six weeks, because his dirty-blond hair was no longer as shaggy as it had been when Billy had first seen him in June. But he'd been bruised and battered some since Billy had last seen him, in the flophouse caring for Cotton's sick guy, and he looked like he hadn't slept in days.

Henry looked just like him, except Henry's hair was blonder and always cut military short, and he had a stockier build. When he had bruises on his face, he seemed like he'd wipe himself off and lunge back into the fray. Jackson would carry the banner and try not to get blown to bits, but Henry would be right behind him, taking out anyone gunning for him.

"Whoa!" Curtis said, coming in behind Billy. "It's a party. What's the occasion?"

"We have news," Jackson told them, smiling tiredly. "Cotton is home."

Curtis, Randy, and Vinnie all went "Hooray!" but Billy caught Sean's eyes.

Sean appeared tired—but then, it *was* his nap time—and his smile was sincere but also a little sad.

"What's wrong?" Billy asked. "Why are all the roommates here instead of in the flophouse hugging Cotton?"

"Lance is with Cotton," Henry said, surprising him. "Cotton's fine, but, well, as some of you may have guessed"—he gave Randy a dry look—"he and Colonel Constant got pretty attached over the last few weeks. The colonel had to go straight back to work, and even though Cotton knew it was coming and is going to get through this—"

"He's a puddle on the floor, isn't he," Billy said grimly. "That asshole. I knew it—yeah. He seemed all helpless and shit when he was wounded and sick, but give him four weeks with our boy and—"

"And he's just as heartbroken," Jackson said dryly. "This wasn't a case of anybody doing anybody wrong, Billy. This was a case of two guys whose timing and plans weren't in the right place." He gave Henry a shuttered look. "I… I suspect Jason Constance isn't the kind of guy to let that get in his way for long. He told Cotton to look for signs. I think you all should help him do that. He didn't strike me as a man who would take what Cotton has to offer for granted."

Randy gave a very adult grimace. "That's nice of you to say, Jackson, but we all know what we are. We're dick on a skewer. Easy to come by, easy to ditch."

Jackson and Henry's eyes both went wide, but it was Sean who spoke up—as much as he could. "That's bullshit," he wheezed, a sure sign that he'd spoken before he could take a deep breath. "You guys, all of you, have way more to offer than what you show on the screen for Johnnies." His eyes searched out Billy's over the crowd, and he said, almost as though they were alone in the room, "I've seen your porn. It's very sexy. I can admit it. But I've spent at least a day with all of you in the last month, and even I can see that there's more to you guys than what you can put out on screen."

"Aww…," Vinnie said. "He likes us!" Vinnie was slender and quick, and his muscles were wiry and tough under skin that was a warm sepia brown. Vinnie tended to be sincere and kind, but not damaged like Cotton. Just a sweet kid who liked sex and, well, had a disproportionately large cock and wasn't doing much else with his life at the moment. He was sort of Billy's acid test of "it takes all kinds."

"I do," Sean wheezed. He was probably going to say more, but judging by the way his chest was rising and falling, he'd been sitting on the couch too long, and he needed to stretch out and rest.

"Yeah, but more specifically, he'd like you all to excuse him while I take him to his room," Billy said dryly. "Don't worry. I'm pretty sure the pizza party will be here until Lance gives us the all-clear, amirite, Henry?"

"Yes, you are," Henry said. He stood and offered Sean his hand, but Sean shook him off and gave Billy a beseeching look.

He really *must* have been tired, because usually he avoided this.

Billy came to crouch in front of him, and when Sean had wrapped his arms around his neck, he stood slowly, allowing Sean to help pull himself up. Once he was there, Sean gave a sigh of relief. "Sorry," he panted. "I was on the couch for too long."

"I know you were. 'Cause you don't fuckin' listen. Now come on. I'm sure Jackson and Henry will tell their story for you when you wake up."

"They already told their story for me," Sean said, with a trace of asperity that made Billy proud. "You'll be getting secondhand story with your pizza, so there."

"You've seen the videos," Billy said blandly as they made their way down the hall. "I like me some sloppy seconds."

"Thank you. Now I've got that image burned in my brain, you bastard," Sean muttered. They passed the point in the hall where anybody could see them, and Billy bent fluidly and caught him under the knees, hefting him up for the last few steps into his room.

"Yeah, you say things like that," Billy panted—his boy had put on his weight again, and he was solidly built—"but I'm pretty sure you just pretend you've never seen those pictures."

Sean was shaking his head even as Billy deposited him on top of his comforter.

"No, you've never seen those pictures?" he taunted.

"No, I wouldn't pretend not to see them," Sean returned, but he was sober. "I told you—you made beautiful pictures. I didn't mind looking."

Billy growled in exasperation, but before he could come up with a smartass retort, Sean threw him one of those honesty hardballs.

"You seemed really angry for a minute," he said softly, his words and breath coming better. "What pissed you off?"

Billy shook his head. "Long story—"

"They're occupied in the living room," Sean said. "You know nobody's going back to the apartment until Lance texts Henry and says it's all okay, right?"

"I figured. Just… just I was supposed to go into the military, right? I was supposed to go. I was the oldest, and the old man was so fuckin' proud. But in the fifth grade I started passing out, like randomly. A fuckton of tests and a hospital stay later, and it turns out I got a heart murmur. Nothin' huge. Nothing that should keep me from playing any sports or nothin'. But I'm not joining the military, and like that, my life means less than shit to the old man. I was already worse than a woman to him 'cause I minded the little kids, but suddenly I'm even less than that. And there was worse to come—I knew there was. I tried to get as much college in as I could before I got outed to my parents. I knew what was coming. But I just... I get so mad at that idea. This fuckin' colonel. His stupid job matters more than breaking Cotton's heart...." Billy's voice was cracking, and he had to stop that right now. *Right* fucking now. He peered at Sean to see if he'd noticed, but Sean's eyebrows were knitted over his eyes, and he was *angry.*

Furiously angry.

"What's wrong?" Billy asked, trying to figure out what he could have said. He'd vented plenty in the last month; it was one of the reasons he loved Sean's company so much. Sometimes Sean would just let that shit roll off his back.

"You have a heart murmur?"

"Yeah, like I said. Kept me out of the military."

"Aren't you *bulimic*? You told me that, right? Eating disorder? You have video conferences with your shrink, calorie diary, all the good shit. I didn't say anything. I figured, 'Oh, hey, this kid's got his act together. He's trying to fix himself. I don't need to butt my big fat nose into his business.' But you have a *heart murmur*. Do you have any idea how bad that can get?" Sean didn't yell—he couldn't—but Billy heard the emphasis even without the yelling.

And realized he'd been caught, damned near with his fingers down his throat.

"It's not like I do meth," he defended weakly. "I mean, yeah, it's self-destructive. It's why I'm trying to quit!"

Sean shook his head, looking like *he* might be the one to burst into tears, which was how Billy felt too.

"C'mon," Billy cajoled. "Don't get all mad. I keep trying to tell you I'm a worthless asshole—"

"I meant what I said," Sean whispered, "when I said there was more to you than porn. I thought you knew that. That I was sincere."

And now Billy couldn't even talk. He sat heavily in the chair by the bed and scrubbed his face with his hand. "Best damned thing anybody's ever said to me," he said finally. "Please don't take it back."

Sean swallowed hard and nodded. "Please keep up with all the work. Don't.... I walked under an overhang, Billy. Rivers, Henry, Cramer, and

I, we all had an exciting day, and we had lunch, and we talked about the case with the kids, and I… I walked into the thruway at the law office, from light to dark to light again, and the light blinded me, and I didn't see the guy until the knife was between my ribs. It was so sudden. There was nothing I could do. You… you have something you can do. To not have your heart stop. To keep breathing. Don't… don't fuck it up, okay?"

Billy nodded. "Okay," he rasped.

"Go… go have pizza with your guys," Sean whispered. He let out a yawn that could not have been good for his healing lungs. "I… my brain is too full, and my heart is too full, and I don't have any wind to talk."

"Okay," Billy whispered again. He stood to leave, but Sean made a noise from the bed. "What?"

"Remember… that thing you did last night?" he asked, looking a little sheepish.

And Billy knew exactly what he was talking about. "You remember that?"

"Yeah. Could you…?"

"Yeah." He turned back toward the bed and bent to softly kiss Sean on the temple. And it was like the touch was magic. It soothed his anger at Constance—at all military men, in general—and his frustration that Cotton had, once again, gotten his heart broken, but this time from a better-quality guy.

And Sean sighed and relaxed against the comforter, his head on the pillows, and closed his eyes in sleep.

BILLY LEFT the room and was surprised to find Jackson waiting for him in the hallway.

"How's he doing?" Jackson asked, green eyes compassionate.

"Doctor says he's healing okay. The wildfire smoke isn't helping." Billy grimaced. "Which means he's going way too slow, and he wants to do more."

Jackson chuckled. "That's about right."

"Everybody," Billy said, remembering the words of Sean's mysterious Russian friend. "Everybody needs to be a fuckin' hero."

"Well, yeah." Jackson Rivers had been through hell. Billy had seen some of it, in the news and in person, and was aware that there was a significant, painful past in his rearview. Somehow it made his wicked smile a thing of beauty. "It's a sickness. I'm just glad that the living sitch seems to be working out."

Billy gave a one-shouldered shrug that he must have picked up from Sean. "Got my own room and three squares a day—"

"I know how you people eat—it's more like three dots a day. But I meant you being a friend to Sean. I think…." Jackson frowned. "I think he's been so focused on his career that until us, his only other friend was Andre. And not that Andre isn't a great guy, but…."

Billy thought of Sean's partner, a trim, meticulously groomed guy in his late thirties who was dedicated to the job and madly devoted to his wife and kids.

"He's not quite in Sean's place," Billy said, remembering Jackson's words about Cotton and the colonel.

"No, he's not. I think they're good partners, though. And I personally love the guy. But if anybody tells you there's a rainbow contingent in the police department—"

"They're lyin' out their ass," Billy said, nodding. "Yeah. I got it."

"I'm just saying—don't leave unless he kicks you out. I think you're good for him."

"I can pay a little rent," Billy said.

Jackson shrugged. "That's between you two. I just…." He blew out a breath. "Don't mind me. Ellery fusses over me, I fuss over all our people. It's a thing. And trust me, I used to hate the guy in the next room. The fact that he's one of us now means he's stubborn as fuck."

Billy frowned, feeling protective. "Why'd you hate him?"

Jackson let out a low chuckle. "Well, for a while, he was crushing on Ellery. That was no way to start a friendship."

A stab of jealousy so powerful it took his breath away pummeled through Billy's chest, and for a moment, he knew how Sean felt, perpetually unable to breathe.

"How… how'd you get over that?" Billy asked, hoping his voice didn't crack.

"He got over Ellery," Jackson said with a shrug. "And he got over himself. Once he realized that the cops weren't always right and they didn't always look into the heart of things, he started working to be one of the cops that *did* look into the heart of things, and we started working together. And while that happened, I guess he realized that Ellery's really only got one blind spot." Jackson raised his hand guiltily. "Sean's a smart kid. He knew when to cut and run. I wish he hadn't run right into the fucking fireman who ripped his heart out in a hospital, but see, that was the rebound guy there, so his heart's free and clear."

"It's funny you think of him as a kid," Billy said. "He's almost exactly your age."

Jackson's expression grew sober. "He's new to the kinds of things you and I know, Billy. And he's mad at himself for all the judging he did beforehand. What he said tonight about how you're all more than porn? It's true, but it's something he wouldn't have acknowledged last year."

Billy nodded. "Lucky me, I got the woke cop."

"Yeah, you do." Jackson grinned but oddly enough sobered again. "And your woke cop is getting bored, but I think I've got a solution for that if you're game."

Billy blinked, suddenly *so* ready to do something besides… *dwell* on the man sleeping in the next room.

"I got no plans," he said, shrugging, throwing his homework to the four winds. He could wake up early and do that shit. Tonight he had people in the house proposing some sort of game, and he was all for that.

Anything to not think about how all Sean had wanted was that kiss on the temple and how easy it had been to give him one, like it was as natural as breathing.

Nose Poking

WHEN SEAN woke up from his nap, the living room was clear, and Billy had cleaned up most of the debris, including spraying down the coffee table with cleaner. Sean had never had to tell him how to do these things. He wasn't sure if Henry had trained him or his mother had, but he was very adept at keeping a house from falling apart.

Or a house's occupant, who'd gotten a little bit overtired and overemotional—Sean could admit that.

"Everybody left?" He yawned as Billy came down the hall to make sure he could walk by himself. "I'm fine. Seriously—unless I overdo it, I can make it around the house."

"I had to carry you to bed, papi. Don't get too excited about yourself."

Sean grunted. "Glad you're here to keep me humble. You didn't answer my question."

"Come sit in the recliner. How full are you from pizza in the afternoon?"

Sean grimaced. "Full enough to only want salad in the evening, why?"

"'Cause I had Randy go get me a watermelon to slice up. It's in cubes in the fridge, all chilling and stuff. Sit in the recliner, and we can have some of that in the evening. It's good."

Sean smiled a little, bemused. "I've never had watermelon for dinner," he said, thinking that if it didn't have a protein, a carb, and a green on it—or be a casserole that combined all three—his mother would have bled out her eyeballs before serving it as a complete meal.

"You've been missing out," Billy said, sounding sincere. "I feel like I should make some popcorn to go with it. In the summer when the air conditioning sucked and my mom didn't want to cook, popcorn and watermelon was practically a food group."

Sean laughed. "Maybe just watermelon tonight," he said. "But we can try it next summer."

For a moment, he panicked. He'd said "next summer," but… but who would they be to each other next summer? He'd been tempted to ask Billy if he wanted to keep rooming at the duplex—he seemed to enjoy the peace and quiet if nothing else—but would Billy go for that? Would his sometimes-prickly pride call a kibosh on it? What if he wanted to bring other men there?

Sean's eyes went wide. Oh dear Lord. Billy's side job was awful enough to contemplate. What if…?

But Billy simply shrugged and nodded like it was a real possibility, and a little voice in Sean's brain said, *Do you really not want to see him again, even if he's with someone? Do you never want to have a long talk with him, seeing those cynical eyes soften in the lamplight? Do you not want to hear him give you hell about being a stubborn asshole? This thing we have, whatever it is, if it's got legs, it'll see us through popcorn and watermelon, right?*

Right.

And God. If nothing else, Sean could use more people in his life to keep reminding him that the Jesses in this world didn't need a Sean in their lives.

"Now dinner's settled," Billy said with satisfaction, "Randy told me about your convo with Dude's owner."

Sean blinked. "Bob?"

"The guy with the Chiweenie that looks like an alligator. You know. Dude the Chiweenie?"

"Yeah." Sean could concede the dog was hard to forget. "Bob is the Chiweenie's owner. I didn't know the dog's name is Dude."

"You didn't know the name of the dog?" Billy asked, looking surprised. "You pet him every day at the park."

"I knew Bob's name!" Sean retorted.

For a moment they stared at each other, and then Billy scowled. "You," he said succinctly, "are a police detective. You don't think you can learn the name of both the dogs and the people?"

Sean grimaced and studied a thread on his couch. "I, uhm, think of the people as suspects. 'Bob, white male, six feet tall, one-seventy, seventy-five years old.' I, uh, don't really think about dog stats."

Billy blinked at him. "You mean like 'Dude, blond Chiweenie, twelve inches tall, twenty-two inches long, twenty-four pounds, six years old?'"

Sean couldn't help it. The laugh started at the bottom of his toes. "That poor dog," he said, his voice barely working. "His little legs go flailing, and he keeps trying to catch up!"

Billy held his hand in front of his mouth and turned his head as he laughed like he was trying to hide his mirth. "Man, I feel bad laughing at him! Dude's daddy keeps feeding the poor thing green beans, and his wife is loving him with bacon treats!" His cackle faded to a manageable level. "It's okay, though. The dog has a *lot* of love." He took a breath like he was getting his shit together. "Anyway. So Dude's dad, Bob, is sort of the pulse of the dog walkers around there. He lives in the neighborhood, right?"

Sean nodded. "Yeah, I know. I'm the one who remembered his name."

Billy rolled his eyes. "So today he starts to talk to Randy—and my God, how Randy can talk more than either of us."

Sean smiled a little. "Lord yes. I remember. I was petting the ladies."

"Isabel and Allison?" Billy checked.

"The golden retrievers." Sean really loved those dogs. Big and graceful, with gracious smiles for anybody with a petting hand, the ladies, as they called them, got along with all the dogs in the park, even the yappy little ones.

"Yeah, well, apparently while you were getting your jollies with the two blonds, Randy was talking to Bob, and he got an earful. I guess there's been some epic criming in the area."

Sean frowned. "What sort of 'epic criming' are we talking about?"

"Well, you know how the park's sort of the neighborhood epicenter, right? So it's this big rectangle and there's a main road running along either side, with cul-de-sacs attached?"

"The cul-de-sacs all have thruways to the park," Sean said, suddenly very, very curious.

"Well, there's been, like, a rash of thefts in the cul-de-sacs. Apparently Bob told Randy that everything from bicycles to vacuum cleaners has gone missing."

Sean frowned. "Have the homeowners reported break-ins?"

Billy rolled his eyes, holding his hands palm up in the classic "I should know?" position. "See, this is why you need to talk to the people instead of doing a threat assessment. Randy and Bob apparently were playing supersleuth while an *actual police detective* was sitting right there."

Sean frowned, thinking about it. "You think we should look into this?"

Billy rolled his eyes again. "You doing anything else?"

Sean humphed. "I can barely walk around the park. Do you really see me running down a guy stealing a bicycle?"

"Well, you won't be alone, genius. I'll be your legs. I mean, I got a lot of pent-up irritation—I bet I could tackle an asshole on a bicycle, and it would be no big thing."

Sean laughed softly, as much as his lungs would allow. "What's this about?" he asked. "Seriously. I'm not Ms. Marple or any of the other heroines in a cozy mystery. I have no intention of hanging out my shingle and being a PI. What are you trying to get me to do?"

Billy's expression went sober. "You said it the other night. You went from the light to the dark to the light, and then you got stabbed. It's gonna take your confidence some, you think? This is something that needs doing. It's not all glamorous and shit, like your day job, but to the people getting their vacuum cleaners ripped off, it's important. I thought…." He shrugged, looking uncomfortable. "You're bored. You watch one more cop show and your head's gonna pop off. This'll keep you from being that guy."

"That guy?" Sean asked, trying to remember if he'd lost his temper or gotten *too* frustrated with his healing body in the last month.

"That bitter guy who yells at all the neighbors and doesn't like kids and screams at the dogs and shit."

Sean blinked. "Uhm… I… I don't *think* I'm that guy yet. How would I turn into that guy?"

Billy gave a snort of disgust. "I don't know. My old man—he seemed okay when I was little, but, you know. Went out on a couple of deployments. Every time he came back there was another kid. Then he quit the military, and everything went to hell. Mad all the time. Hitting us, hitting Mom. I figured he missed the action. He was always such a macho guy, pushing his chest at everyone. He didn't have that place to be a badass, and he's got to be a badass somewhere."

Sean swallowed. "If he was taking his temper out on your family, he wasn't a badass."

"What, your dad didn't yell?" Billy asked derisively.

"Course he did," Sean said, giving a small laugh. "We're Polish. He yelled, he judged, he snapped. It was pretty much all bluster. Only time he ever got pissed enough to hit someone was...." He grimaced. "This is a sucky story. Anyway, he only hit one of us once, and Charlie was almost an adult. But there's a difference, right? Between bluster and abuse. Most of the time when he was yelling, he was funny. 'By God's mother's panties, those assholes better not have forgotten to do the fuckin' dishes!' And he'd be yelling it coming up the stairs after he left us all at home to take Mom out or something. And suddenly we'd realize that all our peace and quiet time had gone, and we'd promised to clean the house, and they'd walk in and we'd be like a little army of worker bees, vacuuming and doing dishes and such. He'd open the door and see that and yell that we'd better be working because we were all worthless little pukes anyway, and then he'd slam the door and say he was taking Mom to ice cream, and we *weren't* getting any."

Billy was laughing by now, but Sean realized his eyes were hot.

"What?" Billy asked, pausing.

"Just… there was all that awkwardness after I came out, and then he was so upset I was joining the force, and I'd forgotten how much I missed the surly old bastard until…." He bit his lip.

"Until now."

"Yeah."

"Sorry," Billy said, voice a little rusty. "I… what was the story you didn't want to tell me? Who'd he hit? You, when you came out?"

Sean shook his head. "No." He blew out a ragged breath. He hated coming-out stories. Many of them were horrible—so many that the good ones broke your heart because they should *all* be that way. But his was sort of a mix of the two, and the mix twisted up his insides.

"Then what?" Billy prodded, and Sean was about to insist that Billy go first, but he saw the way Billy was looking at him, like he was waiting for the flaw.

"See, I came out at school," Sean said, resigning himself. "Not on purpose. I was on the football team, and while I didn't ogle, one kid asked me why I wasn't going out with a cheerleader who was crushing on me, and I told him straight up that she wasn't my type. The guy was a jerk—

and I was probably a jerk back because, you know, still worshipped the old man. Anyway, the whole thing melted down in the quad, and it was me versus three of the other football players."

Billy sucked air in through his teeth. "Anyone need an ambulance?"

"Heh heh heh…." Sean heard the sound and clapped his hand over his own mouth.

"What? What's wrong?"

"That's a *Jackson* laugh," Sean said, aghast. "And Henry's getting it too! Oh my God! Next thing you know I'm going to let my hair grow long and wear my pants dropping halfway down my ass."

Billy arched his eyebrows and raked a glance over Sean, who was wearing a fitted athletic T-shirt—no logo—and khaki shorts that were a little large but obviously would fit when he'd recovered his health.

"No," he said without equivocation. "Judging by the way you freaked out about getting your hair cut last week, that's a super strong absolute no."

Sean chuckled. "Apparently only when I'm channeling my inner devil—good to know."

"Finish the story!" Billy urged him. "What does this have to do with your father?"

Ugh. It was so much easier when he was agonizing over not turning into Jackson.

"Well, I got home, and I was a mess—broke my nose, dislocated some fingers, black eyes, split lip… the works. And my dad turns to my brother Charlie—we were Polish twins, he's about eleven months younger than I am—and goes, 'You don't have a mark on you. What happened?'"

"Good question!"

Sean grimaced. He hated this part. He could never explain why. "And Charlie goes, 'But Dad, he told them guys he was queer! I'm supposed to defend him for that?'" Sean shook his head. "And Dad popped him one. A slap, not a punch, because I don't think he wanted to KO Charlie, but it broke his nose. Said, 'He's yer fuckin' brother, and you defend him till yer dead.' Full-on accent, which I guess he got from my grandpa. And that was it. The family knew I was gay. Mom stopped asking me if I was dating girls, started tentatively asking if I was crushing on guys. And Dad stopped asking me about the police academy. And Charlie…." He sighed. "Charlie did what he was supposed to. Defended me in public. Nobody talked down to us in public. But you know, we shared a room, and...." He shook his head.

"But he wasn't your brother anymore?" Billy asked, his voice catching.

Sean shrugged. "It didn't feel like that. Not until my dad died, anyway."

There was a loaded silence then, and Billy let out a long breath. "I want to ask what happened when your dad died, but it's getting late, and it's been... it's been a weird day. What I really want to do is get you some of that cold watermelon and eat it in the living room and make a plan for talking to all the neighbors around the park, and then watch your stupid cop show with you while I try to get some homework done. Is that... is that okay? Do I lose my empathy card for that?"

"No, that's fine," Sean said, feeling an acute sense of relief. Like Billy said, it had been a strange, emotionally laden day—and apparently, his cop sense really *was* getting rusty if he'd been paying attention to Isabel and Allison instead of to a rash of robberies in the area.

But Billy paused as he was standing up to go get them food. "You and your brother *did* make up, though, right?" And he sounded like it was important to him.

"Yeah," Sean said with a smile. "Night of Dad's wake. All Dad's cop buddies were in the house getting plastered on whiskey, and Charlie grabbed a six-pack of beer and sort of nodded me over. We were both living on our own by then, but we went up to our old room—same bunk beds but all of mom's craft stuff—and we got really buzzed. And Charlie told me he'd been dumb and confused and embarrassed, and he cried and apologized. And I told him...."

"What?" Billy asked. "The guy deserted you when you needed him. What could you possibly have to say to him?"

Sean felt it. This was personal to Billy, and he wondered *so hard* what this kid's story was. He regretted giving them a pass from the hard emotions now; he *wanted* the tough stuff. But *he* was supposed to be the grown-up.

"I said I was sorry Dad hit him. I didn't want him to be forced to be my brother."

Billy's eyes shot open, and then they grew shiny. "What'd he say?" he asked, voice gruff.

Sean laughed a little and shook his head. "Mushy stuff. We were three beers down by then, and it was my turn to go steal the next round. We'd hit 'I love you, man! I love you too!' so I stole another six-pack from the wake—which was still roaring by then, let me tell you—and we woke up brothers again."

Billy's mouth pulled up, like he was trying to chuckle, but it didn't make it the entire way to a smile. "That's a good story," he said. "Why do you hate that story?"

"I hate the part in the middle," Sean told him. "I hate the part where my brother wasn't a good guy all the way through. I hate that my dad felt like he had to defend *me* from Charlie with violence. I just…." He'd never been able to state this—it felt too big.

"You said you used to be a judgy fucker," Billy said. "Like, an asshole cop, right?"

Until he'd crushed hard on Ellery Cramer, yes, he had been. "Yeah."

"And then you learned what you didn't know and felt dumb?"

"So fucking dumb."

"That's why you don't like the story," Billy said decisively. "You like your good guys good and your bad guys bad. Otherwise it hurts your brain. But your people—hell, *all* people—they're not like that. We're all mixed up like that. Good and bad. Angels and devils. I mean, I'm a whore, and you hate that. But I'm also a waiter and a student, and this last month I've been your nurse. That part's not so bad. That's why you hated that story. 'Cause it hurts your brain, but your heart still knows your dad's not a bad guy and your brother's okay. It's hard."

Hunh. Sean almost caught himself making the sound and then realized it was a Jackson Rivers sound. Damn that guy.

"I'll take my watermelon now," he said instead.

Billy grinned. "Yeah. I had a couple of pieces. *Nothing* like the sweet kind of watermelon when it's all cold."

The kid was *so* right.

For a few moments they sat and ate in silence as the long afternoon shadows stretched over the darkened room, and then Billy said, "So, Mr. Detective Cop-Man, how do we do an investigation?"

Sean gave him a smile and swallowed the divine bite of cold fruit in his mouth. "You looking for a hobby?"

Billy grinned. "Why not? You're a smart guy. I'd love to bask in your smartness."

Sean's laugh felt freeing, if still a little weak. "First I text Andre and have him run police reports on the neighborhood. Then tomorrow, when we're petting all the dogs, we start talking to the owners." He gave Billy a sly look. "I'll take the big dogs and you take the Chihuahuas."

Billy grimaced. "I hate being a cultural stereotype."

"It's so adorable I could cry. It's like the reverse of toxic masculinity. All these macho guys going, 'Gotta have a giant fuckin' dog!' and you're like, 'Small dogs love me.'"

Billy had to hold his hand in front of his mouth as he tried not to spit watermelon all over the couch. "You asshole," he choked when he'd mostly recovered.

"Well, we know 'woke cop' couldn't last," Sean said modestly. "Anyway, we each play to our strengths, and when we're done, we compare notes."

"Solid plan," Billy said, nodding. "What are we asking about?"

Wow. Wasn't *Sean* the shittiest teacher ever. "Specific time, specific place, specific circumstance," he said. "Were the things stolen all the same? What was different? Where were they stolen from—which part of the house or yard? Were there dogs there? Did these people share a plumber? A roofer? A gardener? What did they have in common besides living close to the park? Did anybody see anything? Was everybody on vacation? You want stuff as specific as possible so you know what to look for."

Billy nodded and frowned. "This is why you guys are always carrying notepads, isn't it?"

"I'm afraid so." Sean shrugged. "I take notes on my phone, actually." He grinned and made a little pinching motion with his thumb and forefinger. "Got a stylus and an app."

"Very clever, cop-man." Billy rolled his eyes. "My generation knows how to text in our notes. So there."

Sean laughed. "Whatever floats your boat. Just make sure you take notes so we don't have to remember everything, because that's exhausting and inaccurate."

Billy blew out a breath. "You're making this cop thing sound hard. How dare you. Now I have to reassess my opinion of all cops everywhere."

Sean regarded him with sober eyes. "No. Any cop treats you and your buddies like shit, you don't have to reassess a goddamned thing."

"Stay woke, cop."

"Doing my best."

THE NEXT day, Sean woke up with an elephant on his chest.

"Sean?" Billy's voice sounded concerned, and Sean barely managed a raspy, "Yeah?" in return.

Billy appeared in his room as if by teleportation. "You're blue. Goddammit! You spent too long in the recliner, and you're fucking blue."

"'M fine," Sean had mumbled, but Billy probably didn't hear him over the sound of his pounding feet as he went running for his phone.

He didn't remember much after that—Billy helping him into sweats while talking urgently with Lance over the phone, and then Billy helping him into... Lance's Mazda? Again?

"Where's my Charger?" he asked as Billy belted him in from the driver's side.

"We let Henry take it. The guys really wanted a ride. I was going to get it from Henry today after your walk. Lucky us, huh?"

"Sure." He was thinking how much easier the Mazda was on his lungs, but he couldn't say that. Couldn't say much of anything really.

"Stop talking, asshole," Billy muttered, looking over his shoulder while he palmed the wheel. They were going too fast, but Sean couldn't complain about that either. Really, all he could do was pull in one breath after another while Billy broke speed records and sound barriers getting them through morning traffic to Med Center.

Lance was waiting outside with a wheelchair, and Billy lifted him into it with main strength.

"Go park the car," Lance said. "I'll get him admitted." He bent down to Sean's level. "How you doing, Mr. Kryzynski?"

"Bring Billy back," Sean muttered. Henry's boyfriend was almost supernaturally beautiful. If Sean ever saw an actual elf in real life, he'd expect it to look like Dr. Lance Luna. But even that stunningly beautiful face with the delicate cleft chin and the strong jaw didn't comfort him now that Billy was apparently ditching him for a Mazda with primer spots on the side.

"Will do," Lance said. "As soon as you're admitted."

Two hours later, Sean was in a hospital room hooked up to antibiotics and oxygen and trying to understand how this was his fault.

"You sat in the recliner, and you didn't get up for hours," Billy ranted, stalking back and forth at the foot of the bed. "You—you're always doing something. Go to the park, try to do the dishes. Who in the hell needs to shower every day? Always something—"

"What in the hell is he ranting on about?" Henry asked as he came to sit by Sean's bed.

"No... idea...." Sean panted. "Entertaining tho...."

Billy stopped and glared at him. "You. Asshole." That was it—no elaboration or anything.

"Yes, yes he is," Henry said, eyeing Billy like a fighter fish in a tank. "Entertaining. Not you, Kryzynski. As far as I know, you're not an asshole."

"*He's sick!*" Billy snarled, responding to Henry's statement. "How can he be *sick*? I did everything. I gave him his meds, I made sure he got rest, I kept his wound clean I—"

"You did fine, Billy," Lance said, coming in with a chart. "Heya, Sean. How you feeling?"

"High," Sean whispered through the mask. He glared at Billy. "Unappreciated."

The stricken look on Billy's face told him the word had hit home. "You want me to appreciate you?" Billy retorted. "*Don't get sick!*"

"It's not his fault," Lance said gently. "Infections happen, especially with changes in weather. It went from hot to brisk, and there's a few forest fires nearby. The air quality has been sort of shitty. Now you say this came on suddenly?"

"Went to sleep fine," Sean wheezed.

"He was fine when he went to sleep," Billy said.

"Woke up like this."

"He was *blue*. That fucker was *blue*. There I was, listening for him to get up, making sure he didn't end up on the carpet like the first time he tried to take a whizz by himself, and he can barely fucking call my name. I'm so pissed. How could he be *blue*?"

"He's... doing wonders... for my pride," Sean wheezed, but he was smiling as he said it. It wasn't that he was excited about being in the hospital again, but boy, this sure did beat the last time, when Jesse had been having that quiet, angst-filled, one-sided conversation with him about how he couldn't be in a position to be outed, not now. Instead, here was Billy, pacing like a caged tiger and, well, worried sick.

"He's freaking out is what he's doing," Henry said dryly. "Billy, shut up and let Lance doctor."

Billy stopped short to glare at him, and Lance took his opportunity to ask more questions.

"You haven't been overdoing it, have you?" He glanced from Sean to Billy and back again. "Just walks through the park, right? No running, no weightlifting—"

Sean looked away from those perceptive eyes, remembering what he'd talked Randy into the day before.

"Wait a minute," Henry said, suddenly all suspicion. "Randy said he helped you do some bicep curls yesterday, and some chest presses. He was really excited about the Bowflex in your spare room."

Sean gave a weak smile. "Wanted to see… if I still could," he managed.

Billy's eyes bugged out. "*See*! I *knew* it was his fault!"

Henry had to drag a flailing Billy out of the hospital room by his collar so Lance could finish.

"Wow," Lance said, after making a notation on his tablet. "I roomed with that guy for over a year. I never saw him that worked up."

Sean didn't have the wind to answer, but he must have looked puzzled enough for Lance to go on.

"Irritated, defensive, sarcastic, and bitter, but not worked up."

"He's worried… about… Cotton," Sean breathed.

"He worries about everybody," Lance said astutely. "But he tries really hard not to show it. It's like he's been actively fighting not to be a mommy this whole time and boom! You come along and release that shit on everybody."

Sean managed a smile. "Lucky me."

Lance gave him a compassionate look from his beautiful tawny eyes. "Yeah, Detective Kryzynski. You *are* lucky. Not everybody can get Billy that upset. What are you going to do with that?"

Breathe in. "Get better…. Solve crime…. Keep him."

Lance nodded. "Should they rent out his bed at the flophouse?"

Sean closed his eyes. "Will hurt… his…."

"Not until he says so. Gotcha. Now about you. Antibiotics and two nights' stay here, then back home and you start the whole thing again, but this time…?"

"Go… slower."

"Good idea." Lance's eyes softened. "In the workout area—not that other thing. You don't want him to get away."

Sean swallowed and wished he had more wind. "I'm just... another... cop...."

Lance raised his eyebrows. "Yeah. But you see him for who he is. Not even his coworkers have done that much." Lance tapped some more stuff into his tablet. "Okay, now I'm going to submit your treatment plan and go let Henry and Billy back in, provided that kid can calm the fuck down. Visitor's hours end at nine, so maybe get him to go back home and catch some sleep, okay?"

"Yeah." Maybe, if Sean asked nice again, Billy would kiss his forehead or temple before he left. He remembered longing for sweet moments like that from Jesse; it didn't have to be porn sex or dry-humping to turn his key. Sometimes it was just a sweet moment, a kiss on the forehead, a touch of the hand.

Billy didn't seem to mind that.

Lance paused at the doorway and looked over his shoulder. "I remember when you were here before and Rivers and Henry made a big fuss because your department didn't know, didn't show up. My phone's been blowing up since Billy got you here. I don't think that's going to be a problem this time around."

Sean closed his eyes, both in embarrassment and with a little bit of relief. It was so much like the *He's yer fuckin' brother, and you defend him till yer dead* moment of his life—except Rivers and Henry had been the ones slapping people upside the head. The fact that they'd done so figuratively instead of literally helped a little, as did the fact that his department had been mortified that they hadn't known. In the end, though, his brothers had stood for him—and it looked like Billy's brothers would do the same.

EVENTUALLY HENRY came back in, leading a recalcitrant Billy practically by the ear.

"So, what's the prognosis, chief?" Henry asked, and Sean wrinkled his nose.

"Two days... observation. You assholes... leave at nine."

Billy glared at him. "And you don't gotta be a fuckin' hero for a while, right?"

Sean gave a sheepish smile under the mask. "Next week... is fine...."

Billy snorted. "Whatever, man."

"I'm starving," Henry announced. "And Sean, I know you haven't had lunch yet. How about I go get some takeout, text all the guys yelling at me to make sure you're okay—including Rivers and Cramer in case you felt left out—and generally let Billy here tell you all the reasons you completely suck as a roommate."

"I hate you," Billy said, his eyes narrow and voice flat.

"Of course you do," Henry told him, lighting up like it had been the best compliment in the world. "I'm a complete asshole. What's not to hate? Back soon, you two. Ta-ta for now!"

Henry disappeared, leaving Sean and Billy rolling their eyes at each other.

"What now?" Billy asked, and he didn't sound sardonic or bitter. He sounded lost.

"I'll... need... a... nurse... for longer," Sean managed.

"Yeah, sure. But no more being a fucking hero, okay?" So, so lost.

"No... promises. All... ever wanted...."

"Was to be a cop like your old man?" Billy asked, and there it was—the bitter. "Yeah, didn't take a super genius to figure *that* out."

"Sor... ry?"

"Don't be sorry. Don't. Just be healthy. Goddammit, I'm getting *attached* to you—do you get that? You and your military haircut and your up at seven, breakfast by eight, exercise at nine. Oh my God. My morning BMs are actually running on *your schedule*!"

Sean sputtered under the mask and struggled to catch his breath.

"Don't even bother to answer," Billy snapped. "I can tell I hurt your brain. I'm saying—it's not fair. I was just supposed to watch over you for six weeks, and now...." He let out a breath.

"Randy... could...."

"I'd cut him," Billy said, with no mercy left, although Sean knew Billy loved the kid. "No. You don't go replacing me with Randy. You don't go replacing me with *anybody*. You understand? That's a fucking rule."

Sean smiled. Although he hadn't really thought Billy would go for the suggestion, it was a relief to know it was completely off the table.

"Fair," he rasped. "Same."

There was a sudden frozen silence between them as Sean realized what that would mean. How he could take that. That Billy not replacing *Sean* with anybody could mean not being *close* with anybody. Physically. As in Billy's third job, that they hadn't talked about since the last time he'd worked it.

He opened his mouth to try to say "Sorry," but Billy grunted.

"My next shift is in three weeks."

Sean fought not to struggle for breath.

"Don't stress yourself," Billy told him. "I'll think about it. You gotta think about it too. 'Cause if we mean it one way, we're friends for life. But you mean it the other, it's not only that I'm out of a job."

Sean tilted his head and sought out Billy's eyes, which was hard because Billy wasn't looking at him. Finally he turned his head and those bitter, cynical eyes locked with Sean's, except they weren't bitter or cynical anymore.

They were vulnerable.

"Fair," Sean mouthed, and Billy nodded.

"Fair."

They'd think about it.

And given Sean couldn't talk about stupid shit until he could breathe again, that meant he wouldn't be thinking about much else.

Kites

BILLY GLANCED sideways at Sean, checking his breathing, assessing his color, making sure he wasn't too flushed or too pale or too whatever. He'd been out of the hospital for three days and had finally, *finally*, been allowed back in the dog park, as long as he forewent the walk around the soccer field for a whole other week.

Sean had spent his first three days back exhausted, sleeping a lot, and doing exactly what Billy told him to do, which on the one hand had been gratifying but on the other a little bit frightening because their first four weeks together had been nothing but pushback. Neither of them had said a word about the terrifying possibilities of their conversation in the hospital, and part of Billy was a little bit relieved. Nothing to see here, folks. What was it Sean had said? They'd just hit the "I love you, man!" part of their relationship, only they hadn't needed the beer.

Except that's not how it felt.

Sean really *had* stayed in the hospital for two whole days, and Billy had dragged his homework in that first day, after Henry had come back with the takeout, and he'd sat quietly and worked while Sean slept or watched stupid television. That night before he left, Sean had glanced at him, still in the oxygen mask, and pointed to his temple, looking sly.

Billy had almost stalked out of the room, but… but he wanted to kiss the guy. He couldn't kiss his mouth—not under the oxygen mask— but he could lace their fingers gingerly together, avoiding the IV line altogether, and place a simple kiss on Sean's forehead.

Sean had smiled at the touch of his lips, murmuring, "Thanks, Guillermo."

Billy had stared at him for a moment before realizing that of all the things he'd experienced since he'd left home, this right here, kissing Sean Kryzynski on the temple, was the most naked thing he'd ever done.

And he'd done it for the last three nights since Sean had gotten back home. Their days were pretty much the same as they had been—

with an extra ration of shit from Billy about Sean getting sick, that is. But at night, Billy would come in, and they'd talk, each conversation getting a little more intimate, a little deeper, and Billy would stand to leave and… just go tuck the guy in.

Like a big brother, or a father, or a lover.

But mostly like that last one.

God, what was Billy doing?

"What are you thinking?" Sean asked, breaking into his thoughts now. "You look like you smelled something bad. Did my pit-stop expire early?"

Billy gave him a droll look. "Yes. It's killing me. Keep your arms down until the bad guy shows up."

Sean gave a rusty chuckle. "You know, I used to hate Rivers because he had the mentality of a twelve-year-old boy, but I think I'm starting to remember how fun it was."

"You'll never pass," Billy told him. "You eat too much fruit."

That chuckle again. Then Sean changed the subject. "No, seriously. You look thoughtful again?"

"I was just wondering," Billy said, unable to *not* tell the truth this time, "what your laugh sounds like when your lungs are all functional and shit. 'Cause I *think* you might have a really good laugh, but I sort of want to hear it."

Sean was quiet for a moment, so Billy glanced over at him and found he was smiling in a pleased, embarrassed way, and his cheeks were pink.

"You're so easy," he said fondly, and mindful of the people they were going to try to talk to today, he surreptitiously stroked Sean's fingers with his own.

To his surprise, Sean turned his palm up and laced their fingers together, squeezing once before letting him go.

And now *Billy* couldn't stop smiling.

"So you're back!"

They both turned their heads toward the older man walking steadily toward them, his alligator-fat Chiweenie waddling up behind him.

"Dude!" Billy cried, and the amiable creature went right to him, raising his head for a solid ear rub, his little Chi-tail springing about madly against his back. "C'mere, buddy. Haven't seen you for a couple of days. Missed you!"

"I could say the same," Bob said, smiling genially. "Hope you're still healing well." He nodded toward Sean, who looked embarrassed.

"He lifted weights and got an infection and had to be hospitalized for two days," Billy said, feeling a great deal of vindication and glee. "Because he's a stupid asshole, that's why."

Sean grimaced up at Bob. "Stupid asshole," he rasped, and then used both thumbs to point toward his own chest. "Me."

Bob chuckled. "So you were gone for a bit. Did you hear about the break-in over on Cherry Pit Court?"

"Is that really a street name?" Billy asked suspiciously. "Because that's the—"

"Pits," Bob finished for him, grinning. "Yeah, I know it. I think the contractors got tired. The main street was named after his son, Alvin, and then the cul-de-sacs are all Apple Seed, Peach Stem, and Watermelon Rind. It's weird."

"Tired of his job?" Sean asked, surprised, because who thought of street names, really.

"Maybe a little drunk," Bob conceded with a wink. "Anyway, that blue house on Cherry Pit, the one with the yellow trim—"

"I know that house," Billy said, surprised. "It's pretty... not brown. And they've got flags in the front. Rainbow flags, peace flags. Very liberal."

Bob—who called himself a "lapsed republican"—squeezed his eyes shut in self-deprecation. "Of course," he chided mildly, "you'd remember the liberal house."

Billy smiled, all teeth. "It would be wrong if I didn't!"

There was some laughter then, and Billy knew how he *should* feel about politics—all mad at this old white guy for voting for Reagan back in the day—but how he actually felt was that this old white guy was really pretty decent. And his dog was super friendly, which meant the decent went through and through. You couldn't have a super friendly dog if you were a douchebag.

"So tell us about the house on Cherry Pit," Billy prompted. He'd been expecting Sean to do it, but then he glanced next to him and saw Sean working hard to keep his breathing even. Oops, time to pull his weight.

"That got dangerous," Bob said soberly. "That was a mom and her two kids. Dad was out of town on business, and she was all alone. But Charlie and Parker—you know Parker, the big black lab?"

"Good dog," Sean said, nodding.

"He's the best. But they live next door to pretty house, and they heard sort of a clatter. Parker was not messing around when that guy tried to break into the woman's garage. Charlie opened the door because Parker was losing his mind, and they heard a clatter, and when they looked at the space between the houses, they saw the guy had dropped his crowbar next to her smaller garage door. Someone here is going after houses. I tell you, it's not safe at night."

Sean frowned. "Have all the break-ins…," he breathed, "been at night?"

That brought Bob up short. "*Mmm*… no. Some of them have been during the day. The guy on Peach Stem works the night shift. His garage was broken into during the day."

"What… did… they… steal?" Sean asked.

It was Bob's turn to frown. "From his place? His air compressor and his tools. He likes to do home improvement, so he had some good ones."

Sean nodded, and Billy *and* Bob waited for him to pull in some more air. Finally it appeared he had his wind back again. "What was taken from the other houses?" he asked, almost smoothly.

"Bicycles," Bob said thoughtfully. "Power tools, air compressors. Same sort of thing. The house on Cherry Pit has an old Mustang in the garage. The husband likes to work on it on the weekends, to refurbish. I'm sure he's got some valuable equipment in there."

Sean nodded. "Did any of the houses have dogs?" he asked, and Billy glanced at him sharply.

"No," Bob responded promptly, and then, with more thought, "but they all have dogs nearby." He frowned. "That might not mean anything. I mean…." He nodded his chin toward the many dogs currently walking the track with their owners or chasing balls in the middle of the soccer field. "The sidewalks are wide, the bike lanes are plentiful, and we've got this great park in the center. Lots of people have dogs."

Sean nodded but chewed on his lip a little, and Billy wondered what he was thinking. With a little grimace, Sean held up a finger and reached into his pocket for his wallet, then pulled out a plain white business card.

"If you hear of any other thefts, call me," he said. "I'm going to do some snooping and call in some favors, okay? I don't like that he's choosing houses where people are sleeping. It could get dangerous."

"We wouldn't want that," Bob said soberly. "And we appreciate you looking into it."

At that moment there was a deep, ecstatic *woolf* from across the park, and Billy grimaced.

"Oh no."

"Skye!" There was no escaping the way Sean's face lit up, although he couldn't actually call the dog's name across the park.

"Sean, that dog...." Billy shook his head, not sure how he could phrase this. The dog's heart was 100 percent gold—Billy had no doubt. But its body? As muscular as a snake, as tall as a beagle, and as long as a full-grown German shepherd. The dog's tail could break fragile bones, and talk about go! The dog had more go than a nitro-powered race car—and far less control.

But Sean didn't seem to care. His face opened up, and the dog, sensing that here, here was the big brother she'd been looking for all her life, vowed she would prove her love, prove it by throwing that fifty-pound wriggling body right up into Sean's lap!

Sean responded by hugging her, although it probably hurt him like hell, and Billy was forced to take control.

"No," he commanded, standing up and grabbing the dog by the collar.

"Aw," Sean murmured, but his face had gone pale, a sure sign that little leap of faith had hurt him.

"I know you mean well," Billy said firmly, lecturing into the dog's upturned face, "but sit. Sit. You stay. No. No jumping!"

"I'm sorry!" Jim, Skye's owner, was an angular man with a goatee who was about ten years younger than Bob. "Skye! Dammit! Would you sit?"

And Skye, who *had* been sitting, was suddenly in ecstasy again, her anaconda-like tail thumping against Billy's ankle with enough power to bruise.

"I'm sorry," Jim said again, coming over to drag Skye away by her collar. "I almost had her trained to the collar, but the battery went out and she's just a mess! Skye, look, a squirrel!"

Ooh, that dog knew what a squirrel was. With a happy bark, she wriggled around until she saw one down the path, and the chase was on! She hauled ass after the creature, surprisingly quick, and when the squirrel darted up one of the big-boled beech trees, she proceeded to leap up a good six to seven feet, paws scrabbling against the bark in an effort to climb the tree and get the damned squirrel.

"Oh my fucking God," Billy said, watching her.

"Yeah, she'll do that for a good twenty minutes," Jim told them. "Thank heavens. I'm exhausted."

Billy bent down and stroked Dude's little bat ears and his broad back. "You're way too smart for that bullshit, aren't you, buddy?" In response, Dude smiled up at him, reaffirming his supposition that small dogs were far superior to anything over twenty pounds.

Or anything that was *supposed* to be over twenty pounds, he thought fondly, as Dude waddled back to Bob, excited about their walk around the park path.

"So you'll keep us informed?" Sean asked. "And let me know if you see anything suspicious. You guys live in the cul-de-sacs. We drive in from a few blocks over. You've got the inside track."

"We'll do it," Bob assured him, while Jim hollered, "Skye, get down!" He turned to Sean and Billy in dismay. "Oh my God, do you see that? She's *in the damned tree!*"

Jim took off running at a fairly decent clip for a guy in his sixties, and Bob followed a little more slowly, chuckling as he went. As Sean and Billy watched, Skye scrabbled with all four paws as she wiggled, caught by the crotch of the tree that was at least six feet off the ground.

"I'm taking a picture of that," Billy said. "Stay right there." He cast a frantic look behind him to make sure Sean wasn't going anywhere before he ran for a closer shot, because telling his brothers at the flophouse about the hound dog in the tree was not going to have the same impact as a picture.

He caught the whole thing, from the dog flopping around to Jim getting behind her and shoving. Billy took pity on everybody involved and got close enough for the dog to put her paws over his shoulders so he could pull while Jim shoved. Finally the poor dog was down on the ground, licking Billy's face while Jim checked her stomach for scrapes.

"Yeah," Billy said to the poor thing. "You're sweet, but you're hella dumb. I gotta go, baby. That man on the bench is also hella dumb. If

I don't get over there, he'll try to walk around the soccer field again, and that would suck." He stood up and sent Sean a glance over his shoulder, reassured when Sean did an enthusiastic clap from back on the bench. Only the presence of the two older men kept Billy from flipping the bird.

"Thank you so much," Jim said from his spot crouching next to his dog. "I know she's dumb, but seriously—"

"She's sweet," Billy said. "She's just got no smarts. I think she might get them when she's older. Sometimes you got to get older to get your smarts."

Jim nodded, and Bob chuckled. "Just as long as you don't wreck yourself before you get your smarts," he said.

Billy frowned, and Bob looked at his friend.

"Was I being too subtle?"

"About what?" Jim said, looking from Bob to Billy.

"I'm trying to tell him that he and the young man there make a nice couple."

Jim's eyes widened and he shot up straight. "They're *gay*?" he asked, horrified.

Billy grimaced. "You're welcome for your dog," he said. "I'll go now."

"No, no," Jim backtracked. "I'm sorry. I just… you know. It didn't occur to me. I mean, you know. Bob and I are both married to women. Not our scene."

Bob was chuckling and rubbing his eyes, and Billy couldn't help it. He smiled reassuringly at both of them. "I gotta make sure the cop doesn't hurt himself," he said firmly. "See you later."

As he walked away, he heard Bob breaking into a hearty guffaw.

"What?" Jim asked defensively.

"Nothing."

"What? What'd I say?"

"Nothing. I'm going to walk now. Come on."

Billy left them to their lap around the park and made his way back to Sean, who was still sitting patiently on the red bench.

"You okay?" he asked as he sat.

"Getting tired," Sean admitted with a yawn.

"Yeah, we can go as soon as I text these to every single person I know." Billy chuckled again and leaned over to show the pictures to Sean, and Sean laughed like he was supposed to. Billy looked up from the phone to make sure it was a real laugh and not a fake one, and he noticed Sean's eyes on his face.

"What?" he asked.

"You stopped taking pictures to help the dog?"

"Yeah, and then the old guy had to say something about us being a couple and the less-old guy lost his shit. I wish I could have recorded *that*, but sadly, I didn't have my phone open."

"No, it's okay," Sean murmured. "You were just… nice. You were being nice." They were really close now, the wind whipping around them, trying to pry them apart.

Billy didn't answer to the wind.

"I'm not really nice," he cautioned, but he couldn't seem to move away.

"Neither am I," Sean told him, his voice so low that if they hadn't been almost touching, Billy wouldn't have heard him.

The kiss, when it happened, happened so naturally it was like Billy breathed the moment into being. One moment they were static, caught in each other's eyes, and the next their lips were touching and everything around them was warm, soft, and sweet.

A taste, and another, and enough to make Billy want more and more, and finally they pulled apart, reluctantly, and Billy leaned his forehead against Sean's.

"That was good," he whispered. "What do we do with that?"

Sean took one of those deep breaths that said his strength had been taxed to the limit that day. "We do it again, soon. And then a few more times. And someday, when I can run around this park more than once, we maybe take it somewhere private and keep going."

Billy leaned back unhappily. "You're waiting until you can run around the park?" he asked. "Because why?"

Sean's smile was not sweet. It was not kind. It was feral and determined.

"Because I want to take everything you've got to give," he said, nodding definitively. "I want to be in shape to take it."

Billy's eyes narrowed, something in his chest growing cold. "That sounds like something you'd say on a porn set."

Sean shook his head. "I don't want it to be pity," he said. "I don't want you to go easy on me. It's gotta be equal."

"You've got a job and a real life," Billy retorted bitterly. "I'm just a whore. I don't know how equal you think it'll get!"

"You're not a whore," Sean snapped. "You're an engineering student working your way through college. I...." His voice cracked, and the look he gave Billy was miserable. "Man, I got dumped in the hospital, Guillermo. Just let me have a little pride."

Billy's mouth twisted. "Why you gotta… with my real name?" he finished, feeling as vulnerable as Sean professed to feel.

"'Cause Billy's the guy on the porn vids," Sean whispered. "Guillermo's the guy who tucks me in at night and reminds me to poop. You're wrong about wanting it to be porn. I dated a fireman, for fuck's sake. He was an insensitive closet case who was pissed because I had the nerve to get stabbed and my friends called him quietly to tell him. I *know* the difference between the fantasy hero and someone who's a really good person in reality. You… you're a *really* good person." He took a deep breath and then another, and Billy watched his lips move in a "Dammit" as he cursed his inability to make long speeches.

Billy smiled in spite of it all. "Don't hurt yourself," he said fondly. "You're not having sex today, and I get what you're saying. Can you imagine it? I'd be banging away and you'd literally pass out from lack of oxygen. I mean, people talk about passing out from good sex all the time, like it would be fun, but I'd never get another boner after that, so, you know. Wait. I get it."

Sean squeezed his eyes shut. "Tired," he said. "Let's go home. I'll call Andre after my nap."

"Deal."

Billy helped him up and into the Charger, realizing he felt a guilty little thrill at the thought that Sean might need his assistance out of the car, the kind where Sean had to put his arms around Billy's neck and Billy stood up slowly.

So slowly they'd be face-to-face for one of those breathless moments.

And then Billy would positively, absolutely have to kiss him again.

Snooping

"No," Sean said patiently. "I'm not pushing it too far, too fast, and I'm not working for Rivers." He frowned. "Why? Are Rivers and Cramer doing anything interesting?"

Andre Christie's laugh was strained, and he leaned back in the kitchen chair and crossed his arms. "Well, you know how he has a knack for finding the bad apples in any tree?"

"Oh my God, yes," Sean muttered. He'd called Andre after his nap, and his friend—and partner—had asked to stop by before dinner. Sean had been proud of being able to get him some chips and salsa and a beer all on his own since Billy got called in for an emergency wait shift. He couldn't believe he'd thought he'd only have a nurse for a week after he got home from the hospital. It was like functioning *without* that kid should earn him a medal and a commendation.

But it was good that Billy was gone. Besides a chance for the kid to escape captivity with Sean (and it could not have been a whole lot of fun stuck in the house as much as they had been, no matter what Billy said about loving the peace), it gave Sean a chance to talk to Andre alone.

He felt badly in need of a friend, one who was still in law enforcement and had a good relationship and who had hated Jesse with a passion.

"So Rivers," Andre continued, "managed to find a bunch of flatfoots who arrested a guy with mobility issues for doing a thing he could not possibly have physically done, and then these guys put the kid in the hospital for resisting arrest."

Sean grunted. "That's... heinous." God, he remembered how indoctrinated he'd been the year before when he'd met Ellery and assumed that all cops were good and all defense attorneys were sleazy. Sometimes people just needed some help against a massive system.

And sometimes the massive system had big pockets of rot that needed to be rooted out with a dental tool and a backhoe. Ellery was the finely honed dental tool. Jackson was the backhoe—and Henry was the hammer.

"It's even worse than it sounds," Andre said in disgust. "The four guys—Rivers calls them choirboys—are besties with the DA, and the judge, who is normally a decent guy, isn't giving them much of a chance to plead their case." Andre shook his head. "It's a scary world out there, my friend. Be glad you're stuck here for an extra couple of weeks."

Sean snorted. "I'm bored," he said. "Billy wants me to find something to do besides puzzles so I don't make us both crazy."

"Billy…?" Andre raised his eyebrows in a delicate inquiry. Andre—a handsome, slick man in his late thirties—was pretty much the best work partner a boy could ask for. Smart, tough, and a dedicated family man, Andre worked very hard to keep his part of law and order squeaky, squeaky clean. He had a dry sense of humor and a keen sense of fairness, and while the pinball machine aesthetic of Rivers and Henry drove him a little batty, he'd stopped questioning their agenda. They'd pretty much proved—in blood, no less—that they didn't mind when bad guys ended up in prison, as long as they had representation. It was the innocent people who ended up there who made them *really* mad, and they worked hard to keep that from happening.

His question about Billy was all about Sean, and Sean appreciated him to the soles of his slick, shiny oxfords.

"Yes, Billy," Sean said. "Whom we will talk about in a minute. Business first. Can you do me a favor?"

"Anything."

Sean outlined the break-in situation around the park, and Andre nodded, taking notes on his phone. "I'll talk to the property crimes division tomorrow," he said. "If an entire neighborhood is getting hit like this, I should be able to get you times and places."

Sean nodded. "And another thing—this neighborhood is balls to the walls dogs. Everywhere. It's like people found the neighborhood because they had a dog. It's like a selling point. But none of the people hit *have a dog*. I'm thinking it's someone who works in the neighborhood—knows where the milk bones are buried."

Andre nodded, eyebrows up. "That's interesting. You could be right. You and Billy keep your eyes peeled when you're out and about." He paused, leaned back, took a sip of his beer, and smiled. "Now, about that other thing…."

Sean couldn't help it. He blushed, and on his fair skin he knew it was like a giant red flag of guilt and desire, one on each cheek.

"Really?" Andre asked, impressed.

"No, not really," Sean rasped, his chest constricting again. "Do you hear me? Do you think I'm up to *really*?"

Andre grimaced. "Are you up to *possibly*? Because *possibly* could be fun too."

"Possibly is on the table," Sean admitted. He swallowed and reached for his beer, feeling a little guilty. For all he was living with—and pining for—a porn star, Billy was awfully strict about what he could eat and drink while on the road to health.

"Is it?" Andre gave a smile. "I can't wait until I tell Lucinda. She'll be so thrilled. What does your mother think?"

Sean looked at him levelly. "That I'm being cared for by a nice engineering student whose rooming situation got too crowded."

Andre blinked. "Oh," he said. "Is it okay that she thinks that?" he asked carefully. "Do you need to tell her the whole truth?"

"Like when I told her I was doing my own laundry so I could help her out with chores?" Sean asked, eyebrows raised. "No. Telling my mother the whole truth is never necessary—and unlike Ellery's mother, whom I understand has a sixth sense about these things, my mother is happy to go back to Turlock and bother my sisters and sister-in-law and generally make their lives miserable between her once-a-week visits. That's not what I'm talking about."

"What is it?" Andre asked softly. "Do you like him?"

Sean gave him a narrow-eyed glance. "Yes, and during passing period, I'm going to go hang out at his locker."

"Don't be an ass," Andre told him, rolling his eyes. "What's the problem?"

Sean sighed and then regretted it. "I don't care about being out at work," he said flatly. Like Rivers, the snide remarks of the unenlightened had never really bothered him. "I dealt with it through the academy. I dealt with it as a rookie. It was awful, but mostly because so many cops have teeny tiny little brains and it made me ashamed of my profession, but I'm over it. What I'm worried about is what they'll do to *him*. I'll put up with anything, Andre. But...." He swallowed. "I don't care what he does to get through school. I mean, you know, I'd prefer it was wait tables and go into debt, but that's not my call. What is my call is how much bullshit he's going to see if he's my plus-one at the policemen's ball."

Andre sucked in a breath. "I've never gone," he said after a moment, "to the policemen's ball. Lucinda's not really excited about dressing up and going to see my work friends. If she dresses up, she wants to go see a play in San Francisco."

Sean nodded, still catching his breath. That was fair. He and Andre got along great. He knew the officers he could trust—he'd learned a long time ago how to find allies. Maybe just don't hang around anyone who wasn't an ally.

Andre nodded with him and then took another drink of his beer. "The thing to remember," he said after a moment, "is that anybody who recognizes your boy is going to have to admit where he's seen him. If some dumb flatfoot starts screaming the F-word at Billy as he's walking through the station to pick you up or something, ask the guy where he knows him from. That'll shut him up right quick."

Sean chuckled. "It will," he said, nodding his head.

"And other than that? I like coming here for football games. You've got Rivers, you've got Henry, you've got your guy. Do I have straight people I hang with? Well, yeah—my brother and his engineering friends are all very hetero, but that doesn't mean this little rainbow corner of the world doesn't make me happy too. Don't worry about him being at the mercy of the police, *mijo*, worry about him being a cop's husband."

Sean tried not to gasp. "I… I never really thought of that," he admitted. God. The worst thing about dating Jesse had been not being able to keep in contact with him when they both worked extremely dangerous jobs. "I… I need to make him aware that, you know, it's one of the hard things."

Andre nodded. "See, that's the hardest part to me. You… you weren't even doing anything dangerous. I was minding a suspect, you were out to lunch with Cramer and company, getting information, and next thing I know, Rivers is calling to tell me you were in surgery. It was… it was scary, man. You and me, we've drawn our pieces a few times. We've even fired some shots. But there I was, worried about my partner, and it hit me that this was how Lucinda felt every day when I walked out the door. So yeah. Your guy may have a—" Andre rolled his eyes and grinned. "—*colorful* past, but I think if he can handle it, you can deal. But that other thing. That's the one you're going to have to be careful about, you think?"

Sean nodded. "I'll keep it in mind," he said soberly.

"You do that, partner," Andre said, clinking his bottle with Sean's and then finishing off the rest of his beer. He checked his phone and said, "So, uhm, Lucinda's not expecting me for another two hours. You know there's a game on tonight."

Sean grinned. "You move the nachos to the coffee table, and I'll hit the head."

"Fair."

When Billy got home, Andre was jumping up and down in front of the TV, cheering his team on, while Sean laughed softly from the recliner, too winded to even tell Billy who won.

ANDRE FINALLY left, with much bro-hugging and back thumping, and Sean collapsed on the couch, not caring whether it was bad for him or not.

"Good time?" Billy asked, picking up the empty chip and salsa bowls.

"The best," Sean murmured. "Don't clean up. It's fine. I can do it."

Billy gave him an arch look and continued to clean up. "Did you eat anything besides chips?"

"No," Sean said, yawning. "Chips and salsa is legit a food group. Ask any cop. Seriously, man, you're my nurse, not my maid. I can—"

Billy stopped him with a kiss on the temple, which Sean just now realized was a secret weapon. "You're tired, and I'm still all hyped from running around the restaurant. It *offends* me to not bus a table. It's fine."

"*Mmm....*" He'd had two beers with his nightly pain meds, and he was riding the buzz. Dangerous to be this... unguarded. "You're so pretty," he said dreamily. "I could watch you move for hours."

Billy smiled at him, and it wasn't the beers, and it wasn't his imagination—blushed. "You've got a nice mouth, cop," he said. "Says good things."

Sean sobered, remembering his conversation with Andre. "You were only supposed to be here a week," he said unhappily. "But you've stayed for six. And I like you here."

Billy's eyes grew large and almost limpid. "But...?"

"No 'buts.' Just… you didn't have to stay. You're so busy. School. Two jobs. And I'm three. Why did you stay?"

He watched Billy swallow like there was too much to say. "Maybe I like hanging out in the park with dogs and old guys. You ever think of that?"

Sean smiled like he was supposed to but then sobered. "I'm not always a walk in the park," he said softly. "Lots of days are sixteen hours, and I'm surly and pissed off." He paused. "Or, you know."

Billy stared at him, and Sean could see when it hit him. His eyes widened, and that limpid Bambi look returned full force. Hadn't Sean thought his eyes were flat and cynical? He'd liked that—those eyes knew what was in the world and didn't take any crap. This look here? It was vulnerable and sad. No sadness, he thought wretchedly. Billy was competent and terse—and damned funny, Sean could admit it. But not sad.

Until now.

"Hurt," Billy whispered. "Or dead."

Ouch. The hard word. "Can't promise it won't happen," Sean told him. "I mean, I'll probably live longer than *Rivers*, but there's no promises."

Billy grimaced. "Rivers takes stupid chances. Always the fuckin' hero. But you are too. I've seen it. Always the fuckin' hero."

"I'm… evolving," Sean said with dignity, remembering the days when he'd have been the first person to crap on Billy, on his other job, on his feelings. "I didn't used to be."

Billy shook his head. "Naw. You changed. It's hard. Change is hard." He paused in the act of wiping out the chip bowl and rubbed his chest. "Like now. My chest." He took a wobbly breath. "My *heart*. It's changing." He swallowed and put the bowl—a decorative glass one that Sean used for company—in the cupboard. "Change is hard."

"Is it too hard to stay here?" Sean asked, his own chest aching. *Heart. It's your heart that hurts.*

He was relieved and terrified when Billy paused and rubbed his chest and thought. Terrified because what if he said yes? It had obviously just hit him, what Sean did for a living. That this might not be the last time Sean was hurt doing his job. What if Andre was right and *this* was the thing that broke them, their tenuous *evolving* relationship.

And relieved because it meant he was thinking about it—really thinking about it. Sean had learned that this man had surprising integrity. Thinking about it meant it mattered to him.

"It's hard," Billy said, wiping down the counter and not meeting his eyes. "But it'll be harder not to stay." He turned and gave Sean a surprising flash of smile, although he kept his eyes averted as he continued the light cleanup of the kitchen. "And not only because they won't let me pay rent at the flophouse."

Sean smiled a little too. "That leaves, what? Curtis, Cotton, Randy, Vinnie—"

Billy shrugged. "Cotton doesn't pay rent, but Curtis says it hasn't gone up." He looked around as though afraid somebody might be listening in on what was already an intimate moment. "Between you and me, I think John or Lance or someone makes up the difference there. None of us can ever remember renewing a lease, and it's got to go somewhere, right?"

Sean nodded. He'd met Billy's boss, the porn mogul. He was a manic redheaded goober who happened to enjoy watching porn—and filming it, although Sean understood John was letting other people do more of that these days. He was also, Sean had learned, surprisingly philanthropic. The kids—and many of them were eighteen or nineteen—had health and dental and options for life after porn, even if they only filmed a few scenes. The kids who came to him for work weren't exploitable to John, and they weren't disposable.

Given that Sean had *watched* porn when the desire hit him, it made him feel better about the whole thing.

"So they're making rent okay?" Sean asked, making sure.

Billy gave a half smile. "They are. I… I mean, it's the flophouse. The population changes, people get out of porn, more people get in. It's never supposed to be forever."

Here could be forever.

"Then stay here," Sean asked rashly. "I… I mean, I have a spare room…." He swallowed and then figured he could claim the beer made him honest. "Although you don't have to stay there… all the time."

Billy leaned back against the counter, arms crossed in front of his ever-impressive chest. "Let me get this straight," he said mildly. "You want me to give up my bed in the flophouse—and it took me a year to get my own steady bed—in a place where I've got sex on tap with guys who will seriously not even remember we got busy the night before on the promise of a guy I ain't even slept with yet?"

"We could sleep together," Sean said hurriedly and then gulped air. Dammit. "I mean… we could *sleep* together." He tried a smile, but it felt more like a plea. "I… I would like to sleep next to you. Kiss you again." He bit his lower lip. "Touch you. If you'd let me."

"I'd like that too," Billy whispered. "But what if it doesn't work out?"

"I have a spare room," Sean said in desperation. "I mean… worst case here, we make okay roommates."

"What about rent?"

And suddenly the pleasant haze of the beer was burned off. "*Fuck* the rent. I don't care about the rent. I care about the company, dammit!"

Billy looked surprised—truly shocked—and then his expression softened. "Calm down. Jeez, I was only asking. Do you need help putting on your jammies, cop-man? Or did you want to watch some more TV?"

Sean scowled at him. "Another hour of stupid cop shows," he demanded, feeling churlish.

"Good," Billy said. "You make yourself comfortable, and I'll be right there with sandwiches."

Sean opened his mouth to protest, but Billy beat him to the punch.

"And before you argue, I'm starving, so that's what this is about. Not waiting on you."

Sure.

"Fine," he said, turning around and jamming himself in the corner of the couch to help prop up his back and chest. A moment later, Billy came over with a couple of pillows. Expertly, he shoved them behind Sean's back and under his elbow, and then, before Sean could protest, he bent down and kissed Sean's sulky, irritated mouth.

"Let me take care of you a little," Billy murmured. "You said all these pretty things to me, cop, and even if I don't got an answer, I'm feeling sweet, so let me."

Sean parted his lips as Billy withdrew and smiled slightly. "Sweet?" he murmured.

"Yeah. Now find your stupid cop show, and I'll be right back."

"'Kay."

A few minutes later and true to his word, Billy returned with a peanut butter and jelly sandwich on wheat for himself and a turkey sandwich on sourdough for Sean. Sean took the sandwich and his stomach growled, loudly and unmistakably, and he gave a sheepish smile before taking a bite.

"Good?" Billy prodded.

"Dank 'ou," Sean said as he chewed. He swallowed, and the last of the beer sank into the fresh bread, and he felt a little less irritated. Another bite and another, and he let his consciousness slip into the cop show, which was its usual charming, exciting, unrealistic escape from his day.

Billy took their plates to the sink and returned, but instead of sitting on the opposite side of the couch, he sat right next to Sean and tilted his body a little.

"Here," he said softly. "Don't crumple yourself, but maybe if you wrap your arm around my shoulders…."

Sean did what he'd suggested, and Billy put his head on Sean's shoulder, and for a moment Sean's vision went swimmy, but not with lack of oxygen.

Oh, this was nice. So good. Sean's brain, which had been darting with questions like minnows in a pond, suddenly slowed down. Things like "How did you get into porn?" or "Do you still talk to your parents?" which he was *dying* to know, suddenly became so much less important than the very bearable weight of Billy's head on his shoulder.

"So what did you and Andre talk about?" Billy asked during a commercial pause.

"About how hard it was to be married to a cop," he answered.

"Oh," Billy said, and Sean knew he got it.

"I was worried," Sean told him, so relaxed in this moment. "I didn't want to start anything that would hurt you. Andre said don't worry about the people on the force being shitty—he's my partner, and he thinks you're okay. He said to make sure you could deal with that other thing."

"The getting-hurt thing," Billy murmured.

"And the sixteen-hour-day thing," Sean confirmed.

"*Mmm.* He forgot about the big thing."

"What's that?" Sean asked.

"I really want to kiss you," Billy said. "And I want to give you sandwiches when you've had one beer too many—"

"Sorry."

"Don't be sorry. You get a beer with friends. Not a crime. Unless you get mean."

Sean half-laughed. "Mostly emotional. You've seen it. Drunk me."

"Totally livable. But those are the big things," Billy said. He paused. "Not the biggest thing—"

"Later," Sean told him gruffly. "Later. We'll deal with that elephant later."

"Fair."

They watched the show for a few minutes, and when the next commercial break came on, Billy paused the screen.

"Did you really mean it? About me spending the night in your bed?" he asked.

"Yeah."

There was a moment in which Sean could tell something was eating him up inside.

"What?"

"Your ex. Mr. Fire-douche."

"Jesse?" God, Sean didn't want to think about him.

"He ever just spend the night?"

Sean didn't even have to think about it. "Nope. If there was no sex, there was no sleeping over." He grimaced. "In fact, when he came to get his stuff, about the only things he grabbed were his DVDs and his condoms. I don't think he'd even left a toothbrush here."

"Douche," Billy muttered.

Sean took this next question delicately. "Do you have one of those in your rearview?"

Billy shook his head. "No," he said, voice soft. "Mine was… well, he was sweet. We weren't going to be forever, but see," he said, sitting up and turning on the couch so he could hug his knees to his chest, "I was supposed to go into the military, but that didn't pan out—you know that."

Sean nodded. Billy ate with him every day, and Sean had needed to trust that, with intercoms everywhere, Billy wouldn't backslide. "Yeah."

"So I ended up going to junior college. Wasn't bad. Got my job at the café, waited tables. Came home, helped Mom with the little kids. Dad was still an asshole, right, but he didn't hit me anymore, 'cause I was big enough to hit back, mostly, and he left Mom and the little kids alone because I was there. It was tolerable, right?"

Sean nodded, thinking that tolerable was an overstatement, but still. Could have been worse.

"So I get my first boyfriend, and he's sweet. Like I said, not forever, but, you know, lots of necking in my parents' minivan. Very young-adult novel. And that was fine."

"What happened?"

He grimaced. "My little brother, Miguel. We dropped him off at soccer and watched as he ran out to the field, and Sam kissed me, and I kissed back, and suddenly Miguel was getting back in the minivan before we even knew he'd returned because he'd forgotten his shin guards. He caught us, dead to rights, and he didn't say anything to *us*, but he went back to the field and told his coach."

"Oh no."

"Guy was super liberal. Didn't even occur to him that he'd be opening up a can of worms when my mom came to pick Miguel up and he told her. So there I was, thinking, 'Whew, little man didn't even notice,' and Mom gets home, and suddenly Miguel's spilling everything to Dad, and…."

Billy shook his head. "And I'm showing up at my boyfriend's shitty apartment with my schoolbooks in my backpack and my clothes in garbage bags and a face full of bruises. Sam—well, he was pretty stand-up. Let me stay, let me live with him really, but after a year of that, he got accepted to a school down south, and…."

"You weren't invited?" Sean probed.

"I didn't want to go." Billy shrugged. "We… we were mostly roommates, like you said. But then we really weren't that serious in the first place. Just… convenient. It wasn't gonna go anywhere when it wasn't convenient no more." He paused, and those eyes—so much more complex than Sean had ever fathomed. "Not like you."

It was Sean's turn to swallow. "You think we could go far?"

Billy looked down. "It's stupid. So stupid. I… I've hooked up with a lot of guys."

Sean's mouth twisted. "I've hooked up with some losers," he admitted. Jesse hadn't been the only douchebag in his closet. "Only…." He smiled, thinking that when he could see this impulse through to its natural conclusion, what he *wanted* to do was lean in for a hot, hungry kiss, the kind that would wipe all their doubts away. He'd kiss the pulse in Billy's throat and explore the wonders of his clavicles and then his amazing chest. If he'd been in top form, they would be at least *making out*, but instead, they were forced into this horror of horrors: honest communication.

They might never recover.

"Only what?" Billy asked softly.

"Only…." He smiled bitterly. "I think relationships reach critical mass," he said after a moment. "Where what we want in the moment, what we hope for the future, it outweighs all the mistakes in the past. And what I want, right now, is to kiss you."

"Okay," Billy said and leaned forward into Sean's space, took his mouth gently, and oh! He tasted so good. Warm, male—peanut butter and jelly, oddly enough—but earthier, spicier under that.

Sean kissed back, wanting to push, wanting to pounce, but knowing his limitations. Instead he put his hands on Billy's shoulders and kissed some more, lingering, long, drugging.

They weren't going to jump into bed. Acrobatic sex was out of the question. But this… this long, sexy, physical communication—oh *this* they could do. Every rub of the lips, every stroke of the tongue, every breathless sigh made him want more.

Billy's kisses were filled with suppressed urgency, and Sean answered back the best he could, his body tingling, his erection waking up and taking notice. He was surprised and dismayed when Billy pulled back with a soft cry and threw himself to the opposite end of the couch.

"Wha—" Sean blinked rapidly, trying to pull himself together. "What's wrong?"

"*This*!" Billy wailed, pointing to his crotch. Against the placket of his jeans, Sean could see his cock—thick, long, and impressive— straining for release. He gave Sean an agonized look. "I'll just—I'll be back in a minute," he muttered, arching his back.

"No! Wait," Sean said, laughing a little. "Stand up. Come here."

Billy did what he asked, obviously uncomfortable, finally standing in front of Sean with his crotch almost exactly at Sean's eye level.

"You can't," Billy told him. "Doing that gets in the way of your breathing, and you have to move your back and… ah… neck and… oh…."

One button at a time, Sean released the fly of Billy's jeans, tugged at the bottom, and kneaded his ass purposefully as he slid them down to his thighs. Billy's cock pushed out against his brightly colored briefs, and Sean tried not to ogle.

"Impressed?" Billy asked breathily, and Sean tilted his face up, knowing he probably looked stupidly awestruck.

"It's amazing," he said, conceding to the obvious. "I mean, up close and personal… damn." He had a moment of total insecurity. "Uhm, just so you know…."

Billy laughed softly and bent down, capturing Sean's face between his palms. "Want to hear a secret?"

"Sure."

"I hook up with dicks all the time. This isn't a hookup. I think that means it's the guy that's important, not the dick."

Sean grinned and kissed him, keeping his hands on Billy's hips and then rubbing up against his thighs. He teased, sliding his thumbs between Billy's legs, tracing his fingers along the backs of his thighs above his jeans. Billy put his weight on the back of the couch behind Sean's head, leaning over, his stomach rippling to hold the position, and Sean indulged himself in more kneading of Billy's backside, parted his cheeks, slid his fingertips down his crease over his briefs.

Billy hissed when Sean brushed his hole and straightened, pulling away from the kiss with a whimper. "Man, you are teasing me so bad…."

Sean gave him a shy smile. "You are good for an old man's ego," he murmured, finally pulling Billy's briefs away from his package, which unfurled in front of him, erect and proud. "Maybe not," he murmured. "But I don't care."

Smiling deviously, he stuck out his tongue and touched the tip to the end of Billy's cock and licked at the tiny drop of pre in the slit. He was going to tease some more, but Billy threw his head back and moaned softly, obviously sensitive, and Sean pulled his tongue in and swallowed.

Sweet.

He licked again, grasping the long, thick shaft with his fist to hold it steady. The weight of Billy's cock in his palm was electric, sending tingles shivering down his arm, across his chest, and his own erection awoke fully. His groin gave a giant throb, and Sean worked hard not to just jam that magnificent cock down his throat.

Must not obstruct the breathing. Must not breathe too fast, too hard, too quickly.

Absolutely *must* taste Billy's cock, lick its head, work its shaft, swallow his come.

Must.

Billy rested his hands on Sean's shoulders and held his hips absolutely still and let Sean work. Oh Lord. Sean had never really thought of himself as king of the blowjob, but boy, he was trying now. He licked, he sucked, he stroked, he nibbled, and when Billy let out a grunt of frustration, Sean did what was best for *Billy* and not his own pride.

As Billy's noises got more urgent, his hips quivering with the need to thrust, he dropped his hands and clasped them behind his back, like he was avoiding the temptation of holding Sean in place and fucking his mouth, his throat.

Sean reached around and tugged gently, pulling one of Billy's arms forward and then lacing their fingers together.

Then he released Billy's fingers and moved Billy's hand to where Sean's was, wrapped around Billy's shaft. He replaced his own fingers with Billy's, and then moved back to lick the head.

Billy tightened his fist enough to make his cockhead purple and began to slowly jack himself, forward and back, while Sean licked the head and sucked the bell.

"Cop!" Billy gasped. "Gotta go fast. Move back."

Sean did, not wanting to catch Billy's fist in his face as it stroked fast and hard, blurring with motion.

But Sean wanted his come so bad.

Billy gasped and cried out, "Coming! Ah God!"

Sean closed his eyes, opened his mouth, and rubbed Billy's thighs in hope.

The first shot landed in a strip across his face, hitting his tongue, his chin, his cheek. The second landed close to his mouth, and then Billy moved his other hand to the back of Sean's head—gently, with control.

Sean allowed himself to be steered until Billy's cockhead touched his lips, and he sucked hard and strong. Billy gave himself a slow, controlled stroke until Sean's mouth filled with a final thick, slow burst that required him to swallow quickly to keep up.

While he was swallowing, his own body tensed, tightened, and unfurled, and a wholly unprompted surprise orgasm rolled through him, causing him to tighten his mouth on Billy's cockhead and scrape the backs of his thighs with his nails as he clenched his fists.

He issued a muffled groan from his full throat, and Billy cried out again, his fingers tightening in Sean's hair as an aftershock rocked him. Sean grunted, arching his hips off the couch and shaking as he moved his hand down to the front of his sweats to shove them down and squeeze the last of his climax out of his cock. His mouth opened as he gasped, and Billy's last spurt of come dribbled over his lips and down his chin.

Finally he fell back against the couch cushions and worked hard to catch his breath as his vision went in and out of darkness and Billy sank to his knees in front of him.

After a moment, Sean was conscious of Billy pulling down his sweats completely, and then he buried his face in Sean's lap, licking at his still-full cock, cleaning the come from his skin.

Sean's moan was drawn out, luxuriating in the contact, and a little sad.

"Done," he murmured, stroking Billy's hair. "Can't do that again. I'll pass out."

Billy let out a sound of disappointment and turned his head, resting his cheek on Sean's bare thigh.

"We did that," he said, his voice a little bit dreamy.

"We did," Sean rasped, still stroking Billy's hair. "I'd like to do it again." He smiled a little, remembering Billy's shiver of ecstasy as he'd rubbed Billy's hole through his briefs. "I'd, uhm, like to top sometime."

Billy made a delicious *mm* sound. "You caught on to that, did you?"

Sean laughed softly. "Yeah. I like it both ways myself."

"Me too, but everyone thinks, 'Ooh, big cock tops!' Naw. Big cock likes to get fucked like every other vers or bottom."

Sean chuckled again. "We can do this, right?" he said, the seriousness of the words catching him by surprise. "I… I want to sleep next to you tonight."

"Yeah, cop," Billy murmured. "Yeah. I want to do this more. And I don't want it to go away. Not a hookup. Not a one and done. Go you. You caught a porn star by the penis."

Sean suppressed a snort and then let out a small sound of discomfort as his chest gave a twinge. "I'm gonna need to rest up," he rasped. "So I can do it again."

Billy straightened and stepped out of his jeans and briefs, and Sean mourned that there he was, magnificently naked, and Sean couldn't do a damned thing about it. Very carefully, Billy pulled Sean's sweats and briefs up over his hips as Sean sat and then kneeled in front of him to take Sean's arms and put them over his shoulders so Sean could twine them around his neck.

"Ready?" he asked softly.

Sean nodded, and Billy did that amazing, incredible thing where he lifted with his thighs and his core and stood up slowly so Sean could use his strength to push himself up.

They stood for a moment, face-to-face, and Sean leaned his head against Billy's shoulder. Billy wrapped his arms around Sean's waist. For a heartbeat—and then a hundred of them—they stood, holding each other, in the sudden silence of the living room.

Billy kissed Sean's temple then. "Come on," he murmured. "Let's go to bed."

Sean got situated first, facing the door, slightly turned on his good side while Billy turned off all the lights and locked the door. As Sean closed his eyes and listened, it occurred to him that Billy had been doing this quietly, without prompting, since Sean's first night back.

How odd. Sean Kryzynski, cop from the cradle, always the protector, had started this relationship by trusting himself to someone else's care.

The noises changed, and Billy entered the room and put his jeans and henley neatly on the chair. Sean cracked his eyes open to see if Billy was going to sleep commando and breathed a slight prayer when he saw that Billy's briefs stayed on, just as Sean's did under his sleep pants.

"Afraid I'll let the monster out?" Billy asked, keeping his voice low as he moved to the other side of the bed and climbed in.

"Peens are not… practical," Sean returned with dignity. "If they're not contained, they jiggle, they get poked or flop around. And balls are worse. I once woke up late for a test during the academy after a late night, and I wasn't wearing any underwear. I *tripped* on my balls. They got caught between my thighs."

Billy's snort of laughter was muffled by the back of Sean's neck.

"I fell down, hit my face against my desk, and went in with a black eye. I told my entire class I got into a bar fight the night before."

Billy was openly laughing behind him, not even bothering to muffle himself.

"You are *lying*," he whooped. "That is not possible."

"True story," he said—and it was, mostly. He'd tripped on the underwear around his ankles, because it *had* been a good night, but the balls hadn't helped things when it all went south.

"Can't be," Billy murmured, and he aligned himself against Sean's back very carefully. "You are not that clumsy."

"You're missing the point," Sean told him, simply falling into his warmth, his strength. Even his doubt was comforting.

"Which is?"

"You're the only person I've told that to," he said softly. "My entire academy class thought I was a badass. You know I'm just an ass."

Billy snuggled a little more closely and all but purred in his ear. "Still a badass," he said, and then he hummed the AC/DC song in his ear, the one about having the biggest balls, and Sean laughed softly before falling completely asleep.

What Heroes Do

"ARE YOU sure you're not walking too far?" Billy hated nagging, but that relapse in which Sean had ended up back in the hospital seemed to weigh around his neck like an anchor. "This is way longer than your usual soccer field gig."

Sean nodded, but he didn't say anything, probably because he was working on not losing his wind. The weather had taken a blessed turn—there was hope for a little bit of rain to rinse them all off, and Billy was super grateful at the same time he'd started looking up lung ailments to make sure there was *not a repeat* of the hospital thing.

"We need," breath, "to check out," breath, "these houses."

"Stop," Billy told him, slamming his feet together military style. "Just stop right there. Catch your breath. That's an order."

Sean arched an eyebrow at him, but hey! Until he could talk, he didn't get to *talk back*.

"Besides, you're not working smarter. Look." Billy had stopped them at the end of the walkthrough from the cul-de-sac to the park. "See? You can see the main road right there, right?"

Sean nodded, so Billy went on.

"Now see? You've got the list of hits in your paper. There were two houses in this cul-de-sac." Billy frowned. "They... look. They're the one to the left and the right of the walkthrough. That's *weird*. Do you think that's on purpose?"

Sean shrugged and held out his hand, wobbling it from one side to the other. Maybe yes, maybe no. Then he gave Billy a meaningful look and nodded up toward the main road.

Only one way to find out. But first they needed to interview the victims. Billy had seen him dust off his badge case, hoping nobody saw the Homicide Division inscription on the bottom of the badge. According to Sean, badge numbers, people checked. *Divisions* people usually weren't too excited about. And Billy got that they didn't want to scare anyone.

"Ooh," Billy said as they both went for the house on their left. "Can I be your partner? Can I say 'Book 'em, Danno'? Do I get handcuffs?"

Sean paused to stare at him, his dead-on seriousness completely endearing. "Technically we're domestic partners, but don't let that freak you out. No, you can't say 'Book 'em, Danno' because neither of us are named Danno and you *hate* that show. And no handcuffs because I don't do kink."

Billy snorted. "Says you. Domestic partners don't keep saying, 'but you can sleep in your own room,' and give me a month—we'll be doing the kink."

Sean's flush did not disappoint. How this boy managed to pass himself off as a badass would forever be a puzzle, given the way his entire body turned pink when he was embarrassed. "God, you suck."

Billy smirked. "I do. But you haven't experienced it yet, so don't judge."

Billy grinned at him, and Sean glared back, and Billy wasn't sure when that turned into staring moonily into each other's eyes.

Damn. Waking up next to each other that morning had been.... God. Exactly as advertised. Exactly as he'd dreamed. Sean's body trusting his, backed up against Billy's. Sean's soft breathing—or light snoring, depending on who was listening—in his ear, reminding him that they'd done it. They'd taken that step. They weren't nurse and patient anymore—or even adversarial acquaintances. They were lovers. For real.

It was enough to make Billy hope—just hope—that maybe this was a thing that could happen.

Still beaming—and blushing—Sean and Billy walked up the path to the yellow-sided ranch style with the nicely kept AstroTurf front yard. Billy had seen a couple of these—there weren't a whole lot of super-inviting ways to landscape a yard after nearly ten years of drought. And he had to admit, the green was a reminder of times gone by.

In an instant, Sean took a breath and seemed to transform into the cop he claimed to be but Billy hadn't really seen. Without pause he gave a crisp knock to the door and waited for it to open. A harried woman with a baby on her hip didn't let him down.

"Can I help you?" she asked, smiling politely. She had dark hair pulled back in a perky ponytail, brown eyes, and a round face that looked used to smiling but right now was wholly focused on the fussy infant at her side.

Sean pulled his badge out, and Billy could see why; she probably felt particularly vulnerable with two men on her porch, and some sort of legitimacy might help.

"Hi, I'm Detective Sean Kryzynski of Sac PD, and this is my assistant, Bill Carey. We're, uhm, sort of doing a favor for a friend who asked us to look into the robberies in this neighborhood. I was hoping you could help us out?"

Ooh—Bill Carey. Nice one. A lot of John's kids took John's last name—Carey—if their own parents had cut them off.

"Oh!" The woman's nearly hostile sense of distraction lightened up, and she gave a brief smile. "You must be Bob's friends."

Sean grinned in surprise. "You know Bob?"

"Doesn't everybody?" she asked. "Yeah, here. I'm going to put this one—" She gave her hip a gentle bounce, and the little girl gave a quiet gurgle. "—in her crib for nap time. If you two could hang here for a moment until I get back?"

"Sure."

She disappeared, leaving the door open but the screen shut, and Billy said, "Nice catch on Bill Carey. I'd forgotten about that."

Sean shrugged. "All the guys at the flophouse use John's name."

"*Mmm.* I was gonna too."

Sean gave him a look that said he wanted to talk about that later, so Billy asked a deflection question instead.

"We're not going inside?"

"A, we have no authority," Sean said. "B, she didn't ask us because she's a woman alone with a baby and that's a particularly vulnerable position." He gave a sigh. "And C, she's not under suspicion."

Billy *hmmph*ed. "So far all the TV has lied."

"I never claimed it was real," Sean murmured.

"Then why do you watch it?"

Sean gave him a sweet look, showing his heart so completely in his eyes that Billy's throat grew thick. "Same reason we watch porn. We want to buy into the fantasy, and sometimes that's easier when we don't see all the work that goes into it."

Billy nodded sagely but was saved from replying by the return of their young mother. Good thing too, because he still didn't have an answer for that question.

"Hi," she said, coming out of the house and shutting the screen door quietly behind her. "I'm Marla Deeks. So nice to meet you."

"Nice to meet you too," Sean said, smiling. "You're right. Bob asked me to look into this, and, you know…."

"Bob," she said, dimpling. "Well, and Dude."

"And Dude," he affirmed. "So what happened?"

She shrugged and shook her head. "Well, my husband was gone on business. He'd just checked in, we'd talked for a while, and he sang to the baby. We were about to say good night when I heard something in the garage." She grimaced. "I told Todd to hang on while I checked it out, and he immediately put me on hold and called 911. Oh my God. They gave him some shit about calling in from LA about a problem in Sacramento! Anyway, I went downstairs to see what was in the garage, and when I opened the door from the kitchen, I saw someone dressed in black disappearing out the side door to the yard with my husband's bike and his air compressor!"

"Did you get a look at the guy?" Billy asked eagerly, and she shook her head.

"Black hat, black clothes, black gloves. Didn't even see his face, only the back of him."

"Any impressions?" Sean asked. "Old, young, fat, thin, tall, short?"

"*Mmm…* young," she said definitively. "He moved fast. And thin." She shuddered. "Like… scary thin. And midsized, like you guys. Maybe five eight." She blinked. "Oh! And blond hair! It was sticking out from the neck of his hat and sweater like a ponytail. So probably white!" Or dyed that way, Billy thought, but he didn't say anything because she and Sean had a rhythm.

Sean pulled out his detective's notebook. "Well done! And you say he worked alone?"

"Definitely."

Sean frowned. "An air compressor isn't a small thing. Was he riding the bike *carrying* the air compressor?"

She shook her head. "No, not at all. He had it on a skateboard, like a dolly. I think he'd lashed it there with bungee cords because it was fairly stable and he was towing it with, like, one of those dog nooses?

You know, the ones that animal control use? I mean…." She crossed her brown eyes and shrugged. "On the one hand, what an asshole. On the other…."

"Really frickin' clever," Billy said, impressed.

"I know, right? Because that scene could have been right out of a *Benny Hill*, but it went pretty smoothly. The cops got there soon after that. I guess my Todd put on his big-boy voice because the thief disappeared. I mean, even on a bike you'd think the cops would have seen him fleeing, right?"

"Unless he went into the park," Sean offered.

She scowled. "I tried to tell the cops that, but they were like, 'The inside of the park is locked up, ma'am.' But you can see people moving beyond the trees and in the underbrush. I mean, they have to clean the homeless encampments out periodically. There's a lot of nooks and crannies in there where they can hide stuff. And they don't have to sell it the next day, right? Wait a day, sell it then when nobody's looking."

Sean nodded, and Billy could tell the woman had impressed him. "You've been thinking about this quite a bit," he told her.

"Well, the people across the street got hit too, and Linda and I, we have coffee in the morning. She's got a kid Kensi's age, and we let them play. Anyway, her experience is the same as mine but about a week earlier. That's why I think they lay low, hide what they get, sell it later."

"What'd they take from Linda's house?" Sean asked, curious.

"*Mmm…* her house was a big score. I think they got her husband's motorcycle."

"Street legal?" Billy asked, because this was a huge score in the scope of what was going on.

But Marla shook her head. "No. It was more like a dirt bike. He put it in the back of his truck and drove it out to the lake."

"How'd they start it?" Billy asked. Those things were notoriously loud, and getting it out of the garage would have been a trick.

"They didn't, but they did reach inside the connecting door to find the key hangar. I'm not sure if it's a lucky guess or what, but they unlocked the bike to wheel it out but didn't start it."

"How'd she know someone was in the garage?" Sean asked, picking up the thread.

Marla rolled her eyes. "She didn't. Her weirdo cat likes to sleep in the garage for whatever reason. She opened the door for a 'here kitty, kitty' and saw the guy getting away."

"Yikes! That must have been scary. Was the cat okay?" Sean asked.

Billy snorted, but Sean didn't look at him. Billy was worried, though. It had occurred to him these last weeks that he *really liked* animals. Suddenly he didn't want anything—dog, cat, hamster, whatever—to get hurt.

"Yeah," Marla said, but she gave the smile of a demented gremlin. "But I'm not sure about the guy. That cat jumped on his head, he yelled out, and the cat took a chunk out of his face. I mean, Gustav's more of a force of nature than a cat, you know?"

Sean grimaced. "A friend of mine has one of those. What breed?"

"I dunno. American Backyard Bird Murderer?"

This time Sean *and* Billy both laughed, and their helpful neighbor smirked.

"It's a terrible joke, I know, but he's a raggedy tiger-striped disaster. Linda adores him, though. Says a better-looking cat would take away her millennial mom card, and she refuses to even get him groomed."

"Fair," Billy said, and Sean met his eyes and nodded, still laughing.

"Her coolness is totally safe with me," Sean agreed. "But I think you're right. A dirt bike is one of the most valuable things I think they've stolen. I'd wager they sold that, used the money to hole up for a week or so, and then they're back on the take."

She nodded, suddenly looking very sober. "Does that mean they'll be back?" she asked. "I... you know. This neighborhood is pretty safe. I don't want to be scared every time my husband has to leave."

Sean grew sober. "What did the police say when they came?"

She shook her head. "They just filed a report so we could get the insurance, but that was it. I, uh, get the impression that small stuff really isn't worth their time."

"Property crimes are hard," he said, and Billy knew that was the truth. "Like you said, your actual things are probably already sold. But a pattern of break-ins should be investigated." He paused. "So I've got to ask. I notice you don't have a dog, do you?"

She shook her head. "No. Why?"

"Are you allergic," Sean asked, "or busy?"

"So busy," she told him, growing thoughtful. "Again, why?"

Sean shrugged. "Just testing a theory. And your friend Linda only has the terrifying cat?"

"Yeah. She *had* a big bruising pit bull, but Sweaty ran away last summer."

Sean blinked. "Sweaty?"

"Like in those books!" Billy said excitedly. "The *Wimpy Kid* ones." He'd read them to his little brothers and sisters almost nightly. The dog's name was really Sweetie, but the idiot older brother couldn't spell. Suddenly Billy's heart hurt for the unseen Sweaty, who was named after books and apparently loved.

Marla chuckled. "Yeah. Linda's boys love those books." Then she grew sad. "They were heartbroken when she got out. I mean, I said she was a bruiser, but she was really the sweetest dog in the world. Even their *friends* were heartbroken."

"Aw," Sean said. "That's a real shame."

Marla shook her head. "Yeah, but you know, now that you ask, maybe it's time for us both to look into adopting a puppy." She smiled brightly. "Put the kid in the stroller, take the dog for a walk—way to keep the weight off, right?"

"And they make really good friends," Billy said, nodding earnestly.

"They do," she agreed. "And my husband's going to be traveling for a few more years. It's definitely something to think about."

They wrapped it up shortly after that, and Sean and Billy headed across the street to interview the much-talked-about Linda. Linda wasn't home, and Sean said something stupid about walking to the next cul-de-sac, which was the dumbest shit Billy had ever heard, given his complexion and the way his breathing sounded.

"No," he said, grabbing Sean's hand and dragging him to the thruway. There were retaining walls on either side of the thruway, with plants and stuff around waist level as the path dipped into the park. But the retaining walls were built to rise and fall with the path, so at the beginning there were a couple of spots that were perfect for a tired detective to sit on.

"What am I doing?" Sean asked, confused.

"You're sitting here and waiting." Billy scowled and looked over his shoulder, figuring there was about half a mile between where they were now and the Charger in the parking lot, and then a good two miles around the park if he drove the Charger around the side streets. "Okay,

I'm going to run get the car. Do you think you can sit here and not get all winded and sad and stuff?"

"I can walk back!" Sean tried to laugh and ended up wheezing instead.

"Sure you can," Billy said grimly. "Humor me."

"But—"

Billy kissed him as he sat, knowing there was nobody on the path in either direction and reasonably sure nobody could see them as they were, hidden by trees. Ooh... his surrender was so sweet. Billy wondered if this man had been waiting his whole life for someone to tell him what to do with his life so he could figure out what to do with his mouth.

Sean let out a little sound of protest and leaned back. "You're totally bullying me," he muttered.

"I am," Billy agreed. "And you're going to sit there and think of a good reason this won't work. I'll be back in ten minutes. Remember to have your reason ready then."

And with that he took off, hoping Sean had the good sense not to move.

His sprint across the park felt good—really good, in fact. He dodged dogs, people, even leapt over a little kid's head as the poor muffin wandered right into his flight path. He ignored the dog path and crossed the soccer fields, running hard at their steepest hill and then hitting the dog path on the other side. By the time he got to the Charger, he was only a little winded—and a lot pissed off when he saw the teenagers hanging around Sean's car.

"Go away," he snapped. "This isn't yours."

"Guillermo?" one of the kids said softly. "Is that you?"

Billy almost turned around and ran back. Only the thought of the man waiting for him—having faith in him—made him keep going.

"Miguel?" he asked hesitantly. His little brother had been eight three years ago on that fateful day when he'd run back to the car for his shin guards. Now, at eleven, Miguel had shot up in height, although he was still not as tall as Billy, and his face had gone from soft and round to angular and almost... hungry.

"What are you doing here?" Billy asked when his little brother gave a tentative smile. Sean lived in Carmichael, which was close to midtown Sacramento. This little park was a good three miles away from the house Billy remembered growing up in. Their usual park had been a ways away.

"We moved," Miguel said. "Man, shit went crazy after you left. Dad… he, like, lost all control. Put Mom in the hospital. She got a restraining order, and we moved but, you know. She didn't make all the money, so we're in a little duplex now. We all had to change schools and stuff. Teresa moved out and got married, so she gives us money, and Berto—I mean *Robert*—he makes us call him Robert now—he's got some mysterious job and shit. But what are *you* doing here?"

Billy swallowed. "A friend of mine," he said. "He got hurt, and I'm helping take care of him. I left him on the far side of the park. I need to go pick him up." He paused and looked at the other kids loitering near the car—probably to check it out because it was a nice piece, but also looking like disreputable punks at the same time. "You want I should give you a ride home?"

Miguel shook his head. "Naw. Mom gave me the afternoon off from watching the little kids. We got a teacher in-service today."

"Where's the duplex again?" Billy asked, not sure he'd use this information but… but God. His home? Without his father? A surge—a terrible surge—of longing for his brothers and sisters shoved its way next to his heart.

Miguel gave him an address, and Billy frowned. He and Sean had spent some time the night before peering at a map of the robberies and the area. He knew that set of duplexes, and they weren't… savory.

"Yeah, it's a dump," Miguel said, reading his expression. "What can I say, Ghee? They shit on you, life shit on us."

"I'm sorry," Billy murmured, the clock in the back of his mind driving him out of there. He needed to go get Sean!

Miguel shook his head. "Don't be sorry, man. That wasn't your fault."

Billy nodded, swallowing tightly, all the good feeling from his investigative playtime with Sean evaporating. "Take care, little man," he said, and to his surprise, his little brother launched himself at him and hugged Billy tightly around the waist like he had as a little kid. Without thinking, Billy wrapped his arms around Miguel's shoulders, and they hugged hard and desperate before Miguel stepped away, wiping his eyes.

"You gotta go," he said. Then he turned to his buddies, and they slouched off in that particularly middle-school shuffle.

Billy got into the car without another word and drove away as fast as was safe, trying not to cry.

"SORRY I'M late," he said as Sean opened the door and settled in.

"No worries," Sean said mildly. "Did you run into Bob?"

Billy shook his head, not sure if he wanted to talk about it. "No, someone else."

Sean looked at him expectantly, and Billy had the uncomfortable realization that this was the sort of thing you talked to a lover about.

"I, uhm… look. I'm gonna take a detour past Cannonball, okay? I'll explain while we go."

"Sure."

That was it. No questions, no "What the hell?" And Billy became acutely aware of how little he expected that from the important people in his life.

From the men.

Sean's patient acceptance was such a balm to his soul   it was like diaper rash ointment on a part of his body he hadn't realized was chafed.

After a few moments of silence, Billy said, "Look, I appreciate your being chill." He gave Sean a sideways look. "Although I gotta say, when I first got to know you, I didn't think you could *be* this chill—so thanks."

He saw Sean's grimace. "Patience really isn't my strong suit," Sean said after a moment. "But last night was really great. I… I could learn some patience if we can keep doing that."

"Yeah, well, I guess we're both sons of hotheads," Billy conceded. "And stubborn old bastards. But your old man never put your mommy in the hospital, and I guess mine did after I got kicked out of the house."

"And you know this how?" Sean asked, sounding as adrift as Billy felt.

So Billy told him about Miguel and his little band of possible juvenile delinquents, and learning that his mother lived a few blocks away from the park in a not-so-awesome tract of duplexes.

"So we're going to visit?" Sean asked, like he was making sure.

"No! It's your nap time, and I've got a paper to write." He was making excuses to himself—he knew it.

"So what are we going to do?" Sean asked delicately.

"Stalk them." He wasn't even sorry about it either. "I'm going to park down the street, scope out the place, and make sure the old man isn't there and the kids aren't running with more punks, like Miguel, or shooting smack, or any of a thousand shitty things that could have happened while I was gone."

Oh, that rankled. His entire life he'd thought, "Hey, the old man is a complete asshole, but at least the kids are okay." And then he got kicked out, and he thought, "Well, this sucks, but at least the kids will be okay." Except his little brother was at the park looking like he was about to break into Billy's boyfriend's car, and Billy's sister had gotten married and moved the fuck out of the house. Where the fuck was Berto—erm, Robert? He was the next oldest; he'd be, what? Seventeen? A senior in high school? Lily would be a freshman? Then Miguel, and finally Cora—short for Corazon because she was the family's heart, right? She'd be nine years old. Was she home *alone*? Three years Billy had been building a wall between his heart and these kids he'd spent his life caring for, and one hug from his little brother and the wall was crumbling, and he was falling apart.

"Hey," Sean said softly. "It's not your fault. You were kicked out of their lives. You didn't run away from them."

"Yeah, but I didn't make a whole lot of effort to go back, either," Billy retorted bitterly.

"You were beaten and kicked out," Sean snapped, and Billy was actually heartened because all that patience worried him. "And you know what? *You were a kid too*."

"I was twenty years old when I got kicked out!" Billy retorted. "Remember? Me, skating on the old man's rent?"

"You think that's the reason you didn't leave?" Sean sounded disbelieving. "You really think that?"

"Yes!" He paused. "No." He sighed. "Yeah, no. Probably not."

Sean sighed too. "I get it—you were the oldest. So was I. I made sure my little sisters weren't picked on, and Charlie and I had each other's backs. I fed the kids when the folks were at work, and I made sure the other kids were dressed before school and occupied everyone when the grown-ups were doing what they had to do to have a household. I *get it*. You were responsible."

"They were mine," Billy said, turning onto Cannonball and all but groaning. God. He'd known his parents needed both incomes, but this street.

"Sure they were," Sean said gently, looking around. "But your parents were the ultimate authority, and you know what? They let you down. They ripped that part of your life away from you. You want to know why you didn't go back? Because you were too busy trying to figure out who you were without them. *That's* why you didn't go back. So that's fine. Let's go stalk your family."

Billy scowled and parked the car across the street and a couple houses down from the duplex his brother had indicated. The house they were in front of had a neatly trimmed lawn, and while all the shutters were drawn, the porch was at least swept. But that was not the case with the rest of the duplexes on the block. There were a lot of ragged lawns on that block, a lot of cracked driveways and sidewalks. Trees that had only been trimmed by the city to make way for power lines and cars but still hung dangerously over the duplexes themselves, and cars that had been parked for months, if not years, each one with an accretion of dust, pollen, and detritus.

Billy muttered the house number he was watching, and together he and Sean monitored the outside of a beige stucco duplex with cracked walls and sagging gutters. The lawn was too displaced by the roots of a giant tree to be even, and the tree roots had cracked the sidewalk in front of the house and in the driveway as well.

The garage door opened, and Billy could see a battered minivan inside, and then a young girl—high school age, probably, with generous curves and a messy bun of curly black hair on top of her head—came out with a baby on her hip.

"Lily," Billy murmured. "The baby is probably Teresa's. Miguel said she got married and got out."

"Cute kid," Sean said, and Billy smiled.

"Yeah, well, the old man's genes don't suck. Just the old man." The baby had the unmistakable features of Billy's family. Pointed chin, wide-set brown eyes, little dimples they could see from across the street. This baby had a big happy smile, though, and Billy thought wistfully that he would have loved to bounce Teresa's baby on his shoulder when it went through the colicky time, and how he would have been a proud uncle with a stroller, probably from the first day it had been born.

Billy swallowed hard, not sure he was going to get out of there without losing his shit and feeling like a complete asshole. His hand went to the ignition, and he thought desperately about bolting, when Lily, who had been about to set the baby—probably nine months old—on a blanket under the tree, paused and looked up at their car.

And she froze.

Reluctantly, Billy made eye contact with his younger sister, and the excitement he saw flash across her face almost made him want to run faster.

"Oh God," he moaned. "I gotta… I gotta go."

Sean's hand on his thigh stopped him. "You're an engineering student," Sean said softly. "You're helping a friend out while he heals. That is all any of them have to know for now. You understand me? Look at her."

Lily waved madly, scooped up the baby, and walked across the street in her bare feet.

Against his will—not even with his permission—Billy found his hand had lifted and he was giving her a tentative wave back.

"I'm an engineering student," he repeated. "I'll be at Sac State next fall."

"I'm just a friend."

Billy turned to him fiercely and reached down to grab the hand on his thigh. "You're my boyfriend," he said. "And I'm helping you recover. Because you're a police officer, and you were wounded in the course of doing your job."

Sean's lips quirked. "Detective," he reminded Billy softly.

"That's even better."

"Damned straight."

And with that Billy took a deep breath. "Stay here," he rasped. And then he stepped out of the car.

Lily had gotten to the Charger by then, and she gave a little squeal and gave him a hard one-armed hug. "Guillermo! Oh my God! You're… how did you find us? Holy crap, wait until Mom hears. She'll be so excited. I have so much to tell you. Damn, it's so good to see you!"

Billy had to laugh. Lily had always been effusive. A babbling baby and a mischievous child, Lily, along with Cora, had been the family's sunshine, doing their chores cheerfully, working hard at happiness when happiness wasn't always an option with their old man hanging over their heads.

"How you doing, Lil?" he asked softly. "Saw Miguel down at the park. He looked—"

"Like a juvenile fucking delinquent," Lily said with disgust. "And if you think *he* looks bad, you should see Berto—excuse me, *Robert*—'cause he's an asshole. Do you know what that pendejo did? Dyed his hair *blond*. Can you imagine that? Like he's going to wake up one day and totally not be Mexican. It's obnoxious."

Billy couldn't help laughing. "Hey, I changed my name too."

Lily frowned. "To what?"

He winced. "Billy?"

"Oh God, why? You used to be such a badass about it all. Guillermo was a good Mexican name. Didn't you tell a teacher that once?"

Billy grimaced. "Well, yeah," he said softly. "But then I wasn't part of the family anymore, Lil. Didn't seem to matter."

She sobered. "Dad's an asshole. You heard what he did to Mommy, right?"

"Miguel told me," he said. "I'm sorry. You guys, it seems like shit sort of fell apart after I left."

Lily let out a bitter laugh. "Only because you were the one holding it together, Guillermo. Wasn't your fault Dad's an asshole." She grimaced and rocked the baby on her hip. "Teresa's baby," she said, confirming his suspicions. "Dimitri." She grinned. "Teresa married a Russian guy—can you believe that?"

Billy had to laugh. "No, I can't."

Lily reached down to grab his hand. "Come inside, Ghee. Cora's making sandwiches, and Mom went out to get cookies. It'll be a celebration."

Billy glanced behind him to Sean and bit his lip, shaking his head.

"Lily, I want to, and I'll come back, I swear. But not today. My roommate—"

Suddenly Lily looked down into the Charger, her face lighting up. "Is that like roommate as in *code*? Like, is this your boyfriend? Ghee! You've got a boyfriend? That's great!"

Billy had to laugh, and he went with the easy explanation to save time. "Yeah, well, it is. But he's recovering from an injury, and look at him—he needs to go home and rest." Sean was pale, his head tilted back and his eyes closed. He didn't even see Lily with her face pressed against the glass. "This wasn't planned. I saw Miguel, and you guys were so close, and I thought I'd—"

"What, watch us?" She laughed up into his face, because like most of the women in his family, her full growth had stopped at around five foot two.

"Well, yeah." Billy smiled down at her, and he found he was reluctant to let her go. "I missed you all," he admitted. "I… I wanted to see you. But I really got to get him home. He'd go inside and have cookies and milk and probably even hold the baby—he comes from a big Catholic family too, so he gets it. But he's not a hundred percent yet, and…." He grimaced, trying to think of a way to put this.

"You got feelings," she said astutely. "We're like, 'Guillermo, our long-lost brother,' and you're like, 'Please don't break my nose again.'"

"Well, Pop broke my nose 'cause he was an asshole," Billy admitted.

"Yeah. He was. But he's gone now." In an abrupt move, Lily suddenly shoved baby Dimitri at him. "Here, hold this. It wiggles."

Billy laughed and took the baby, all the baby-holding skills from his childhood coming up in a rush while she shoved her hand down his pocket with so much casual familiarity he wondered if she remembered he hadn't seen her in three years. Then she pulled his phone out and held it in front of his face to open it.

She worked at putting numbers in it, and he stared down at the pudgy little Russian–Mexican-American baby in his arms.

Dimitri grinned up at him and blew a raspberry.

"You," he accused, "are unfairly cute. That's just wrong."

Dimitri laughed like he was the funniest thing in the world, and finally Lily gave him his phone back.

"There. I called my phone, and I'm going to give everybody your phone number. But not Dad, because don't worry. Once Mom filed the restraining order, went to the priest and got an annulment, he hasn't been back. Apparently the fact that the priest thought he was garbage was enough to make him stay away and stay drunk or whatever." She shook her head, and again, that bitterness he hadn't remembered tinged her movements. "I don't care. But *you* I care about. Get your guy home. Get your head in a place where you can eat cookies. And be prepared for me and Corazon and Teresa and Mom to start pestering you about your life, because…." Her voice broke a little, and she stood on her tiptoes, her feet still bare on the ragged blacktop, and kissed his cheek. "God, Guillermo, we all missed you so bad. Even Miguel and Roberto, and don't let them pretend they're too badass to admit it. I'm so glad to see you."

She wiped under her eyes with her hand and waved at him. "Go," she sniffled. "Just go."

And he did.

Lingering Touches in the Shadows

SEAN REALLY was tired—but not so tired that he couldn't feel the pulse of anxiety emanating from Billy's—*Guillermo's*—body as they walked through the garage and into the duplex.

"Go lay down," Billy said crisply. "I've got—"

But Sean stopped him and grabbed his hand, then continued his journey down the hall with Billy in tow.

"Where am I going?" Billy asked, and Sean was relieved to hear some humor in his voice.

"You're going to lay down with me until I fall asleep, and talk."

"I don't want to talk about it," Billy muttered.

"You don't have to," Sean replied shortly. "Just come talk to me. Anything. Let's open the drapes, because it's pretty outside, and lie on the bed, and touch. It'll be fine. The earth won't move. Heavens won't open. And I'll fall asleep."

And you'll feel like the world isn't closing in, crushing the breath out of you.

Sean knew that feeling, that look on Billy's face. The feeling of family sitting on your chest. He'd felt it his entire senior year when Charlie couldn't even look at him. He'd felt it his first two semesters of the criminal justice program, when his father gave him anguished looks over the dinner table because he was afraid Sean's sexuality would get him killed on duty. Billy had other demons—and other memories—but Sean knew, without a doubt, that he needed someone to help him get those elephants off his chest.

"Sure," Billy said. "That's five minutes out of my life."

"You'll never miss it."

They got to the bedroom, and Sean slowed down long enough to undress, taking his shoes off and putting them in the closet and his jeans off to fold over the chair. He was bent over slightly, getting his sleep pants out of the drawer, when Billy's warmth along his back soothed the urgency from his blood.

"We didn't get lunch," Billy murmured, trailing intimate lips along Sean's neck.

"We can have an early dinner," Sean said, turning into his chest and wrapping his arms around Billy's waist so he could lean his head against Billy's chest. "And this is wonderful."

"*Mmm.*" Billy took a deep breath. "I told Lily you were my boyfriend. I know it's too soon, but I didn't want to explain."

"*Mmm.* New," Sean said. He got it. He'd never been of the "one blowjob equaled an engagement" school himself, but he'd also known—and made clear—that he didn't take physical intimacy lightly. The situation between them was odd; they'd become so emotionally intimate in the span of five weeks that the physical intimacy seemed secondary.

And yet so important.

"I don't mind," he said. "I am unimportant to how you and your family interact. If you want to see them, get involved with them again, I will make the visits and have the lunches if you need me to. Or I'll stay hidden here while you pretend I don't exist."

"Hey!" Billy pulled back from him. "I'm not your douchebag ex—and don't confuse us either. If I'm gonna be out to my family, I'm gonna be out. None of this 'Yeah, I'm gay, but this is my good friend who's wearing my shirt' bullshit."

A weight on Sean's own chest lightened. "Understood."

"No," Billy muttered, still clearly miffed. "Not understood. You.... I mean, my dad beat the shit out of me, and that sucked, but your dad made you think that being gay was all fine as long as it didn't make waves, and that's a different kind of suck."

Sean grimaced because he was right, but before Sean could say anything, he kept talking.

"Besides, Lily was all excited about you. I... when I go back, I think I sort of need to go back with a boyfriend, so, uhm, even if we're not there yet, I appreciate you letting it slide."

"Who says we're not there yet?" Sean asked softly.

Billy frowned. "We're exclusive," he said, and then looked away.

"Except for work." Sean tried not to sigh. He got it in a way, because Billy *had* been left high and dry before, and he had a right to not depend solely on Sean for support. But… gah. Sex. Sex was such a big deal, drilled into every Catholic boy from catechism on. It was the hallmark of a relationship, right?

Except… except Billy's kisses on the temple had felt so much more important than every sex act he'd ever performed with Jesse—or most of his other exes, for that matter.

"I'm—"

Sean pressed his fingers against Billy's lips. "You're not sorry. You shouldn't be. If I couldn't deal with your job, I shouldn't have ever kissed you, never allowed myself to want you. But I did. So now I deal with it or *I'm* the douche."

"That's not true," Billy whispered. "I'll look for other jobs. Pick up other hours."

"Only if you want to," Sean said. "Or can afford to. For your comfort level." He rubbed his face against Billy's neck. "I get the feeling that sometimes porn isn't only about the money for you guys. Sometimes it is. But sometimes it's about more. When you're ready to tell me about that, tell me."

Billy sucked in a breath, like he'd been socked in the stomach. "You're very perceptive."

"Well, you know. I *am* a detective," Sean said softly. "And yes, I know it rhymes."

He heard Billy's dry chuckle, but it was very soft.

"I'm going to lie down under the covers," he murmured. "Because it's getting chilly outside. Kick off your shoes and jeans and join me. Just for a minute. Please?"

"Yeah."

He could only sleep on one side, which was sort of a pain in the ass, but Billy spooned behind him again, and he thought he could get used to it if Billy's hard body was a perk.

He closed his eyes, toying with Billy's hand as it draped across his stomach and listening to the sound of the wind in the trees outside his open window.

He thought, *This is it. He's going to let me fall asleep and then slip out of bed and start his homework*, but Billy began to talk.

"It's that," he said softly, "I was so lonely. Sam had left, and I was desperate for money and about to lose my place to live, but it was more than that. It was that I didn't have anybody to tell about how shitty it all was. I'm not a joiner. There's not a club at Sac City with my name on it. I wasn't gonna rush a fraternity or anything like that, not even if it had all the alphabet in the front. What did I know from LGBTQ? I wanted to kiss a boy—that was it. My ambition. And my family… they were gone. As far as I knew, Mommy, she just let me go. I didn't know she was gonna make a big last stand or anything. And those two guys—Reg and another guy who's not there now—like I said, they had the brotherhood thing. And they were gay, and it didn't seem to matter. They were friends too. And then I found out about the flophouse, and I was like, 'Hey, I can figure shit out. I can date a girl and see if that's what I want. I can bang all the guys if that's what they're doing. I've got brothers.'"

"Did it work out like that?" Sean murmured.

"Yeah, a little bit," Billy said in wonder. "I… I'm still not a joiner. There was all the damned drama going down, and I managed to sidestep that easy. But the guys were solid. I didn't see, I guess, until Henry showed up, how they might have needed more of the Guillermo guy who would have run their lives and less of Billy, who sort of let shit slide as long as he got his." He let out a soft snort. "Henry—he's all about the responsibility. And I remembered that Pops—he'd been an asshole, but he'd drilled that shit into me. And for a while I blamed the military for all the bad shit too, but then you figure out that people bring what they got into a thing. I guess Pops had all the meanness, and he brought that into the house too."

"*Mmm.*" Sean wanted to hear this so badly. It was the only thing keeping him awake.

"So… you know. To me, the flophouse means family. All the sex was great—and man, I did all the guys, all the ways—but that was just, I dunno, a perk. You never had to sleep alone, so I didn't."

"You can sleep alone here," Sean murmured.

"But I can sleep with you and don't have to put out." There was some soggy humor in his voice, and Sean attempted a laugh.

"You're almost asleep," Billy said softly.

"Mm-hmm."

"But you managed to calm me down."

"Good."

"I… I never got calmed down like this before."

"Even better," Sean slurred, and then he was out for the count.

WHEN HE awakened, the blowing wind had turned into a blowing autumn rain. He paused to close his windows, thinking wistfully that he wished there was some way to leave them open—he loved the smell of the rain—but that all the moist air was probably not good for his healing body. He made his way down the hall and into the kitchen and saw Billy at the table, doing homework as promised, his phone on the table next to him. As Sean entered, the phone buzzed, and the screen lit up, and Billy glanced at it and gave a patient sigh.

He picked up the phone and responded to the text and then set the phone down again, only grimacing a little as the phone lit up almost immediately.

"C'mon," he muttered. "I already answered this."

Sean let out a soft puff of air as a chuckle, and Billy glanced up at him, smiling sheepishly. "Suddenly everybody wants to know my business," he said, but he couldn't hide the fact that he was pleased.

"Feel good, coming back to the living?"

Billy shrugged. "Yeah, a little. But I forgot how much time they take, you know?"

Sean texted his mother at least three times a day. "I know."

Billy set his phone firmly aside then and closed his notebook, marking the page. "Hey, my sisters aren't the only ones texting me today."

"Yeah? What's up?"

"Well, Henry was supposed to spend a night at the apartment with the guys, but he texted them to say he and Rivers were neck-deep in it, and he had to bail. The guys wanted to know what they were working on—Cotton said he sounded stressed—and I told them I'd ask. I mean…." He gestured to the sound of the wind and rain on the roof, and Sean nodded.

"Shitty night to be out," he said softly.

Billy nodded. "I sort of lost track. Rivers and Henry—they're always up in somebody's business, right? What do you think they're doing?"

Sean didn't have to rack his brains. Ellery had actually asked him a couple of questions the week before as they were prepping for the case.

"It's an ugly one," he said softly. "The one where that kid with special needs got accused of attacking the woman in the park with a knife. You remember."

Billy snorted. "It was so dumb. Witnesses were like, 'That guy had to work to walk unassisted!' and the cops were like, 'He resisted arrest!' Yeah, I remember. How'd that even make it to trial?"

Sean shrugged. Jackson and Ellery really *had* been neck-deep in the case pretty much since they'd brought Cotton back, but Sean had followed some of the details on the news, and they hadn't been pretty.

"Cops lied," he said, feeling the heaviness of this in his chest. "They lied, and then they beat the kid to cover it up. I would imagine Jackson and Henry are out trying to find who really did it. I mean, you gotta admit, that would make a pretty cool surprise at any trial, right?"

Billy nodded and gave a crooked smile. "Well, yeah. But isn't that shit only for the movies?"

Sean held his hand out and wobbled it back and forth. "I imagine there's plenty of drama out there if you look. But yeah. That's probably what Henry's doing tonight."

Billy blew out a breath. "I should go over and check on them," he said heavily, and Sean opened his mouth to say, "Yeah, we should both go," but Billy cut him off. "Just me. It's cold and wet out there, and you are at risk for infection. So no. No you joining me. I don't want to leave you alone…." His face softened. "For one thing, you'll watch that stupid cop show without me, and I'll get all jealous that I missed it."

Sean smiled softly. "I'll find a movie you're guaranteed to hate," he said, "so you don't miss anything."

Billy stood and put his hands on Sean's shoulders, bending down to kiss the top of his head. "No going out in the storm to help Rivers, okay? Not without me? Deal?"

Sean closed his eyes and let Billy's heat sink into him. "It's been a long time," he said softly, "since somebody *not* my mother was worried about me like that. Don't worry. No heroics. I promise. I'll just sit here and be a couch potato." He yawned, hating how long it was taking him to come back from this. "As long as you get home and turn me over, broil my other side…."

Billy laughed like he was supposed to and set about making dinner, but thoughts of Rivers and Henry brought up worry Sean didn't think he'd had in him. It was funny how people grew on you. He'd hated

Rivers when they first met. He'd spent years trying to ingratiate himself to the people on the force, trying hard to follow the rules and do the right thing. But then he'd met Ellery Cramer, and he'd crushed so damned hard. Here, he'd thought, had been a man who had his shit together, who knew and respected the law, and who was willing to work hard for justice.

What he hadn't understood then was that the fire that had lit Ellery Cramer from the inside had been Jackson Rivers. And watching Jackson—and Ellery—take risks with their lives over the past year and some change had made him more and more aware of exactly how he risked his own life. He loved being a police detective, but he'd better be on the side of the angels when he went out. That was his only requirement.

Even if his captain or his colleagues didn't agree with him on where that line was.

The thought that he'd been backup—no matter how unwary—for Jackson and Henry as they tried to get an innocent kid out of jail when he'd gotten stabbed had been the only way he'd been able to make any sense of his injury.

Like he'd told Billy, he'd gone from light to the dark to the light.

The light had been the idealism that had carried him into the force, and the dark had been the assumption that he'd have to go along to get along.

The light had been when he'd remembered he could think for himself, he could draw his own conclusions, and he didn't have to follow the department line if he didn't want to. His soul was worth way more than any promotion, than any money or the accolades of his peers.

Even if it meant getting stabbed as he followed his friends back to the office from lunch.

And now he was laid up while his friends went into the cold and the dark and the rain and looked for evidence to defend a kid from the corruption of the institute Sean represented.

He wanted so badly to be with them. Goddammit, he wanted to help.

The least he could do was let Billy go to *his* friends and help be the stabilizing force they needed.

Billy hustled around the kitchen, working on grilled chicken and preseasoned brussels sprouts as Sean set the table—quietly so as not to earn any censure. When dinner was ready, they both sat down, and Billy frowned.

"You're not talking," he muttered. "You're almost always talking, even if you can barely breathe. Why aren't you talking?"

Sean shrugged and smiled ruefully. "Just wishing I was in any shape to be out in the cold and the dark, right?"

Billy scowled. "I know, and I'm not happy that you want to be out with them. They're crazy. You know that, right? Rivers is a hero—we all know it—but he's certi-fuckin'-fiable. And Henry's like his mini-me. No, I'm super glad you're here and trying really hard not to ask me why there's no potatoes tonight."

"Why aren't there potatoes tonight?" Sean asked.

"'Cause my skinny jeans are getting tight," Billy replied with a scowl. "Ugh. This calorie diary is for shit when you keep saying, 'I'm Polish! I need starch!' You do not. That's like me saying I'm Mexican and I need beans. It's a hurtful stereotype, so no potatoes."

Sean scowled at him. "I've seen the stats. Your people live longer than mine because beans and rice form a perfect protein, *and* it helps you poop. Maybe now that you're talking to your family again, you should get some recipes from your mother and we'll both be happy."

To his surprise, Billy's face split into a huge smile, so bright and so shining that he immediately had to ruin it by putting his hand in front of his mouth. "I can, right? I... I used to *long* for my mommy's cooking after I left home, and now I can ask her or, you know, my sisters."

The smiled died abruptly, and Billy dropped his hand.

"At least until somebody finds out what I did for a living." He blinked. "Do. Did. Fuck." Now he covered his eyes. "I'm so confused! I'm supposed to shoot a scene next week! What do I tell John?"

Sean sighed. "Nothing right now," he said. "Right now eat your sad chicken and veggies with no potatoes and go visit your friends while I sneak cookies from the pantry and watch *The Black Phone.*"

Billy swallowed, and then Sean watched him do what Sean was telling him to: to wait until he could think clearly and to do what must be done in the now.

"You will not watch *The Black Phone* without me," he said. "We've been planning to watch that movie together for a week!"

"You could always watch it with the flophouse, and we could compare notes," Sean suggested.

Billy shook his head adamantly. "No. You and me, watching it together. Promise."

Sean rolled his eyes but was secretly warmed. "Sure. Fine. I can't watch our cop show, I can't watch the movie—should I sit here with the lights off and stare into the dark, pining for you?"

Billy snorted. "No, you're going to watch the movies that your ex-douchebag stole from you when you were in the hospital and I spent an hour setting up in the streaming services. You're welcome. Just...." He paused and bit his lip. "I, uhm, like watching stuff with you. Don't... don't—"

Sean gave him a lopsided grin. "Won't watch those things without you," he said softly. "Don't worry. I, uhm, like watching stuff with you too."

Billy grinned again. "Yeah, this is all sweet and gooey and stuff, but I give you a week or two before you can run laps again, and suddenly all you want to do is work out."

Sean snorted. "How stupid do you think I am? If I'm running laps, you and me are having some sex!"

Billy's throaty laughter warmed him from the toes up, and filled him too.

Better than potatoes, hands down.

SEAN WAS halfway through *Baby Driver*, and texting Billy another effusive thank-you for streaming all his favorite movies, when there was a knock at his door.

It took him a minute to get up and answer it, and he chided himself for growing used to Billy waiting on him at the same time he wished Billy were there now. It didn't matter what people were selling—cleaning products, magazines, religion—Billy's acid tongue and give-no-fucks attitude usually had them hauling ass to another neighborhood in one or two sentences, and Sean really envied that ability sometimes.

He especially envied that ability when he opened the door and saw Jesse standing there.

God, that man was still good-looking.

Tall, with salt-and-pepper temples, Jesse was one of those men who proved that whiskey and steak weren't the only things that could get tastier with age.

But that didn't mean Sean's mouth watered when he saw who was standing on his porch.

"What?" he asked, eyes narrow and expression flat and unfriendly.

"Hey," Jesse said, giving a sort of sheepish smile and jiggling the grocery bag in his hand. "I, uh, realized that, uh, I maybe confused some of your movies with mine when I left. I thought I'd bring them back."

Sean grabbed the bag from Jesse and realized that, in addition to *two* DVDs when Sean knew Jesse had taken at least ten, there was also a six-pack of beer, a quart of Jack Daniels, and a box of lubricated condoms.

"Fuck off," he said, shoving the bag into Jesse's chest before backing up and slamming the door.

Jesse stopped him with a booted foot between the door and the frame.

"Come on, Sean," he said, his voice low and smooth. "You know it doesn't have to mean anything. You, me, some good times—"

"I'm still on pain meds, you insensitive fuckhead," Sean snapped, although mostly it was ibuprofen, but Jesse didn't know that. "And no 'good time' with you is worth the shitty emotional hangover. Now move your foot before I—"

"What?" Jesse taunted. "Call the cops?" Behind him, the trees rustled in a particularly vicious burst of wind, and Sean's next breath was a little rustier. Damp air—goddammit, it sucked when everything your mother said about "You're gonna catch your death" was right.

Sean growled. "You think it's the cops you should be worried about?" He held up his phone, which had Billy set to speed dial. "One touch of this button and I've got five bored porn stars here on my doorstep, ready to come take pictures with you and post them to the internet. Think carefully, Jesse. Is your dick today really worth your reputation as a straight man tomorrow?"

"Sean," Jesse wheedled, but he'd straightened his posture, which demanded him pulling his foot out of the door, which was all Sean needed.

He slammed the door in Jesse's face and slid the deadbolt home. He heard a frustrated crash of glass against his door as he stalked to the couch and tried not to groan. Fuck. He needed to clean that up before Billy got home.

He pulled out his phone and texted, *Where'd you put the cleaning gloves?* Although he could picture them hanging under the sink as he did so. As he sagged into the recliner for a second, he just wanted that contact with Billy before he got up again and confronted the evidence of his bad choices on his concrete stoop.

I'm not telling you. Whatever it is, ignore it. I'll get it when I get home.

Sean smiled and touched the screen. *There's glass on the porch. I want to clean it up before you get home.*

The phone erupted in his hand, and he almost fumbled it as he took the call.

"Glass? Who in the fuck threw glass at your porch?"

"It's not a big deal," he hedged.

"And now it is," Billy snapped. "Those little words just made it a *huge* deal. *What happened?*"

"My ex showed up with booze and condoms, and I slammed the door in his face."

There was a stunned silence on the other end of the line, and for a moment Sean wondered if Billy had just dropped the phone to come storming over.

"Booze and condoms?"

"Yup."

"Fucking. Classy. Are you sure he's gone?"

Sean stood up and went to check through the peephole and the window. "I don't see him," he claimed. "I threatened to have porn stars show up and post pics with him to Instagram. He took off."

Billy snorted. "They would never—"

"I know," Sean said, smiling a little. "Your guys are too sweet to out him on social media, but he doesn't know that. Look, I just wanted to know where the gloves are—"

"So I'd come home and clean up the glass."

"So the glass wasn't there when you got home." Sean scowled. "I really can take care of myself—"

"On a dark and stormy night when you shouldn't be out. Sit down, cop-man. Me and the guys will be there in twenty."

The screen went dark when he hung up, and Sean stared at the phone in shock for a moment before he got up to go find the gloves.

WHEN BILLY got there, Sean was at the point of wiping the Jack Daniels off the front door, his chest hurting from the cold air, but feeling energized and a little bit angry and a little bit triumphant. He could *too* take care of himself, right?

Billy wasn't alone—the Johnnies kids were still unloading from the Charger as he marched up to the porch, took the cleaner and the rag and the gloves from an unrepentant Sean, and proceeded to chew him out for doing exactly what Billy had known he was going to do and be stupid and independent and stubborn.

"Fine," Sean said shortly as Billy slipped the gloves off his hands with absurdly tender fingers. "The next time I have to deal with that guy, I'll call you, and I'll tell him you've got my testicles in a jar under your bed and I'll stand up for myself when I can get those back."

Billy's mouth—set in a stern, irritated line—wobbled slightly, and his shoulders relaxed. He paused and stroked the back of Sean's knuckles with his thumb.

"You can keep your testicles where they are, papi," he said softly. "I just wanted to take care of you is all."

Sean smiled, acutely aware of the entire flophouse watching their entire interaction from the walkway in the rain. "How about we take care of your guys," he said. "Do you think *they* want to see *The Black Phone*?"

Billy grinned at him. "Well, *yeah*. But you go sit down and cover up, and I'll make popcorn." He paused, growing sober. "And yeah, I know you can do it, but let me? Please?"

How could he say no?

IN ALL, it turned out to be a good night. The guys stayed over, two of them taking the guest room, one taking the couch, and one taking the recliner. Billy slept next to him, giving Sean all the news before they fell asleep.

"How's Cotton?" Sean asked softly, fighting sleep with every breath. The boy had watched the movie breathlessly, leaning quietly against Billy's shoulder as they sat on the couch. Looking at them, Sean hadn't experienced jealousy, although he'd expected to. Instead he heard Billy talking about how the flophouse guys had become his brothers. Yeah. Sex was confusing sometimes, but the trust Cotton put into the guys around him—that was crystal clear.

"Cotton's sad," Billy told him. "But something happened. Something really exciting."

And then Billy told him that his friend had gotten—completely unsolicited—an offer for a full ride at a nursing school down south. And the director of the nursing school had the same last name as the "soldier guy" Cotton had fallen in love with.

"So," Sean said slowly, "is he going?"

"Yeah," Billy said with a sigh. "At the worst? It's a career I think he'd be really good at."

"At the best?"

Billy laughed a little. "His top-secret boyfriend will come visit, and Cotton will get his Happy Ever After."

"Do you believe in that?" Sean asked, almost holding his breath.

Billy breathed softly on the back of his neck. "I might," he murmured. "I'm working on it."

Sean smiled. "Fair," he said.

"Hey, cop-man?"

"Yeah?"

"If you're feeling up to cleaning off your porch, think you'd let me do sexy things to your body sometime when there's not a dozen other people in the house?" On that note, he thrust his groin gently into Sean's backside, letting him know that while it wasn't exactly urgent *now*, they could maybe make it urgent if Sean was interested.

"God yeah."

"Good."

Hero's Due

BILLY DROPPED half the flophouse off at school the next day, leaving Randy at Sean's house—just in case.

"Just in case what?" Sean asked suspiciously. "I do something crazy like fold laundry or take an extra lap around the park?"

"You can't go to the park," Billy sniffed. "I've got the Charger, remember?"

"It's only a mile," Sean told him. "We can walk there and then walk back." He grinned at Randy, who grinned back. "It'll be an adventure."

Billy looked at Randy and shook his head sternly. "It's Friday," he said. "I've got one class. I'll be back by lunch. We can go then."

Randy nodded with the eagerness of a puppy. "I hear you," he said. "Only *you* get to take him to the park. Understood." He smiled obsequiously, and Billy fought the temptation to pat him on the head.

"He overdoes it," Billy said.

"I've only got two weeks more before I go back to work!" Sean argued. "I mean, I'll be on desk duty, but my PT regimen says I should be walking two miles by then!" Billy knew very well it infuriated Sean that Rivers had gone in for heart surgery and had been back to running in the mornings at six weeks, and Sean was still walking with the same amount of recovery time. It probably didn't seem fair, although from what Billy understood, in Jackson's case they had been clearing out scar tissue from an old injury to his heart, and in Sean's, he was trying to recover not only from the knife wound but also the trauma of having his chest cavity fill up with air, as well as the surgery to relieve the condition. Both had their lives threatened, but Jackson's procedure had involved more delicacy and less raw tissue damage than Sean's.

And Sean had suffered the setback from trying to do too much too soon.

"You will be," Billy reassured him, but inside he quailed. He'd come to care for the snarky, patient, irritable, tender man he'd shown up to nurse. He'd *said* he could handle being a cop's significant other, but truthfully, the idea scared him a little.

Couldn't they just… just *be* right now?

But they couldn't. He knew that. Sean had to make a living, but more than that, Sean *wanted* to make a living doing something important. The guy who would clean up glass on the front porch so Billy didn't get hurt coming home was not going to hide out in his duplex when he could be doing something to make the world better, right?

"We need to keep up our own little investigation," Billy said. "That's why I need to be there."

"Oooh!" Randy perked up. "What kind of investigation? Can I help? I'll take notes while you guys ask questions!"

Billy looked at him thoughtfully. "Actually, if you want, you can come with us, and then, if we've gone too far, you can stay with Sean while I go get the car."

Sean cast him an evil look. "How do you know I won't be able to walk back this time?"

Billy gave him a look of compassion. "Because I've clocked it at a mile and a half, papi—you're not there yet."

"Augh!"

"Yeah, you hold that thought. I've got to go get the guys home, so you and Randy be good." With that he dropped a kiss on Sean's forehead and ran, Curtis, Vinnie, and Cotton in his wake.

"What was that?" Curtis asked after everybody was belted in.

"What was what?" Billy replied absently, backing out of the driveway with careful attention. The tenant in the other side of the duplex drove a giant SUV that wasn't always easy to see behind.

There was quiet in the car until he'd gotten completely out and had stepped on the accelerator, going forward.

"The thing you did before you left," Curtis said.

"Synced our schedules?" Billy didn't get it.

"The kiss," Cotton said patiently from the back seat. "You kissed him."

Billy grunted. "Have kissed lots of guys. In fact, all of you." He paused. "Except you, Vinnie. Sorry. You're still new."

"Maybe someday," Vinnie said cheerfully from the back.

"I wouldn't count on it," Cotton said mildly, his big sloe eyes peering at Billy from the rearview mirror. "That wasn't the kind of kiss you give when you're going to kiss other guys."

Billy grunted. "I still have a job," he said, remembering that his next film date was coming up.

"Yeah," Curtis said, "but you also have FAFSA coming, and a job waiting tables, and, hey, you don't have to pay rent. You don't have to *do* that job if it's incompatible with your new monogamous lifestyle."

"You guys," Billy muttered, "I don't want to talk about this. It's all weird in my stomach, so could we not?"

"Sure," Cotton said, because he was a sweetie-face who would never press things. "Just... you know. It's okay. To be happy with him. You don't have to feel bad for being happy with him. Someone who knows all of you, right?"

Billy had to tear his eyes away from the rearview mirror so he could drive and not wreck the car. "Sure," he said gruffly. He absolutely would not look in the mirror again, because it was possible that Cotton's enormous brown eyes had held the faintest look of reproach.

BILLY HAD managed to shake that look from his memory by the time he finished class and got back to Sean's place. When he arrived, it was to find that Randy had—on Sean's directions—broiled a bunch of marinated chicken breasts so Sean could show him how to make a week's supply of sandwich filling and stack it neatly in plasticware to put in the fridge.

It was a good home-ec lesson, and Billy was not surprised to hear that Sean's mother had texted the instructions to him while Billy was at school.

Unfortunately it was not the only thing Sean had heard via text while Billy was gone.

"Good sandwich," Billy mumbled through a full mouth, then caught sight of Sean's intent expression as he checked his phone. "What's wrong?"

Sean grimaced and showed Billy one of those courtroom drawings that sometimes got released to the press. "Christie sent me this while you were gone. Apparently Jackson and Henry were *really* busy last night."

Billy took a moment to study the picture, and as its import hit him, he sucked in a gasp.

"Is that—oh my God."

The scene was drawn from the gallery's perspective, as they often were, and featured Jackson Rivers on his feet in the witness stand, his back turned toward the jury as he peered over his shoulder.

His back was one giant series of bandages, following the track of what Billy would guess was a helluva knife wound, going from his shoulder blade down to his waist, where it turned into a puncture.

The caption read, *P.I. Jackson Rivers produces evidence of a cover-up and a murder attempt by the Sac PD.*

Ellery Cramer, who had apparently been the one to ask Jackson to produce the "evidence," could be seen in the foreground, his face hard and angry as he looked at Jackson's wound.

And the jury was appalled.

"Oh Jesus," Billy muttered. "Is Henry okay?"

"Yeah," Sean said. "See? There's a sketch of him behind the defense's table. I texted Christie to make sure."

"So," Randy said, looking scared and worried, "I guess they won their case."

Sean shook his head. "From what I understand, the DA's office is refusing to concede. I mean, I have faith in Ellery to get the kid off the crime but…." He shook his head. "I don't think the cops who did this to Jackson are going to be charged."

Billy found himself suddenly furiously angry. "And this—*this* is the system you want to be a part of? This is what you want to go back to?"

Sean swallowed, and Billy realized that he'd probably cut his lover—a cop who was the son of a cop—to the bone. "Can't fix it if I walk away from it," he said softly before standing up. "I'm going to go grab my jacket. It's a little chilly out there today."

He made his way down the hallway, moving at a good clip for anyone whose life *wouldn't* depend on their physical fitness in two weeks. Billy watched him go, setting his sandwich down not because he was afraid of gaining weight but because suddenly the nicely marinated meat and whole-grain bread didn't taste nearly as good as it had before he'd seen that appalling picture and realized that Jackson Rivers had sacrificed his dignity, his safety, and literally the skin off his back to get a kid off a trumped-up charge, and he was probably never going to get payback.

He glanced apologetically at Randy, who was giving him a surprisingly adult look from those bright green eyes.

"Wow," Randy said.

"I'm sorry," Billy returned. "I don't want to see him get hurt again."

"Well, yeah," Randy agreed, nodding his head. "But the world needs good guys, Billy. You should know that. The other kind are everywhere. It's like, even if there aren't enough good guys to go around, just knowing they're out there gives you hope, right? I mean, even if the bad guy fucks us raw or blows us away, we can hope a good guy is out there to protect our brothers."

Billy stared at Randy in horror. "Randy, my brother, why wouldn't the good guy save you too?"

Randy's mouth twisted, and again an adult self-awareness that Billy could have sworn the kid didn't possess was written all over his angular face.

"I'm the dorky redheaded kid with all the allergies and the runaway mouth, Billy. I get killed first in all the scary movies, and my death is comic relief. I mean, you're all nice to me at the flophouse, and my own family couldn't love me more. In fact they didn't, because I got the shit kicked out of me and then found myself homeless, right? Anyway, I know who I am. I'm not the guy who gets the cop or the soldier or the doctor. If I'm lucky, someday I'll figure a way out of porn and end up with a guy who works at a gas station but doesn't mind my fifty-dozen allergies and big mouth." He gave that crooked smile again, and Billy wanted to cry. "But if I *am* lucky, it's because John took pity on all of us and I managed to live that long. So, you know, maybe give your cop guy a break."

Billy swallowed. "Yeah. Sure. I'll think about it. Do you still want to come to the park with us?"

Randy perked up. "And see all the dogs? Yes! Maybe that one you showed us climbing trees will be there, because I *like* that dog!"

Randy *was* that dog, Billy thought, his throat a little tight. Awkward and intense and too big for its body and pure of heart right down to the big feet and big ears and ginormous protrusion from a private area.

"Me too. I'm going to go drop my books," Billy lied. He usually dropped his books in a corner of the kitchen, but he suddenly needed to talk to Sean privately.

He found Sean in the bedroom, staring sightlessly into his closet. Without a word, Billy put one hand on his shoulder and reached in to grab a fleece vest, which he held up for Sean's approval.

"I'm sorry," he said softly, helping Sean into the vest, one arm and then the other.

"It's not easy," Sean replied, his voice just as soft. "These last weeks have been really…." He smiled a little. "Well, awful and wonderful. I'm still waiting for my body to recover so we can…."

Billy felt the flush rising from his cheeks and nuzzled the back of Sean's ear. "Me too," he murmured.

"I'll still be a cop when we do," Sean told him.

Billy nodded. "I'll still be worried when you go back in the field," he said.

"But you can't—"

Billy buried his face in Sean's neck, not proud of himself in that moment. "I won't," he whispered. "I won't be mad at your job no more. I swear."

Sean nodded this time. "Okay," he said softly. "I… it poisons a lot of relationships, you understand?"

Billy nodded, remembering his father's anger, his temper on being in a quiet place when he seemed to long for the movement, the violence, the decisive action of deployment.

"Dangerous jobs do." He swallowed. "But I can't be a jerk about it. I know. I just…. Rivers isn't gonna get no justice for himself, you know that, right?"

Sean's mouth turned up a little. "It's never like the movies," he said, and then rolled his eyes and corrected himself. "It's *rarely* like the movies. Sometimes the system can hand out justice, and sometimes it takes a little more than good guys with guns and badges to cart away the bad guys."

"Like what?" Billy asked.

"Well," Sean said thoughtfully, "I would watch the press in the next week. Ellery hasn't wanted the case tried in the press because his client would have a really hard time with all the people in his face. But Jackson took off his shirt, and that's going to get people on alert. Jackson *can* take that sort of flack, and if Ellery's smart about it, the story behind that wound is going to make the rounds. Just… pay attention," he said softly. "I know you're not good at politics. Neither am I. But have a little faith, okay?"

Billy took a deep breath. "Sure. Now let's go. Randy wants to meet all the dogs again."

"Sure." And then Sean turned his head and kissed him, long and deep, surprising Billy with the intensity, the tenderness, and the passion. When they separated, Sean was the one who kissed *him* on the forehead, and Billy had to admit it.

He sort of liked that.

RANDY ENDED up throwing balls to, like, half the dogs who went to play in the park that day, so Billy showed Randy which thruway they were taking for their investigation. Sean's movement had improved enough that they managed to question the three houses hit in the next cul-de-sac and then make their way down the connecting street to the cul-de-sac over.

Pretty much everybody had the same story to tell. They'd either heard a noise in their garages or they'd awakened to find something portable but high value missing from their jimmied-open garage door. This wasn't a wealthy neighborhood—most people didn't have high-tech security, and on the few occasions when an alarm had gone off or a security camera had captured footage, the perp had either been gone before anybody got down to see more than a flash of a black outfit, or the only salient feature the camera had captured had been a wisp of blond hair.

After viewing some footage—people were really accommodating about showing the two of them the videos on their phones—Billy and Sean waited on the main road for Randy to come pick them up.

Sean was tired but not overly so, and Billy was reminded once again that he really would be ready to go back into the fray in a couple of weeks.

"You're sure Randy has a driver's license?" Sean asked seriously.

"Yeah. Henry helped him get it when Rivers was laid up." Billy shrugged. "I mean, not that I'm not taking over when he gets here, but I'm pretty sure he'll get here. What do you want to do after your nap?"

"Want to stop on the way back and get a whiteboard and some magnets and a map? I need to… you know. See what's going on. And then we need to maybe phone interview the people with the dogs to see if there's anything *they* have in common that we're missing from the people who got hit."

"We can talk to more of those people at the park," Billy said. "So get their addresses and put them on your little murder board here."

"Good thinking. But it's only a map. Nobody's been hurt." Sean gave him an almost flirtatious smile. "You know. We're just doing this as a hobby."

Billy rolled his eyes. "Yeah. Sure." Then quickly, before he could back out, "So, uhm, if we're just doing this as a hobby, is there any way we could take tomorrow evening off? My, uhm, mom would like me to come to dinner, and, uhm…." He took a deep breath. "I need backup," he explained, feeling weak and awkward. "I… if I don't have someone there who knows how to make grown-up noises come out of their piehole, I'm going to end up screaming 'I'm a porn star!' and then running off into the night."

Sean chuckled. "And into the family histories forever." He made his voice deep and authoritative. "Dear Reader, he was never seen again."

Billy covered his eyes with his hand. "Please?" he begged in a little voice. "I swear, if you and me weren't a thing, I might ask Lance if I could borrow Henry. I, uh… you know. Need proof of adulting. Seriously."

"Don't you have report cards?" Sean chided, and Billy dropped his hand and gave Sean a gaze of mute appeal. "Oh my God!" Sean clutched at his chest. "The eyes! The Bambi eyes! No wonder you work so hard at being an asshole. Those forest animal eyes—so limpid. So cute. They should be classified as a weapon!"

"So you'll come eat at my mommy's table?" Billy begged, aware that he was being pitiful but beyond pride at this point.

"Yeah, of course," Sean told him, his voice dropping softly. "I bet she can cook, right?"

"If she's forgotten, I haven't," he promised fervently. "I swear, if you do this for me, I'll make her enchilada casserole. It's got *cheese*!"

"Wow. This *is* serious!" The subdued roar of a powerful engine sounded, and they both looked up to see Randy pulling alongside the curb.

To Billy's intense relief, the car appeared to be in one piece, and the joy on Randy's face was worth the two miles of potential disaster, he figured. "And here's our ride," Billy said, happy to get out of the embarrassing asking-for-help conversation.

But Sean didn't let it go. Instead he paused and touched Billy's hand as Billy got ready to take Randy's place behind the wheel. "I would have done it without the bribe," he said.

"I would have made her casserole if you hadn't done it," Billy told him, kissing him briefly on the cheek. "But this way we're both a lot happier."

"Yeah."

THE NONMURDER board looked cool and official, Billy thought critically, as he carefully overwrote Randy's eccentric handwriting. Randy had gone home after dinner. He'd been a huge help with the presentation, remembering details and suggesting ways to organize information. It was easy to forget that the kid was super smart, but he really was. Sean had treated his suggestions respectfully, explaining why he didn't take some of them and building on the ones he did take.

By the time Randy left, the board outlined everything they had on the thief—or the perp, as Sean called him—as well as where he'd struck, which houses had dogs, and what had been stolen. When Billy got back from driving Randy to the flophouse, he found Sean sitting at the table, staring at the board and obviously deep in thought.

Billy didn't want to think about the mystery anymore. Instead he stood behind Sean and looped his arms around Sean's neck, bending over to nuzzle his ear.

"Please tell me," he murmured, "that you're not super tired already."

Sean turned his head into Billy's embrace, and their lips caught in one of those tantalizing over-the-shoulder kisses.

"Not that tired," he rasped.

Billy moved to the front of the kitchen chair and offered his hand for help up. Sean took it, not because he needed the help, Billy thought, but because he appreciated the offer.

And because it brought them up close and personal and made it easier to kiss.

Oh, he tasted good. Their lips started out soft and tender as Billy let himself be walked backward down the hallway, but as they neared the bedroom, Sean's hands found Billy's bare skin under his T-shirt and fleece, and Billy was suddenly quivering, wanting this more than he could ever imagine wanting before.

Sure he'd been turned on—had made a career of it in fact—but that need, that craving in the pit of his stomach for just *this* touch, just *this* lover, surely that was new. It felt new. Like sex was a thing he'd never heard of and he couldn't wait to know what happened next.

Sean paused in the doorway, kissing along his jaw, moving his lips down Billy's neck, licking along the line of his collarbone, and Billy gasped.

No! No, he had to be in control. He couldn't let Sean take over. Sex was *his* thing.

With an effort he pulled away and captured Sean's mouth again, his hands moving surely under Sean's sweatshirt. He pulled it over Sean's head, careful of the bandage that they still protected from the shower, and turned so Sean was the one being backed to the bed.

"Okay," Sean murmured, reaching behind him to pull down the covers. "Okay."

"Okay what?" Billy needed to touch him, needed it so badly he almost couldn't breathe. He ran his hands up and down Sean's back, then down under the waistband of his pajamas, thrusting under the pants and the boxers and kneading his backside.

Sean moaned and ground up against him, his own hands worming under Billy's clothes again to palm his chest.

"Okay, you can be in charge this time," Sean told him. "Okay."

Billy paused, suddenly pulled out of their moment. "I... I didn't mean—"

Sean captured his mouth again, and Billy was lost, lost and needing and almost out of control once again.

Well, he *did* know what he was doing, after all.

He sank into the kiss, shoving Sean's clothes down his legs and then crouching to strip them off. Sean's cock smacked against his thigh, thick, turgid, and ready.

So pretty. Straight, flushed pink with a purple head, Billy took it into his mouth and down his throat with one thrust, the fullness against his palate comforting. All of him—Billy could take all of him.

He pulled back and swallowed him again, reveling in Sean's fingers tightening in his hair as Sean gasped.

"Gotta sit down," Sean murmured. "Let me—"

Billy pulled off and gave him a playful glare. "Lay down and spread your legs," he ordered gruffly. "Bend your knees a little. I'm gonna make this good."

Sean did as he was told, and by the time Billy had stripped off his shirts and his jeans and briefs, Sean was spread out on the bed like an offering—and Billy wanted to take him so damned bad.

He started out a little slow, kissing from Sean's ankles up his calves and spending a moment on the inside of his knees. Sean laughed a little and gasped a little, protesting at the same time he spread his legs wider.

Good.

"Tickle?" Billy asked, moving his mouth up along the inside of Sean's thigh.

"Yes," Sean breathed.

"Do you like being tickled?" Billy taunted.

"Not when I'm hoping to get—" Realization seemed to set in. "Oh God. I'm going to get fucked. You want to fuck me. God yes."

Billy ran his tongue carefully up and down Sean's inner thigh, scooting up on the bed and grinding his own cock into the mattress as he flicked his tongue out to tease the base of Sean's.

"You really want that?" Billy asked, tonguing his shaft again and palming Sean's thighs to spread them a little more.

"It's terrifying," Sean admitted. "Yes, please."

Billy chuckled and tongued his cock again, this time pulling the head into his mouth and sucking on him.

Sean squirmed on the sheets, bucking his hips, and Billy pulled off immediately.

"Nah-nah," he whispered. "No doing that."

"Please?" Sean begged. He let his knees fall open completely, and Billy practically melted. He loved seeing men like this. Loved having their most vulnerable parts on display for him to touch, to suck, to lick.

It was the one time in his life he felt powerful, and for it to be a man he cared about….

He felt like king of the world.

His palms were already on the inside of Sean's thighs, so he slid them lower, parting Sean's cheeks and exposing his taint and his little pink asshole.

This man had not been fucked enough, he decided, and licked lazily down Sean's crease. Sean gasped and thrust his hips again, and Billy grasped his shaft firmly as he continued to lick.

He really loved rimming a guy. Loved watching him fall apart, loved penetrating him with his fingers slick with lubricant. Having his fingers inside somebody as they stroked their own cock was enough to bring him close. He was doing something powerful, something important to their bodies, and he had the control to make it amazing.

"Need the lube," he commanded and paused to watch Sean stretch his arm over his head, making sure there were no hitches or hisses in pain.

Nope, and Sean must have planned for this. The bottle was under his pillow, and Billy knew for a fact it had been in the bedstand that morning because he'd checked to see if they'd need any since Sean's ex had cleaned the place out.

Apparently not of everything.

Billy took the handoff and clicked the bottle cap, dumped some on his fingers before snicking it closed again and fingering Sean's hole gently. Sean moaned and reached for his cock, but Billy caught his hand.

"No coming," he commanded, and he heard the faint tremor in his own voice. "I need to be inside you. I need to see."

"No coming," Sean mumbled, but his hand was shaking, and Billy wasn't sure he could keep that promise.

He'd try. That's all Billy needed.

Gently, he helped Sean wrap his fingers around his shaft, and then he went back to fingering him, stretching him, tonguing his balls and sucking them delicately, one at a time, into his mouth.

"Guillermo?" Sean rasped, his fist tightening around his cock, his cockhead bulging purple from the circle of his thumb and forefinger. "Guillermo, please."

Oh, there was something about hearing his name—his *real* name—in the earned intimacy of Sean's bedroom that made his pulse quicken.

He'd wanted to overpower, to rule, to possess, but he hadn't counted on needing to be inside Sean as much as Sean needed him inside.

He scissored his fingers gently and lifted up on his elbows. "You ready?" he asked, totally serious. "I… I'm an assful, Sean. If you're not ready—"

"Please, Guillermo," Sean moaned. "I need you. Go slow, but please…."

Billy added lubricant to his cock, not wanting this to hurt even a little. He pulled himself up into position, careful not to crush Sean's torso or his lungs. With a grunt, he grabbed a pillow from under Sean's head and thrust it under his hips, opening Sean's body for him and leaving his breathing and lungs clear before finding Sean's stretched, ready hole and thrusting slowly in.

It was a good thing Sean had relearned how to breathe.

Billy watched him work to pull in oxygen as Billy shoved out everything but sex with his cock.

Oh man. Tight, slick, warm, Sean's body sheathed him, protected him as nothing else ever had. Billy found himself shaking and absolutely needed to move.

"Please?" he begged, surprised to hear the word coming from his mouth.

"Yeah," Sean whispered, stroking his shoulders as he wrapped his legs around Billy's hips. "Go."

Slowly at first—so slowly. Sean groaned, he begged, he pleaded, but Billy couldn't make himself go any faster.

He absolutely must not hurt this man.

Finally he was seated all the way in. And he had no choice but to pull out again, all but the tip, and then thrust inside again.

Out and in.

Oh God. It was a rhythm as old as the seas, but until this moment, this moment here, sheathed inside someone he cared about more than he'd ever imagined, he hadn't recognized how destructive it could be if unleashed without control.

He fucked slowly, and then as Sean started thrashing on the sheets beneath him, his fair skin flushing with their sex, he fucked a little faster. Sean's cries grew hoarse and breathless, and Billy grabbed Sean's hand, which had fallen limp at his side, and wrapped it around his cock again, urging him to stroke.

They could do this. They could come to completion without hurting Sean's healing wound. They could—

"Ah!" Sean arched, and the ripple through his body took him slowly as a long jet of come arced from his cock. His ass tightened around Billy's cock, and climax rushed Billy like a tidal surge or a freight train or a comet hurtling to destroy. It took over his body, blew out his circuits, blanked his mind, and he started to spurt, coming again and again until he was left convulsing in his lover's body, at a complete loss for control, overwhelmed and powerless at the roll of emotion coursing through a heart and mind he thought he knew so well.

He barely had the energy to push himself to the side, his cock disengaging slowly, still caught in the clench of Sean's ass.

He lay there for a moment, chest heaving, shoulders shaking, fighting the temptation to sob with surprise and confusion.

"Hey," Sean said, his own chest heaving. Tentatively he reached up and pushed Billy's hair off his forehead. "You good?"

Billy nodded and gave in to the impulse to capture Sean's hand and kiss the fingertips. "Just… just sex isn't like this," he managed.

Sean nodded, one corner of his mouth quirking up. "Great, you mean? 'Cause…." He gave a sensual little stretch, his hips and groin undulating provocatively. "That was great. We'll have to wash that pillowcase, but, uhm, *great*."

Billy smiled faintly, still at a loss. "You… uhm, your chest, your lungs—you all okay?"

"Yeah," Sean said softly. "Still catching my breath, but yeah."

"Good." Billy let out a soft sound of wanting and decided to fuck it all. "'Cause I need to hold you."

"Good," Sean whispered, and rolled gingerly into his arms. Against Billy's chest he murmured, "I really wanted to be held."

Somehow that moment, holding Sean in his arms, listening to the true miracle of his breath, seemed more significant than the sex.

Except the sex was hugely important, and that was *boggling*.

"Hey," Sean said while Billy crushed him into his chest. "What's wrong? Are you sorry?"

"No. Not sorry. Not for that."

"Then what—"

"Just hush, okay? Just…."

"Yeah. Okay."

Billy didn't have any words. None at all. What was the use of having sex like that, he thought wretchedly, if he had no words to explain how it was different from all the other sex he'd ever had?

SEAN FELL asleep against him, and Billy wriggled out of his embrace to put on his briefs and go around the house turning off lights and locking the doors. A part of him told him to put on sweats and stay up late, studying to write a paper due the next week, but that's not what he really wanted to do.

What he really wanted to do was slide back into bed next to Sean and hold him some more, and sleep. Just this once it would be worth it to save his homework for the weekend and hold Sean's pliant body next to his.

When he crawled back into bed, Sean snuggled into his body, trusting and happy, and Billy wondered, *What do I have to do to earn this?*

"OH GOD," Billy muttered the next evening as he piloted Sean's Charger through the suburbs to his mother's house. "This is a mistake. We didn't even get our stories straight!"

Sean snorted. "About what?" he asked.

Billy gave him a sideways look, checking to see if the fatigue that had dogged him all morning had finally been napped away. The day before had been busy, and the lovemaking had been strenuous, and Billy had called a moratorium on the park that morning.

"You can make phone calls," he'd decided while Sean gaped at him in irritation. "And I'll get my homework done, and you might not have to fall asleep at my mommy's kitchen table."

Sean had fumed, but in the end he'd conceded, and Billy reflected that maybe—just maybe—it was a sign of how much the guy respected Billy's judgment—and Billy himself—that he was willing to put up with all Billy's shit.

But Billy wasn't willing to put up with much backtalk. The texts coming to them about Rivers weren't encouraging. Henry had put out that he was sick and cranky, and that Ellery had his hands full over the weekend, and Sean's partner, Christie, had said the entire department was running around like a kicked hornet's nest because Ellery had implicated the four officers who had hurt his client—and Jackson—during the trial. Henry had asked Billy if maybe he could take Sean over to Rivers's place on Monday because Jackson wasn't looking like he'd be up to going back to the office by then, and that way he'd have company.

At first Sean had chafed at that. He felt like Rivers should have the chance to work if he felt like it, but Henry had actually *called* him and

told him that Rivers did not have the sense God gave a goat when it came
to his own help, and that he'd needed keepers the night before because
Ellery and Jade had been going to a political function and they didn't
want him home alone.

Billy hadn't heard all of the conversation then, but when Sean hung
up, he'd looked troubled.

"What's wrong?"

"You forget, don't you? That every cut leaves a scar. I don't know
all the shit going on with him, but you know he avoids hospitals like the
plague. They give him panic attacks."

Billy cocked his head. "Didn't he visit *you* when you were in the
hospital?"

Sean nodded. "Yeah. Because that's the kind of loyalty you get
when you're his friend. Best to return that if you can."

Billy chuckled. "Good, because Henry told *me* that they picked up
a dog on their last adventure, and the guys at the flophouse have been
trying to take care of it. Apparently they put down a pad for him to piddle
on, but he whines until they take him outside, and Henry says all the guys
love him, but they're afraid the little dude is getting freaked out with
all the people coming and going. He was sort of hinting… you know…
since you've got a little yard in the back…."

Sean had groaned. "God, is it a you kind of dog or a me kind of
dog?" he asked suspiciously.

"It's a me kind of dog," Billy told him. "Which is good because
you've got a me kind of dog kind of yard. But it might not happen. It's
all still in flux, right?"

Sean nodded. "But, uhm. A dog. That would be… you know. When
I go back to work. Company when I'm not home. Someone to take to
the park." He'd given a brief, almost pleading, smile, and Billy realized
what he was really asking.

"Yeah. Walks to the park might be even better with a dog," Billy
said. "Even a temporary dog."

And that had seemed to sober both of them.

So preoccupied with that, it hadn't even occurred to Billy that he
and Sean would need to agree on their stories about Billy's job. About
his life in general.

And it didn't help that Sean was super casual about it either.

"Our stories?" he asked now in the car. "Like how you're rooming with a bunch of college students to save the rent, but now that you've tasted the delights of my spare bedroom, you might move out?"

Billy snorted. "I thought we were boyfriends," he said, and then hurriedly backed that up with, "at least for my mommy."

"We can be boyfriends in real life too," Sean said softly.

"We are," Billy conceded. "I just... uhm don't want to... you know...."

"Tell everybody in the flophouse and announce you're moving out and ready to quit porn," Sean said with a sigh. "I get it, Billy. But we're not going to tell your mother that. We're going to say you were living with a bunch of other college students when Henry asked if you'd want to help me out to get a break on the rent. It's pretty much the truth—"

"Except Rivers was the one who asked," Billy pointed out.

"Yeah, but Rivers makes things complicated. Henry used to room with you, now he's got his own place, an interesting job, that sort of thing."

"Yeah, that's great. But what do I tell her about *me*?"

Sean let out a breath. "That you're still gay. That your first boyfriend moved away and waiting tables alone wasn't enough to make the rent. That you've played the field, and now you and I are sort of a thing. None of that is a lie, Guillermo. None of that should make you ashamed." He paused. "*Are* you ashamed? Because you shouldn't be. You fed yourself. You paid rent. You hurt nobody. And you stayed safe."

Billy grunted. "You do realize... I mean, you *know* sometimes we went out there and sold it, right?"

Sean grunted in return. "I thought maybe," he said softly. "It's... well, it follows sometimes."

"Still safe," Billy assured him, feeling low, lower than low, even if Sean never once tried to make him feel like that.

"Billy, I'm not going to tell your mother anything you don't want me to. I promise, sweetheart. I won't betray you."

Billy fought the absurd urge to cry. "I... I don't know how to thank you for that," he said hoarsely.

"Trust me," Sean said simply. "I know your father was a bastard, and you haven't found someone to believe in since then, but maybe... maybe... you could trust me?"

Billy let out a breath. Wasn't that what it came down to?

"I'm trying so hard," he whispered. "I don't know why this is so hard."

Sean let out a short laugh. "Because we're human. We just are. You've got a guarded heart, Billy. You learned early not to leave any part of you out there to get wounded. It's kept you alive, and I get it. But… but…." His voice dropped. "Last night meant a lot to me. I think it meant a lot to you. If we're going to build on that, you've got to trust that I won't throw you away, right?"

"Yeah," he said, swallowing.

And then Sean said the thing that made it click. "Like you feel like *they* threw you away," he said softly. "You were their rock, Guillermo. Don't think I don't know that. You kept all the kids in line, and you kept your dad away from them. Took the worst of the bad shit. And they found out the one thing about you they didn't like, and that was it—ripped out of their lives. And you make a good show of it, but it hurt you. It hurt you bad enough that you backed away from the kids at the flophouse, even though every instinct you've ever had was probably screaming to step in and be an older brother. But you were done with that, because it only ended up hurting, am I right?"

Billy grunted because hey, that was even deeper than his shrink had gotten in the last few months.

"And you tried to make your body perfect, because that, at least, you could control," Sean finished on a rush.

Billy took a moment at a stoplight to scowl at him.

Sean scowled back. "Am I wrong?"

"No," Billy muttered, looking back at the road. "I don't like talking about it."

"I get that," Sean said softly. "But you're going to have to figure out how to negotiate those waters, because your mom's going to want to know why you're not eating her food."

Billy groaned slightly. "I've got a scene next week," he muttered. "I should start fasting on Monday!"

Sean *hmm*ed noncommittally, and Billy let out a frustrated groan. He was hurting Sean with this—he knew it, and while he admired Sean's refusal to force a decision, he almost wanted it. Did he really have to be the grown-up about this?

Except the answer to that question was yes. And so was the answer to all the questions he had now. Keeping his family in the dark about what he did was a valid choice, but if he made that choice he was going to have to stick with it. He didn't want to hurt his mother—and frankly he didn't want to open himself up to more hurt. He was just so thrilled to have his family back again. He felt like he needed to make sure they wouldn't… what had Sean said?

Throw him away?

"Gah!" he groaned. "Why are you so good at adulting!"

Sean's laughter was bitter. "Billy, you've heard me talk to my mother for nearly six weeks now. Have I even once told her about Jesse?"

Billy's answer was a growl because he hadn't even met the guy, but he *hated* that guy.

"Yeah, no," Sean answered for him. "So I get not telling your mother everything, even if your family is super tight knit. Just, whatever story you're going to give, make sure you stick to it. I'll back whatever play you make."

Billy let out a groan, and then, almost like his hand had taken over because his brain seemed stuck on Neanderthal noises, he reached out and grabbed Sean's hand as it rested on his thigh and squeezed.

Sean squeezed back, and that was sort of the end of conversation for the rest of the trip.

He remembered that moment in bed when he'd said, "Sex isn't like this." He was starting to understand that sex may actually *be* like that, all-encompassing and all-consuming when there were whole lives attached.

Color him surprised.

Outside Observations

BILLY'S MOTHER was like the female mold for all the women in his family, Sean thought. Five two to five four, with dark glossy hair that might be streaked or dyed blond but definitely could not be tamed, as well as wide hips, tiny feet, Billy's enormous limpid eyes, tiny noses, and smiles that could knock a cat off a wall from fifty feet away.

Beautiful—his mother, Lucia, his sisters, Teresa, Lily, and Cora—all four of them were simply stunning, and as they gathered around Billy, hugging him and burbling mostly in Spanish about how much they'd missed him, Sean understood to the bottom of his toes where Billy's no-nonsense brand of dishing out orders must have come from.

There was a lot of maternal chaos in that room.

His brother Miguel was there, hanging with Teresa's husband, Alexei, and Sean sensed a deep bonding between the two men in the room that he could appreciate.

Roberto—or Robert, apparently—was not there.

But as Lucia led them into the living room, where battered couches vied for space with a battered recliner, desk chairs scavenged from the kid's rooms, and kitchen chairs, so that everybody had a place to sit, Lucia was full of nothing but praise for her second-oldest son, who, she said, had helped her make rent and car payments with his business walking dogs.

"He's really been a miracle, Guillermo," Lucia told them, smiling through tired eyes. "I'm still working at the hospital—they always need nurses—but your brother got us through some tough times in the last months."

"Fuckin' Dad," Miguel muttered. "I can't even believe him!"

Lucia sent her son an unhappy look, but she didn't seem to have any defense for her ex-husband.

"What did he do?" Billy asked. "I mean, you're divorced, right?"

Lucia nodded, but Lily was the one who spoke up. "Mom didn't change all her bank codes when they first split, right after you left, Ghee. She got back from the hospital, Dad was still on a bender, and she had us grab our clothes and then moved us out and found this dump before he even knew what she'd planned."

Teresa, who was perched on the arm of the recliner, which Lucia was sitting in, reached down to grab her mother's hand. "Mommy was really brave," she said softly, glancing at Billy with pleading in her eyes. "She told us all that she wouldn't live with any man who had done what he'd done to you, Ghee, and who would chase one of her children away. But Dad...." All the kids in the room shuddered, but their mother kept her expression carefully blank. Sean had checked out his share of domestic dispute calls, and he had seen that expression on the faces of abuse survivors. He looked at Billy, sitting next to him on the couch, and saw an identical expression.

Billy had borne the brunt of the abuse, along with his mother, until that final beating when he'd been kicked out —Sean had known that— but sitting in this spotless house with the spare furnishings and eclectic decorations, Sean could see the enormity of Billy's childhood hit him.

Sean didn't know what Billy's rules for holding hands in front of his family might be, so he very carefully shifted his weight until their thighs were touching. It was casually done. It might have happened to any two people sitting on the broken couch, but if Billy needed it, Sean's warmth was right there.

As if reading his intentions, Billy reached over and grabbed Sean's hand, apparently almost without thinking. Sean laced their fingers and allowed himself to be pulled back into the family, this time knowing his touch was anchoring Billy to the here and now instead of letting him get lost in the past.

"What did he do?" Billy asked, voice hard.

"He waited until I had some money saved," Lucia said bitterly. "By the beginning of this summer I was going to try to get a house— get a loan. I was getting my paperwork in order, and suddenly my savings disappeared. I have no idea how he got my passwords and bank information. I know Teresa thinks I didn't, but I could have sworn I changed everything. There should have been no loopholes, but it was gone. Roberto—I mean Robert—called him up and said he'd confirmed everything." She shook her head. "Oh, your brother was so angry. *So* angry. But we couldn't make it not happen. We couldn't press charges. The police wouldn't believe I hadn't given him the bank information in the first place. If Teresa hadn't gotten a job at the hospital as a ward clerk, we may have gotten evicted. And Roberto's job walking dogs was the only reason we ate for at least two months."

"Yeah," Miguel said. "And even that was sad. Somebody let one of the big dogs out. Robert was all ripped up about that, man. So pissed. Thought somebody in the neighborhood had let the dog out on purpose. It was sad. Berto—dammit, *Robert*—was really ripped up."

Sean couldn't help searching out Billy's gaze. "Sweaty?" he mouthed.

"Hey," Billy said, "was the dog named, uhm, Sweaty? Like after those books I read you guys?"

"Yeah," Teresa said, looking sad. "I think that's one of the reasons Robert missed that dog so bad." Once again she squeezed her mother's hand. "We missed you, Ghee—all of us. And… and once you were gone, it hit us. How much you'd been hiding from all of us. How much you'd held us all together. How hard that must have been."

Miguel snorted bitterly. "Yeah, until some ignorant pendejo put you out of your misery."

Billy gave him a sharp look. "That was *not* your fault, mijo. I never blamed you for that."

"Did you blame *me*?" Lucia asked softly, and Billy tightened his grip on Sean's hand.

Sean squeezed back again, and Billy looked his mother in the eye. "Yeah, mami, I did. You…."

"I let him," she said, her voice choked. "I was so afraid. But the kids missed you so badly, and I had time to realize how much I'd put on your back, you know? How much of the protecting you were doing, how much you'd kept from your father. All of it on your back, from the time you were younger than Cora to the time he… he beat you and turned you out with not much more than your schoolbooks. It's okay, *papacito*. You can be angry."

Sean heard his dry swallow. He remembered his own words about how porn was sometimes so much more than rent or sex for the people in it.

Sometimes, it was a way to be seen.

Guillermo Morales had not felt seen for much of his life, but he probably did right now. What would he do with that information? Would he shout, "I'm a porn star!" like he'd threatened, and bolt out of the room? Would he give his mother absolution? Sometimes being seen wasn't comfortable—or comforting. Sometimes there were too many shadows in the heart that people wanted hidden.

"Thanks, mami," Billy said faintly. "I'm... I'm working on it."

His grip on Sean's hand tightened to the point of pain, but Sean wouldn't have let go for the world.

Into the uncomfortable silence, Teresa spoke, and Sean smiled gratefully at her. "So, Ghee, you gonna tell us what you been doing over the last three years? Enquiring minds want to know!"

Billy gave Sean a sideways glance, but he stuck to the script. He'd sought out Sam, they'd shared an apartment, and after Sam moved on, he'd survived on tips and student loans and had roomed with a bunch of guys in a flop.

His family didn't seem to see anything amiss with this, and Billy's grip on his hand eased up a little bit. In a moment, he asked how Teresa and Alexei had met, and then about Lily and Cora's grades and whether Miguel was doing any sports in school, and by the time dinner was served—pot luck style in the tiny kitchen/dining room so they could all eat in the living room—Sean could feel Billy's complete relaxation into "Guillermo, the good son," and knew that for the moment, he would be all right.

"MY GOD," Sean muttered as he loosened his belt on the way home, "you weren't kidding about how your mom could cook."

The family had left Sean alone for the most part. In a way, he figured he was window dressing, Billy's boyfriend, proving Guillermo was doing okay and living a stable life for the family that hadn't seen him. But being left alone during a chatty dinner where everybody caught up with everybody else's business meant Sean's only entertainment was his next forkful, and, well, Lucia could cook.

"Yeah," Billy laughed gruffly. "Be careful. My mom's table can be dangerous that way."

"Hm." There was a thoughtful silence, and Sean thought he'd escaped all the emotional landmines, but then Billy spoke up again.

"What did you think?" he asked, his voice suddenly young. "About my family? You were quiet, but I get it. I think we snark a lot at each other, but we don't talk a lot."

"I think your family was lovely," Sean said, meaning it. "In fact, I think they're a lot like mine. Loud and obnoxious and in each other's business and… and important. I think it must feel good to hear that they cared that you'd gone. That they missed you." There was more, but he wasn't sure if Billy was ready to go there.

"Then why do you look so pissed off?" Billy asked, which meant apparently he *was* ready to go there, and Sean wasn't sure if he was going to be okay with that.

Sean let out a breath. "Because they took you for granted," he said bitterly. "From the time you were a baby. And I get it. The oldest gets the burden, but you took care of the little kids and you protected everyone from your father and nobody noticed until you were gone, and… and you deserved better. You deserved to be *celebrated* before you even left. So I'm pissed for you. And you may never be pissed about this, but I am, and you know what else? If I ever meet your father, I'm going to pin his balls together with his service medal. So there's that. And now you are aware."

Billy let out half a laugh. "Well, my dad's gonna look great next to your ex-boyfriend, because someday I'm gonna pin *his* balls together with his badge. They can be a matched set."

Sean shook his head. "Your old man's got a lot more to answer for than Jesse the douche. I'm telling you, Ghee, there's something very calculated about how he ripped off your mom. I…." He didn't want to say this because Billy might not have thought about it yet.

"I wonder if one of the little kids helped him," Billy said thoughtfully.

Sean must have made a sound of surprise because Billy shrugged.

"Yeah, it occurred to me. You… I mean, you probably don't know how this works. Everyone was afraid of the bastard, but the little kids, they wanted a father too, so they were always trying to please him. And he'd play them like little dolls. 'Yeah, kid, your mother was bad, but I'll be nice to you since you got me a beer.' Berto, he was the worst."

"Robert," Sean corrected almost absently.

Billy shook his head. "Nope. Unless the little shit can show up and give me his new name, he's gonna be Roberto the squid to me, just like when he was a little kid."

Sean made a pained sound. "You know, growing up with an abusive parent—"

"Yeah, yeah," Billy said with disgust. "Doesn't breed heroes, I get it. But he was my shitty little brother, and if he wants me to think of him like a grown-up, he's gotta be a grown-up to me, and that's the truth. If I could come back and see the family, the least he could do was be there to curse me out or whatever."

Nobody had given them an explanation for why Roberto hadn't been there, and Sean felt a deep stirring in his gut, an unsupported hunch that he was unwilling to voice.

God, Billy was only now trusting him. Did he really want to jeopardize that with an unsupported hunch?

"Your mom wants to see you once a month," Sean said instead. "I'm sure you'll run into him. I mean, Thanksgiving and shit."

Billy gnawed on his lip and made the final turn into Sean's neighborhood. As he came to a stop in Sean's driveway, he murmured, "I… I think Thanksgiving needs to be with the flophouse this year," he said, almost to himself.

"Oh," Sean said, voice neutral. It *was* nearing the end of October, and Halloween was just around the corner. There were already decorations up in the front yards of Sean's neighborhood—some of them quite elaborate: skeleton tableaux, ghosts in trees, the big inflatable characters. Thanksgiving was also just around the corner, and Sean had rather been hoping for a reason not to have to drive to Turlock this year to watch his mother suck up to his sisters and sister-in-law for grandmother privileges.

"You'd be with me," Billy said, the unconscious arrogance making Sean smile. "I'm not leaving you alone or to drive out to southeast of hell's asshole, or wherever your mother talks about driving in from."

"Turlock," Sean said dryly.

"South*west* of hell's asshole," Billy retorted. "I stand corrected." He raised the garage door, and they both were silent as he pulled in and then shut the door behind them. He killed the engine, and it was just the two of them with the silence and the honesty that had driven them since the day Billy had become his reluctant nurse—and then so much more.

"So," Sean said into the closeness of the garage, "why are we going to the flophouse for Thanksgiving?"

Billy swallowed. "Because… because I think, no matter what happens between you and me, I think it might be my last Thanksgiving and Christmas with these particular brothers." He let out a sigh. "That doesn't mean I won't see them again. I mean, I'm tight with everyone except Vinnie, the new guy, really, but see?" He turned in his seat. "We're all moving on. Me and Curtis are going to Sac State next fall, instead of Sac City. Cotton's going down south to nursing school. And even if Randy's stuck in porn for a while, I think he's going to find his way too. He's ready to grow up—you can see it."

Sean nodded. "Yeah," he agreed softly.

"And for two years these guys were my family. I mean, there were others. We might ask Zep and Fisher if they wanna come by. You wouldn't know those guys—they left in July. But...."

"It's like college graduation," Sean said, getting it. "Your guys are graduating, and things are going to change."

Billy nodded. His eyes, when they fell on Sean's face, were bright and shiny. "It's getting time for us all to grow up," he said. "Last night? You and me? That was... that was grown-up. That was so much more important in my heart than anything else I've ever done with my body. I... I can't go back after that. I can't move back into the flophouse and fuck everything with knees again. It would *dishonor* that thing we did last night. You understand?"

Sean's throat tightened, his chest too. For a moment, he was back to six weeks ago, where he could barely breathe. "I do," he rasped.

"But...." Billy bit his lip. "This is gonna sound stupid to you, but this last scene.... I promised Dex and John. I mean, guys bail on their contracts all the time, but you saw." He looked away. "You saw my family, all the fuckin' promises my dad made that he tried to keep with a backhand or a sock to the stomach. Johnnies—they've done me better than that." He grunted. "Besides, I'm still getting my health insurance from them. I need at least two months to figure out how to stay with this shrink, 'cause I'm telling you, if I hadn't wired your duplex for sound, I'd be destroying your plumbing tonight." He put his hand on his stomach. "I am *not* feeling good about everything I ate, and my usual MO for that sort of thing was to throw it all up."

Sean wondered if there was any sort of safety device he needed for that roller-coaster drop in the conversation. "That's both appalling and good to know," he said, mildly nauseated now himself.

Billy rolled his eyes. "Yeah, but you yelled at me about my heart, and I've already got one big lie in with my family that I refuse to correct. I need to learn how to just kick back with an antacid and learn moderation," he said.

Amen to that. "Yeah," Sean said, his mouth twitching up for a moment. Then because it needed to be said, "And last night was important to me too. I usually work over Thanksgiving, but this is my first year as a detective, so I think Andre was going to have me over. But...." His smile reached a little further this time. "I'm so excited to be planning holidays with you. I know it's stupid, but it anticipates us being together when they come."

Billy's expression grew suddenly sober. "We're doing this, aren't we?"

Sean nodded. "Yeah. We're doing this."

The soberness turned to a frown. "Are we telling people? Are you telling Christie or Rivers? Do I tell the flophouse?"

"We do what we do," Sean said. "People will figure it out."

Billy shook his head. "So secret, right? Until you trust me."

Sean blinked. "No. No, that's not—"

"It's fine," Billy said, and the hell of it was, he didn't sound resentful in the least. He sounded like he'd expected this. "Just... you know." And those cynical eyes with that hard jaw were suddenly vulnerable and soft and absolutely naked. "Let me know if you need me to move out or anything."

Oh God. "C'mere," Sean murmured, leaning forward to kiss him. A kiss. Another. And more. Billy pulled back with a groan, leaning his forehead against Sean's as they steamed the car's windows.

"We should go inside," Billy panted.

"Yeah, but you gotta know.... I'm not going to make you leave, Billy. You have the spare room. It's yours. You have my bed, for as long as you want it. It's yours. I—"

"I have a scene this week," Billy said bleakly. "You... you can't make promises about anything until you know how you feel about that scene. You can't." His voice rose sharply, and Sean realized how much this had been haunting him. "I can't take it if—"

If someone he was regarding as family rejected him.

"Then let's go to bed," Sean murmured. "And when the scene comes and goes and we're still standing, we're still here, then you'll believe me, okay?"

"Don't you want me to be faithful?" Billy asked, his voice ringing bitterly. "Don't you want me to be yours?"

"*Of course I do!*" For once Sean was grateful for his injury because it kept him from shouting. He pulled in a painful breath—and then another. "Jesus, Billy, I don't like the idea of what you'll be leaving me to do. But right now, with you, it's better than… God. A thousand nights of Jesse going, 'At least I don't cheat,' or some guy I'm only sort of meh about talking about how our stock portfolios could let me retire early."

Billy pulled back and frowned. "You've had those dates? I thought they were only in sitcoms."

"Yes, I've had them, but *that is not the point*."

Billy swallowed. "What is the point?" he asked, suddenly very much in the moment.

"Do you think you're the only one who thought last night was special?" Sean whispered. "Do you think you're the only one who wants to plan for Thanksgiving? Or the future? Let's… let's do that. Yeah, relationships end. And yeah, we've got some roadblocks. But I think it's worth it to hope, right?"

A faint smile flirted with Billy's full mouth. "You don't look all happy and sweet, cop. But you've got a good heart."

"So do you," Sean told him. "Can we go inside and, you know, make more good moments to outweigh the bad?"

"Yeah." Billy grimaced and put his hand on his stomach then. "But, uhm, maybe some antacid and TV first. I'm sorry. It's funny how sex is something you do with your body and shit, but sometimes your body has way other ideas."

Sean laughed softly. "Guillermo, you are absolutely perfect. Please don't ever change."

"Whatever, man. Here, let me help you out."

Sean didn't really need the help—not tonight. But he loved the way Billy supported his weight, loved the way they ended up chest to chest, face-to-face. Loved the security of Billy's hands around his waist as he met Sean's mouth with his own.

They pulled away again, some of the sadness, the desperation brought on by their conversation fading with this unhurried kiss in the dark.

"I never knew how much I needed to feel safe," Billy said, "until I realized how much I wanted *this*, this thing with us, to not go away."

Sean leaned his head against Billy's shoulder. "I never realized how important it was to be a safe person until you said that."

They stayed there for a few more heartbeats before they made their way into the house.

THE NEXT morning, Sean walked steadily around the soccer field, Billy at his side, both immersed in their own thoughts. Sean wasn't sure what was in Billy's mind, but Sean's mind was a montage of making love the night before.

There had been no penetration—Sean was still a little sore, and Billy had muttered something about his "window at work."

"What do you mean, window?" Sean had asked, feeling stupid.

"No sex three days before or after," Billy said, shrugging. "I go in tomorrow to test." He let out a tiny, embarrassed sigh. "I think the time period is left over from when it took a lot longer to get results, but Dex and John say over and over again they really want us healthy."

Sean nodded and fell into the kiss again. They'd been on the couch, necking like teenagers in front of the television, and the moment had been so pure, so easy, he hadn't wanted to pull the painful things—Billy's job, his past, even his family—up to talk about.

He'd only wanted that kiss, that moment in time, that feeling of Billy's cock in his mouth, the joy of Billy's mouth on him. He'd wanted the pleasure of Billy's hands on his skin, the sensations of tongue and fist, finger, cock and... oh! Oh! Oh!

Climax, pain and stress free, the two of them twining on the couch, the gloriousness of them.

They'd stumbled down the hall naked after shutting off the lights, locking the door, closing the drapes, and then they'd brushed their teeth and slid into bed, almost tipsy on the lovemaking, on the aftermath of the painful conversation in the car.

Sean went to his customary side because he was used to sleeping that way now, and Billy spooned him, arm securely around his middle.

"Guillermo?" Sean had breathed as sleep took them both.

"Yeah?"

"I'm weak. This—what we just did—that was delicious. I don't want to lose this. I don't want to lose you snarking at me over breakfast. I don't want to lose you giving me shit and then being so sweet. Whatever

I have to do, whatever I have to say, I'll do and say it to keep this. To keep you here. I used to think it was a black-and-white line—cheating, no cheating—but the way you touch me, I've got to believe it's special."

"Oh God. So special," Billy had whispered. "Sean?"

"Yeah?"

"Keep calling me Guillermo, okay? I like the way you say it."

"Okay."

"But only between us. Because it's special. It's mine."

Sean smiled. "Okay."

"And you don't need to work so hard to keep me. I'm easy. You may be weak, but I'm easy. Remember that."

Sean had chuckled softly because Guillermo was anything but easy, and he wanted to say that. Wanted to tell him that he was prickly and independent and snarky, and Sean loved him anyway, but then there was the big scary word, the one he wasn't sure they should say yet, so he'd let the moment carry him off to sleep.

"What are you brooding over?" Billy asked now, catching up with him as he started his second loop.

"Did you have a nice talk?" Sean chided him. "Did Bob and Jim have good stuff to say?"

"Uh-huh. Bob's dog is getting fatter, Jim's dog is getting spazzier, and somebody broke into another house last night."

Sean tried not to trip over his own feet. "Dammit!"

Billy chuckled. "Thought you'd like that."

"Where was it?" Among other things, when Sean and Billy had put up their "murder board," they'd tried to anticipate where the next robbery might be.

"Exactly where you said," Billy said. "No dog, no man there at night, no cameras."

"What did they take?" Sean asked, regaining his stride around the park.

"Bicycles—nice ones," Billy said. "Two, three hundred dollars resale. Seriously."

Sean nodded. "This guy's smart," he said as they continued to charge their way around the path. "Nothing big enough for grand theft. Even the dirt bike—under a thousand dollars resale."

"So we gonna do some cop shit?" Billy asked, sounding excited. "Stakeout? Talking to bike shops? What?"

Sean was on the verge of breaking his heart and telling him they were probably going to turn this over to the property crimes division when his phone buzzed in his pocket. He pulled it out and frowned at the name on the screen before holding a finger up to Billy as he put it to his ear.

"Yeah, Ellery, what's up?"

"So how're you doing?"

Sean came to their usual bench and sank gratefully onto it. "Getting a little better," he said cautiously. "I can move. Why?"

"I know Henry asked you, but I'm making sure you're still up to babysit."

Sean frowned at Billy, who shrugged back. "Your boyfriend? I thought he was housebroken."

"You heard about Friday, I take it," Ellery asked, his voice flinty with that Boston accent and to the point because that was Ellery.

"Yeah," Sean said. "We heard. Why?"

Ellery let out a breath, and Sean heard the weariness in the sound. "This weekend was rough," he admitted. "Fever, chills, and God, the wound. It's a nightmare. Anyway, I don't want him home alone tomorrow. Since you're still convalescing, you know, I thought...."

Sean shrugged. "Yeah, we're planning to come over tomorrow. Rivers can beat the shit out of us on video games."

Billy's eyebrows went up. "That's unlikely," he said with a certain amount of swagger. He did love to practice, but Sean shook his head.

"Jackson's got his own control," he said, preparing the kid for disappointment. "I think he plays it in his sleep."

Billy's cackle could probably be heard over the phone. "Game *on!*"

Sean smiled. "Yeah," he said into the receiver. "It'll be fun. Pet the cats, give your boyfriend shit—it's all good."

The relief in Ellery's voice warmed him. "Thank you. Seriously, thank you. If I could lock him in the hospital until this is all over, I would, but...."

"Yeah," Sean said softly. "No worries. We'll be over around nine. How's that?"

"Perfect," Ellery said. "I leave at eight. I mean, how much trouble can he get into in an hour, right?" And before Sean could curse him out for jinxing the entire day, Ellery had hung up.

"What was that?" Billy asked. "Your voice got all quiet. What was that?"

Sean shrugged, still troubled about how much trouble Jackson could get up to on a day that ended in Y, and tried to work up the energy to stand up off the bench.

"He should be in the hospital," he said after deciding they'd wait five more minutes and see if maybe that pack of Chihuahuas would come say hi.

"You said he was really terrified of them," Billy remembered, and Sean nodded.

"He's got history."

Billy frowned. "You mean last year when he caught the Dirty/ Pretty Killer?"

Sean laughed a little. "No, I mean ten years ago, when he was shot by a sniper because he'd worn a wire on his partner for three months, and the DA he was turning evidence over to decided to take over his partner's drug and prostitution ring and take Rivers out in the process."

Billy's jaw had literally dropped. "Oh my God. For real?"

Sean stared at him. "You didn't know this?"

"Oh my God. Wasn't the Dirty/Pretty Killer enough?"

Well, it had been a pretty spectacular story, but Rivers had been in the hospital while all the media excitement had gone on.

"It should have been," Sean agreed. "But you know. The guy keeps trying to be Superman in Batman's body. Anyway, Ellery was making sure we could show on Monday. Because Jackson should still be in a hospital, but dollars to donuts he's going to try to follow a lead or something while we're there tomorrow."

Billy nodded, then smiled as the Chihuahuas came up to them, standing on their little hind legs to sniff at their hands. "I'll be strong," he said, but Sean could tell he wasn't convinced.

"We'll both have to stay strong," Sean warned him. "Because you've met the man. He's sort of a force of nature."

And that was how Sean planned to deal with Rivers. Stay strong, say no, keep the guy from running into danger. That was what he resolved to do as he bent down to pet the delicate little dog-goobers who were looking to sit on their laps.

HIS FIRST inkling that that plan might get kicked out the window came at seven the next morning, when Andre called him, sounding stressed.

"You'll never guess where the DA sent us this morning," he snarled into the phone.

"Hell? Purgatory? Bakersfield?" Sean asked groggily in return.

"Worse. Cramer and Rivers's place."

Sean sat up too fast and hissed. "Because why?"

"Because the DA is dirty, Sean. I get you haven't seen it—you've been on medical leave since the guy got put in office. But he's dirty, and Charlie Boehner got capped last night, and Cartman the crooked DA is trying to pin it on Rivers."

Sean slow blinked. "That's unlikely." There was no way Rivers would even know the president of the policeman's union. For one thing, everybody's favorite ex-cop and PI was persona non grata at the department. True, Jackson had been making goodwill inroads after Ellery started his own firm, starting with Sean himself, but a guy with his history had an automatic handicap when dealing with the department.

"I know it's unlikely," Christie snapped. "But this entire morning has been a trip to banana-bonkers land. De Souza and I got kicked *off a crime scene* to drive across town to interview a guy who could barely move, to see if he shot a guy he didn't know in the middle of the night. Rivers had a bombproof alibi, though, so it's okay."

"He's sleeping with Ellery Cramer?" Sean hazarded. Ellery's integrity was rock solid.

"Even better. He was up at fuck thirty in the morning playing video games. We have his times *and* his prints on his personal controller as proof."

Sean snorted, thinking he'd like to see Billy's face when he heard *this*. "Does he ever sleep?"

Andre made a pained sound. "It didn't look like he did last night. He's looked better. I'm giving you the heads-up because I understand you're babysitting?"

"Yeah, why?"

"Because de Souza and I are going back to the crime scene after a stop at the station. Thought you might want to come by. You know, get Rivers some… perspective."

Sean's eyes popped open, and all vestiges of sleep went away. A case. A real one—no matter how sideways he was involved.

"We're going to be at his place at nine. I'll see what he says and text you."

"Your nurse gonna be with you?" Andre asked.

Sean looked to where Billy was propped up on his elbow, those remarkable eyes sharp with listening to his side of the conversation. "Yeah, why?"

Andre voice went from hard and "cop mode" to personal. "'Cause you're still not a hundred percent, and I know he won't let you overdo it. Text me. Keep Rivers alive. See you later."

"So what's doin'?" Billy asked. "And come back to bed for a minute. There needs to be a snuggle."

Sean grinned at him and did as he asked. "Not too much of this," he warned, enjoying Billy's chest and his kiss on the temple. "We can't be late to go meet Rivers."

"Why? What was that about?"

Warm and secure and rested, Sean explained the situation, and Billy even laughed at the part where Rivers *did* have his own personal gaming controls. But when Sean wrapped it up, ready to go shower, Billy made him pause.

"This was your union president?" he asked for clarification.

"Yeah."

"You don't seem all broken up about it."

Sean's face got grim. "He wasn't a very good person," Sean said. "He wasn't taking our department in a good direction. I know it sounds bad, but I'm not sorry he's dead."

Billy nodded. "Maybe I need to get better at politics so I can keep up with which cops are good cops and which ones aren't."

Sean smiled at him, feeling a little dazzled. So cute, so smart, so cynical—it was like he'd been made for Sean. "Just remember I'm a good one," he said soberly.

Billy nodded. "Yeah, cop. I'll do that."

He kissed Sean on the temple, and it was time to start their day.

Reckoning

BILLY GLANCED at Sean, sitting in the passenger's seat on the way home from Jackson's house with a tiny brown dog cuddled in his arms, and tried not to be too mad.

It had been one hell of a day.

Sure, yeah, let's go babysit the guy on medical leave—it'll be a blast! He thought sardonically.

Except Sean had gotten that phone call in the morning, and by the time they'd gotten to Ellery Cramer's *very nice* house on American River Drive, their easy morning had been rewritten into fifty-dozen stops, including one in which a very sweet woman who reminded him of his sister Teresa had fed them *pan dolce* and horchata, and another in which Sean snuck him inside a crime scene and tried to triangulate a sniper's bullet.

The whole thing had ended back at Cramer and Rivers's place with everybody—like *everybody from the flophouse*—frantically searching through traffic footage looking for the guy who'd killed a guy that Sean had proclaimed a political douchebag who made the police look worse than they already did.

Billy understood none of it. Oh yeah, he understood his specific tasks.

"Here, look through the window and see where the red laser pointer goes!"

Well, that was easy; it landed on Henry's shirt half a mile away. Even through the binoculars, Billy had seen Henry almost shit his pants when that little red dot showed up on his chest. It would have been high comedy, except he and Sean had been standing in a room that still had a bloodstain from the last guy who'd seen the little red laser pointer dot on his chest. They'd felt bad for scaring Henry, even with a little pencil light.

"Here, pick up some Chinese food while we gather everybody from the flophouse to study traffic cam footage to see who might have killed the guy from half a mile away!"

Done. Billy even knew where the place was that had the vegan noodles, although he was a little bit surly that he couldn't eat any, since he'd pretty much pushed his window with the pan dolce that morning. He'd gotten a carton of veggies and figured a little bit of noshing on that was what he usually ate three days before a scene, so it should be fine.

"Here, look for someone suspicious on the traffic cam footage on your laptop, with all your flophouse friends!"

Well, that had been easy, and fun, really, like a work party. The whole lot of them had been chatting back and forth while the tiny dog that Rivers and Henry had rescued had been passed from guy to guy, all of them trying to comfort the poor thing after he'd been separated from his owner in the mess that had gotten Jackson wounded in the first place.

So Billy had lots to do during the day, but none of it felt as if it was under his control.

Particularly watching Sean and Jackson exhaust themselves over this case.

In the end, it had been the animals that saved them.

Jackson Rivers was domesticated by two three-legged cats, one approximately Siamese in lineage named Billy Bob and one adolescent black cat named Lucifer. The cats got along—Billy Bob seemed content to be Lucifer's big brother—and together they stalked the house, being badasses of the feline variety. The small dog who had landed in Henry's custody on the night Rivers was wounded, however, had *not* been part of their little club.

Poppy had spent his time in Cramer's house being handed from lap to lap as they all concentrated on a variety of monitors at Cramer's kitchen table. One unwary person had set him down, and all hell broke loose.

Jackson had taken the cats to the bedroom to calm them down, and Billy had put the dog in Sean's lap and told him to go sit.

Finally—*finally*—after a day filled with activity and hard work, the two guys who were *supposed to be on leave* had taken time to rest.

Sean had fallen asleep with the dog curled up in his lap, and Billy assumed Jackson had done the same in the bedroom with the cats. While they were out of the way, everybody else had found the perpetrator and his entry point to where he'd taken his shot, and Cramer had enough evidence for whatever legal maneuvering he was going to do. It must have been enough, since Billy had been able to convince Sean they could leave then, although he was fairly sure he had not heard the last of whatever it was they'd been chasing on the monitors that day.

Rivers had offered to pay for every guy in the room to get the hell out of town for a day or two, because whoever had killed the dead guy in the apartment had an "unknown agenda."

Billy figured he was probably only after other bad guys, so he and *his* guys were okay, but he also guessed you didn't get to be like Rivers and Sean, carrying the weight of the world even when you were broken, by thinking only about your own guys.

Hell, Billy had even opted out of being the leader of the flophouse because he just didn't like being hurt.

But Rivers's dedication to keeping them all safe had softened Billy's frustration with both of them, Rivers and K-Ski (as Rivers insisted on calling Sean), as the two of them had pushed themselves to exhaustion.

Now, finally, they were returning home, and all Billy could think was that Sean needed to go to bed immediately—and Billy had a paper to turn in the next day.

Oh, and they should probably show the tiny dog where to crap, since it seemed they'd be caring for the little goombah until he got returned to his owner. Or the guy who was going to be his owner as soon as that guy got out of rehab.

So maybe he was a little bit brusque as he herded everybody in the door. He stood with Poppy the puppy out in the little duplex side yard for a moment while Sean got ready for bed, and then gathered one of Sean's old blankets from the garage to put on the bedroom floor for the little dog to sleep. When he came back inside, figuring he'd set the dog up and kiss Sean's temple and go out to do homework, he found Sean, in his pajamas, asleep full length on the couch with the dog cuddled to his chest.

"*Aiie,* papi," he murmured, more and more of his family's Spanish coming up in his language now that he was thinking about them more. "What're you doing to me out here?"

"You gotta stay up late," Sean mumbled. "I'll keep you company, okay?"

Billy's eyes burned, and for a moment he thought about herding them both into the bedroom where they belonged, to leave him out there alone in the kitchen, burning the midnight oil. It was what his mother had done when she'd been going through nursing school, he remembered. She'd put all the children to bed, make sure her husband was fed and had a beer, and then she'd sat at the kitchen table and done her homework.

But this wasn't like that. This was Sean, asleep, maybe, but not forsaking Billy to work alone.

"Okay," he whispered. "Not too late, I promise."

"Good work, Guillermo," Sean murmured.

"Thanks, cop."

And even though his mind was racing with things—snipers in the city, thieves in the suburbs, heroes working when they should have been resting, tiny furry dogs who suddenly appeared in their lives—he was suddenly set to sit down and write a paper for his humanities class.

Weird how one really good thing in his life could do that for him. He wondered vaguely if it was magic before he settled into his work.

He MANAGED to finish the paper in two hours and get it printed out at Sean's desk in the corner of the guest room. While waiting for the printer to work, he looked around the room, thinking he hadn't really slept there in nearly a week, but it hadn't mattered because he hadn't brought anything to add there anyway. Mostly his clothes, right? And he'd brought almost all of them to Sean's after it became apparent he wasn't going back after the first week. He'd never been a clotheshorse— he took up about three-quarters of the dresser, with a few hangers in the closet for his best shirts and slacks.

And then it hit him.

He hadn't really left anything back at the flophouse. Maybe a few posters that he and Cotton had put up in the last few months in a desperate bid to prove that they'd left their mark, but really, the odds that six other people had already had sex in his bed were pretty much an even bet.

He wasn't "going" to move in here—he *had* moved in here. And he wasn't using the spare bedroom either. The mattress was great, and Sean bought the good sheets, but Billy didn't want to make a cave in here. Although some framed prints would be nice, this time ones that he'd picked, since Sean liked sports and Vincent Van Gogh and that was about it.

But Sean *really* liked *him*. Billy hadn't been trying to get laid when he'd shown up here. He hadn't been aiming for a sugar daddy. He'd been trying to give back a little, like Jackson did, and Henry, and now that he knew it, Sean.

But the fact was, he wanted to *belong* here.

That morning, Billy and Sean had arrived at Rivers's house with super-sweet coffee drinks in hand. Billy had been appalled, but apparently the two of them were determined to destroy their bodies with sugar, and dammit, they were grown-assed men, so he only got a limited say about what they put into their bodies. But Jackson hadn't been ready to go yet, and Billy had gone into his bedroom to help him put on his shoes.

Something about seeing the great detective staring at his tennis shoes with the realization of exactly how screwed he'd be if he tried to put them on himself had hit Billy just right.

In a rare moment of vulnerability, Billy confessed his worst fear.

"I'm a whore, Jackson. How can he trust me if I'm a whore?"

"Whoring's honest work, if an honest man does it," Jackson had replied.

"Why me? Why'd you send me to come help him?"

"I don't know. I figured you were ready to get out of the life, and he'd just been dumped in the hospital. I mean, hurt guy, pretty nurse—at the very least I thought you two could become friends."

And they had. They'd become more than friends. They'd become lovers.

And Billy had fallen in love.

Without invitation—or warning—Billy remembered his first scene filming at Johnnies.

"So we're starting this one in jeans," Dex said. *"You can fold your other clothes—there's cubbies behind the camera line here, okay? And we have robes for you guys between takes. You look all freshly scrubbed—did you read the pamphlet I gave you? Eat lots of fiber three days before and nothing but water two days before?"*

"Yeah," Billy replied. He'd blushed on a dime back then, and his face had burned. *"All pooped out. No worries."*

Dex was tall, stunningly beautiful, and still innocent looking, although he'd spent ten years in the business himself, and the look he turned to Billy had been kind. "Don't worry—we won't ask you to bottom your first time out. But, you know, keeps everything fresh. Like if you were planning on a really exciting date, right?"

Sam had been gone for about three months at this point, and Billy had brightened. "I can pretend," he said, and Dex nodded and then sobered.

"Try not to get attached," he said softly. "At least not while filming scenes. A lot of guys—myself included—have hooked up with someone they met in the business and made it work really well. But not during a scene. The scenes are... well, think about it like playing basketball or skateboarding with friends. You're doing something physical that hopefully you love doing—but you're not gonna marry any of the guys on the court, right?"

Billy had laughed involuntarily. "God no," he said with feeling, thinking about his soccer teammates in high school.

"Yeah," Dex said, and again, that kind look in his eyes. "Sex in here," he gestured to the faked bedroom beyond the door of the office suite, "isn't about love, Billy. It's like those big fiberglass castles at theme parks. We can dress the place up to look like a bedroom and make sure everybody's having a good time, but at the end of the day, you have to go home and live your life. Have a good time here. Come out your eyeballs and enjoy the fuck out of it. Be friends with the guys you meet—there are some great guys here, and going out to concerts or playing ball or seeing movies is a whole lot of fun with people who know you. But...." He sighed.

"But it's not love," Billy said, getting it.

"Not usually," Dex had agreed, looking relieved.

At that moment, Lance had shown up. They were filming their scene together, and Billy had been thrilled because God, Lance Luna was one of the most beautiful men he'd ever seen. They'd kissed, they'd stroked, they'd fondled, they'd fucked, and they'd come. And when it was done, Lance asked him if he wanted to go eat afterward and then asked him if he needed a place to stay.

But a week later, he was hooking up with another guy from Johnnies, and Lance was too, and he realized he felt nothing more than happiness for his friend and sex for himself.

And he'd gotten it then, what sex was when you were at work as opposed to what he and Sam had been fumbling for when he'd been in Sam's bed.

And even though he got very proficient at it, very polished, he'd assumed he would never, ever feel that sort of hope in human touch again.

THE MEMORY left, blown away as though by a desert wind, and Billy found himself on the floor of the spare room, hugging his knees and wiping his wet cheeks on his shoulder.

And he tried to think, *Tomorrow I have school. The next day, I have a scene.*

And what came out of his mouth was, "I can't. I can't. I can't. I can't I can't I can't—"

EVENTUALLY HE managed to pull himself up, get his paper, which had long since printed, and set up his schoolwork so he'd be good to go in the morning. He turned off the lights and then roused Sean, gently, to come to bed.

Poppy seemed more than content to curl up on the old folded blanket by the bedstand, and Billy slid behind Sean exhaustedly, making sure to set his phone on his own bedstand with the volume way up because he was really not looking forward to waking up in five hours for school.

When he was finally snuggled up against Sean's backside, his breathing beginning to settle, Sean tugged his hand—which had been at Sean's waist—to Sean's chest and laced their fingers together.

"You sound sad," he mumbled. "Are you okay?"

"Yeah," Billy whispered, surprised Sean had noticed. Billy assumed he'd sleepwalked from the couch to the bedroom.

Sean squeezed his hand. "You'd tell me, right?"

Billy felt the tears, which he thought he'd vanquished, burn at the back of his eyes again. "Yeah, but not tonight, okay? Tomorrow, after school." The thought comforted him. It wasn't that he thought Sean would forget; he just thought that maybe the whole thing would feel less dire, less impossible choice, if he only had a little bit of sleep under his head and his paper turned in.

"Promise?"

Billy smiled. That promise, at least, would be easy to keep. "Sure. You like being bored."

"You're never boring," Sean mumbled. "Night, Guillermo Morales."

His own name—it was a balm to his heart. "Night, Sean Kryzynski."

That's all he remembered until morning.

THE NEXT day he beat Sean to the shower and had breakfast on the table for him before he left. Sean had looked at the egg frittata and grimaced.

"You know, I can cook for myself, especially when you're not eating."

"Yeah, I know. I love your guilt. It feeds me like my mother's enchilada casserole—mm-mm-mm, so filling." He rubbed his stomach to emphasize the point.

Sean squinted at him, and if he'd been a dog, his ears would have been pinned back in irritation. "As soon as you run out of here with your coffee-no-cream, I'm putting cheese on this. Gooey, drippy cheese. *Mmmmmm....*"

Billy's eyes narrowed. "Now you're playing mean."

Sean stood and moved to the cupboard. "Yeah, and I'm so mean I'm going to show you where the good thermos is. That one you've been using doesn't stay hot, and it only holds a cup or so. This one holds three, and it'll be hot until you get back." He paused in the act of reaching up, and Billy watched him assess his body, making sure that was the smart thing to do. Carefully, he stood on his tiptoes and reached again, grabbed the thermos easily, and turned around with a look of triumph on his face.

Billy took in that joy and swallowed unhappily, hating himself for what he was thinking.

"What's wrong?" Sean asked.

"You don't need me," Billy said gruffly. "You can even drive again. I'm taking rideshare today. You... you could do everything here yourself."

At that moment Poppy ran into the room from his blanket, where he'd apparently stayed, and started scratching at Sean's pantleg. Without thinking, Billy scooped him up, ready to take him outside before he bolted from the house, but Sean took him instead. The action brought them close—as close as they were when Billy helped him stand up with Sean's arms around his neck.

"I do need you," Sean whispered. "Just in a totally different way."

Billy opened his mouth to refute him, to be cynical and snarky and stupid, but Sean pressed their mouths together, the dog in the middle, and pulled away, whispering, "You have to go. But I need you to come back. I need to find out why you're sad. I need you to kiss me again. Okay?"

And Billy nodded dumbly while Sean took Poppy to the side yard and left him to pack a really big, really nice thermos with an entire pot of coffee with sugar.

At the last minute, Billy threw in a dollop of cream. He'd missed cream since he'd started showing his body off for a living. Suddenly, that dollop of cream was the only thing getting him out the door.

He paused by the sliding glass door to the side yard to see Sean, crouched down as he couldn't have been six weeks earlier, rubbing the little dog's stomach. He'd done it strategically. There was a small patio set out there, and he was close enough to the chair to use it for balance as he stood. Billy smiled at him.

"Don't spend too much time in the shade, papi," he called through the screen. "You can still catch cold."

"Good luck on your paper," Sean called back—not loudly, but he could breathe enough to be heard. "See you in a bit."

Billy practically jogged to his car, wondering at the uneasy feeling in his stomach.

HIS HUMANITIES class was his third class of the day, right after lunch, and the students were like the walking dead. The professor was funny and dry, as always, but Billy could see the midterm blues haunting the exhausted eyes of all his students as they tried desperately to take notes. Curtis sat in the desk behind him, and he kept poking Billy with his pen whenever he nodded off.

The clatter at the doorway was enough to wake the dead, though, and he and Curtis met eyes as a cop, fully decked in SWAT gear, barked at their professor.

"We need everybody to clear out. Don't run, don't panic, just go to your cars in the front parking lot or cross the street to where the busses are and go. Grab your stuff and leave. Now."

Billy's stomach sank to his toes as Curtis said, "Today? You don't have the super car *today*?"

"He was going to drive to the park!" Billy muttered, but he was pulling out his phone as they went.

Sean answered on the first ring.

"We're getting cleared out of the school. Is there anything I should know?" Billy pulled back into an empty alcove to watch the students streaming by. Away from the stadium side of the school, he thought, and he remembered the day before. They'd spent an entire day tracking a guy who could make a shot from half a mile away.

Like from a stadium.

Shit.

"Stay on the line," Sean said tersely. "And stay put. Give me five minutes."

"What's up, man?" Curtis demanded. "Randy, Cotton, Vinnie, and Henry are all at the shrink today. I don't think we've got a ride home."

"Text them and find out," Billy muttered. "Sean's calling someone right now. Give me a minute."

One minute. Two minutes. His heart beat so loud in his ears he wondered if his heart murmur had risen up from the depths of his fears to attack him now.

Sean's voice when it came back was clipped. "They think the sniper's at the stadium. You and Curtis catch a bus to my place—"

"Where are you going to be?" Billy asked, the fear in his chest a real thing.

"Andre and Rivers and a few others are going to be at the stadium to see if they can talk the sniper down. I think Henry's on his way too. I'm going to meet them there. You guys can go home, but I'm about to drop the dog off, and then I'm on the way." Fifteen minutes, Billy thought. Ten if he floored it, and he had no doubt that Sean would be standing on the accelerator.

"Fuck. That."

Sean sounded out of breath, like stress had done what his physical activity hadn't been able to. Like he'd overdone it again or was so worried his heartrate had spiked.

"Please, Guillermo," he pleaded softly. "Go somewhere safe. I want to see if my friends need me—"

"And I want to make sure you're fine," Billy snapped. "Look, we've got to find a way back where the cops can't see us, but we'll be there. Don't do anything stupid."

Sean's voice crackled. "Like let a college student boss me around?"

"Okay then, don't be an asshole," Billy snarled. "Wait for me. I'll be there."

"I want you to be safe—"

"*You fuckin' think*? Now wait for me!"

And then Billy hit End Call and looked at Curtis, who was busy texting.

"I'm going to make my way to the stadium," he said, glancing around. For the most part, the SWAT team had herded the students to the parking lot, and now they were busy directing traffic. Casually, Billy started moving as though he and Curtis were heading down the sidewalk, but they came to the end of the building around the back where there was a shortcut to the other end of campus, and both of them started to sidle that way.

"The front of the campus is a zoo," Curtis said. "I'll go with you."

Billy grimaced. "I may leave you to go chasing after the dumb-as-shit cop who thinks he's going to help when he can barely fucking breathe. You understand that, right?"

"Yeah, Billy. I got that impression. I'll stay out of the way and let you do that. Just…." Curtis sighed. "Just don't want to let my brother go without backup, you know?"

Billy grinned at him. He and Curtis, they were the two practical ones. The ones who were hell-bent on getting their degrees. The ones who refused to commit to any of the drama, but who were always down to fuck if they were ever hard up.

But Curtis thought of him as a brother, and Billy realized it did something good to his heart to realize he wasn't the only one whose ties to the flophouse had gone deeper than he'd planned.

"'Preciate it," he said gruffly. "Now keep an eye out. We're going to hug the buildings here and try to stay out of sight of the SWAT guys, okay? We're both brown, and you know they'll be thinking about shooting us first."

"God, thanks for that, asshole. Let's find our way."

SEAN GOT there too late, wheezing because he'd been halfway across the soccer field when Billy had called him and he hadn't caught his breath during the entire frantic drive over.

He arrived in time to watch Rivers send Andre and his interim partner, Leslie de Souza, as well as two uniformed police officers and Henry, to take the passage with the stairs into the stadium proper. Billy was nowhere to be seen, and as Sean climbed out of the car, wishing for Billy's no-bullshit help up, he heard Rivers say, "Go brief Sean about what we're doing."

He looked up to see Ellery Cramer trotting across the parking lot, dressed in a natty suit and shiny shoes while Jackson disappeared into the stadium behind him.

Ellery wasn't stupid.

He gaped at Sean for a moment before turning toward where Jackson had disappeared, and they both realized Rivers had literally said, "Look over there!" while he ran to put himself in harm's way.

Sean gaped back, fighting the hurt of being left behind but knowing that *he* couldn't catch Rivers and Ellery needed to.

It didn't take much urging to send Ellery flying in the opposite direction, looking furious and worried because his idiot boyfriend was about to go get between a sniper and his target.

Sean locked the Charger and started after him, hating how slow he was, hating how his breath labored in his lungs. He'd almost reached the stadium when he heard running footsteps behind him and a familiar, dear, angry voice swearing at him in Spanish.

"Are you hearing me, cop-man?" Billy demanded, screeching to a halt in front of him. "Where the fuck do you think you're going? Lookit you—your lips are fucking blue!"

"Rivers," he panted, "is still bleeding from his back. He's going to help." Wheeze. "Ellery too."

"But I don't need them, you stupid fucking pendejo!" Billy yelled. "*I need you!*"

Sean remembered his time in the hospital and how angry Billy had been that Sean was sick, and he knew without a doubt that this was the same thing.

"I need you too," he said with a little smile. "Now come on, let's go make sure Rivers doesn't get himself shot. Again."

Billy turned around, and for the first time Sean saw Curtis standing near the Charger. "Stay here!" he called. Sean handed him the keys, and Billy ran close enough to pitch them while Sean walked toward the small, practically invisible thruway into the stadium.

As they entered the shaded passageway, Sean's breath almost stopped. Sudden inescapable panic squeezed his chest, and he found himself fumbling for Billy's hand.

I went from light to darkness to light again, and then....

Oh God. The only difference here was that he *knew* there was something scary on the other side of the darkness. He *knew* somebody was waiting there with the potential to hurt, to maim, to kill.

And this time, he was holding Billy's hand as he went, and Billy was in danger too.

"You okay, cop?" Billy asked when they were halfway through.

"Stay back from the entrance," Sean managed to say. "When the light changes, pause for a second and let your eyes adjust."

It wasn't the same, he thought. The day was mildly overcast, the gray skies a good foil for what they'd see but not blinding like sunlight. Rivers and Cramer were on the other side too, drawing fire, and Henry was probably up in the stands, getting ready to kill to defend them.

It was that thought that gave him the courage to go on.

His friends—the guys who had made sure he wasn't alone in the hospital, who had brought Billy into his life, and who had cared about him, in spite of his shitty attitude when they'd first met—those guys were in trouble.

He needed to help.

They came to the opening of the thruway, right where the light hit, and Sean tugged on Billy's hand, pausing to let his eyes adjust and to peer onto the track to see what was happening.

"Jesus," Billy breathed.

Sean made a hurt sound and got ready to launch.

BILLY HOPED that Jackson Rivers was never mad at *him*, because the guy he was yelling at on the track in the stadium had obviously pissed him off.

Rivers was standing about forty feet away, angled with his back toward them, and was very deliberately baiting the sweaty guy in the SAPD sweatshirt. Neither of the men seemed to notice the tiny red dot tracking their movements from one to the other as Jackson accused the man of assaulting him, of deserting his fellow policemen, of being a dirty cop, while simultaneously trying to back up toward the tunnel where Billy and Sean stood, looking for a move to make.

And definitely neither of them noticed Ellery Cramer, standing behind and a little to the side of them, until the dot lingered for a heartbeat too long and—

"Oolf," Sean muttered. "Nice one."

Jackson let out a yelp worthy of the dog as Ellery made the world's clumsiest tackle. He landed on top of Jackson, who hit the track on the still-seeping knife wound on his back. A shot rang out, passing through where they both had been and fracturing the screen that ran in front of the empty first row of seats in the stadium.

The stupid dirty cop Jackson had been trying to save said, "Hey, is somebody shooting at us?" and Jackson called out a name.

"Adler! Adler, don't do it!" He was yelling from flat on his back, with Ellery on top of him, obviously working hard for oxygen, and when the sniper answered back, tearfully, Billy saw Jackson take his first real breath since Ellery had leapt on him.

And then he looked up at his boyfriend and begged. "Baby, please get off me. Please. You're in the line of fire."

What followed was something Billy would never forget. A dual conversation between a guy up top of the stadium pointing a sniper rifle down at them, a guy with every advantage and nothing to lose, and Jackson Rivers. And in between that, there was Rivers begging Ellery to get up and run toward safety.

Billy clutched Sean's hand like a lifeline, like he could keep Sean from running into danger today, tomorrow, or for the rest of Sean's life.

"C'mon, Ellery," Sean muttered. "Get up and let him work."

"He won't," Billy replied, neither of them taking their eyes from the terrifying tableau.

Sean glanced at him. "How do you know?"

Billy caught his eyes. "I wouldn't."

Sean swallowed, and they both turned back to the scene, listening as, one painful moment at a time, Jackson Rivers talked the sniper down.

Henry's voice sailed across the stadium, calling, "Jackson, we've got him!" and then the dirty cop—the sniper's intended victim, who, it seemed, hadn't been innocent in the least—attempted to flee through the tunnel Billy and Sean were standing in.

Billy was aware that Sean was reaching for the weapon he'd apparently strapped on when he dropped off the dog, but the dirty cop was coming too fast.

Billy stepped out of the thruway in front of Sean and threw all his fear, all his frustration, into a solid punch to the guy's jaw.

Dirty cop went down, and Sean muttered, "Damn, Billy!" as he sank to one knee, pulled a pair of handcuffs from his gun belt, and started to cuff the guy while reading him his rights.

Billy saw him, busy, looking purposeful, and his stomach gave a lurch as he realized this was his lover in his element, and Billy had a moment of disconnect, of "What do I do now?"

Then his eyes fell on Ellery and Jackson. Ellery was scrambling up, careful not to put any pressure on Jackson's prone form, and Jackson was squeezing his eyes shut. As Billy approached them, he heard Jackson say, "I think I popped all my stitches."

Oh Lord. *That* was a lot of pain. As Ellery leaned forward to leverage Jackson up, Billy crouched behind him, and using the same idea he'd used when helping Sean, he hoisted Jackson's elbows while Jackson held his arms stiff at his sides. After he was partway up, Ellery took over, and for a moment the two men simply stood there, holding each other's faces, while Ellery begged Jackson not to take chances like that and Jackson begged Ellery not to put himself in danger like that either.

Billy wanted to laugh—or yell at them both for being idiots, but then Jackson Rivers did something truly magical.

He proposed.

Billy's jaw dropped, and Jackson told Ellery that since they couldn't seem to promise to stay out of trouble, the least they could do was promise to be together forever.

For a moment time stopped, and two of the most practical men Billy had ever known shared the most romantic moment he'd ever seen, and in that moment, he wondered if this was why people still believed in love.

And then he saw the mess of blood seeping through Jackson's sweater and realized that, oh my God, *he* was the grown-up here, and he needed to speak up. Ellery Cramer seemed about to pull out a tablet to schedule the wedding, and Billy said, "Later! Right now, he's bleeding like a stuck pig."

A few words of sanity in that madness—that's all he had to offer, but it was enough to get them out of the stadium and to the parking lot, where an ambulance awaited. Ellery and Jackson left in that, after Ellery shoved his keys into Billy's hand and begged him to get Ellery's Lexus to Med Center. Billy tightened his hands around the keys and promised he'd get it done, and they were gone.

Sean was over by Christie and the interim partner's unmarked vehicle, helping Christie book the dirty cop. Billy had no idea for what—being target practice? But it was sort of fun to watch the guy fume, "You guys are supposed to be my brothers!" when Billy knew that if Rivers said he was dirty, he was *really* fuckin' dirty.

But Billy had nothing to do. With a sigh, he wandered over to the Charger, where Curtis sat in the passenger's seat with the door open, watching everything with interest. The fire department showed up as he talked to Curtis about which one of them got to drive the Lexus and which one of them got to drive the Charger to *pick up* the guy who drove the Lexus, when one of the firemen—a tall, stacked salt-and-pepper daddy—strode up to Sean and… holy shit!

"Is that guy macking on your cop, man?" Curtis asked in disbelief.

"Oh *hell* no!"

This—*this* was purpose. Billy didn't even remember striding up to the guy, but he had a very clear image of Sean pushing against his chest in an obvious effort to free himself from the man's long arms and unwanted attention.

"Yo!" Billy snapped. "Are you Jesse?"

Surprised, the guy turned to him. He was wearing a uniform but didn't have the helmet or the fireproof jacket or anything, and Billy realized he was probably six-foot-plus tall if he was an inch.

Billy didn't care. "Are you?" he demanded, craning his neck to stare the guy down.

"Sean, who's this?" Jesse asked, confused.

"I'm the guy who helped him clean glass up off his porch, you fucking douchebag. *Get away from him*!"

He wasn't aware he was shouting—or advancing on the guy, shoulders back, hands coming up like he was going in for the attack—until Sean tugged at one shoulder and Henry tugged at the other.

Whatever the fuck Henry had been doing—and it probably had something to do with the sniper in the stadium—he had his real soldier game face on, and Billy was reminded that Henry had spent a lot of time on deployment before he'd ended up in the flophouse.

"Billy, calm down," Henry was saying in his ear, and Sean was breathing heavily, which told Billy he'd overdone it, which only made him angrier.

"*This* guy," Billy snarled. "*This* fuckin guy—he's the one who dumped Sean in the ICU."

Suddenly he and Henry were shoulder to shoulder, and Henry bumped him subtly so they were both standing in front of Sean.

"I remember you," Henry said, voice flinty. "Go away."

"Guys," Sean gasped weakly.

"You show up with a fifth of Jack and a box of condoms and you think that's okay?" Billy snapped. "And then when he says 'no,' you throw the bottle at our front door? Are you fucking kidding me? Whatever you think you're doing here, you're not wanted. Go away. *Get out*!"

"Billy!" Sean tried again, and Billy turned toward him.

"Are you okay?"

Sean struggled for a deep breath and gave him a look of mute appeal.

"He needs me," Billy told Henry. "But you know what he needs more?"

"For this douchebag to go do his job," Henry answered. "Did you hear us, douchebag? Go do your fucking job."

And suddenly there was another grown-up on Billy's other shoulder. "Jesse," Andre Christie said, his voice icy.

"Detective," Jesse said, looking worried. "I was just checking on Sean, er, Detective Kryzynski."

"I think Sean's boyfriend has the right idea," Andre said. "Go do your fucking job, Mr. Carver. Leave us to help Sean. You are not fucking qualified."

Jesse's eyes grew wide. Apparently Henry and Andre scared him, and the idea that Billy was his boyfriend pretty much tied him in a knot.

"Boyfriend?"

"*Fucking go!*" they all snarled, and that was it. He spun on his heels and went to ask Andre's partner some questions about the scene.

Andre, Henry, and Billy all turned toward Sean then, and Andre murmured to them, "This place is about to become balls to the walls cops. You guys go ahead and leave. I was with Henry, and I'll get Rivers's statement in the hospital." Andre chuckled. "And see if that proposal we all heard him make really sticks."

"Weak shit," Henry muttered in disgust. "He needs to do better."

"Right?" Sean rasped, and Henry gave Billy an urgent look.

"Get him home before he ends up in there with Rivers and they kill each other."

Billy grimaced and held up the keys to Ellery's Lexus. "I promised Mr. Cramer that somebody would get his Lexus to Med Center. Curtis can drive it, but somebody needs to pick him up or—"

Henry scooped the keys out of his hand. "Good catch," he praised. "I'll go fetch Curtis. I'll drive the Lexus, and he can drive the haunted minivan."

Billy and Sean both shuddered. They'd ridden in it the day before—Godspeed to Rivers and Henry, but neither of *them* wanted another ride.

"Deal," Billy said, and then he turned toward Sean, taking his elbow and steering him toward the Charger. "Come on, Mr. Hero. Let's get you in bed and down for your nap—"

"And probably pick up dog crap," Sean breathed. "I just dumped the poor dog in the house."

"Well, thanks for that, but I guess that's my job too."

"Sorry."

"No you're not. Nobody's ever sorry they don't have to clean up dog poop. Now sit down and let me take care of you, okay?"

"Sure," Sean rasped, doing exactly what he said. "No problem."

Best news Billy had heard all day.

AN HOUR later, Sean was lying in bed, the dog had been taken out to the side yard and was lying on his bed, and Billy... well, in spite of having a thousand things he *could* be doing, Billy was sitting in his customary chair in Sean's room, watching him sleep.

"I know you're there," Sean murmured, his eyes still closed.

"Good for you," Billy returned without heat.

"What are you thinking about?"

Billy breathed out. "Well, I was thinking about what to cook you for dinner. And then I thought, *I would really like a hamburger*, 'cause, you know, I haven't really eaten since Sunday."

"I can make my own—" Sean began.

"I'm not done," Billy said, and to his horror, his voice clogged, and he hated that, but there was nothing he could do about it now.

Sean's eyes opened, and he began to focus. "Carry on."

"And then I thought, 'But I really want to make him a hamburger. I want us to sit down together and have a hamburger, and I want him to tell me I did a good job cooking it—'"

"'Cause you would."

"Of course I would. But back to me thinking, 'And I want to sit on the couch with him leaning in my arms, and then I want to rub my hands all over his body in bed and see where that leads.'"

"Good places," Sean murmured.

"The best," Billy confirmed, his voice growing thicker as he saw Sean's eyes were totally focused now in the lengthening shadows from the window. "You and me touching only goes good places. And I thought, 'I want him to forget that douchebag ex—'"

"Hard not to when you, Henry, and Andre scared him away," Sean said on a rough chuckle.

"He got off easy," Billy told him. "Henry and I were ready to pound him. I think the only reason that asshole is still up and breathing free air is that Christie showed up and pretended to be the grown-up in the room."

"He *is* the best grown-up," Sean agreed.

"But back to you forgetting your douchebag ex, and you and me touching you and sexing you and—"

"Making love," Sean supplied, his eyes not leaving Billy's face. The first tear slipped by, and Billy let it and thought that should have been where he stopped and walked away, but he couldn't seem to leave, couldn't seem to break this moment when Sean's big blue eyes drank in his every expression and didn't judge and didn't contradict. Sean simply joined his thoughts seamlessly, like fibers spinning together to create yarn.

"Yeah, that," Billy rasped, and there went the next tear. "And nowhere in any of those thoughts that started with hamburgers and ended with us making love and maybe having a cookie with some milk was the thought, 'But I can't because I have to go get naked and have sex with a guy I don't care about for a paycheck.' Not once. I mean, I actually pulled the hamburger meat out and was about to make patties so they'd be ready when I was making dinner. And then my phone buzzed, and it was Dex, making sure I was ready to go tomorrow. And he's never texted me before. I've always shown up and done my job and enjoyed it, but tonight he sent me a text, and there I was with a package of hamburger in my hand, and I was thinking…."

He swallowed, not sure if he could go on, and then Sean prompted him softly. "What, Billy? What were you thinking?"

"I can't," Billy said, coming completely undone. "I can't. I can't. I can't. I… I can't put sex in a box again. It was in a box, things you did for fun and money." He made a box with his hands. "But see, me and you touching—that doesn't go in the box. You and me touching is like the opposite of being in a box. It's like… freedom. And I've tasted freedom, right? And I can't go back in the box anymore. I can't… I can't—"

Sean pushed himself up on the bed and held out his arms. "Come here, Guillermo," he whispered. "Let me hold you and set you free."

Billy practically threw himself at Sean, mindless of his healing body, only wanting his comfort, his embrace, his kindness.

His caring. His love.

And Sean wrapped him up in all of that, rocked him softly, and told him he was free.

AN HOUR later, they were lying side by side in bed, clothes still on because they weren't in bed to make love.

Sean turned on his side and studied his lover, the "porn kid" who'd been there to take care of him because he'd been at a low point in his life and who had stayed because…. *Because he belongs here.*

He belonged there, in Sean's bed, eyes closed, turned toward Sean by an angle of his shoulders, a cock of his lean hips.

A buzz interrupted the silence, and Billy pulled his phone out of his pocket.

Wordlessly, he turned it toward Sean. It was from Dex, and it said simply, *Billy?*

And Sean, who had vowed to stay out of it, to let Billy make his own decisions, to not get possessive or weird or old-fashioned on a guy who'd been making his own way in the world without Sean for the last three years, said, "Tell him you can't."

The relief on Billy's face was stunning.

He typed simply, *I'm sorry. I can't.* and sent the text.

"I feel so bad," he said hoarsely. "That wasn't a lie, but I left Dex and John in the lurch and—"

His phone buzzed again, and he read it, eyes wide, and then his eyes started to spill over again. Wordlessly, he showed Sean the phone.

Had a feeling. Stop by tomorrow and we'll talk about job options that will help you keep your bennies. Pet store manager needed!

Sean glanced at the phone and smiled, but as he turned toward Billy to share in the relief, perhaps the joy of not having to leave the people he worked with, Billy buried his face into Sean's shoulder and wept silently while Sean held him some more and gave a silent Catholic-boy thanks that it really might be all right.

"I WON'T make as much," Billy said for the tenth time, but not like he was mad about it—just like he was worried Sean didn't know what it meant.

Sean took a bite of his hamburger—seasoned to perfection, Sean thought—and nodded. "I know," he said when he'd chewed and swallowed. "You've said that before. Is that a problem?"

Billy gave him a sort of guilty look from across the table. "I can pay rent," he said, his cheeks flushing.

"You don't need to," Sean said, not getting it. "I mean, I'm not expecting you to. You signed on to take care of me for an extra bed and food."

"And the car," Billy said, one corner of his mouth twisting up. "I totally would have taken care of you to use your car."

Sean grinned. "Just so you know, before I got hurt, I didn't let *anyone* use my car."

"So I'm special?" He said it like they were still kidding, but suddenly Sean knew there was a right answer to this one.

"Very," he replied. "Don't ever doubt it." He started to chuckle. "I don't know if I've ever had any boyfriend defend my honor before."

Billy blinked. "Wait, when did I—"

"You, Henry, and Andre defending me from Jesse?" Sean gave a slantwise smile of his own. "Man, I don't know if I've ever seen anybody put in their place like that. There I was thinking, 'God, I wish I could sock this guy in the jaw.'"

"You couldn't even *breathe*!" Billy cried, mad all over again.

"Yeah." Sean sighed. "My doctor's checkup is tomorrow to see if I'm okay to go back. I'm sort of afraid of what Lance is going to say." Billy was staring at him darkly, like he would be very glad to keep Sean home and on disability for the rest of his life, and Sean spoke up hurriedly. "Anyway, suddenly you were in Jesse's face—and, you know. You and me, we're not that tall, but you were yelling at him, and he was backing up, and then Henry was at your side and doing the same thing, and Andre. Never thought I was a damsel in distress, but suddenly I've got two knights and my own Prince Charming defending my honor." He smiled to himself at the memory. "It was pretty awesome."

"Guys like that," Billy said with disgust. "They think 'No' means 'You just didn't ask with enough hands.'" He shook his head. "Not dealing with that shit was the best part of getting jacked up for porn. I mean, I could fight before—our old neighborhood wasn't much better than my mom's new one. But once you got the muscles, people don't even pick on you." Billy snorted. "Unless they're seven fucking feet tall and have a fireman's badge. Oh my God, you need me to save you from fucking douchebags!"

Sean laughed then, content to let Billy go off because he was so fun when he did it. "I totally do," he said happily. Then he sobered. "I'm, uhm, glad you volunteered."

Billy was chewing as Sean spoke, and he finished slowly as though thinking. "I meant it, what I said. I've never felt anything like I've felt with you. I know I should probably get my own place. I just…." He smiled sheepishly at Sean. "In two weeks, you're going to wake up and go out and work insane hours and come home to an empty house, and I hate the thought of that. I hate that you'll be coming home to someplace without another heartbeat, you know? Even at my loneliest, I had my roommates, and sure"—he grinned—"they were usually good for a quick one, but they were also…."

"Your brothers," Sean murmured. "I get it. You want me to have family here."

"Yeah, but not your mom, 'cause I'm sayin', she's a lot."

Sean chuckled. "And the fact that you get that qualifies you for the position of roommate," he said.

"But more," Billy added, meeting his eyes. "More. We're a real couple."

"Yeah," Sean said.

"And I'm gonna tell people that. I'm not making anybody guess anymore."

Sean nodded. "That's good, because after the way you went after Jesse today, I think the cat's pretty much out of the bag."

Billy smiled with satisfaction. "Yeah, you're not making me hate that moment."

Sean chuckled and said, "My God, I love you."

The kitchen went so still they probably heard stars explode from light years away. Even the dog, who had been quietly pawing Billy's pantleg for bites of hamburger, stopped moving.

Billy stared at him in quiet surprise. "I love you too." He studied his hamburger—eaten protein style, wrapped in lettuce, with pickles and ketchup. "It's sort of stupid we haven't said that before, right?"

"Yeah," Sean agreed. "But that's okay. I gotta tell you, Guillermo, I don't think either one of us are all that bright."

Billy grinned at him, and the mood of relief, of quiet celebration, filled the room again.

Sean did the dishes after dinner, and they watched stupid television. About midway through Sean's favorite program, the one Billy claimed to hate with all his soul, Billy started to kiss his ear.

Down the back of it—oh! Nibbling on the lobe—nice. And smooth lips down the side of Sean's neck—*mmm.*

"How you feeling?" Billy asked softly.

Sean turned his head to capture Billy's mouth. "Like topping first," he murmured, "but bottoming at the end."

Billy sucked in a breath and nipped at Sean's ear. "Aren't *you* adventurous—but your lips were blue this afternoon. I'm saying—you need to pick one and go with it."

Sean groaned because Billy was probably right, and also because he'd slid his hand under Sean's shirt and was rubbing his stomach, his chest, skin to skin.

"Bot—" Billy tweaked a nipple. "—*tom!*" Sean squeaked at the end. "Bottom. I'll bottom. It's not fair. You're so good at topping, though. God, I'd have bottomed a lot more if I'd known there were guys who could top like you."

Billy laughed gruffly, pinching Sean's other nipple. "I'm sort of glad you haven't," he growled. "'Cause that makes me special."

"Oh, Guillermo," Sean moaned as Billy slid his hand down under the waistband of Sean's jeans. "You were already *so* special."

Billy nipped his earlobe again. "Good."

Abruptly his hands and his warmth were gone, and Sean was scrambling up after him.

"Go get naked," Billy ordered. "I'm going to put the dog out for a pee, okay?"

"Yeah," Sean murmured. Poppy the tiny rescue dog was going to his new owner the next morning, one of the people who'd been hurt the most by the dirty cop Jackson had tried to save that day. Sean would miss the little creature, and suddenly he wanted one of their own more than anything. A dog to keep Billy company when he was gone, and a dog to get him out of bed and out of the house on his days off when he thought the job had taken all he had to give.

Sean knew those days; he knew every cop had them. As he made it to his room and stripped—first himself, then the comforter down to the foot of the bed—he thought that having a lover, a partner, who got him, who could make him laugh and who kept him on his toes, *that* would make all the difference.

But the dog would be nice too.

But not now. Now Sean lay in the bed naked, unapologetic about what was going to happen next. He grabbed the lubricant from under the pillow and squirted some on his fingers. When Billy came in, still air drying his hands after washing them and ordering the dog into the corner on his blanket, Sean had moved his fingers down to his cleft and, with his back to the door, was penetrating himself slowly, lost in the stretch of it, the anticipation.

The freedom.

Billy made a sexy, wanting sound, and Sean glanced over his shoulders to see him frozen, watching Sean's hand as he slid his finger in and out, and Sean looked him in the eyes, added more lubricant to his fingers, and thrust a second one in.

"Can you go ass-up?" Billy asked, and as Sean did that, he heard Billy taking off his clothes, folding them neatly onto the chair like he did every night.

In a moment Sean was crouched on the bed, his knees underneath him, his bottom in the air, two fingers sawing in and out of his asshole.

It was the most decadent thing he'd ever done in front of a lover, and he had no doubt, none at all, that Billy wouldn't let him down.

But that didn't mean he wasn't surprised when Billy's cock prodded near his cheek.

Sean opened his eyes, and Billy cupped his face. "Can you suck it, pretty man?" he whispered. "Get it all wet and hard and drippy? 'Cause I'm gonna put it in your ass, and we both need to be ready."

Sean groaned at Billy's words, at his cock teasing Sean's lips, and at the feeling of his own fingers in his ass. He went to pull his hand out so he could use it for balance, but Billy whispered, "No, baby. Keep stretching. It's okay if we get sloppy here."

And then he thrust his cock gently into Sean's mouth.

For a moment Sean simply accepted it, let it stretch him as he stretched himself, but then, as he got used to multitasking, he started to *appreciate* it, licking the bell, sucking it into his mouth, running his tongue up the vein on the underside. Billy let out a breathy moan, urging him on, and Sean started to take him in farther while he penetrated deeper, deeper, driving his two fingers all the way in to the hilt.

At the same time, Billy thrust into the back of his throat and held there, and Sean started shaking, suddenly so close to coming he couldn't think straight. He felt a burst of precome on his tongue and knew Billy was in the same place. Billy pulled out slowly, letting Sean taste him, and then bent down and whispered in his ear again.

"So good, papi. But now I'm gonna fuck you real hard. You gotta let me know if it's too much, okay?"

"Okay," Sean mumbled, soothed by Billy's hand on his arm, by the closeness of his mouth to Sean's ear.

Billy nuzzled him a little and moved into position, his hands gliding over Sean's shoulders, down his spine, along his flanks. Those touches, sure and warm, made Sean feel wanted, made his body feel *needed*, made him hungry for what was to come.

Billy's cockhead at his entrance while Billy rubbed those confident hands along his backside was enough to make Sean beg.

"God, please."

Slowly and gently, but this time Sean knew he could take it. This time Sean knew it would be wonderful. He closed his eyes and let Billy possess him, and when Billy was all the way in, Sean pleaded for it, because now he knew Billy wouldn't hold back.

"Please," he groaned again. "I can take it, I swear."

Slowly, Billy pulled out, and Sean's ass clenched over the loss of his shaft with every inch. Then Billy thrust in a little more quickly, and then again, and then again and then—

"*Yes!*"

Sean cried out, welcoming the whole of his shaft, the plum-sized head of his bell, *all* of it plunging into his body while Sean clung to the sheets and let it happen.

"Stroke yourself," Billy panted. "You gotta work for this ride!"

Sean wanted to laugh, but his own grip on his cock took the laughter from him. He gibbered instead, squeezing himself as Billy pounded. Maybe he was begging, but there were no words, and all he knew was that the fucking absolutely positively couldn't stop.

And then—oh heavens. Billy bottomed out inside him as he squeezed his own cockhead, and suddenly, in a burst of stars, his body exploded. He lost all cohesion and blew apart, Billy's cock and his hands the only thing keeping him on the planet while the rest of him shot through the heavens in streaks of light.

Behind him Billy groaned and came, and Sean could feel his come deep inside, all of him taken over by Billy's cock, by his warmth, by the pleasure of being with a lover who would give him everything, anytime Sean asked.

Sean moaned, aftershocks rocking him as he squeezed every drop of pleasure from himself and wrung every last shudder from the man inside him.

Billy stayed there for a moment, rutting, his hips still fucking even if he'd already come. Then Billy groaned and shot one more time, deep inside, before he fell to the side, pulling out of Sean's ass.

His very absence drew one more spasm from Sean's cock before Sean collapsed, facedown, turned just enough toward his lover to see his face.

Neither of them spoke for a long time.

Finally Billy said, "I'd give up every porn scene I ever shot for a chance to do that with you."

"You just gave up all the ones in the future," Sean murmured. "I'm so glad it's worth it."

Billy rolled over enough to kiss him softly. "For you and me together, fucking like bunnies? Totally worth it. Best decision I've ever made."

Sean smiled dreamily. "Wait until I top," he promised.

"I'm gonna be waiting a long time for that, papi. Topping you is officially my new favorite thing."

Sean laughed semihysterically. "I can't even argue," he mumbled, his ass aching and tingling, his nipples tingling. Hell, even his cock and taint were tingling, every part of him still quivering from good, hard use.

"Don't argue with me," Billy said smugly. "Not 'bout this. Gotta tell you, I'm a dumbass about a whole lot of stuff, but about you and me fucking like bunnies? I should get my degree in *that*!"

Sean giggled again, and so did Billy, both of them deliriously happy, sexed, and replete.

It was a good moment, Sean thought, and he savored it.

Deep down, he knew they'd have their biggest challenge in the days to come.

A Matter of Trust

BILLY WAS surprised when he met with Dex in a different part of the office suite the next day.

Johnnies—or John Carey Industries—was housed in a mostly deserted office complex down J Street about two blocks before CSUS. Built in the seventies, it was one of those weirdly shaped places with a big open courtyard in the middle. John had leased two side sections of the one-story building and essentially divvied it up into sets—mock bedrooms and living rooms with cubbies before the filming line—and refurbished part of it into locker rooms with both a "set" shower that was super luxurious and photogenic in case the models got frisky after their regular scene and wanted to film some more when they were soaping off, and a regular bank of gym showers for practical use.

The set showers were also excellent for just chilling out after filming—Billy could attest to that. Fucking on the cold linoleum was really only exciting for a couple of scenes, and after that most of the models took a pass.

So that's where Billy was expecting to go, but after he walked in and talked to Mrs. Bobby's Mom, telling her that he had an appointment with Dex, she grinned at him.

"He's got a new office—wait till you see!"

"A new office?" Billy said dumbly, glancing over to where Dex's office used to be, adjoined to John's office with a partition giving Reg a desk and an office of his own in a corner.

The partition was gone now. Instead, Reg sat at Dex's desk, and his smaller desk had been moved out. He'd replaced Dex's watercolors, as well as his pictures of his husband, Kane, and his niece with pictures of houses that Reg's boyfriend had built or helped refurbish. Billy waved as he peered in, and Reg gave him the biggest smile in return and waved back before turning studiously back to the paperwork in front of him.

"Today's balancing the books day," Mrs. Bobby's Mom said, her comfortably worn face looking at him worriedly. "He tries to do it by himself, and then I go in and double-check his math, and then we go get Bobby and go out for dinner with ice cream to make him feel better." Her son and Reg had been a couple for nearly two years now. Bobby had made a stop at the flophouse during his first days with Johnnies, and Billy remembered the big, raw-boned country boy with the old-soul eyes with fondness. Bobby still did the occasional scene, even with his mom working the counter, and Billy remembered Sean's too-accurate observations about how porn was a last-ditch way to make money for some of the guys, but for a lot of them, there was something more.

Bobby wanted to be seen, and Reg, who had never had anything good in his life, wanted people to see Bobby too. Reg had shot his own porn for nearly ten years, but Bobby was beautiful—one of the best models Billy had ever seen or worked with—and Reg was just so proud that this big, beautiful man who could fix anything in the house—including Reg's life —wanted him.

In a flash, Billy understood what Sean had been saying.

Bobby had grown up in a tiny town where everybody expected him to be ground under the bootheel of the rich and powerful family that controlled it. He had a real need to be seen as somebody beautiful, desirable, and in charge.

Reg had a learning disability—possibly several—and had spent much of his life taking care of his mentally ill older sister. He had needed to be seen as normal, as worthy, and as an adult, an equal, as capable of giving and receiving pleasure as the next guy.

Guillermo Morales, invisible good boy, the older child who rode herd on the others, had needed his time on camera showing he was sexy, showing he was bold and individual and in charge.

Sean had always seen him that way. From the moment Billy had walked into his house and said, "So Rivers says you need a pretty nurse," Sean had regarded him as an equal, an opponent, an obstacle—a formidable human being in his life. And then he'd insisted on them being friends.

And neither one of them had been able to stop at just friends.

But Billy had always, always been seen.

"Billy?" Mrs. Bobby's Mom called his attention back to her desk.

"Sorry," he said, pulling himself from epiphanies to practicalities.

"No worries—you went somewhere for a minute."

Billy looked at her, at her office space, which was filled with pretty little cross-stitch samplers, as well as pictures of Reg and Bobby and one of all three of them.

"What's your name, Mrs. Bobby's Mom?" he asked, feeling a little tearful.

"Elaine," she said, smiling. Even her business placard read "Mrs. Bobby's Mom."

"Elaine, can I still come visit you if I'm no longer shooting scenes?"

Her face softened even more. "Oh, baby. Of course you can." And she came around the desk and hugged him hard while he tried to figure out what had happened to his testicles because he was crying like a little tiny baby at the drop of a hat and he couldn't seem to stop.

That's where they were when Dex walked in and with that inevitable Dex kindness, said, "A hug? A group hug? Do I get in on some of this action? I wanna hug!"

Dex smelled like leather and citrus, and he was strong and warm, and his arms reached around them both. The hug seemed to go on forever, and Billy was okay with that.

Eventually Dex and Mrs. Bobby's Mom led him down past the public office space of Johnnies and into the back hallway. Except instead of turning left, which led to the places Billy was familiar with, Dex turned right and, in a few steps, came to a doorway as wide as the hall that had been sealed as long as Billy had worked there.

It wasn't sealed any longer. In fact it was brand-new, a sliding frosted-glass door with JonDex Industries on the front, and with a faint shock, Billy realized that this had been the signature on his last residual check.

He hadn't even thought to question it, but it occurred to him that just as the flophouse boys had grown up, so had John Carey Industries. They passed through the doorway, and Billy realized the office suite to his right had been refurbished. There was another plate on the door announcing JonDex Industries, and Dex took them through that one too.

The office was beautifully decorated, with an open floor plan and a big desk in the corner, complete with visitor's chairs that didn't look hellishly uncomfortable, all made with maple and leather, looking very rich without looking gaudy. The carpet looked like a carpet of leaves, and the walls were a cheery pale gold. Across from the windows, there was an accent wall with a mural of tree leaves and a logo overlaid—strong roots, a strong trunk, and JonDex Industries woven into the leaves themselves.

Damn—this was a whole thing, wasn't it?

A voice, thick with Boston and irritation, spoke up from the opposite corner of the desk. "Geez, Dexter, took you long enough. What, did you have to stop and hug everybody? You did, didn't ya? You big soppy, uhm, goober."

A smaller voice chirped, "Goober!" and Billy saw there was a children's corner too, complete with adult chairs and children's chairs, toys, colorful mats, and a coloring table. Sitting in one of the adult chairs was a truly beautiful man with dark hair and snapping dark eyes, and a golden-haired toddler with dimples in his cheeks and a sturdy chin played across from him.

"Chance, who do you love, huh?" Dex said, going to the desk and pulling out a package of animal crackers. "Who's your favorite? C'mon, kid, don't let me down!"

The toddler squealed, "Unca Dex!" and raced across the carpet on sturdy legs. "Cookie!"

"That's cheating," said the dark-haired man with the street Southie in his voice.

"Nothing's cheating when it comes to getting a child's love, is it, Chance?" Dex scooped the boy up into his arms and, with the ease of familiarity and practice, threw him in the air just high enough to make it fun but not high enough to make it dangerous. "Who's my boy? Huh? Who's my boy?"

"Eeeee!" The kid squealed again, and if Billy had to hazard a guess, he figured that would be "Unca Dex!"

Mrs. Bobby's Mom stepped forward, smiled indulgently at Dex and the child, and said, "I do believe it's my turn. Chance, how would you like to run up and down the halls with me?"

"Run!" the boy gasped as Dex put him down.

"Mrs. Roberts," Dex said, "nobody's shooting out in the quad today if you want to take him out there."

Elaine's face lit up, and she said, "C'mon, Chance, would you like to go see the birds? Your Uncle Kane set up an aviary—there are *birds* outside!"

"Burb!" the boy cried, apparently doing everything at top volume, and Mrs. Bobby's Mom smiled happily as he took her hand and then took the lead.

"Oh my God," said the dark-haired stunner. "That woman's a lifesaver. Chase has been orienting with his new job these last six weeks, and we've had to get used to Daddy One not being there until dinnertime. Kid's been driving me *nuts*."

"You love it," Dex said gently. "Tommy, let me introduce you to your new employee, I hope. This is…." He paused and looked at Billy. "How do you want to be known?" he asked. "Some guys keep their names, some guys were never really that invested. Tango here was either or. I still slip up and call him Tango, you know?"

Billy thought of the way Sean called him "Guillermo," and how it felt personal and just between them. "Billy," he said, "although you might hear my boyfriend call me Guillermo, so if that sort of slips out, that's fine too."

Dex grinned. "Officer K-Ski? Am I right? We had Rivers and Cramer over for dinner a few weeks back. They were worried about him, but super glad you were watching over him. How's Rivers doing, by the way?"

Billy blinked, remembering what a small world it was. Dex was Henry's brother—of course he'd know Rivers and Cramer. "Rivers popped all the stitches in his back, man," he told them. "It was gnarly. He's back in the hospital now."

Dex groaned. "Man, that sucks."

"Yeah, but he proposed to Cramer right after he did it." He remembered a text he'd gotten that morning. "Apparently your brother's on a mission to make him redo that proposal. I mean, you know, something that didn't involve blood and bullets might be nice, right?"

Dex covered his face with one hand. "Doh! Yes. Yes, it would. I'll text my deadbeat brother and see if I can get in on that action. Those guys have been really solid for us. We owe them flowers or something." He pulled out his phone and punched a few buttons and then waved them both to the desk. "But you guys are here for something totally different. Sit down, and let's talk. Billy, from what I understand, you're about two years from finishing your degree in engineering, right?"

"Yeah, sort of. By June I should have my A.S. in science and have all my lower division classes done, but it's junior college. The upper division that lets you know if that's what you really want doesn't happen until then."

Dex nodded. "Well, as you may have noticed, we've branched out a little. John and I have wanted a place to engage our employees after porn for a long time. Or even before porn, if they come in to audition and realize it's not for them. We felt like there needed to be places young people could go to make an honest living and get paid a living wage while they worked their way through school or even just stayed doing something they enjoyed doing. And because my best friend here had a thing for fuckin' animals—"

Billy gigglesnorted, and Dex squeezed his eyes shut.

"Let me rephrase," he said, trying to do damage control. "My best friend here platonically enjoys his amphibians."

"So does your *husband*," Tommy retorted. "Let's not forget, we're both the assholes with the giant turtles intent on breaking our houses."

Dex shrugged. "And a snake who loves my balls—"

"That's all you and Kane," Tommy said affectionately. "Keep me out of your kinky shit."

"God, seriously." Dex shuddered. "Anyway, we started by buying a pet franchise. Cashiers, stock personnel, animal health technicians, groomers, adoption centers—we're working on placing as many people who want to be there in that business. We've got our eye on a café—"

"I would love to quit my job waiting tables," Billy said. Two four-hour shifts a week had been all he could handle. Boy, was he not a fan of people drinking too much coffee.

"Good," Dex said. "Because that'll give you more hours and, well, we need managers. Of course we'll work around your school schedule, and we'll pay you a living wage. Tommy here is the GM of the store. He'll show you the ropes, let you work the stocking and cashiering jobs so you know what their life is like, and show you how to write the schedules and manage the staff. Now...." Dex looked embarrassed. "I shouldn't have to say this, and I gotta work on my schtick, but this ain't porn, kid. All clothes stay on. Anybody caught having sex at work *will* be fired. This is a way to have a legit job out of porn, with people who won't judge you, doing a thing you hopefully like. It's a way to keep your health and dental, and maybe keep contact with your Johnnies brothers and sisters too."

Billy had never gotten to know any of the girls—but then, he'd really only tried with a girl in a relationship, not in porn. But the guys. Oh, he really *would* like to keep tabs on Curtis, Cotton, and Randy, and even Lance and Henry, although he had a feeling that last one was not going to be a problem.

"I'd like that," he said softly, and the sudden relief was so powerful, it left him feeling weak. "I… I would *really* like that."

"Awesome. Now you said you had somewhere to go after this?"

Billy glanced at the clock on the wall, a silly cartoon animal clock with big-gloved hands pointing to the numbers. "Yeah, I gotta go pick Sean up from the doctor's in an hour. They're running stress tests and shit to see if he can fucking breathe well enough to go get shot or stabbed again. I should leave in about forty minutes."

Dex let out a snort. "Well, I can't fix stupid, and I can't fix cop, but hopefully after you fill out some paperwork, we can fix your job sitch, since you're all monogamous and shit. You ready?" He pulled out a file that appeared to be the standard hiring file in any business ever, and Billy peered around the office again.

"You and John aren't doing porn anymore?"

Dex shrugged. "We both made a commitment to go visit the sets once a day and meet all the new hires, like we did before. But we hired some guys we could trust who, like you, were ready to get out of doing scenes but didn't mind the business so much."

Billy blinked. "So why'd you ask me to be a pet store manager and those guys to film porn?"

Dex cocked his head. "I don't know, Guillermo. I think because you have always been, in your heart, such an upright guy. I mean, don't get me wrong—you shot beautiful porn. But you've always been a fan of order, of rightness. I'm surprised you haven't quit before now."

"Were you going to offer this to Cotton?" Billy asked.

Dex nodded. "Yeah, but we needed Cotton to get a little stronger. I'm just so excited he got strong enough to take that opportunity down south. That kid needed a break, you know?" He grinned at Billy. "Had the feeling you always sort of made your own breaks."

Like volunteering for nurse duty and falling in love with his prickly, irritating patient.

"Maybe we both got lucky," Billy said, but he took a pen from the desk and started writing, noticing the picture of Dex's husband and their niece on the corner of the desk. "So," he said as he wrote, "kids. How in the fuck do you make that work?"

And as he filled out his paperwork, Dex and Tommy took turns regaling him with kid stories, and by the time he was done, he realized he'd been able to remember a few of his own from his days of helping his mother.

It was the first time he'd really told those stories since he'd started porn, and as he stood and shook Dex and Tommy's hands before taking the JonDex exit out to the parking lot, he realized that he'd locked that part of him away. Porn had been all about being the star, being seen, being selfish about his looks, his body, his sex, and his paycheck. Kids were all about giving to make sure someone else was happy.

As he hopped in the car to go get Sean, he realized that he had that part of himself back now, and he'd missed it.

And he never wanted to give it away again.

SEAN WAS not nearly as happy after his meeting with the doctor.

"Two more weeks," he'd growled, getting into the passenger side of the Charger.

"You had that setback," Billy reminded him, wondering if this was what he had to deal with for the rest of the night. He'd been sort of happy himself.

"I'm going to get on your nerves," Sean warned.

"There were wildfires for two weeks," Billy recalled. "Lance told you that was going to cause problems."

"You're starting a new job, and I'm going to be stuck at home—"

"Let's get a dog," Billy said, out of the blue.

Sean turned to stare at him. "Are we moving a little fast?"

"If we get a dog this weekend and I move out the next week, are you going to let the dog starve?" Billy asked.

"No! I'm not a monster!"

"Good. You needed a dog before I moved in. You need a dog now. Let's get a dog. It'll give us an excuse to go to the dog park before we catch the thief."

Sean glared at him. "Big dog," he said, although Billy knew he'd regretted giving Poppy back to her human, even though he'd been in rehab and more in need of a little dog companion than any human in history.

"Little dog," Billy said equably. "Little dogs make little poops. Big dogs leave big steamers."

"We get one of those septic pits installed—a hosepipe, some enzymes, you dump the poop into the hole, add the little enzymes and it becomes dirt."

Billy's eyes got really big. "I did not know that. That needs to be common knowledge. Two dogs."

"Are you kidding me?" Sean asked, bewildered. "What are we going to do with two dogs?"

"What do you have—a month? You have a month before you go back to work full-time?"

"Three and a half weeks," Sean groused.

"Yeah, and I'm working three days a week and going to school two and a half. So those dogs are going to be alone in the backyard, and they need to have a buddy. So a big dog and a small dog who love each other, and a pet door."

Sean scowled. "They are going to destroy everything we own."

Billy snorted. "All I got is clothes, and they're already in your guest room closet. I say we buy ourselves a new comforter now, and then when the dogs rip up the one on your bed, we have it ready."

"Jesus, Guillermo, you've got this all planned," Sean said, sounding baffled.

"Yeah, Sean Kryzynski, I really fuckin' do," Billy replied, proud of himself. "You and me are going to live in your duplex 'cause it's a nice place. I'm gonna decorate because you offered, and I'm gonna make it my place. There needs to be some color in there. Right now it's like a blue jeans ad. I mean, my name is Guillermo Morales—I need some Mexican in my place, you understand?"

"And a small dog," Sean said, and Billy had stopped at a long light, so he had time to turn his head and give him a sly smile.

"And a big dog," Billy said. He grinned. "They can take turns bossing each other around."

Sean chuckled, and Billy felt the last of his pout dissipate into the bright fall day. "At the very least," he said, "we should put out Halloween decorations."

"You know what?" Billy said happily, "I got nothing but time today. Let's do that now."

THE NEXT day, Billy's phone blew up with texts between Henry and the Johnnies boys because Rivers was getting home that afternoon and he and Henry were planning a *real* proposal. Everybody wanted in. Sean and Andre went in on a glass vase that Billy got to pick up from the store—it was engraved and everything. Sean had wanted to put Billy's name on the tag, but Billy said he'd go in with the flophouse guys on the table setting and the flowers.

Billy had spent part of the day at school and part of the day running around helping Henry run errands for Jackson, and when he got home, he collapsed wearily on the couch, looking at Randy in admiration.

The kid had not just hung with Sean while Billy was out, he'd also hung the decorations they'd bought the night before, and now their porch and the tree in front of the duplex looked commercially spooky and fun. They'd bought ten pounds of candy the day before—Sean said there were usually lots of trick-or-treaters—and Randy had put some of it out in a bowl shaped like a skull so company could eat a Starburst if they were so inclined.

"Good job," Billy said, grinning. "You want to dress up and give out candy on Saturday while you're at it?"

Randy's eyes got big. "I could do that? I mean, Mr. Sean, could we do that? The flophouse really doesn't get anybody—we buy candy every year, and we've got a fake pumpkin out with a light, but so far, no action."

Billy glanced at Sean, who grinned. "Sounds good. Invite the other guys too."

"Yes!" Randy cried, and then he paused. "I started dinner, Billy. Sean walked me through kielbasa and sauerkraut, and we've got some whole-grain bread and some veggies to sauté."

"Sounds great. You staying for dinner?"

Randy peered at them shyly. "Could I? I mean, you two seem pretty cozy, but it's nice to eat with friends."

"You're always welcome," Sean said. "You know, we're going to start haunting the dog adoption places. I was thinking, on the days Billy's gone all day and I work, we could maybe use a friend who would come check on them, maybe take them to the park to play. I could pay you—"

"*Can I help pick out the dog?*"

Billy almost jumped, because the request was so raw, so needy, and he sent a panicked look at Sean, wondering what they'd unleashed.

"Sure," Sean said gently. "You like dogs?"

Randy looked at them both and nodded, biting his lip. "See, I had a dog at home, Skipper, but… well, after I got kicked out, I asked my friend to check on him, and I guess my dad had him put down and… God. I miss having a dog. You guys, if I could, you know, pretend I had my own dog. I've got all the allergy medication and stuff. I… I miss my dog."

"We can share," Sean said softly. "That's fine. We'll keep an eye out on the websites, look for a good one to adopt. Billy says a smaller one and a bigger one. We can do that."

Randy nodded and wiped his eyes on the shoulder of his shirt. "I gotta go check on dinner," he said, although Billy was fairly sure kielbasa and sauerkraut mostly just got warm in the pot.

When he'd moved into the kitchen, Billy came and sat knee to knee with Sean, took his hand, and kissed it.

"Good job, cop," he murmured.

Sean shrugged and used his free hand to rub his chest meaningfully. Billy did the same thing and remembered the text he'd gotten from his sister that day.

"Lily asked Mom if she could bring her and Miguel and Cora over too. I meant to ask you. It's just that your neighborhood is so much better, and they're old enough to not want a grown-up, but—"

"But too young to turn loose," Sean said, and Billy nodded.

"You get it. So, I guess you're gonna have a lot of people here Halloween night. My people, I guess. Sorry about that."

Sean shrugged. "I didn't get partnered with Andre until last January. So last year I filled a bowl with candy and went out to have a drink with the guys in my department." He sighed. "I… well, they weren't exactly rainbow friendly. I realized I was killing their convo and came back home to find the candy gone and toilet paper in my tree. I, uhm, sort of want to see your people all dressed up and being happy and drinking spiced cider. Invite who you want, okay?" He grimaced. "But we may need to go grocery shopping Friday after you get back from school."

Billy nodded. "What about, you know, Project Cop on Vacation?"

Sean let out a little groan. "Yeah. See, I went back over our notes— when this guy hits houses, which nights, all that. Sundays and Fridays, and he's due. He's hit one of the thruway houses in Peach Stem. That was last Sunday, and he should either be out Friday or Sunday this weekend. Now I want to put my money on Sunday because Saturday's going to be loud and obnoxious, and I bet a lot of people will be out Friday too. Sunday's probably going to be quiet. The cops will be tired from Saturday, and—"

"It's perfect," Billy said.

"But then it would suck to have Bob call us up tomorrow morning and tell us that another place was hit."

Billy grimaced and took a good look at Sean. He tended to overdo things when Billy wasn't there, and the day before had been a lot of errands as well.

"We'll take that risk," he said, and Sean glared at him.

"You're just going to decide that for me? I thought—"

Billy shook his head. "No," he said. "See, I get it. In a month you're part of the cop force, and there's going to be danger every day, and you know what you're going to do?"

Sean cocked his head. "Not tell you a fucking thing about it?"

Billy thought his head was going to explode. "You're going to tell me fucking *everything*. I want to know if you get a hangnail or a paper cut or if the smell in the elevators made you puke. Henry says it's heinous, by the way. I'm going to Febreze you the minute you walk into the house. Anyway, so you tell me everything, because if you're not telling me shit, I'll worry."

Sean made a sound. "*Mmm…* when I was in the hospital, Rivers showed up on the internet driving a giant SUV into an apartment complex that had erupted into gunfire. I'm not sure how excited Ellery was about that."

Billy glared at him and mimicked his sound. "*Mmm…* you can bet Ellery Cramer watched every last second of that footage, though, because that's what you fuckin' do when you love someone. Trust me on this."

Sean's eyes widened. "Okay. Okay, fine. So we've established that I can do my job if I don't try to hide when it's rough. Understood. What does this have to do with not going out tonight?"

"Tonight it's cold, and you're still on leave. Nothing about what the doctor said made you magically better, faster. I'm sure you tried to *jog* around the dog park this morning, and you probably feel pretty good about that, but you're beat. Tell me you're not."

He grunted because Billy had him dead to rights and he knew it.

"Yeah, that's what I thought. So when you're on cop time, you do cop things, and I don't got no say. But you're here and you're on *my* time, I *do* have a say, and I say you get a little better, you rest tonight, you have fun tomorrow night, we get sexed up all Sunday, and then we do the thing. And if we're wrong, we're wrong. So far this guy hasn't hurt anybody."

"He's actually been pretty smart about it," Sean conceded.

"So I sort of get why cops in property crimes are so laid-back now. They're like, 'It's stuff. You're not dead. We'll do our best.' We'll do our best, but you need to rest and eat your sour wieners and shit."

"It's kielbasa, sauerkraut, and french bread, and it's delicious."

"If it gives me gas, you're gonna live with it, so I'll believe you."

Sean chuckled. "Fine. So since you've apparently taken over my life and my schedule and pretty much everything else because you're, like, a control freak or something, what was that first item on Sunday? I need you to repeat that. It sounded interesting, but, you know, maybe you meant 'go running at the dog park' inste—"

Billy kissed him, hard and no bullshit, showing him that he'd wanted Sean's scrawny recovering cop body all day. About the time he sensed the fight had leached out of Sean and they were going to spend a nice Friday night at home, maybe practicing for Sunday, Randy called out, "Hey, guys, want to look for dogs on the internet—it's fun! I do it all the time when I want to destress… erm, sorry."

Billy pulled back and smiled softly. "Yeah, Randy. We can do that. Dogs on the roster for next weekend, after the Halloween madness is all settled down and I've started my new job, okay?"

Sean smiled softly at him and winked. "Where have you been all my life, Guillermo? You do make the best plans."

Billy grinned, kissed him gently on the forehead, and went to pull out his laptop.

Apparently Randy had a powerful need to look at dogs.

HALLOWEEN WAS really pretty awesome, Billy had to admit it.

Randy dressed up like Frankenstein because he said his height made him a natural, and he greeted every kid at the door with a growl, making them scream. Curtis, Cotton, and Vinnie all showed up dressed in black shirts and black pants with different dayglow painted jack-o'-lantern faces on their shirts. They put fun scary movies on Sean's TV—*Ghostbusters, The Nightmare Before Christmas, Gremlins*—and watched them with Billy's mom while Billy's three youngest siblings went trick-or-treating around the neighborhood. It wasn't until after the party that Billy realized he hadn't asked any of the flophouse kids to hide what they'd done for a living—it had never come up, and they'd never had to lie.

Sean ordered sandwich trays and had veggies and vegetable chips on the table for a buffet dinner, as well as apples galore, and Billy wanted to kidnap him to a desert island and give him a world-class blowjob for being considerate of Billy's people.

Henry and Lance were enjoying the night couple style, as well as giving out extra candy in case there *were* any trick-or-treaters in the apartment complex, and that was fine, but Andre Christie brought his two kids over to make the rounds of Sean's neighborhood too. His neighborhood was nice, he said, but apparently a lot more spread out than Sean's. Billy thought it was more so Andre could keep track of Sean, make sure he was doing okay, and that made him feel better about the next month, when Sean went back to work.

In all, it was a raucous, fun, safe and sane kind of night, and the kids showed up after their rounds with pillowcases full of things like full-sized Snickers bars and little cellophane bags full of mixed candy.

By the time every last person had gone —and the Johnnies kids had driven Lance's Mazda home after staying to clean up—Sean had been asleep in the recliner for a good hour, and Billy had that happy, tired feeling of not wanting to talk to another person for at least a year and a half.

After he'd shooed Sean to bed and turned off all the lights, he realized that he and Sean really *did* have Sunday off, and they could spend the whole day in bed.

And he wondered if he'd ever been this happy in his life.

He determinedly tried not to think about how Roberto hadn't shown up again, with his blond ponytail and mysterious job and his connection to the neighborhood they were investigating. They'd find the culprit the next day, it would be some random stranger, and Sean could go commando on his ass, and that would be that.

Because otherwise, what were the fucking *odds*?

Trust

SEAN SHIFTED in his seat in the Charger and thought that maybe he should have taken his doctor's advice and spent the next three weeks sleeping. Something about this car's seats that used to feel like they were cupping his body with the love only leather could bestow on him was now hard and uncomfortable and making him want to wiggle.

Or maybe it was his ass, which had taken a pounding that afternoon and would probably need a good three-day rest before he and Billy did all of *that* again.

It wasn't a *bad* problem to have, but it wasn't a comfortable one either.

"Would you sit still?" Billy muttered. "I swear, this car's gonna be knocking, and whoever is breaking into these places is gonna be, 'No, I can't do no criming here because two homos are getting busy inside.'"

Sean did a slow pan to Billy, horrified by that entire sentence, and Billy met him with a giant grin.

"You're being an asshole," Sean said mildly.

"Only because I still have mine. Yours got destroyed today," Billy replied smugly.

Sean couldn't stay irritated. He chuckled softly. "So worth it," he admitted, and then shifted again. "But, you know—"

"Yeah, I'll buy us some witch hazel pads. They'll make sitting so much easier after we spend a day like that. Trust me."

Sean chuckled again because Billy was done with porn but he still knew more about sex than Sean, and Sean totally *could* trust him.

And at that moment, Billy sucked air in through his teeth. "Look."

They were in the Peach Stem cul-de-sac, facing the park thruway, and Sean grunted because he saw it too.

The figure was dressed all in black, including a watch cap over a ponytail that looked like it was tucked under the person's collar.

"What do we do?" Billy murmured.

"Wait until they go into the garage," Sean said softly. "Then get out of the car and hurry to the end of the thruway, because they have to go that way." There had been just enough rain the week before to fill in the creek and keep it running, so there would be no going through the creek bed with the stolen merchandise.

"We can't stop them midtheft?" Billy asked, outraged, and Sean sent him an annoyed look.

"We aren't even supposed to be here!" he retorted. "I don't have my service weapon with me. I mean, yeah, if we hear thumping or shouting, we call for backup, but this way we can be credible witnesses to a theft."

"This is so disappointing," Billy muttered, and then they both slunk farther down in their seats and shut up so as not to draw any attention to the Charger as it sat with the other cars that didn't fit in the driveway or the garage.

Their perpetrator didn't give them a second look. Thin and lithe, a young man or a woman with easy, athletic grace slid in through the side gate and, Sean assumed, started to pick the lock, which they'd done in the previous heists. It didn't matter. As soon as he was out of sight, they were out of the car, closing the doors gently with silent clicks and then sprinting to the thruway so they could be invisible.

Or Billy was sprinting. Sean was jogging and wishing he *could* sprint. It was okay, though. They were virtually silent and in place shortly, Sean's breath coming in quick little puffs of the cool night air, but not labored. He felt absurdly proud of that.

Together they crouched in the deep shadows of the overhanging trees, behind the walls that separated the thruway from the yards of the adjacent houses. Sean peered out over the top of the wall, making sure to keep his face out of the light from the streetlamp and blessing the angle that gave him a full view of the house their thief had just entered.

They had finally situated themselves when Sean heard footsteps coming not *from* the house but behind them. He glanced at Billy and then peered in the direction of the footsteps.

From the shadows came another figure, also dressed in black, this one older, moving purposefully. Sean's first thought was "military," and his second thought was "violent."

Billy bumped his arm, and Sean mouthed "partner" at him. Billy nodded and then frowned, squinting at the figure. It was a man—that much Sean could see—with a watch cap on his head but his face exposed.

There were trees planted for shade here, but the canopies were big and the trunks were far apart, so light from a bright harvest moon illuminated him every few steps, and he and Billy got an eyeful.

Billy's muttered "Oh no" in Sean's ear was enough for all the pieces to fall into place.

Sean's eyes went back to the partner, who was now hugging the shadows as though he knew he was being observed. He had a square jaw that came to a point of a chin, a hawk-like nose, and a craggy brow. But if he looked beyond the nose and the brow, he could still see the resemblance. He wondered if this man's eyes were flat and cynical, made characterless with anger, if his mouth was thin with cruelty.

He wondered if Billy knew who the other perpetrator might be, the lithe young person with the bleached ponytail and the ingenious ways of stealing large objects.

He wondered if he should call Andre now or if he should wait until this played out, wait to see what Billy would do, trust in his lover's adulthood in a situation that might test the trust of any man, old or young.

Before he could make a decision, their thief emerged from the house, steering two new mountain bikes down the sidewalk and into the thruway. When he got to the park proper, his partner stepped out of the shadows.

"Fucking mountain bikes again? Are you kidding me?" he growled.

"I'm sorry," said his younger counterpart. "He had some good woodworking tools, but I can't carry all that stuff."

"You've done it before," the guy snapped, grabbing one of the bikes for himself.

"You stole my fucking skateboard!" the younger one said, and Sean could have predicted the fist that came out and struck the younger figure in the face, but it still surprised him.

Apparently it didn't surprise Billy, because he stood, hopped the wall, and practically flew to the shadows to clock the guy in the face.

"You leave him alone, you sonofabitch," Billy yelled. "You too much of a coward to fucking do your own goddamned crime? You gotta get your son to do it?"

"Guillermo?" Roberto said, his voice shaking. "The hell are you doing here? You gotta go! Your cop boyfriend's gonna find out and—"

"Too late," Sean said, approaching from the wall with a solid stride, hoping he could make up for in imposing what he lacked in speed. "His cop boyfriend is here. Mr. Morales—"

"Guillermo Senior," Billy spat with disgust, his hands still tangled in his father's sweatshirt.

"Guillermo Morales Senior," Sean said, wanting to kick the guy in the balls on general principles. "You are under arrest." He pulled his badge from his pocket and his handcuffs and got ready to do some fancy footwork here, if he was going to make everything turn out okay.

HE CALLED the local police and identified himself by badge number, asking for a unit to come pick up one adult male suspect of local robberies. Then, while Billy held his father's handcuffed hands behind his back and frog-marched him toward the street, he called Andre. He was going to need Andre to give this whole thing some respectability.

He'd just finished hanging up on Andre's sputtered promise to be there in ten when the cruiser arrived.

It took ten minutes and some hot badge flashes to get Senior (as he would forever call the man, because in Sean's mind he had no relationship to the man in Sean's life besides sperm donor) handcuffed in the back of the unit for safekeeping. Then he took in Billy, standing with his arms crossed and glaring at his little brother, who was mirroring his posture with the exact same expression on his narrower, softer face.

Sean had known—deep in his gut he'd known. As soon as Roberto had failed to show up for dinner with Billy, he'd known. As soon as he'd heard about the dyed ponytail and his mother's mysteriously missing money, Sean had known. The dog-walking business, the missing dog— all of it had told the story.

And as soon as he'd seen Billy's father on the walkway, he'd known why.

But what to do about it now?

"The fuck you doing here, Roberto?" Billy snarled, breaking the silence at exactly the same time Roberto did.

"The fuck you doing in my life, Ghee? You fuckin' bailed, remember?"

"I was *thrown out*, you little shithead! Dad beat the shit out of me, remember? He broke my nose, and I pissed blood for three days! You had a chance to be *free* of that motherfucker, and you came crawling back?"

Roberto took a step away, and his aggressive, upright posture folded a little, his shoulders hunching in. "He… he…."

"He tricked you," Sean said, glancing at Billy. *C'mon, Billy, trust me here.* "Didn't he?"

Roberto wasn't a hardened criminal. His lower lip quivered, and he swallowed loudly. "Nobody tricked me into nothin'," he snarled.

Sean lowered his head, rubbed the back of his neck, and pulled Billy aside. "Work with me here, Guillermo," he said softly.

"Let him get what he deserves," Billy snarled, his chest heaving and his blood obviously up.

"What he deserves is a second chance, just like you got," Sean said, but he didn't raise his voice. "You don't get it. You know what happens if Roberto gets arrested here?"

Billy froze. Yeah. He knew. "He goes into the system," he rasped.

"Yeah, he does. And even if they seal his records since he's a juvenile, it doesn't matter. He's seventeen. He'll be in the system as an adult because enough stuff of enough value has been stolen to make a case for grand theft. He might even end up doing gen pop time, and look at him." Roberto was Billy's height, but he hadn't worked out for years, turning his body into a machine. In fact, he looked like he was on the verge of an ulcer, which, given what Sean guessed, only made sense.

"He'll get slaughtered," Sean said, hating that in his bones. "And once he's in the system, if he so much as looks at a cop funny, he'll end up back in the same place."

Billy growled and then glanced at Roberto surreptitiously. Sean saw what Billy did—the kid wiping under his eyes with the back of his hand and looking around to see if anybody had taken note.

"Fuck." Billy's next breath sounded decidedly shaky. "What do we do?"

Sean glanced at the kid again and then saw Andre's unmarked pulling into the cul-de-sac. "Wait for the officers to take the statement of the homeowners," he said, because that was already in progress. "And wait for Andre to come and witness this since I'm not officially anything right now."

"And then what?" Billy asked, and this time the pleading, the supplication in his voice, was evident.

"Trust me," Sean said, ordering his thoughts like little soldiers. "Can you do that for me, Guillermo? Can you trust me?"

Billy looked at him for a long time and then nodded. Given how the man in the back of the unit had let Billy down, Sean knew this for the huge furry deal it really was. "Please," he said. "Please, cop, let's do my little brother right."

"I'll do my best," he promised. Inside, he was shaking. God, please let this turn out okay.

IT TOOK him five minutes to finish briefing Andre, who was both irritated and impressed.

"This?" he asked, clearly exasperated. "This is what all those, 'Hey, could you just get me some info,' calls were about? You were trying to bust a robbery ring while on leave?"

Sean winced. "I was bored," he said. "We were walking in the park daily—it sort of evolved." They'd hidden the "murder board" in the guest bedroom during the Halloween party; if Andre didn't know "evolve" was a vast understatement, he probably had a good guess.

Andre snorted. "Well, you've managed to evolve a successful relationship and a healthy career bump out of a punctured lung. Maybe next time you'll really get shot and figure out world peace!"

"Not funny," Billy said direly, and Andre held out his hands.

"No, no—you're right. And judging by the way Sean's breathing, this was a big deal. I hear you."

"Fucking night air," Sean rasped. "Who knew your mother was right about that shit?"

"It's terrifying, I know." Andre nodded fervently, making Sean wonder if he didn't have an overbearing mother in *his* family roster. "But what do you have for me?"

Sean shot Billy a look. "You guys, follow my lead. I'm going to talk to Roberto, and Andre?"

"Yeah?"

"Let's see what we can do to keep this kid out of the system. I think you're gonna see he's had a raw deal."

"You go first, partner."

Sean remembered Roberto's and Billy's arms-crossed, spines-upright glowers, and as he walked up to Roberto, he relaxed his shoulders, put his hands in his pockets, and made sure his expression was neutral. Not too pleasant—people didn't trust that. If he could get Roberto to respond, he might try smiling a little.

"So," Sean said quietly, "Roberto. I'm a friend of your brother's. My name is Sean Kryzynski, and I'm a detective for Sac PD. This here is Andre Christie. He's my partner on the force, another detective. Our usual beat is homicide, but your brother and I started looking into the local robberies while I was on medical leave."

"Good for you," Roberto said sullenly.

"No," Sean replied. "Good for *you.* Because this bust was off books until I cuffed your father and called the cops. And the only people who know *your* name are standing right here."

Roberto swallowed and automatically glanced at Billy, whose anger had melted as he'd realized his little brother's options.

"Sean's a good guy," Billy said, his eyes on Sean's. "He's going to try to do right by you, but you've got to cooperate."

Roberto nodded. "Fine. I'll cooperate. What's that mean?"

All the attitude. Well, apparently it ran in the family.

"Let me tell you what I know, or what I think I know. You can correct me if I'm wrong, okay?"

Roberto appeared a little more animated. Sean was asking for his input and not bullying the kid with his world view or his badge.

"Okay, cop. What do you think you know?"

"Well, I think this all started when your mom had a little bit of money. You were being a good kid—walking dogs for pocket cash, getting to know the neighborhood. Was that when you ran into the old man?"

Roberto swallowed. "Yeah. He was getting drunk in the park."

Sean nodded. "And he told you how bad his life was now that he'd lost his family, didn't he?"

There was a miserable nod. "Started talking about how he shouldn't've hit mami that way. How he missed us. Sounded really fuckin' sorry." That bitter stinger at the end told Sean all he needed to know about how truly disillusioned Roberto had become.

"Yeah," Sean said. "Abusers like your father? They're pros, Berto. They hide that shit all the time. They're like con men, but your bruises are the con. Don't feel bad that you got taken in. You wanted a dad—there's no shame in that. And you wanted not to have to struggle for money. You remembered when your folks could afford a better place, better food. You wanted that back. You were vulnerable, and you're only a kid. Every kid wants two parents, right?"

Roberto crossed his arms again, but this time it was to protect himself. "Yeah. It was stupid. I bet mami didn't want nothing to do with him. I was dumb."

"You were a kid," Sean said again. "And suddenly you were the grown-up. You'd lost Guillermo, you'd lost Teresa—you were the new man of the house, and you were scared."

Berto didn't answer, but he blinked rapidly, and that was enough for Sean.

"And your old man says, 'Kid, I got some money with your mom. I know she doesn't want to talk to me right now, but I think maybe if I get a little of my money back, I can get back on my feet.' Am I right?"

The rapid blinking spilled over, and Roberto nodded miserably.

Billy said, "Aw, Berto. No."

"Yeah," Roberto whispered. "Like, word for word."

"That's how mami's money disappeared," Billy surmised, and Sean could see him trying to swallow the anger, trying to work on the empathy.

"Yeah." Roberto lost the battle and wiped his face on his shoulder. "And she cried, Ghee. For two days. She almost couldn't work. It was like… like having that money disappear, it took all the fight out of her. *I* did that."

"And then you called him," Sean reasoned. "And you yelled at him and tried to get him to give the money back."

"He'd spent it," Roberto spat. "Fucker had *spent* it, on drugs. On a shitty house that's falling apart. On a fucking hooker that does more meth than dick. He spent mami's money, and then he laughed in my face."

Sean nodded. "And then he told you how to earn more."

Roberto shook his head. "I didn't want to. I told him no. He said, 'That one house has a sweet bike in it,' and I said, 'Yeah, it's also got a hella big dog.'"

"He let the dog out, didn't he," Sean prompted. He'd known this had to be connected.

"He *shot* the dog," Berto burst out, and then he broke down sobbing, and Sean nodded to Billy, who took his little brother into his arms and held him like a father should have and let him cry himself out.

While they were doing that, Andre and Sean held a quiet conference.

"So the old man got the kid to start robbing houses for a cut," Andre said quietly.

"Yeah. The kid picked the places without dogs—he didn't want another dog on his conscience, so he avoided those places. He knew where they were from his dog-walking days." Poor Berto. Like Billy, he must have really loved working with the animals.

"And dear old dad just keeps blackmailing him. Keep stealing or he'd tell the kid's mother. Keep stealing or he'd turn the kid over to the cops," Andre reasoned. "The kid's the one taking the stuff, right?"

"Yup," Sean said. "He doesn't know corruption is a crime."

"He does not," Andre agreed. They met each other's eyes, and Andre nodded. "In fact, it carries a stiffer sentence than the actual crime, doesn't it?"

Sean nodded grimly. "It does."

"I'm thinking maybe we have a talk with Senior and he confesses to the robberies, and we leave Roberto out of it?" The question at the end was because Andre wanted to confirm what Sean had been thinking.

"Yeah," Sean said. Then he grimaced. "And because I'm sort of living with the kid's brother...."

"Maybe my name should be on all the paperwork," Andre finished, sighing. "That's no good, Sean. That gets me the commendation and you the bupkiss."

Sean shrugged. "Yeah, but otherwise who knows when the next DA is going to jump in and start screaming about cleaning up police corruption, and then this is going to be a whole big thing again. I think we learned from the last DA that sometimes staying outside the system is really what's best, you know?"

Andre shook his head. That wound on Jackson Rivers's back and the four cops who would have murdered him and his witness rather than let the truth come to light about their false arrest would haunt the department for a good long time.

"We're supposed to help people," Andre said bitterly.

Sean grimaced. "Yeah, but if we keep Roberto out of the system for this one and let his dad go to prison, we've helped my boyfriend's entire family, and we need to count that as a win."

"Fine," Andre muttered. "I still say we should put your name on the paperwork—"

Sean put a hand on his wrist. "And I say we don't take that chance. Now we've only got one thing to do."

Andre growled. "Convince Senior that this is the best course of action for him."

Sean nodded. "Think we should call Cramer? Maybe explain the sitch to him and have him plead out?"

Andre shook his head. "Normally, I'd say yes. But Cramer and Rivers—they're going to be calling attention with their big names on this small potatoes. Let's see if we can maybe be good guys without the training wheels, yeah?"

"Yeah."

THE BACK of a police cruiser was a really, really shitty place to be. There were bars and bulletproof glass between the front and back seats, and no amount of cleaning could get out the vomit, urine, and feces that had been released there by the previous residents. There was an aura of despair, of anger, back there that would take sage and an exorcist to remove.

Sean got in on one side of Senior and Andre got in on the other, and then they shut the doors, knowing that the vehicle, being off, would have zero ventilation, and the close, sweaty smell of bodies and past residents would be nasty and uncomfortable, and their perpetrator was weak.

Soon he'd be doing anything to get out of there.

"What?" Senior asked, after about a second of silence. "Is this where you tell me it's in my best interest to talk?"

"No," Sean replied pleasantly. "This is where I tell you that if I ever see you outside of a prison cell, I'm going to pin your balls together with your service medal for beating the shit out of your family, you gutless fucking weasel. This is where my partner offers you the deal of the century while you imagine what a testicle piercing would feel like."

Senior sneered at him, but he didn't say anything, which was good. Sean would have given—quite literally—all the breath in his body to shut this fucker up.

"Wow," Andre said. "I've never heard him threaten someone like that. You should listen to him, man. I think the joint's the best thing for you."

"For what?" Senior asked, keeping his eyes carefully off Sean. "I didn't do nothing. That useless kid did all the robbing."

"Are you sure?" Andre asked. "Are you *sure* the kid did all the breaking and entering? Because, you know, if you, say, *coerced* him into doing the breaking and entering, that's corruption of a minor. That carries the sentence of grand theft *plus* the seven years for corruption of a minor. But, say, if it was *just you and nobody else*, then that's just grand theft."

"Much smaller sentence," Sean said.

"Would a lawyer tell me that?" Senior asked suspiciously.

"Yes." They both nodded, because it was the truth.

"But only," Andre added, "if you phrase it as a hypothetical and keep your son's name out of your ungrateful rotted mouth forever after, amen."

"Which one of the little fags blew you?" Senior asked meanly, and they knew the interview was over—but they also knew they'd won.

"You have the right to remain silent," Andre began, reciting the Miranda rights. "Anything you say—"

"Okay!" Senior whined. "Okay, okay. It was all me. Not the kid. All me. I stole the shit. I shot the fuckin' dog. All me. Ungrateful little bastards. Their mother was a stupid bitch, and—"

Sean hit him in the nuts and didn't even feel a little bit guilty for punching down.

Guillermo Morales Senior was still retching and sobbing as Sean got out of the car and Andre finished reading him his rights. Idly he wondered if he was going to get cited for brutality, but deep down he knew he'd take that citation, and if he never hit another perp, that one would be worth it in a thousand different ways.

But that momentary satisfaction wasn't going to make the next few hours okay, no matter how much he wished it could.

Trusting the Future

BILLY YAWNED and stretched in bed, trying to figure out what was wrong.

Then he heard the shower and sat bolt upright, wondering where his head was. Monday morning. Sean was up! He was in the shower. How late was it? Did Billy have anywhere to go?

He took a deep breath and calmed down. He went into work orientation on Wednesday. He had school on Tuesday and Thursday and Friday morning. This morning, after he and Sean had gotten home at fuck you in the morning, was free.

His eyes narrowed, and he leapt out of bed and stomped into the bathroom.

"You looked like shit last night, cop," he snapped, shucking his boxers and pulling the shower curtain open. Sean was standing there—not sitting—squinting through shampoo. "What are you doing up so early?"

Sean squeezed his eyes shut and wiped the water from his face. "Good morning, sunshine. I thought I'd get up at my usual hour and go to the dog park today and tell people that we found the bad guy and he's in jail."

"The bad guy—"

"Who has no relation to you," Sean said soberly. "Get in or get out, sunshine—you're letting all my nice steam out, and we only have so much hot water."

Billy glared at him, but he got in, turning Sean's body so his back was to the spray, then ducking so he could rinse his hair.

"And that part about you looking like shit?" he growled, still afraid for Sean's health.

"I'm going to overlook that as concern, because I already have one mother, and she hasn't seen me naked since I was five."

Billy tried not to chuckle. That was a good one. "Seriously—"

Sean wiped the water from his eyes again and straightened up, turning to kiss Billy full and long on the lips, with tongue and wandering hands, until Billy's senses were suffused with warm, wet, slippery man.

For a few blissful moments, all the events of the night before slid away. His brother robbing houses, that pathetic story of being taken in by their father, and his father, who had barely recognized Billy's existence—all of it went rinsing down the drain. The awful conversation with their mother after they'd taken Berto home, the terrible confession, their mother's heartbreak and guilt—God, all of it, all of it swirling with the hot water down, down, and away while Billy allowed himself to be overwhelmed, to be taken over by pleasure, by security, by love.

He'd heard what Andre had said while Billy had been comforting Roberto. Sean had given up any credit for the bust, any commendation, any mention for taking his own initiative, all so Billy and Berto's no-good, gutless, asshole sperm donor could go to prison and leave Roberto out of it to have a second chance.

Trust me, Sean had said, and Billy had—he'd trusted his cop. But he'd thought Sean would do a minimum best, a "sorry, man, them's the breaks," best.

Sean had given everything for Billy and his ungrateful punkass little brother, and Billy…. Billy didn't have any way to pay him back.

"You're thinking too much," Sean murmured into his mouth. "Turn around."

"Turn around to do what?" Billy mumbled, but Sean was bossing him around this time, and Billy found himself facing the spray while Sean… sat down? Was that what Sean was doing? Sitting down behind—ahh….

Sean started with the washcloth, which was probably a good idea, the gentle pressure, the nubbly pleasure, stroking down his crease, probing delicately into his hole. Billy propped himself on the rails recently installed on the sides of the shower and thrust his rump out a bit, giving Sean easy access, and Sean chuckled and obliged.

Some more cleaning, and some rinsing, and some—ah! Probing with a finger and… oh… oh…. Sean's tongue swiped across him, and Billy moaned, suddenly needing this so badly he didn't even realize he'd slipped directly into subspace, limp and willing, ready to allow the man behind him to do anything to him, anything at all.

Sean obliged, and damn, his tongue was a thing of magic. So were his fingers, gently thrusting, teasing, stretching, before Sean moved his hands to other places—the backs of Billy's thighs, which were really sensitive, and the front of them, which just sort of teased him until—oh! Oh yes! A perfect reach-around, Sean grasping Billy's cock while he went to work with that wicked, wicked tongue.

Billy began to gibber, his body shaking, until finally he managed, "Gonna come. Gonna fall! Gonna—"

But Sean had pulled back and let go as soon as Billy said he was going to fall, and Billy, adrift and on the ledge of orgasm, welcomed Sean's hands as he stood and helped Billy out of the tub, as he dried them both off and led Billy, dazed and still shaking, into the bedroom and onto the bed.

Billy slid on first and lay on his back, legs spread, knees flopping lewdly to the side, not sure if that's what Sean wanted but knowing that's what *he needed*. He needed to see Sean's face while they were merged, needed to know Sean was there, holding him, *grounding* him, keeping him from flying off the edge of the cliff without a parachute or a place to land.

Sean reached above him under the pillow for the lube, and Billy opened his mouth to try and tell him, "Hey, this isn't my first rodeo!" but Sean kissed him instead while simultaneously clicking the lubricant and oiling his own cock.

Billy groaned, grabbing Sean's shoulders just to hold on to his own sanity, and Sean chuckled.

"Patience, okay?"

Billy swallowed, but the word came out anyway. "Need." And oh, he needed all of it like he'd never needed before. Sean's touch, his tenderness, his gentle care. How did Billy not know this was necessary? It was like rediscovering sex all over again when he thought he'd had a handle on things by taking Sean into his bed. But this was Sean taking *him* to bed, taking his pleasure into consideration, taking his time, just taking *him*, and when he breached Billy's entrance, Billy wasn't thinking about size or length or professional pride in the timing of the orgasm or turning his hips or his face to the camera or any of the other things porn had taught him about sex.

He was thinking, *Thank God, Thank God this man is inside of me, making me his own.*

But that didn't mean it didn't feel *really* good as well.

Sean didn't ask him if it was okay or too much—Billy's groan, the way he wrapped his legs around Sean's hips—he knew that spoke for him, and Sean took him at his word. He thrust slowly at first, establishing a rhythm, and as Billy blissed out in the fog of sex, Sean moved faster… and faster… while Billy begged him, spurred him on, pleaded for his come.

"Grab yourself, Guillermo," Sean whispered. "You come first. It's your turn."

Billy remembered he could and slid his hand between their bodies, grabbed his cock, and reveled, the first time in forever, at how good his own fist felt around it. Sean's face contorted with effort was the sexiest thing he'd ever seen, and Sean's cock, stretching him and knowing him, was the first time being fucked had almost felt like too much.

It was too big inside him, not the length or the girth but the *man*, the person he'd given himself to, heart and soul, and as he squeezed his own cock and felt orgasm approaching, overwhelming him, destroying him, he wondered how he was going to survive when it had wrung him out and left him empty and aching and needing more.

And then it hit.

He must have screamed because his throat was sore, and he knew his body convulsed from his taint to his asshole to his arms, one flailing for purchase on the sheets and the other gripping his cock like a lifeline, but Sean kept fucking, kept thrusting, kept rutting until he gave his own cry of orgasm and collapsed, face buried in Billy's neck, his hips still twitching as he filled Billy up, completed him, shot hot and dripping in his ass—but more than that, bigger than that, filling his heart, his throat, his brain, his *soul* as well.

Billy's body surprised him then, bunching up for one more leap, one more jump off the ledge, but this time Sean was holding him, gasping in his ear, and Billy closed his eyes, held his lover to his heart, and together they leapt into the ether and floated down, down, gently to the earth.

Sean lay on top of him, his cock sliding out of Billy's ass, leaving a trail of come against his thigh, but Billy didn't care. His breathing! How was he breathing after that? But before Billy could lecture, worry, or fret, Sean slid to his customary side but this time facing Billy and throwing his outer arm across Billy's chest, keeping him anchored, keeping him safe.

Billy closed his eyes, feeling them burn, surprised at the rush of emotion that swept through him now that sex had left him full and sated, vulnerable to the things in his heart.

"Hey," Sean whispered, brushing under his cheekbone. "How you doing?"

Billy was absurdly glad he didn't make an "I didn't think I was *that* bad!" joke because what they'd just done, it was too big, too important for self-deprecation.

"My heart feels broken and remade," he said, eyes still closed. "And it's a little sore, but I think it can hold the both of us still."

"Yeah?" Sean's voice shook a little, and Billy turned his head and smiled faintly.

"You make it stronger, cop. You take care of me really good."

Sean's smile was slow and warm, like honey. "I do, don't I."

Billy heard the pride and had to chuckle a little. "You worried?"

"I've been sort of helpless," Sean admitted. "I… worried a little that… that you wouldn't love the caretaker as much as you loved the patient."

Billy searched out his eyes and rubbed his lower lip with a come-stained thumb. "And I worried that you wouldn't love the mess as much as you loved the bossy porn guy."

"Weird how we fret about the stupid stuff, isn't it?" Sean asked gently.

Billy nodded. "I really love you."

"I really love you too."

They lay there for a while, talking about everything and nothing. About prepping the house for a dog and changes Billy would make when he got his paycheck. And about synching their schedules when Sean went back to work. And maybe helping Randy get a car so he could be more independent now that Billy was giving up his bed in the flophouse.

Practical things that belied the momentous, magical thing they'd just done.

In the middle of their discussion, Sean's stomach growled, and Billy smiled. "Go ahead. Let's get dressed. Let me feed us. If my knees still work, we can go to the dog park, okay?"

Sean had just slid on his briefs and his jeans when the doorbell rang, and Sean hauled a clean shirt and sweatshirt on over his head. "That's probably Andre," he said over his shoulder. "Get dressed and join us."

"Aren't you going to shower?" Billy asked, because he felt like he smelled like Sean and probably vice versa.

Sean squinted at him. "The only one who's going to get close enough to smell that we had sex is the guy I had sex with, Guillermo. Get your brain out of the porn studio and get dressed!"

Billy chuckled then and rolled out of bed, found some of the clothes he'd moved into Sean's dresser, and pulled them on, wondering as he did so how long it would be before they started wearing each other's shirts.

As he heard Andre's voice in the front room, he frowned at the dresser and reached into Sean's drawer to pull out one of his SAPD sweatshirts in white and black. He threw it on with a certain possessiveness that he didn't question before hustling into the front room.

Loose Ends and Happy Beginnings

ANDRE GREETED Sean in the way of their people—with a box of donuts and two large coffees. They liked theirs with cream and sugar because drinking it black was masochism. It was one of the ways they'd bonded as work partners nearly a year before.

There was nothing weak about not liking your coffee to taste like crap.

"Oh wow," Sean murmured. "Come in quick. Let me eat a donut before my better-looking half comes out."

"He's moderating your diet?" Andre asked. "That's terrifying."

"He's very nutrition conscious," Sean told him, thinking that was an understatement. "And it's probably a good thing too. It would have been easy to pack on pounds these last few weeks. Now come sit and let me eat sugar and tell me what's doing."

"Well, eat fast, because you need to wait for Billy before I talk. I don't want to tell the same story twice."

Sean nodded and sat down at the kitchen table, going to work on the donuts with Andre between gulps of delicious artisan coffee.

Billy emerged right as he was reaching for his second, and seeing him in Sean's sweatshirt was surprising enough to almost—*almost*—make him drop the donut.

Andre turned to see what had caught Sean's attention and smirked. "Makes a statement, doesn't he?"

The sweatshirt was a little tight on Billy's amazing chest, but it was loose in the waist and generally looked really magnificent. That, however, was not why Sean was speechless.

Sean spoke shared-wardrobe too, and that was a very big way of saying, "Mine."

He smiled. "You have no idea," he murmured before taking a bite of donut while looking Billy in the eye.

Billy blushed, and Andre snorted. "You know, my wife wears my shirts too—I think that's a universal language there. But come sit down, son. Have a donut."

"I'm having a frittata, no cheese," Billy said, "and I'm making one for each of you, too, so you have some protein to balance that out because…." He shuddered. "Bwah. No. Bad cops. No donuts. Shame."

Andre raised his eyebrows at Sean, who smirked and took another bite, and then Andre surreptitiously reached for his second, sticking his tongue out at Billy's back like one of his children.

Sean chuckled and then gestured with the rest of his donut, talking through a full mouth.

"So we're here. Billy's made his entrance. Now speak."

Andre sighed and took another bite before setting the rest of his down. "Okay, so the DA went for the deal, and Billy's dad signed off on it, without a lawyer. I have to tell you, though, the only real loophole in this deal is that without mentioning Roberto's name, Billy's father can still try to contact his wife and kids. Did you talk to their mother?"

Billy grunted, and Sean winced.

"It was rough," Billy said. "She was so hurt—and so mad. But I think she'll forgive Roberto eventually. Why?"

"Because you two may need to help her get a permanent restraining order, something that keeps him from calling her up from jail. Also help her change her numbers. You can get a notification telling you when he's getting out, but hopefully by then your mother will have a chance to move, to update the restraining order, and maybe he'll leave her alone."

"With luck he'll get killed in jail," Billy said, sounding truly optimistic about the whole thing for the first time.

"We can always cross our fingers," Andre said soberly. "Because if he vows he's reformed—"

"He's lying," Billy finished, turning toward them both. "I think my family knows that now."

"Good," Andre said. "Now, the reason I came here with donuts as an offering is because I wanted to talk about Berto. You need to think about how you're going to mentor the kid. He's lost his one male influence, and you guys, he's going to need some attention. I've seen kids like this. If someone doesn't step in—"

"I was thinking about Jackson's duplex, with the young ex-cons," Sean said, because he'd thought of nothing else since the night before.

"They have work parties, and Jackson and Henry organize community service parties for them to help them sign off with their parole officers."

"That's a good idea," Billy said, sounding surprised. "Berto, you know, he was a squid—but he also wanted someone to tell him he was a good boy." His voice got sad, and he paused for a bit in the act of chopping chives. "Probably why he was such an easy target for our dad, right?"

"Exactly," Andre said gently. "So get him involved with the ex-cons—who will also talk about how much prison sucks and what they're doing to try to quit their old lives—and maybe get him a job doing something he loves. Nothing official. I understand his grades have gotten really bad in the last year—"

"That's what mami said," Billy muttered. "He's smart. He can fix it. But you're right—no official job until he's going to graduate high school. But what can he do?"

Sean grinned. "He can help Randy watch our dogs," he said happily.

"What dogs?" Andre asked, glancing around the mostly tidy house looking baffled.

"The ones Billy and I are getting next Sunday," Sean told him. "I've been haunting websites. I've got some ideas."

Billy expertly flipped a frittata and then turned to graze Sean's temple with his lips. "You really mean that?" he asked, his voice low and quaky like it had been after sex. "You'd do that? Open your duplex to my thieving little brother?"

"He needs to be trusted, Billy," Sean said softly. "And he loves dogs. Watching your father shoot Sweaty was a big deal for him. I think being able to care for a couple of dogs—really be the dog walker like he wanted to do at first—that would mean a lot to him."

Billy nodded. "And, you know, I'm going to be working at the pet store until I'm out of school, probably. Maybe when he's out of high school, I can get him a job."

Sean nodded. "Exactly. We can give him options. Let him see that not all adults are douchebags. Not every path leads to something that feels awful."

Billy cleared his throat and went back to cooking, and Sean and Andre watched him for a moment. Sean didn't know about Andre, but he knew that a lot of thinking was going on with all that industry, but they were both wise enough not to say anything until Billy turned back around with their plated frittatas.

Andre and Sean ate gratefully—the donuts really had sent them on a sugar spiral—and then Andre left to get back to work.

Billy had started the dishes against Sean's protest, and now Sean stood up behind him and wrapped his arms around Billy's waist.

"Whatcha thinking?" he asked softly.

"That I don't got no guarantees," Billy rasped. "About Berto. He could steal all your stuff. Murder us in our sleep and run away with our dogs. It could all go horribly wrong."

"Very true. But I have faith that your mom will help keep him in line, and so will the dogs. And so will Jackson's guys. I mean, there's no guarantees with kids, you know. My own mom goes off on my brother's girlfriend all the time because she doesn't like the way she's raising the kids, but I've met them. They're fine. I don't see a lot of screwups in their future. I could be wrong. It's a crapshoot."

Billy chuckled and gave up on the dishes, taking Sean's hands where they were clasped around his stomach. Billy's hands, warm and soapy, were comforting somehow.

"What if I hate my new job and I have to go back to waiting tables?"

"Happens all the time," Sean soothed. "You'll find something you like more."

"What if I get to my upper-division classes and I suck at them, and I realize I hate engineering and should have been a chef instead?"

Sean finally laughed outright, tilting his head back so he could really put his stomach into it.

Billy caught his breath and turned around in his arms, his eyes searching out Sean's face.

"What?" Sean murmured, caught by the intensity of those not-so-cynical, very vulnerable brown eyes.

"Your laugh," Billy said, as full of wonder as a little kid. "I used to wish I could hear it when your lungs worked, because I thought it would be really amazing."

Sean's smile felt shot with sunshine, like glorious light was filling his soul. "Is it?"

"It's even better than I thought it would be," Billy said, sounding choked.

"See?" Sean whispered. "Have some faith, Guillermo. Have some hope. That turned out all right for you, right?"

"Yeah," he said, lowering his mouth to Sean's. Their mouths meshed, the kiss a benediction, and then a prelude, and then becoming all it needed to be in itself. He pulled away and engulfed Sean in a hug, strong and gentle, everything Sean had ever wanted when he'd dreamed about being in a man's arms. "Maybe we should have some faith."

"We're going to get dogs," Sean promised.

"We're going to be in love forever and ever," Billy promised back. "I'm going to graduate, and you and me are going to get married in a park, like Rivers and Cramer are threatening to do, and our mothers can come be a lot together, and we'll invite the flophouse and your people and—"

Sean kissed him again. "Wait until I ask you," he murmured. "Don't worry. It'll happen."

"It'll happen," Guillermo Morales replied, going back to that tight, greedy hug. "We can do things like that."

"Together, we absolutely can."

Sean could stand holding his sunshine to his heart forever, but they'd get bored just standing around saying I love you. Their lives were busy, and when they held hands and got to work, they could accomplish so much.

Like all of their friends, they had so much to do.

Nothing Happened

A Fishlet

ELLERY STARED at his two PIs—technically one too many for such a small firm—and flailed for something to say.

"You… you were just going to… you were supposed to pick up a file," he said, well aware that he'd said such things before.

"We did," Jackson told him, nodding excitedly like a puppy who'd fetched. "Right, Henry?"

"Sure." Henry gave his partner the side-eye—through the one eye not swollen shut. "We got the file. See? On Jade's desk."

Jade, who was rifling through the file, gave them both the stink-eye. "Right file," she confirmed. Then, "*Whose blood is this?*"

"Blood?" Jackson said, his most innocent voice at odds with the ice pack held against his broken nose. "There's blood on your file? How'd that happen?"

Ellery looked at Jackson's sister, hands open, palms up, as if begging her for an answer. "Can you believe…?"

"The actual fuck?" she asked them both. "Jackson, you need a new Kleenex. Your nose will *not* stop bleeding. Henry, sit down and I'll wrap your knuckles and find you another ice pack for your eye." She shook her head. "And somebody had better tell us what in the hell went on."

Henry and Jackson met eyes again, and Jackson was the one who said it. "Nothing happened."

They smiled at Ellery and Jade, who stared back in outrage, and the word "impasse" permeated the room.

Three Hours Earlier….

"DO WE have everything?" Jackson asked. "Baby gift?"

"Chcck," Henry said, pointing to the package on the console of Jennifer the minivan.

"Subpoena in triplicate?"

"Check," Henry confirmed, pointing to the folder *under* the baby gift.

"Cookies from the bakery at Midtown?"

"Chempk," Henry mumbled through a mouthful of the cookie he'd stolen from the bakery box just as Jackson asked. "Wam half?"

"Oh my God, yes." Jackson took the offered cookie from Henry and bit into it, trying not to let his eyes roll back in bliss. "Damn, that's good." Brown sugar, toffee, chocolate… what was not to love?

They took a few moments to enjoy their stolen cookies, and then Jackson was back on the case.

"Stolen schedule identifying Lindstrom's, Craft's, and the choir boys' schedule so we can successfully avoid every asshole we've pissed off in the last two and a half months?"

Henry held up the highly marked-up document. "According to Jade, who has studied this extensively, we're good. If we walk into the building and present our subpoena, the desk sergeant—our favorite new mother who we saved with ice cream this summer—will simply hand over the folder, accept the bribes, tell us she adores us, and we can leave. Eas—"

"If you say 'easy' I'm asking Jennifer to stop so I can kick your ass out of the car."

Henry looked around and grimaced. This was one of the streets downtown where the homeless tents were a thick stratum around the businesses. There was a hierarchy here that didn't extend to sympathetic PIs who had business keeping people out of jail. Getting kicked out of the minivan here was not a great idea.

"Understood," he said, only a hint of panic in his voice. "No jinxing this. We're too close."

Jackson and Henry had been trying—one good deed at a time—to have a good working relationship with their local police force. Their favorite detective, Sean Kryzynski, had gone back to work a week before, and while they trusted Sean and his partner, Andre Christie, they didn't want to put too much of a burden on their friends as they negotiated crime in Sacramento. They had Fetzer and Hardison in the flatfoot division, but they were near retirement, and, well, it would be good to have some more cops on their side.

Some PIs worked very well with their local po-po, but Jackson had history. Ever so much history.

Their one good lead—and it was a great one—was with the desk sergeant. Desk Sergeant Clara Kensington had been a godsend that summer when they'd needed to find out who had worked a case. Henry, picking up on how miserable she must have been at eight months pregnant in August, had endeared himself to the woman with a shameless use of ice cream and a little sports cooler full of popsicles. Win!

And today, when they had a judge-issued subpoena for the police files related to a case they were defending, Jackson and Henry were going to *capitalize* on that win by bringing the desk sergeant—newly returned from maternity leave—a present for her baby and a box full of delicious pastries.

And hopefully a lot of sincere goodwill. Henry had told Jackson after the last time that he felt like the woman was his own sister. He wanted to see baby pictures, dammit!

Clara—Sergeant Kensington—lit up visibly when Jackson and Henry approached her desk. She was a lovely young woman, probably not yet thirty, who wore her raven-wing-black hair in a double braid tucked into a bun. The look she gave Henry was particularly precious, especially when he said, "We have gifts and then business, but none of that until we see pictures."

She looked shyly around, as though afraid to admit she even had a child. When she saw that no other cops were nearby—Jackson and Henry had chosen this time of day in particular because K-Ski told them it was often dead after two and before four o'clock in the afternoon—she reached into her pocket and pulled out her phone. She was calling up a picture, smiling softly to herself, when Carruthers—one of the cops from the old guard who had hated Jackson the most—strolled in from the back of the station.

"Rivers," he grunted, and Jackson didn't miss the way Clara hid her phone in her pocket when she heard his voice. "The fuck do you want?"

Jackson took a deep breath and was not surprised when Henry answered for him. "Why? Do you need to mop the floor with your face again?"

Jackson grunted. Oh, this was so not what they were here for.

Carruthers sneered. "Lucky shot. We were in a hospital. Who expects a guy to throw down in a hospital?"

"You were being shitty about another cop," Jackson retorted. "Who expects a cop to be shitty about his brother in the hospital?"

"No brother of mine sucks dick," Carruthers spat, and to their surprise, it was Clara who reprimanded him.

"Do I need to refer you for sensitivity training?" she asked crisply. "Because in this department we don't discriminate."

Carruthers's face contorted. "Yeah, you wish. Go spawn another monster, sweetie. I'm tired of hearing about your harelipped little bastard."

Jackson gaped at the man, who stalked away, his obviously mortified rookie partner at his side, and then snuck a look at Sergeant Kensington.

She was stricken, her eyes red-rimmed, her lower lip trembling, everything about her annihilated in one cruel statement. Jackson looked back at the two cops heading for the elevator and then turned to Henry.

"I'll be right back," he said.

Henry started talking a mile a minute to Kensington. "Here, you just… watch this, eat a cookie. What we need is written up on the subpoena. We'll be right back."

He caught up with Jackson as Jackson was rounding the corner.

"You were supposed to stay put," Jackson muttered.

"This way we can have adjoining cells," Henry said, and Jackson could hear the fury in his voice. Yeah, if he was a better person, he'd tell Henry no, but he was not.

Which was a good thing because there was a *mess* of cops waiting for the elevators, all of them laughing and elbowing Carruthers in the ribs.

"Good one!"

"God, I wish she'd stop showing those pictures. That kid gives me the creeps!"

"Stupid cow. Can't she just do her job?"

Jackson counted six of them, including the rookie, who looked like he might be going to cry. Rivers tapped the rookie on the shoulder and gestured with his chin, away from the elevators, out of sight of the bane of his existence.

The kid—God, so young. Did they have to recruit so young? Male, Caucasian, brown hair, green eyes, still had the occasional spot—winced as one of Carruthers's cronies said something particularly crass about Kensington and her baby, and then nodded and slipped away without notice.

He could always say somebody called his name as they were getting on the elevators. Plausible deniability—it was a thing.

The elevator doors opened, and all the laughing, joking good ole boys got on. Jackson and Henry waited a beat to make sure nobody else got in with them and followed, Jackson pressing the Close Door button as he did so.

Instead of turning around to face the doors—that strange human custom—Jackson and Henry stayed, shoulder to shoulder, to face the five assholes who had conspired in the nastiest way possible to make a decent cop's life a living hell.

About the time the five guys facing them realized there was something amiss, Jackson hit the Emergency button, the elevator stopped between the first and second floors, and all hell broke loose.

IN RETROSPECT, it could have gone so very, very wrong. They were, in fact, facing five guys with guns, tasers, and nightsticks. But they were facing them in an enclosed space, and, well, Carruthers swung first. Jackson ducked, Carruthers's fist hit the stainless-steel elevator door, and the melee was on.

Jackson and Henry did good fighting back-to-back. They called out plays—"Duck!" "He's coming for you, Jackson!" "Here's his stick!" At one point, somebody hit the Go button on the elevator, and it made it to the third floor. The doors started to open, and Jackson and Henry met eyes and took stock.

Four of the officers were down, clutching broken noses, sprained wrists, and groins. Or one groin. Carruthers's groin. Jackson might have given the fucker a ruptured testicle, but he was okay with that. One guy was still up, glaring at them, as together they stepped backward into the surprised group of people waiting for the elevator. Quickly, before those people could react to what was inside the car, Jackson reached in, hit the Close Door button, and sent the car all the way up to the sixth floor.

"Wait for the next one," he said as he snatched his hand away. He and Henry didn't even spare a glance at the crowd before bolting for the stairs.

When they got down to the first floor, to their surprise, the rookie was standing with a file folder in his hand.

"Quick!" he urged, shoving the folder at Jackson. "Clara's holding the door."

They followed his direction from the stairwell to a half-hidden utility exit, where Clara stood making sure the door—which apparently needed a key to open and had an automatic lock—was kept open enough for them to shove it wide and sprint outside.

They paused first to make sure she was okay. "You won't catch hell for this?" Jackson asked worriedly. When they got to the car, they'd take stock of their injuries, but mostly everything was minor.

"Not after I file a complaint," she said with a small smile. "If you guys could do that for me, the least I can do is talk to my IA officer."

"That's a tough thing to do," Jackson said soberly.

"My baby's beautiful," she told him, her face crumpling.

"Just like his mother," Henry said, kissing her cheek—and leaving the faintest blood smear. Over the intercom they could hear somebody mustering police for intruders in the building, and it was time to go.

They'd gotten out early enough that nobody was there to stop them as they pulled away from the parking lot and into traffic. Heigh-ho, heigh-ho, it was back to work, heigh-ho.

Henry was on the phone to AJ before they hit the street, asking if maybe, pretty-pretty please, he and Crystal could hack into the cameras at the police station and erase everything that had happened in the last twenty minutes?

Crystal said she'd already started, and Jackson gave thanks for psychic friends.

Adele Fetzer called them before they'd gotten to the office.

"Where are you?" she asked, all irritation.

"In traffic, Adele!" Jackson said brightly. He sounded a little congested; he'd broken his nose. Again.

"Do you have any idea who just walked into a police station, beat the hell out of five officers in an elevator, and got away clean?"

"Nope. What do the security feeds say?"

"Nothing. The whole system went down five minutes ago."

"That's a shame. Was anyone hurt?"

She let out a low chuckle. "According to the guys in the elevator, they just ran into walls."

Jackson held his closed fist up, and Henry bumped it delicately. Both of them had torn knuckles and strained wrists, and that was as violent as they wanted to get for a high five.

"A *damned* shame. I'm sure they're the nicest people," he said, acid dripping from his voice.

Adele's whoop of laughter put *that* lie to bed. "Oh, kid. I'd say you didn't make any friends today, but that little baby-faced hamster kid— Kenny Kinsey, bless his heart—has asked for a different trainer, and he had a *thumb drive* of moments his phone got after Carruthers asked him to turn off his body cam. Carruthers is going to be lucky if he's allowed to retire with his pension."

Jackson sucked air in through his teeth. "So, uhm, body cams— were they on?"

"No," she said pleasantly. "They were all off. The guys were in the station and all. What was going to get them there?"

"Not a thing."

Adele rang off shortly after that, and Jackson let out a breath.

"We got the folder?" he asked.

"Got the folder," Henry affirmed. "I think. My eye's starting to swell shut. What, uhm, are we going to tell Ellery."

"The truth?" Jackson hazarded.

Henry snorted. "Sure."

"NOTHING HAPPENED?" Ellery repeated in disbelief.

"Nothing," Henry agreed, but he was staring at Jackson as though not sure he'd actually said that.

"Nothing," Jackson told them both. "According to the police department, five men just ran into doors."

"In an elevator," Henry added.

"In an elevator," Jackson repeated, as though that somehow made it more credible.

"Five men *including* you?" Jade asked, eyes narrowed.

"In addition to!" Jackson retorted, and Ellery could tell he was stung to his core.

"You and Henry," Ellery said slowly, "beat up five police officers *in the department elevator*, and...."

"There's no record of that," Jackson told him virtuously. "You can't prove that. Nobody will testify to that. It didn't happen."

"Nothing happened," Ellery said, and his eyes widened. Oh my God. He narrowed his eyes and glared. "You...." He pointed his finger directly at Jackson's chest. "*You* should have been a lawyer."

Jackson clutched his heart. "You take that back!"

"Not until you tell me what happened!" Ellery shouted.

"*Nothing happened!*" Jackson and Henry shouted back.

"Hey!" Galen entered in his stately way and thumped on the floor with his cane. He peered from Jackson to Henry in surprise. "What in the hell happened?"

"*Don't* say it!" Ellery ordered, and Jackson and Henry both leaned back, hands to mouths. "According to those two, nothing."

Galen's eyes narrowed. "Is anybody pressing charges?"

"No," Jade said. "I just texted the desk sergeant. She said, and I am quoting here, 'Your employees were kind and supportive and did nothing to warrant any investigation.'"

Galen blinked several times in rapid succession and peered at Jackson and Henry again. "Oh dear God. *Somebody* needs to tell us what happened."

"Nothing." Jackson's voice had taken on that stony ring that told Ellery he wasn't getting a thing out of him.

"Which is probably the same thing that will happen tonight when we get home," Ellery said sweetly. "Not a goddamned thing."

"Fine," Jackson said.

"Fine."

"Fine."

And for the rest of the day, that was that.

THAT NIGHT, Ellery climbed into the shower with Jackson and proceeded to seduce him—gently, of course, because he was covered with bruises.

When it was over, and they'd both dried off and mopped up the excess water on the floors and put on pajamas, Ellery lay, head pillowed on Jackson's chest, and tried to map his injuries.

"Ooh, this one's bad," he murmured. "Someone caught you pretty hard with this one."

"Telescoping nightstick," Jackson mumbled, half asleep. "If he'd had room to swing it, my wrist would be broken."

"*Mmm*...." Ellery kissed his bruised wrist. "Why did this happen again?"

Jackson let out a sigh that told Ellery he was out of fight. "They were being shitty to the desk sergeant. Her kid was born with a cleft palate, I guess. They were telling her to stop showing pictures of her ugly baby. Worse shit, too, but...." He sighed. "Go ahead. Tell me it's stupid."

Ellery's eyes burned. "Nope. Not stupid." He grimaced. "Just... you know. You and Henry are really lucky that nothing happened."

"Yeah. Maybe next time we try to make nice with the police department, nothing can involve fewer ice packs. That'd be nice."

Nice, Ellery thought, but not necessary. Sometimes the biggest somethings were revealed by the most important nothings.

Like Jackson's—and Henry's—enormous hearts.

Zoomies

So I was *trying* to finish *Sean's Sunshine*, and my brain didn't want to do it. Apparently not just kittens have a case of the zoomies.

AH, SUNDAY morning.

They had things to do, Jackson was well aware. Joey was coming by tomorrow to deep clean the house, but he and Ellery needed to tidy up and do laundry before they got company. Ellery had some sort of idea about the two of them "picking out a menu" for a caterer and buying extra food for the entire week after Thanksgiving, since Jackson's brother was going to be in town for a couple of days and Ellery's parents and sister with *her* family were going to be in town *forever*. Or a week, from Wednesday to Wednesday. Whatever. Jackson understood Chanukah would be included in those days, and he and Ellery had gone shopping accordingly with the understanding that a small gift and a card would also be welcome at Christmas.

Jackson had greeted this clarification of holiday tradition with narrowed eyes.

"You do realize that one year, my Christmas gift to Jade and Kaden was that I might live to the next year, right?"

Ellery had blinked. "And yet this year that's a given, and you get to expand your horizons. How fortunate for all of us. No, you're not excused."

"Is this an excuse for your mother to send me goofy cards with reindeer on them and some sort of reminder of the childhood I should have had and she would like to give me as a gift?"

"Do you object?" Ellery asked, and now he looked sober and serious, because that was also what his mother had given Jackson for the last two birthdays.

"No," Jackson said, rubbing his chest. "It's just, I have the feeling that every time she does that, some therapist gets his wings. It's weird."

"Well, if you believed in therapy, I'm sure you could have funded an entire mental health wing by now," Ellery told him, and Jackson was quite done with that conversation, thank you, so he stopped grousing about Christmas.

And started "planning," which mostly consisted of Ellery saying, "And now we have to do this. Which option do *you* want?" and Jackson staring at him in horror while trying to decide if vegan turkey would get him disowned by Jade and Kaden if it was only an option and not the main course.

He was *exhausted*.

So now, lying in his now-customary position of mostly on his stomach but a little on his side—a leftover from when he'd still had stitches in his back—he was thinking that he didn't want to get up. He wanted to hide his head under the pillow and never think about what sort of sauce should be served with vegan turkey or wonder if his brother had an allergy to red wine ever again.

"Jackson," Ellery murmured.

"Jackson's on hold. Please try again," he mumbled.

"Very cute. Jackson!"

"I don't know whether the kids prefer banana cream pie," Jackson wailed. "*I* prefer banana cream pie. Get pumpkin for yourself!" And with that he grabbed the extra pillow and plastered it over his head, thinking if he was lucky, he'd suffocate and not have to "plan" anymore.

"*Jackson!*" Ellery snapped, ripping the pillow off his head. "Can you not hear what's going on in the next room?"

Jackson frowned. His dreams were often violent, with crashes and angry noises. The sounds coming from the living room and dining room were on par with that, with the addition of what sounded like two mountain lions in full roar.

"World War Three?" he mumbled. "The actual fuck are they doing in there?"

"*Destroying my house!*" Ellery wailed. "Could you go stop them?"

Jackson turned to Ellery Cramer, Esquire, Attorney at Law, the man who had saved him body and soul, the man he would die for, the man he would live for.

"I thought you loved me."

"I do. And if *you* love *me*, you will go stop whatever's going on in the next room."

Jackson narrowed his eyes. "If I do that, can I go play pickup with the kids from the flophouse and the kids from the duplex?"

"That's a thing?" Ellery asked in surprise.

"It was going to be," Jackson said. "I was talking to Sean about it, and he and Billy seemed to think the flophouse kids—this generation anyway—wanted to stay tight, and the kids in the duplex miss their old gangs, but you know—"

"They're actually gangs," Ellery said dryly.

"Well, yeah." It was hard to stay away from a bad thing if you didn't have a good thing to replace it. It was why a lot of junkies took up handicrafts in rehab. "We thought, maybe, add Henry in the mix, it would be a good thing."

There was a mountain lion scream from the other room and a crash from what Jackson hoped was a lesser grocery-store vase and not the really nice cut green crystal vase Sean and his work partner, Andre, had gotten them for their engagement.

"You were going to miss the game?" Ellery asked, his eyes big and limpid, and he must have been really taken by this because he didn't notice what sounded like ripping. Oh God, please let that not be the drapes.

"Well, yeah. You kept saying I was supposed to plan, so I said I had to bail." He tried to keep the resentment out of his voice, he really did, but gah! He was so tired of planning!

Ellery swallowed, his eyes even shinier. "I'll tell you what," he said. "You go deal with—" *Crash!* "—that, and clean up the worst of it so I don't see, and I'll let you go play with the other boys. When are they meeting?"

"Around eleven," Jackson said, hope lacing his voice. Oh wow. *Freedom, sweet freedom* was only a few household chores away! They might even have time for some happy naked things in the interim.

The shininess left Ellery's eyes, and the look of pure calculation that crossed his face told Jackson he was on the same page. "Done," he said. "But go get them while the house is still standing!"

"Woohoo!" Jackson practically leapt out of bed, still in his boxers. Without bothering to put on any clothes—or slippers—he ventured into the chill of the morning. "C'mon, you no-thumbs-having motherfuckers. Daddy's gonna give you a *real* lesson in zoomies!"

ELLERY CHUCKLED a little as Jackson ventured into the living room, because the initial phase of curing the zoomies, he'd learned, had nothing to do with trying to calm things down. If anything, Jackson was going to spend a good fifteen minutes racing around the living room, yelling at the furry little reprobates, waving his arms, and making dives to smack their tails as they fled. The first time Ellery had seen him do this, he'd been appalled. The whole purpose of Jackson intervening was to stop the devastation, right?

But then he'd realized that Jackson was *playing* with the cats, and he was also *controlling their flight path.* He'd trap them behind the couch, feinting going one way and then the other, until they both gave up and fell asleep. He'd zoom them into the guest room, where they'd hide under the bed panting until they started cleaning each other's ears and forgot what they were doing to get there.

Once when they'd been particularly destructive, he'd herded them into the guest room *bathroom* and then into the shower, which he'd shut them in for the half hour it took him to clean up.

Ellery lay in bed now, listening for Jackson's trajectory, trying to decide where this mishigas was going to see exactly how much damage he was going to have to repair on the fly.

For a moment it was all Jackson's footsteps and "Ha! Gotcha, no-thumbs! You go that way motherfucker!" and "Jesus, Lucifer, if you were any clumsier you'd starve to death!" Finally, there was the opening of the guest room door (uh-oh), and then the opening of the guest room bathroom (oh no), and then the slamming of the guest room shower, (fuck fuck fuck fuck bugger fuck fuck!), followed by Jackson snapping, "Now calm the fuck down, you little bastards, or your next stop is the swimming pool!"

Ellery buried his head in the pillow, much like Jackson had, and his hand found the lubricant they'd put there two nights ago when they'd made love.

As Ellery heard Jackson's cleaning-up sounds—accompanied by a lot of swearing—he remembered that thought about having all the time in the world before Jackson took off to do boy things, leaving Ellery home alone to plan by himself, which would take him a tenth of the time it was taking to drag the reluctant Jackson through his Thanksgiving planning.

They might even have time to… to…. Oooh….

He hedged his bets first, used the bathroom, brushed his teeth, took a short shower, getting all the creases. When he got out, Jackson was still stomping around swearing, and Ellery wondered if he wasn't going to have to fake it through Thanksgiving dinner with rips in his drapes and divots in the tiles under the fireplace.

Such things bothered him, but not as much as they used to before moving in with Jackson and Billy Bob and now Lucifer. People and pets were messy. Houses got banged up. He would replace the drapes when it was possible, and perhaps wait until Lucifer got over his clumsy stage to replace anything else. (Jackson had suggested sewing a penis-shaped patch onto the corner of the couch because both the cats had been dicks about using it as a scratching post instead of the cat mansion in the corner of the living room. Ellery had simply gotten it reupholstered.)

When he got out of the shower, he heard Jackson moving around in the kitchen, which suggested he'd been sweeping, and Ellery was pretty sure he'd heard the vacuum going, which suggested the Ficus might need to be repotted. As Ellery was drying off, Jackson came stomping into the bathroom, irritated and frustrated and growly. He stepped into the shower muttering something about "Fucking no-thumbs-having-motherfuckers-oughta-be-a-law," and Ellery took that to mean that the next part of his plan was very necessary.

Still wrapped in his terry-cloth robe, he went looking in his closet for his old shaving kit and was ever so pleased when he found it easily. A trip to the sink while Jackson was still grumbling, to wash all the things, and then….

JACKSON STEPPED out of the shower and gave himself a cursory swipe with the towel, stopping to brush his teeth and make sure all parts of him were cleaned of the potting soil and the ceramic dust of the (thankfully) mass-produced vase that had no sentimental value but had still been one of Jackson's favorites.

The cats had done a number on the living room, and he was going to have to make a trip to the hardware store to fix the place where the cats had literally ripped the drapes off the curtain rod and then torn the curtain rod down as well. Jackson had removed everything and left the drapes neatly folded and the curtain rods propped in a corner, and he figured it would be his job after the pickup game. He might get Henry to help him since Henry seemed to be handy like that—together they should be able to make it not look awful on Thanksgiving.

But he was still in a grumbly, growly funk when he entered the bedroom, and Ellery blew his mind.

He was lying naked, which was unusual because even when he was feeling sexy, he was still Jackson's occasionally shy Counselor who didn't go for the Tinder pose. But that wasn't all. His cock—well oiled— was in his hand, and he was stroking it slowly, for his own pleasure as well as, Jackson hoped, for Jackson's appreciation.

Jackson appreciated—oh, how he appreciated.

And he especially appreciated that Ellery's knee was cocked, and between his taut asscheeks, there peeked… oooh. A handy, sexy toy that Ellery and Jackson had talked about using a lot but—until now—had never broken out to play with.

The no-nonsense black handle was clearly visible against Ellery's pale flesh.

Jackson wasn't even aware he'd dropped the towel.

Ellery's body—slightly cooled by the air but still moist and clean from the shower—was smooth under his as he rubbed their chests together, and Ellery let go of his cock to wrap his hands around Jackson's biceps.

"We still mad?" he purred.

"About what?" Jackson asked, sucking on his neck, his shoulders, his collarbone.

"Nothing," Ellery moaned, his hips thrusting a little, his cock bumping up against Jackson's, turgid and dripping.

"Good." Jackson moved his mouth to Ellery's nipple, and Ellery whimpered in the back of his throat. "Do you have any needs, Counselor? Any particular wants you need me to fulfill?"

Again that sexy, half-strangled whimper. "I'd like to get kinkier," he confessed on a mewl, "but I really need to be fucked."

Fire roared through Jackson's blood, and he tugged gently on the plug, glad Ellery believed in lots of lubricant, because it slid right out. Then he was poised at Ellery's entrance, and Ellery took him on one hard push, crying out in relief as he seated.

The rest of it was a blur, a gorgeous, sexual, sensual blur, as Jackson went from zero to orgasm in the time it had taken the cats to wreck the house. His climax hit him with a rush, and he wasn't shy about crying out and pumping into Ellery's body, conscious that Ellery was moaning and coming and coming and coming as he did.

Ellery's convulsions started him up again, squeezing and stroking Jackson's cock through his ass, and in a moment, a long, slow moment, Jackson was thrusting hard and slow and powerful, and round two was *on.*

FUCK THE plans, Ellery decided an hour later. He wanted to go to the pickup game and watch Jackson play basketball in the thin November sunshine. He could bring his tablet and do all his ordering and organizing there, and when they got home, they could see if the guest room was still standing after letting the cats out of the shower. They had a litter box, they had food and water—Ellery was hoping the solitary confinement would chill them out.

So he and Jackson pulled up to the park where the rest of the guys played, and Ellery—walking with the faintest bit of stiffness—took his place on the bleachers. Jackson was greeted with a ration of shit for bringing his boyfriend to the game until he pointed out that Henry and Lance were playing, as were Sean and Billy.

There was some hooting and hollering, and then Jackson took one team and Henry took the other, both of them picking whoever cracked them up the most at the time they were choosing.

Ellery watched the game with interest, noting that Jackson had picked Lance, Billy, AJ, and Jael for his team, and Henry had picked Sasha, Sean, Randy, and Curtis for his own team. On the one hand, it seemed evenly matched. On Jackson's team, AJ was a little bit timid, and Jael was a little bit uncoordinated. On Henry's, Randy was all ears and elbows, while Sasha, one of the ex-cons, was all chest.

But that's not what it came down to.

Ellery watched as Henry missed a shot and then made a stiff little wince of recovery as he ran and then Sean did the same thing.

And then Randy did the same thing.

Ellery's eyes widened as he suddenly deduced something very personal about a bunch of guys hanging out sweating in tank tops and shorts as they said crude shit each other in a stunning display of smack talk.

But not once did the real smack get talked.

Finally it was over. As Ellery watched, fascinated, Jackson, Lance, and Billy ran circles around Henry's team, giving AJ and Jael plenty of chances to play. When the game ended, all the guys gathered around the bleachers, guzzling water and continuing to talk shit.

"Hey, Ellery," Henry called with a grin. "Your fiancé cheats. There's no way his team beat us, you know that, right?"

Ellery gave him a prim glare. "He doesn't *cheat*, Mr. Worrall. If you want your team to beat Jackson's, Billy and Lance need you and Sean to top."

There was a sudden shocked intake of breath as everybody stared at him in horror, apparently for saying the one obvious thing that nobody had thought to talk shit about. Ellery was about to turn red and rethink moving back to live with his mother when a raw cackle of glee broke the silence, and then another, and then another, and Jackson, Billy, and Lance all sank to the blacktop and howled.

Sean and Henry gave them a narrow-eyed glare, and then they broke too and laughed until all ten of the players were hanging off each other and laughing, and Ellery was left, mildly embarrassed, sitting on the bleachers with his tablet on his lap, wondering what the statute of limitations was on outing the sex lives of two entire basketball teams in the middle of what was apparently a bragging ritual.

Eventually the laughter subsided, but the general happy chaos followed them to Jennifer the haunted minivan, where Henry said goodbye to Lance—Lance had a shift in an hour—before Henry hopped in back.

"I'm sorry," Ellery confessed humbly to Henry as Jackson started up the vehicle and headed to Lowe's. "I didn't mean to—"

Henry cackled some more. "Don't you dare apologize. That's the best laugh I've had in forever. But oh my God, Ellery, next time you've got a hot tip like that, could you maybe tell me in private?"

"Yes, of course," Ellery mumbled, still embarrassed. Jackson's hand on his knee cheered him up a little, as did Jackson's insistence that he buy new drapes, which he and Henry spent the rest of the afternoon hanging up.

They were still talking about how to fit sixty-million different Thanksgivings into one day when Henry took Jennifer and went back to his apartment, leaving Jackson to clean up and then shower again before starting dinner.

He was busy sautéing some chicken and vegetables and steaming some rice when Ellery finished his food order and place settings and other plans and moved behind Jackson as he worked, wrapping his arms around Jackson's waist and rubbing his cheek on his shoulder.

"Good day," he murmured.

"Very," Jackson said, rubbing Ellery's knuckles with his thumb.

"Good enough to let the cats out?" Ellery asked.

Jackson turned around in his arms, grinning. "I don't know, Counselor. If they wreck the house again, will it be your turn to top?"

Ellery chuckled, his cheeks heating, and he buried his face in Jackson's neck. "If it is, I promise not to tell a soul," he mumbled.

"You can tell whomever you like," Jackson replied, nuzzling his temple. "As long as I'm not on the blacktop playing a pickup game."

Ellery groaned into his chest, and then Jackson kissed him, kissed away the embarrassment, kissed away the awkwardness, and left only the bright, shining day that had started off badly, then gotten wonderful, and then gotten worse.

But here in Jackson's arms, it was all wonderful. Ellery had never been bright and popular. He'd often had the ability to send common sense like a wet blanket on top of the heads of any peer group he'd ever tried to enjoy. Leave it to Jackson Rivers—and the friends he'd gathered to himself—to turn what could have been one of the most awkward moments of Ellery's life into something fun and magic and joyful.

The cats could have their zoomies. It was worth all the torn drapes in the world.

Keep reading for an excerpt from
Constantly Cotton
The Flophouse series, Book #2
by Amy Lane

The Long and Winding Road

"MR. JASON, what was that?"

Lieutenant Colonel Jason Constance, Commander of Covert Operations, self-named Desert Division, wondered if it was possible for his stomach to sink past his balls.

He hadn't been in this much trouble out on the field, looking at a trained assassin through his sniper's scope. And even then he hadn't felt fear.

But then, his ass had been the only one on the line.

"Hang on, Sophie!" Jason called to the back seat of the "borrowed" medical shuttle. He blinked hard to clear the grit of sleep from his eyes. He had managed to pull over to catch a nap for an hour or so, but his internal monitor was pinging danger, and he'd started the bus up when he was certain the kids had all dropped off to sleep.

He couldn't shake the thought that someone was on their tail.

Around lunchtime, his life had seemed so simple.

Stressful—yes. Lonely—*hell* yes. But… fuck.

Simple was relative.

He was in charge of one of the most complicated, gawdawful tasks on the planet. For years, a powerful man—a commander in the armed forces named Karl Lacey—had utilized his ties to the covert ops community to try to create the perfect assassin. He'd used everything from psychics to behavior modification to outright torture to get men to forget their better angels and to find joy only in the hunt… and the kills.

The results had been predictable. To everyone but Lacey.

He'd set a batch of highly trained serial killers loose on an unsuspecting world.

Jason and one of his best operatives, a man named Lee Burton, had stopped the operation before it went international. They'd had help. Burton's boyfriend, Ernie Caulfield, a psychic Lacey had trained up and then tried to have Burton assassinate, had been their compass, and a batch of civilians who'd seen Lacey's psychological Frankenstein's monsters in action had become weapons.

The fallout had left Jason in charge of Lacey's old hidden military base in the desert outside of Barstow, with Lee Burton. Jason and Lee had spent the better part of the last eight months tracking down Lacey's abominations, and it was grim, dangerous, dirty work.

And painful.

They called it Operation Dead Fish.

Not every man Lacey had turned loose on the world had started out a monster. So many of them were left with tortured bits of soul and heart mangled in the wreckage. But it was hard to bring a patient in when that patient was trained to dismember people with his teeth and a plastic fork. Not a lot of their targets were brought home alive to fix.

The only thing that had kept Jason from hollowing out, becoming the man he and his small contingent of fifty or so operatives, agents, and trackers hunted, had been the other part of that fallout.

Burton's boyfriend, Ernie, was so psychic he really couldn't function in a crowded city or urban area, but he was also sort of a sweet, goofy angel who liked to feed people their favorite pastries and could pull a future out of thin air with a rather spacey look into the clouds. Burton's best friend, Ace Atchison, and Ace's psychotic boyfriend, Sonny Daye, had proved staunch and loyal friends and good soldiers, as had Ace's friend and employee, Jai, no last name, a mobster who had been "given" to Ace because Ace had risked his life to save Jai's boss's granddaughter.

And Ellery Cramer and Jackson Rivers, the lawyer and his PI boyfriend, who had not only stopped one of the first serial killers to escape Lacey's control but had tracked the man to Lacey independently, had proved invaluable, both in a fight and as allies in a dangerous secret war.

And all of them, in one way or another, had become something Jason Constance had never thought to have when he'd signed his name on Uncle Sam's bloody dotted line:

Friends. Family. People who knew who he was and cared about *him*—not what he could do for the juggernaut corporation that was the US military.

So Jason had started his morning depressingly early, resolving a crisis that had been brewing for a week and then checking with his far-flung agents, who were currently tracking a number of the rogue operatives through various countries, including their own, and then making contact with his field agents, who were keeping tabs on dangerous targets and trying to find a way to take them out without alerting—or hurting—the civilian population, and then finally with his wetwork agents to make sure that killing people for a living hadn't turned them into killers who did it for fun.

By lunchtime, all he'd wanted was a goddamned tuna sandwich. That was all. The limit of his ambitions.

And then Ernie had called him, out of the blue, and complicated his world.

Ace Atchison and Jai were chasing down an RV of trafficked children, he'd said. They would need help. "Jason, you know we can't just let this happen," he said.

And Jason, so desperate to do something *good*, and do something *real*, had agreed. He'd had Anton Huntington, his transport guy, fire up the old helicopter and take him out to I-15, that long stretch of nowhere between LA and Vegas, and he'd gotten there just in time to watch the big Russian ex-mob guy and a staff sergeant with a high school education take out the guy ferrying kidnapped children from Sacramento to Vegas.

Literally without trying.

That didn't stop Ace and Jai from being glad to see him. No. But it did feel anticlimactic. Right up until Jason had called his own CO, Brigadier General Stephen Collings, and told him that he'd intercepted some trafficked children and would like permission to use military transportation to take them back up north to Sacramento.

It was a basic request—a courtesy, really. Jason, whose real rank was actually heftier than the silver-leaf Lieutenant Colonel insignia he wore on his uniform, had sort of thrown it out there in the name of keeping to protocols in case he ever had to act civilized.

And Collings, one of the coldest fuckers Jason Constance had ever dealt with, including the assassins in his charge, said, "My division is, at this moment, tracking the group trafficking these minors. We need to see where they're going and follow the money trail. Please put them back on their original transport and designate a soldier to continue to drive them to their original destination."

Jason remembered a feeling of blankness blowing through him, a cold desert wind scouring the duties and the paperwork and the must-dos and the protocols right out of his blood, like the abrasive cleanser used in plumbing.

Every nerve ending was suddenly pristine and alert and awaiting a different set of orders from Jason's tattered, thin soul, as opposed to the ones he usually followed from Washington.

"No, sir," he'd said, his voice sounding tinny, far away, shouted from a mountaintop, even to his own ears. "No, sir. I'm not putting these kids back in that piece-of-shit tin wagon and shipping them back to hell."

The conversation had devolved from there.

And when it was over, Jason turned to Huntington almost as though he was surfacing from a deep pool—or a deep sleep.

"Sergeant Huntington?"

"Yessir?"

"I'm about to do some things my superiors don't approve of. Doing what I ask may get you called in on a court-martial. Let me know if that bothers you."

"You go, I go, sir," Huntington had replied smartly. He was young— late twenties or so—with thick blond hair, Iowa farm-boy blue eyes, and a chest almost too big to fit behind the helicopter controls. Jason had been nursing a crush—a very, very secret crush—on his transport sergeant almost since Anton had joined covert ops, but since he was pretty sure Anton Hungtington was straight (and even if he wasn't, Jason wouldn't hit on someone in his unit, ever), he'd indulged in the crush like other officers indulged in nudie magazines.

He only brought it out at night, when nobody else could see.

But still, it did his heart good to know that he inspired loyalty in somebody.

He'd had Huntington radio for a military transport bus and taken responsibility for the kids, while Jai and Ace had driven off to meet Burton and take out the people on the receiving end of this horror perpetrated against children.

Jason felt like his job was more dangerous.

As soon as the transpo arrived—with cases of water, thank God— Jason had sent the driver back to the base with Anton and hopped behind the wheel.

The trip from the middle of the desert had gone fairly quickly, or as quickly as the old bus could go, given that it overheated if Jason pushed it past fifty miles an hour.

Ernie called him halfway to the I-5 interchange and told him to stop off at a hospital close to the freeway in East Los Angeles. Apparently Jai's boyfriend worked there, and he'd volunteered to take a look at the kids and make sure nobody was suffering from heatstroke or lingering effects from their imprisonment in the back of the sweltering RV.

Jason had pulled into the ambulance bay and been directed toward the side of the big building that was closest to the parking structure. A small, almost hidden, employee entrance sat there, and Jason turned off the laboring engine while he and the kids waited in the shade.

And then the door had opened, and Jason had gotten a good look at another member of Burton and Ernie's hidden family.

He had only the occasional glimpse of Jai, the giant Russian who had been helping Ace Atchison tend to the children as they were moved from the horrible, stench-ridden RV to the slower, air-conditioned military transport bus, but he knew the man existed. When he had dinner with Burton and Ernie, Ernie gossiped to him about all of the denizens of Victoriana, and Jason started listening to their stories like some people paid attention to television shows. Jason Constance, covert ops, living in a hole in the world and tracking down people the US government denied creating, had no family. Or at least in his uniform, he pretended he didn't. His sister was alive and well and living outside of San Diego, teaching, and his parents had retired to Arizona. He texted them from a secure phone reserved for family interactions and exchanged pleasantries because he'd been brought up right and he was loved. But he didn't talk about them to anybody but Ernie and Burton. Ernie was semiofficially dead, and he liked it that way, so Jason felt safe there, but that was the only place. He hadn't had a lover since he'd gone into covert ops ten years ago. Back then, the stigma against being gay was such that any contact, any at all, would have compromised him and the people he worked with beyond forgiveness and redemption.

Things were different now, and even if they weren't, watching Burton and Ernie build their private bastion of tender civilization in the middle of the unforgiving desert would have inspired him to find somebody, anybody, to make the world a warmer, more welcoming place for his stripped-bare, desiccated soul. But his emotional centers felt battered and rusty, like a once-functioning piece of equipment that had been dipped in salt water and left in the sun to rust and gum up with sand.

He wasn't sure he could even touch a lover right now, not with the reverence and joy he seemed to remember that involved.

So seeing George, Jai's boyfriend, jumping into the military bus to smile gently at all of the children and tell them that he had meals prepared and was going to take everybody's temperatures and make sure nobody was sick—that was like watching a movie star walk into his life and invite him to the party.

And to realize that this perfectly average slender blond man with gray eyes and an engaging smile belonged to Jai, the almost terrifying ex-mobster who stayed very intentionally on the periphery of Jason's vision whenever they met? If Jason hadn't just flushed his entire career down the toilet, he would have been almost giddy.

As it was, he'd been up since 4:00 a.m., following an op going down in Europe, and it was nearly eight in the evening by the time George and his boss, Amal, managed to sneak Jason and the children onto a medical transport, practically under Stephen Collings's nose.

He was too tired for giddy. He'd settle for relieved.

Jason pulled out into the thick of Los Angeles weekend traffic, knowing the only way to get the kids away from the military and the mob was to take the 14 through the mountains and then turn back toward I-5 north of Palmdale.

Which would be like a flea taking a tour on a hairless cat. Sure, it could get from nose to tail faster, but it could also get caught and squashed. There wasn't much up in that area—lots of bare stretches of road with housing developments parked in acres of succulents so the wind didn't scour the dirt from the mountaintops.

And not a lot of places to stop.

But the kids had been fed—twice, because he'd stopped for fast food while he'd been clawing his way through traffic to get to the hospital—and they had water, fuel, and AC. If he could tough it out over the mountains, he could find a place to park in Palmdale or Lancaster, before driving the relatively short six hours to Sacramento, where hopefully he could find the authorities to get the kids home.

It was a plan. He liked this plan. There was sleep in this plan; there was another chance to feed the kids. Hell, because it was a medical transport, there was even a bathroom in this plan. This plan was a go!

And it had been a go as he'd made his way through the mountains and found a small town before Palmdale with a gas station.

It wasn't that he needed the fuel—as far as he could see, he had plenty to get him to Sacramento—but having the level place to park the bus was a plus. Once they'd descended from the mountains, and the temperature had leveled out a little from ice fucking cold to warm night breeze, the level place was pretty much his only requirement. There were thin polyester blankets in the compartments above the seats. He, Sophie, and Maxim broke those out and distributed them to the other young people, aged around ten to fourteen as far as he could see, and he had Sophie and Max tell the other kids they were stopping to sleep before he finished the drive. It should be easy, right?

A few hours, that's all. Four hours of sleep, right? He was a soldier; he'd run on less, certainly. But he'd been running on two hours at a time for the last four nights, and it wasn't like he wasn't used to being perpetually tired, but this was stretching it.

He was trying to pilot a land yacht through a traffic tsunami, and the kids in the back were depending on him.

A few hours of sleep.

So he parked the bus and had the kids crack the windows to let in some of the night air, and then he wadded up one of the blankets under his head and leaned against the window and closed his eyes.

He dreamed about the desert.

Not this one here, the one at home, but the one far away, where his job had been to kill people in a war he didn't understand. Half the reason he'd risen up the ranks, really, was so he could understand why he was ordering young soldiers to their death and making them kill people they didn't know.

But back then he'd been barely out of OTS and trying to get the attention of his CO. He remembered all of them in the coms tent, the beginnings of an epic windstorm gathering around the barracks.

"But look," he'd said, pointing to the blips on the screen. "General, these aren't our guys. I know you think they're our guys, but they're not moving in our patterns. We need to get eyes on them because if they get any closer—"

About then the first missile was launched at their fortification, from what they later discovered was the back of a captured Humvee.

He'd seen the trouble, all right—but only when it was right on them.

He woke up in the front of the bus with a strained breath. Fighting his way to consciousness, he knew the one thing he had to do was listen.

He heard the grumble of a big vehicle—a badly tended SUV, he thought—as it exited Highway 14 and rode the hairpin offramp toward their current location.

Where the big medical bus was sitting like a fat bird.

Quietly, so as not to disturb the children, he hit the starter and watched as the warm-up light glowed on the dashboard. These things usually took about two minutes to warm up. Two minutes. That was enough time for the SUV to see them on the way by and to turn around and come back and check on them. Was it enough time to fire? Was it enough time for the men inside to see who was sleeping there and come back to kill them?

"Sophie," he hissed.

The girl—wide gray eyes, a pink stripe in her hair, and a razor-quick mind—had apparently been sleeping as lightly as he had.

"Mr. Jason?"

"Tell everyone to get on the floor. We need to pull out as soon as the engine's ready."

"Yessir," she said. No questions, no whining. God, it was too bad she was twelve years old; he'd like to recruit her.

The SUV passed them, and for a moment he wondered if he wasn't getting on the road too soon. It was an SUV for God's sake. Somebody lived out here, right?

But he got behind the wheel and started up the bus as soon as the light went out.

And as he was pulling away from the gas station, the first bullet zinged by, and the second too. The third didn't zing. Fired from a silencer, he figured, the third bullet ripped through the side of the bus and then tore through the seat where Sophie and Maxim had been sleeping, before it lodged itself solidly in Jason's shoulder.

"Mr. Jason," Sophie said breathlessly from the floor. "What was that?"

And as pain tore through him, every synapse declaring a magnesium fire in his shoulder, and now in his side, all at the same moment, he realized they were fucked.

"Hang on, Sophie!" he called, stomping on the accelerator and going straight. Not toward the freeway, which would take him right by the people shooting at them, but straight, which would take him into some of the least populated places of California and possibly Nevada.

But hopefully, it would not take them to where there would be bullets.

Award winning author AMY LANE lives in a crumbling crapmansion with a couple of teenagers, a passel of furbabies, and a bemused spouse. She has too damned much yarn, a penchant for action-adventure movies, and a need to know that somewhere in all the pain is a story of Wuv, Twu Wuv, which she continues to believe in to this day! She writes contemporary romance, paranormal romance, urban fantasy, and romantic suspense, teaches the occasional writing class, and likes to pretend her very simple life is as exciting as the lives of the people who live in her head. She'll also tell you that sacrifices, large and small, arc worth the urge to write.

Website: www.greenshill.com

Blog: www.writerslane.blogspot.com

Email: amylane@greenshill.com

Facebook: www.facebook.com/amy.lane.167

Follow me on BookBub

SHADES
of HENRY

AMY
LANE

A Flophouse Story

One bootstrap act of integrity cost Henry Worrall everything—military career, family, and the secret boyfriend who kept Henry trapped for eleven years. Desperate, Henry shows up on his brother's doorstep and is offered a place to live and a job as a handyman in a flophouse for young porn stars.

Lance Luna's past gave him reasons for being in porn, but as he continues his residency at a local hospital, they now feel more like excuses. He's got the money to move out of the flophouse and live his own life—but who needs privacy when you're taking care of a bunch of young men who think working penises make them adults?

Lance worries Henry won't fit in, but Henry's got a soft spot for lost young men and a way of helping them. Just as Lance and Henry find a rhythm as den mothers, a murder and the ghosts of Henry's abusive past intrude. Lance knows Henry's not capable of murder, but is he capable of caring for Lance's heart?

www.dreamspinnerpress.com

CONSTANTLY COTTON

AMY LANE

A Flophouse Story

When Jason Constance rescued a busload of kidnapped children, he didn't expect a parade. He didn't expect to be hunted by mobsters and the military either. Wounded and half out of his mind, Jason finds himself at the tender mercies of an angel-faced nurse named Cotton.

Cotton has just flunked out of porn, and as far as he can tell, he's flunking life too. Having an injured colonel in his bed seems par for the course, but he's too busy keeping Jason alive to question how fate brought him there.

But fate isn't done with them. When they go on the run from the mobsters who shot Jason, there should be no time to fall in love, but neither man seems suited for an average life—or relationship. Jason and Cotton can probably survive homicidal mobsters and rogue military operations. The question is, can they survive the work they'll have to do to forge a place just for them?

www.dreamspinnerpress.com

Guess who's swimming in the
same pond...

FISH
OUT OF
WATER

Amy Lane

Fish Out of Water: Book One

PI Jackson Rivers grew up on the mean streets of Del Paso Heights—and he doesn't trust cops, even though he was one. When the man he thinks of as his brother is accused of killing a police officer in an obviously doctored crime, Jackson will move heaven and earth to keep Kaden and his family safe.

Defense attorney Ellery Cramer grew up with the proverbial silver spoon in his mouth, but that hasn't stopped him from crushing on street-smart, swaggering Jackson Rivers for the past six years. But when Jackson asks for his help defending Kaden Cameron, Ellery is out of his depth—and not just with guarded, prickly Jackson. Kaden wasn't just framed, he was framed by crooked cops, and the conspiracy goes higher than Ellery dares reach—and deep into Jackson's troubled past.

Both men are soon enmeshed in the mystery of who killed the cop in the minimart, and engaged in a race against time to clear Kaden's name. But when the mystery is solved and the bullets stop flying, they'll have to deal with their personal complications… and an attraction that's spiraled out of control.

www.dreamspinnerpress.com

AMY
LANE

WEIRDOS

Not all
dogs are
Lassie.

If Taz Oswald has one more gross date, he's resigning himself to a life of celibacy with his irritable Chihuahua, Carl. Carl knows how to bite a banana when he sees one! Then Selby Hirsch invites Taz to walk dogs together, and Taz is suddenly back in the game. Selby is adorkable, awkward, and a little weird—and his dog Ginger is a trip—and Taz is transfixed. Is it really possible this sweet guy with the blurty mouth and a heart as big as the Pacific Ocean wandered into Taz's life by accident? If so, how can Taz convince Selby that he wants to be Selby and Ginger's forever home?

www.dreamspinnerpress.com

A LONG CON ADVENTURE

The Mastermind
AMY LANE

"Delicious fun." — Booklist

A Long Con Adventure

Once upon a time in Rome, Felix Salinger got caught picking his first pocket and Danny Mitchell saved his bacon. The two of them were inseparable… until they weren't.

Twenty years after that first meeting, Danny returns to Chicago, the city he shared with Felix and their perfect, secret family, to save him again. Felix's news network—the business that broke them apart—is under fire from an unscrupulous employee pointing the finger at Felix. An official investigation could topple their house of cards. The only way to prove Felix is innocent is to pull off their biggest con yet.

But though Felix still has the gift of grift, his reunion with Danny is bittersweet. Their ten-year separation left holes in their hearts that no amount of stolen property can fill. A green crew of young thieves looks to them for guidance as they negotiate old jewels and new threats to pull off the perfect heist—but the hardest job is proving that love is the only thing of value they've ever had.

www.dreamspinnerpress.com